The Scot Who Loved Me

"Find another mon."

"No. It must be you."

His scowl deepened. "Why me?"

"Because only a highlander will do."

Tension thrummed in her veins. Fierce, knowing eyes searched her hood pulled low as if he had an inkling of her identity. Beside her, one thigh shook a wide strip of tartan to cover Will decently. The beast was getting down to business.

"Now why would a Sassenach ask so prettily for *my* help?" His tone was deceptively soft. "Time to show your face, lass."

Her soul's frayed parts called for readiness.

She scraped back her hood. "Because a Sassenach isn't doing the asking."

His gaze smashed into hers. Startling. Incendiary. A glare to blast her back into the night. The shed's wretched air suffocated, yet Will's nostrils flared and his chest rose and fell with ragged breaths. His only sign of life. Otherwise, he didn't move, didn't speak, didn't blink.

She was hanging by a thread.

"Anne Fletcher MacDonald," he said at last.

Also by Gina Conkle

The Scot Who Loved Me

A Scottish Treasures Novel

GINA CONKLE

AVONBOOKS

An Imprint of HarperCollinsPublishers

THE SCOT WHO LOVED ME. Copyright © 2021 by Gina Conkle. All rights reserved. Printed in the United States of America. No part of this book may be used or reproduced in any manner whatsoever without written permission except in the case of brief quotations embodied in critical articles and reviews. For information, address HarperCollins Publishers, 195 Broadway, New York, NY 10007.

First Avon Books mass market printing: June 2021

Print Edition ISBN: 978-0-06-299899-6
Digital Edition ISBN: 978-0-06-299895-8

Cover design by Patricia Barrow
Cover illustration by Gene Mollica Studio, LLC.
Cover photographs © VJ Dunraven Productions/Periodimages.com;
© margit777/Shutterstock (plaid); Sandratsky Dmitriy/Shutterstock
(dress)
Chapter opener illustration © Uncle Leo / Shutterstock, Inc.

Avon, Avon & logo, and Avon Books & logo are registered trademarks of HarperCollins Publishers in the United States of America and other countries.

HarperCollins is a registered trademark of HarperCollins Publishers in the United States of America and other countries.

FIRST EDITION

21 22 23 24 25   BVGM   10 9 8 7 6 5 4 3 2 1

This book is dedicated to Laurie Schnebly Campbell,
an excellent teacher, encourager, and guide.
She is a writer's secret weapon and the
reason many romance novels shine.

The Scot Who Loved Me

Chapter One

August 22, 1753

*T*orchlight flickered over a monster of a man sitting on the ground, his braw arms manacled to the wall of Marshalsea Prison's strong room, the outbuilding for troublesome criminals. The floor reeked of piss. Night soil's scent clogged the air. Rebellion had a cost, and it was paid for in the shed. Anne crumpled a handkerchief doused with lavender oil against her nose and stepped gingerly inside.

The warder's bruised eyes searched her hooded face. "There's less beastly men I could show ye, miss."

"No, he's the one I want."

Chains clinked, the cold noise rippling over her skin. The sleeping beast stirred, shifting a tattered MacDonald kilt on massive thighs, and the bottom of a hairy ballock swung into view.

"See what I mean?" The warder sniffed. "Not fit for the kindness of yer bosom."

She was eyes on the beast, a generous purse dangling from her fingers. "It's my bosom, Mr. Ledwell. I'll thank you to keep your concern to yourself."

Grasping hands cupped the offering. "Yer payin' a lot for one worthless highlander."

In the shadows, eyes of molten gold glared through lanky hair, riveting eyes that stripped lesser souls. The brute was bound but not defeated with his head tipped back and arms resting in fetters as if he took his ease. The English could never conquer him. He'd rotted on a prison hulk at Tilbury Fort for his part in the Jacobite Rising of '45 and lived to tell the tale.

But this imprisonment he'd done to himself.

Why?

She winced behind her scented cloth. Untended cuts and nasty bruises showed through his torn shirt. Still, he was a sight. Blond-brown hairs glinting on rock-hewn thighs. A thickly carved chest whittling to a lean waist. With his size came a large nose and a wide, once familiar, mouth. Passionate, soft (the only part of him that was), and utterly kissable.

But those eyes had the power to mark a woman. Brash on his best day, moody on his worst. Spite flashed in their depths at the warder sifting a bony finger through the purse.

Ledwell raised a polished coin to the light. "A Queen Anne half guinea. Don't see much of this fair lady." His thumb rubbed the stamped profile. "Looks newly minted too."

"You have thirty pieces of gold, as agreed," she said.

"No' thirty pieces of silver?" Mocking words climbed out of the dark.

He speaks. She stepped closer, dank straw submitting to her foot.

"Ledwell is greedy, but he's no Judas."

Husky laughter floated from the floor. "And I'm no savior."

The warder's face scrunched in confusion. The beast, however, fixed a keen gaze on her. With her hood pulled forward, a single torch lighting the shed, and a cloth muffling her voice and hiding her face, Will couldn't know it was her. Yet, for all her confidence, his presence tied her in knots, and he was the one in chains.

"What makes ye think ye can handle him? Three men couldn't." A leering Ledwell slid the purse into a pocket inside his coat. "Countin' on yer feminine wiles to get that filthy rag off him?"

She bristled at the unseemly question. "Where did you find him?"

"At the Ram's Head on London Bridge. Tavern maid said he sauntered in wearing his kilt, demanding ale. She obliged him 'til he was drunk as David's sow. That's when the Night Watch was called."

"Raised the hue and cry, did she?"

"She did, an' two Watchmen hauled him here in a cart." Ledwell hiked up sagging breeches and sniffed. "But it was me who bound him to the wall."

Preening man. There was no need to glory in the downtrodden. It was bad enough the Dress Act of 1746 outlawed kilts.

"If he was tied up, how did you come by those bruises on your face?"

Ledwell's chin jutted at two large feet covered in loose leather boots, the tops folded under big square knees. "Kicked like a madman, he did, when we tried to cut off his kilt."

"Try cuttin' it off again, and I'll break your nose," the highlander boomed.

"It's within my rights."

The two were ready to brawl, and manacled or not, she knew who'd win. She'd witnessed the former MacDonald enforcer train with one or both hands tied behind his back. Will's booted feet had probably knocked sense into the Watchmen's witless heads when they tried to cut off his kilt, but the skirmish was less instructive for Ledwell. He paced the shed's tight confines, arguing his point.

"The man can't be gaddin' about in a torn kilt. It's an affront to the crown."

"I daresay the king would be more bothered by a naked man roaming Southwark." She smiled thinly against her handkerchief. "Now, I believe you owe me a key."

"It isn't proper," he blustered.

Her patience waned. "That is not your concern, sir. It's mine."

Ledwell planted his legs wide. "A prisoner died yesterday. Big man, he was." Squinty-eyed, he sized up Will. "His breeches might be large enough—"

"I'll no' wear a dead mon's clothes." Will's snarl was deep.

"Ye will if I say so!"

She tucked away her handkerchief with the utmost care. *Men.* Strength was their vernacular. They lived and breathed it. She wasn't born with that knowledge, but being a fast learner, she'd acquired it as one must to survive London. For that reason, casual as you please, she reached into her lacy cuff and freed a knife with lightning speed.

"When you tried to cut off his kilt, did you use something like this?" She buried the knife tip in Ledwell's soiled neckwear.

Hot breath steamed her blade. Eight inches of sharp metal kept Ledwell against the wall, hands high and his bloodshot stare on the weapon under his chin.

"Here now, miss. I'm only doing what's proper for women. Keeping a man covered an' all."

"Proper?" Now that amused her. "What delicate sensibilities you have." She dragged the knife down his waistcoat, the metal *clack, clack, clacking* over wooden buttons. "Let me assure you, any woman roaming the streets at this hour has seen a Man Thomas or two."

Ledwell's eyes bulged when her knife stopped at his Man Thomas.

"You, sir, have a problem—my blade on your baubles."

Throaty laughter rumbled in the dark. "She's go' you there."

Ledwell gulped. "Ye made yer point, miss."

"I fear I haven't. You've wasted my time carrying on about breeches and kilts. Why, I feel quite ignored, and men who do that do so at their own peril," she said in a voice one saved for difficult children. "Let me remind you of our arrangement. You get a bag of gold, and I get the key to unlock the prisoner."

"Y-yes—it's—it's here." Ledwell's shaky hands searched his waistcoat and produced a time-worn key.

She snatched it. "Leave."

The warder quit the room, muttering about unruly highlanders and unrighteous women. She sheathed her knife, confident Ledwell wouldn't return with reinforcements. If he did, the boastful man would have to explain how a woman had bested him.

Beyond the shed, terse footfalls echoed in the night. She listened, head cocked, until a door banged shut.

Finally. She was alone with the former enforcer of Clan MacDonald of Clanranald.

Steel infused her spine. She'd need it to face the man whose stare burned holes in her back. Foggy wisps curled through the doorway, the damp chill welcome. It'd keep her alert. Her purpose was clear: his freedom, her proposition, and a promising future for the people who depended on her. Well-laid plans, all of them, yet they wavered like a stack of children's blocks about to fall when she swung around and faced the smirking highlander.

"Go' any more weapons I should know about?" he asked.

"Only the knife."

The weapon was snug against her skin, security in an insecure world. The blade left an awful slash

for those who didn't understand the word *no*.
Tonight she needed the former enforcer to say *yes*,
a Herculean task since she would do the asking.

"You've gone to an awful lo' of trouble to see
me, lass. Why no' come closer?" Head lolling on
the wall, he hitched up a knee, and shorn wool
separated over a swath of hairy thigh.

A spark burst inside her. The boor wanted to
scare her off.

"That's rude, Will MacDonald. Even for you."

Mischief played on his face. "Have we met?"

She squeezed the key, its metal teeth biting
through her glove.

"Yes. A long time ago."

He shrugged and stared at the wall, indifferent
to her presence. The younger, hot-blooded highlander she once knew was gone; the older one
who took his place was rougher and dangerous
with his careless air.

An unpredictable man. A challenge, to be sure.

She gathered her skirts and crouched boldly
between his legs. Will grunted. He searched
her hood, shock warring with irritation across
handsome features. A wealth of unbound gilded
gold hair draped giant shoulders. With the key
in hand, she brushed back those gnarled locks,
admiring his breastbone's dip in the middle of a
meaty chest.

"My name is Mrs. Neville."

Stern eyes slanted when she toyed with a strip
of his shirt. He resented the intrusion, but his
body didn't. Brown nipples tightened. Skin pebbled in waves of uninvited pleasure. Grit covered

Will, adding to what made him attractive, the gruff man unafraid of getting dirty and twice as nice when he cleaned up.

"Beg pardon, lass, but our meetin' must no' have been a memorable night." He rattled the chains, his smile none too friendly. "As you can see, I'm in no position to make this one any good."

Will's voice was pure Western Isles, full of softened vowels and hints of Gaelic behind every relaxed turn of a phrase. He could recite a tax roll, and a woman would count herself content, listening to his whisky-smooth brogue.

"Aren't you the brazen one."

His scrutiny swept each stitch and fold of her cloak. "Forgive my bad manners. A mon gets few social calls in the shed."

She dropped the cloth strip. "Have you had female visitors? *In here?*"

"You're the only one."

His chin tilted, cocky as the first day she'd laid eyes on him eight years past in Edinburgh. A strapping young man of twenty then, Will had stood on her father's doorstep, took one look at her sooty apron and the rag fisted on her hip, and he'd flirted outrageously, mistaking her for a charwoman. She'd let him carry on until he announced he was Anne Fletcher's protector for the journey to Skye—to meet her betrothed, Angus MacDonald.

A forbidden spark had been lit, and damn her eyes, it burned hotly still.

The years had been kind to Will, having chiseled away youthful arrogance to reveal solid male. Yet something was amiss. Chained to the wall, he wore assurance with a touch of . . . madness. Up close, his eyes gleamed in the same manner as the lost souls hauled off to St. Luke's Hospital for Lunatics. Nor did he question a woman purchasing his freedom at midnight.

"Gossips say you've never lacked the companionship of women."

A half-crazed smile split his face. "Rumors, lass. Just rumors."

"I heard you were a busy man, protecting London's wealthy widows."

Really, there was only one. The Countess of Denton. She fought the vile taste that woman's name left in her mouth.

Will's smile went cold. "State your business, or I'll yell for that *bodach* Ledwell to give you the boot."

A warning twitched inside her. They both wore old wounds. What good was there in poking them? Will had done what he had to do to survive, so had she. Everyone, rebel or not, had paid a price for the Uprising.

"My business?" She checked the door, survival's reflex. "I dare not explain all the details here. But the truth is you need me as much as I need you."

By the devil-take-you shine in his eyes, Will didn't share the same conviction.

She held up the key. "You are mine now."

He snorted and gave her the once-over. "You're a scrap of a lass with nothin' more than a needle up your sleeve. What makes you think I'd give you the time o' day?"

"Because you are a man of intelligence who

knows the wisdom of listening before rendering judgment."

Lines bracketing his nose deepened. A moment crawled by, but her fine appeal must have struck the right note.

"It's your gold." Iron-clad wrists knocked the wall. "I'm a captive audience. Start talkin'."

An ugly shiver skipped across her back when a beady-eyed rat tottered out from a pile of straw. Before setting out for Marshalsea, she'd thought about what to say and how to say it. Facing Will, those practiced words crumbled on her tongue. Nothing was right. Her gaze slid over hair in need of washing, a jaw in need of a shave, and eyes a touch fevered.

All she could manage was, "I want to hire you."

His glower was monstrous. "Those days are over. I won' work for a woman."

Insufferable man. "This is not about you warming my bed. I need your talent for . . . finding things."

"Finding things?" Disdain twisted his mouth. "You go' to do better than that."

"You would be well paid. Ten times your earnings from the docks."

Torchlight flickered on unconvinced features.

"Ledwell gave me your arrest record." She rummaged for the rolled-up document tucked inside her pocket. "I can burn it tonight, and you would be free."

"Free is a questionable word these days." A shake of his head and, "Find another mon."

"No. It must be you."

His scowl deepened. "Why me?"

"Because only a highlander will do."

Tension thrummed in her veins. Fierce, knowing eyes searched her hood pulled low as if he had an inkling of her identity. Beside her, one thigh shook a wide strip of tartan to cover Will decently. The beast was getting down to business.

"Now why would a Sassenach ask so prettily for *my* help?" His tone was deceptively soft. "Time to show your face, lass."

Her soul's frayed parts called for readiness.

She scraped back her hood. "Because a Sassenach isn't doing the asking."

His gaze smashed into hers. Startling. Incendiary. A glare to blast her back into the night. The shed's wretched air suffocated, yet Will's nostrils flared and his chest rose and fell with ragged breaths. His only sign of life. Otherwise, he didn't move, didn't speak, didn't blink.

She was hanging by a thread.

"Anne Fletcher MacDonald," he said at last.

"Anne Fletcher MacDonald . . . Neville. Mrs. Neville to you."

Will's brows thundered. "You married an *Englishmon*?"

She braced herself. "Yes."

Teeth bared, he blistered her ears with a string of Gaelic curses. She flinched but held her ground. Having spent much of her childhood in London with her English grandmother, tutors had scrubbed her diction clean, though not her vocabulary. Her brothers had made sure of that.

Will's face was inches from hers. "Ask your English husband to protect you."

"I can't. He's dead."

"Like the first one?" Wildness glittered in his eyes.

The jibe struck hard. She quaked with emotion stuffed behind a cool facade, an inborn skill she'd honed to perfection. By the sour sentiment twisting Will's rugged features, she could no more talk sensibly with him now than she could eight years ago.

If her heart had turned to ice, rage had flamed in his.

"We share too many secrets," she said.

"Secrets, you say?" His laugh drew blood. "No' secrets, lass. We share mistakes. Too many of them."

Torchlight lit half of Will's face. The other half was murky and hostile, belonging to a feral creature who should be left alone to lick his wounds. But this was the beast she needed, a man to exact justice. Little by little, tendons on his neck relaxed. Will slumped against the brick wall, his mouth set but calmer. Anger taxed a body, even a dauntless warrior. Humbled, she stuffed the arrest papers in her pocket and fingered the crude medallion hanging from her neck. Memories of distant, tear-stained faces seared her.

Their suffering . . .

Never forget.

Will had borne his share of suffering too. A wee bit of compassion would not be out of order. A bucket of what looked to be barely touched water sat near his hip. She filled the ladle and set a peace offering to his lips.

"I will have to burn these skirts, you know."

Will guzzled water, his vivid eyes singeing her.

He finished and shook his head at having more. "Too much, too fast and I'll retch."

"When was the last time you ate?"

"The night I was arrested. Though I recall more ale than food goin' down my gullet." His brogue was heartwarming and his half grin cocky.

"That would be three nights past. And now, though it pains me, I am asking for your help. In return, I can help you."

"No." He shook his chains. "I'm otherwise detained."

His jaw was mulish behind a mud-flecked beard. The truth was he'd rather not be indebted to her. The jaunty angle of his head told her as much. Though sorely tempted, now was not the time to respond in kind. She set the ladle in the bucket and chose her words with care.

"You understand, if you stay here, you will be dragged before the magistrate, and you will be given six months imprisonment. Wear the kilt again, and you will be transported to the colonies—to serve *seven* years on one of the king's plantations."

"No' a bad idea," he said, studying the ceiling. "Been thinking about going to the colonies. My father's there." Will met her gaze with a taunting glint. "It'll be my pleasure to sail on King George's coin."

"We shall make it worth your while."

"*We* is it?" His brows shot high. "Go' another Englishmon waitin'? Husband number three?"

She massaged her forehead. "No."

Lavender oil smeared under her nose was losing its effectiveness. Whiffs of Marshalsea and

Will's unwashed body assaulted her. Not half an hour in the shed and she was in danger of casting up her accounts. How did he survive three days? He'd not stay, not if she had any say in the matter. The Dress Act was too bitter an edict to swallow.

"Be as stubborn as you like," she muttered. "But I will set you free."

She rammed the key in the manacle, and their bodies brushed.

Fine hairs on her arms lifted, a rush, delicate and soft. Very out of place for the man she was nose to nose with. She did her best to quash the flutter.

"You truly want to go to the colonies?"

Will's lashes dropped half over his eyes. "It's time I leave, lass."

His graveled voice sent cracks across her heart. He was leaving her. It made no sense. They'd not seen each other in years, yet she knew it in her bones.

Pinching the key's bowhead, she tried to force it. The lock's internal mechanism wouldn't budge. Like her, it was a little rusty about opening up.

"You're still freein' me?" Will's head was at her shoulder.

Molars gritting, she cranked the key. "I cannot turn my back on you."

"You did once."

She froze. That hurt. Deeply.

There was no reason to explain her choice. Will wouldn't believe her; he was too busy clinging to his version of the past, and she was too busy fighting for her future. So many people depended on her. Pushing up on her knees, she steeled herself and twisted the key again. Iron grated iron until the metal bracelet opened. Will hissed at his sudden release, his gaze digging into hers, bright with pain.

Three days in chains would leave a man stiff and sore. She cleared her throat and reached for his meaty shoulder. Under the circumstances, rubbing it wasn't out of the question.

"This will help," she murmured. "Warm you, ease the hurt."

Will absorbed her profile. She flushed the more he watched, rather demoralizing for a woman who lived a shade outside the law. By the slash of his brows, the monster of Marshalsea's shed was unpleasantly baffled too.

"I canna believe you're here."

The highlander was wistful, his voice set to the *shush* of leather rubbing skin. Will's body was a familiar map of ridges and furrows. Bigger than most, he was brute force in the flesh. His livelihood required brawny arms to career ships and powerful legs to turn a quayside treadwheel. A creature of that world. Skin darkened at his elbow, a laborer's stripe. She traced that suntanned line, careful not to look him in the eyes.

"You roll your sleeves here. When you work the docks."

Will's breath stirred hair by her ear. "Of all the women to walk through that door . . ."

His voice was achy and soulful, the timbre striking tender notes.

"You know, it's not just me who needs you. There are others, Aunt Maude and Aunt Flora."

"Those two are in London?"

"They live in my house," she said, bundling her skirts.

She straddled Will's leg and reached for the other iron clamp. Her inner thigh glanced his. Masculine leg hairs tickled her. She aimed the key at the lock and missed.

"Careful, lass. Don't fall on my account." Even in chains, he hinted at humor and seduction.

Embers sparked on tender skin above her garter. *Sinister little hairs.* Will's leg skimmed hidden places, featherlight under her petticoats.

She took a bracing breath, fit the key into its hole, and nudged her thigh away from his.

He nudged his closer. "I'm no' complainin'. You're warmin' me nicely."

Will. He'd flirt with the devil if the devil was a pretty woman.

Years ago, she'd loved the highlander passionately. Young and foolish, both had believed they could be together. But ardent, youthful promises didn't stand a chance against the tide of war and family obligation. Worst of all, Will had been for the rebellion. She and her family had not.

When she gripped the key harder, a big dirt-smeared hand covered hers.

"Let me."

Will's hand. Long fingered, scarred, the knuckles scratched and bruised. His hands were good at wielding clubs and pistols, yet gentle enough to woo a headstrong virgin into giving heart, body, and soul to him.

Nodding mutely, she pushed off the ground and swallowed an angry cry when he got up on one knee. His ripped shirt split wide, revealing a back full of cuts and purple welts, likely from cudgel strikes.

The beating he took . . . all in the name of donning his kilt.

She was in a daze when the second chain clinked against the bricks. Will stood to full height, his brooding eyes watching her while he nursed his newly released arm.

"I cannot believe you won't help us," she said.

"You'll no' guilt me to your biddin' because of Aunt Maude and Aunt Flora." Will stretched his neck, the bones cracking. "Find another mon."

"I need *you.*"

His eyes dulled. "Never thought I'd hear you say that again."

Chin high, she was done asking. He'd never forgiven her for what happened in the ruins of Castle Tioram years ago. Truth be told, she'd never forgiven herself. It made Will's sudden touch on her jaw all the more poignant.

"Who did this to you?"

The pads of his fingertips were warm and rough grained. With murderous fury in his eyes, it took her a moment to understand. The bruise on her temple. She'd forgotten about it. When they were on the ground, Will couldn't have seen it for the shadows.

"It happened a few nights ago when I was alone in my warehouse."

"I didna ask when it happened. I asked who did it."

She jerked her chin free. "I don't know."

Torchlight guttered beside her. Life stopped— no past, no future. No right or wrong. She was a woman with a man. Will had to feel it. He searched her bruised hairline, her eyes, her mouth until a subtle veil dropped. She lost Will again—if she ever truly had him in the first place. One summer of sex and endearments wasn't love. It was . . .

A formative experience?

Carnal escape?

Freedom for a young woman expected to put family first?

Within her cloak, papers crinkled. Will's arrest record. She pulled it from her pocket and fed the document to the fire. Ashes floated bit by bit like fall leaves until it was gone. Will ground those gray scraps under his heel.

"You're a riddle, madame. What kind of trouble follows you that your head is bruised and you wear a knife up your sleeve?"

Dignity squared her shoulders. "The less you know, the better."

Will was proud. Forlorn. Mighty as ever, filling the room with his torn shirt and shredded kilt over naked thighs. A quick stride would flash his male parts. The tartan's untouched back hung long and properly pleated, but if he gave it to a laundress, she'd heave it into a fire. There was no saving it. Could be there was no saving Will.

She grabbed her petticoats and headed up a short stack of stairs. Will wasn't far behind, his shoulders brushing the door frame. He watched her scrape muck off her shoe, stark hunger lighting his eyes, but he'd made it clear she was not the woman to feed him.

"Shaking off the dust of your feet?" he asked, a touch belligerent.

"What I do is the least of your concern." She raised her hood with an eye to the moon-drenched road beyond the open gate. "The better question is, what are you going to do now that you are free?"

Chapter Two

Tattered wool slapped Will's legs, and cold glommed on his skin. Slouching timbered buildings loomed, old plaster smeared on their creviced faces. Southwark was a coarse bawd, and time had not been kind to her. When the Stuarts reigned, crowds teemed her narrow streets to gorge on violent sports, brimming brothels, and colorful theaters. Not anymore. Her soggy lanes were empty. Her reputation in tatters.

Prisons, breweries, and warehouses crammed close quarters now. A place easily forgotten. A place Anne called home?

He kept a respectful dozen paces back to make sure she arrived safe . . . wherever she was going. The lass was taking a long stretch of her legs on this midnight walk, cutting through low-hanging fog better than a river barge. Swan Alley to Long Lane, a quick turn onto Tanner Street, this last thoroughfare blessedly peaceful save a dog barking at a trio of drunks staggering out of a seedy chophouse.

Two whores idling outside a tavern snickered as he strode past.

"Never mind them, luv," a henna-haired doxy cooed. "It's me ye want." She flashed a winsome smile and scarlet stays.

He grinned and plodded on. "No' tonight. I'm otherwise engaged."

"Yer loss." She snapped her cloak shut and gave Anne's back the gimlet eye. "I'll be right 'ere if Miss Stiff Skirts turns ye down."

Miss Stiff Skirts. A fair description. Done with hanging back, he jogged to Anne's side, the smell of fresh-cut wood growing stronger. They had to be close to the wharfs. Much of England's timber and stone trade passed through this part of Southwark.

"You should have taken Red Bess's offer. She is generous with the occasional man. Allows him to stay all night in her bed." Two more steps and Anne's gaze slid to his legs. "She might even have a pair of breeches for you."

Whistling low, he matched her stride. "Stickin' a knife at a mon's baubles, and, if I'm hearin' right, you're familiar with the habits of local harlots. Times have changed, Mrs. Neville."

"Indeed, they have, Mr. MacDonald."

His midnight rescuer was frosty, her gray hood slipping low when she turned onto Mill Lane where the Iron Bell Tavern lived. Anne was long of leg but more than a head shorter than him. If he didn't know any better, he'd say she wanted to shake him off.

"You know you've still no' answered my questions," he said, trying to be congenial. A congenial man got answers.

"I recall answering a fair number of them."

"No' the ones that counted."

Candle lamps outside the odd door lit Anne's profile. The other side of the river was well lit, the Southwark side not so much.

Her footsteps quick, she was nose forward. "I won't tell you more because the two of us working together is a bad idea."

"So just like that—" he snapped his fingers "—you unlock me from Marshalsea and leave."

"Yes—" she eyed him and snapped her fingers "—just like that."

Irritation coiled. She was blood-pumping sauciness and tight lips, a bayonet's jab and feint in her conversation. Growling at her in the shed hadn't worked, but he'd keep their skirmish going . . . for Aunt Maude and Aunt Flora's sake.

Anne turned onto Bermondsey Wall, the slender road tracing the river's embankment. An orange tabby cat slinked across the low wall, a mouse wriggling between its teeth. Aside from the cat, its prey, and a veil of fog, not another soul inhabited the road, save him and one headstrong woman. When she stopped at an iron gate askew on its hinges, he nearly tripped over his own feet.

Rusty reflexes. Three days in chains did that. Left his bones cold too.

"This is my home." Anne's honeyed smile came with a bite. "If you happen upon a highlander willing to help a woman in need, send him here."

He chuckled low. *Woman in need.* Anne never needed anyone. He pushed the squeaky gate wide open and ambled forward, hands on hips into the yard. Weeds grew in the flagstone path. A lonely lamp glowed beside the black-lacquered door of a brick and flint stone house facing the river. An empty lot sat on one side of the house, a burned-out building on the other.

Looking up, he spied a bricked-over window frame on the second floor. "This is no' the home of a wealthy woman."

"When did I say I was wealthy?" Her silken voice sent a quiver over choice places.

The moon painted Anne a fey temptress. Cheeks sharper than he remembered, her flesh-pink mouth was the same, a mouth that did shameless things to a man—like convince him to walk midnight streets just to hear her secrets. The bruise. The knife. This run-down house and her bulging bag of gold. Nothing added up to the Edinburgh lass he once knew.

Well, not everything had changed. She was mouthy as ever.

This version of Anne could be otherworldly. Fascinating, beautiful, yet worthy of caution. She'd deceived him years ago. He had no doubt she'd do it again.

Fool that he was, he wanted inside.

"You saw me safely home," she said. "Your gentleman's duty is done."

Her wry tone insulted him as if she found his protective nature amusing.

"I followed you because I wanted to, no' because I had to."

Anne jingled a key ring out of her petticoat pocket. "Then I thank you for your kindness."

"I'm no' bein' kind."

Pale green eyes flashed with irritation. She was older and wiser than the maid who'd kissed him senseless from one side of Scotland to the other. Their kisses had been hot, their tangle of limbs hotter. He couldn't recall who had seduced whom back then. Young Anne had sported a ramrod spine and give-no-quarter spirit.

Fierce, mouthy lasses . . . his weakness.

While on the prison hulk, he'd come to believe she'd marked him, a young woman quenching her sexual curiosity before entering a loveless marriage. A nasty chill climbed down his back. Could be she'd marked him again. A woman who wanted something else from him.

Calm as a summer breeze, Anne nodded at London Bridge rising in the distance. "If you cross the bridge, the Night Watch will haul you back to prison." Brows arching, she eyed his nearly naked thighs. "Or to St. Luke's."

"The Night Watch can bugger off."

Her mouth quirked. "Then it's a ferryman for you. Go to Marigold Alley and tell Henry Baines I sent you. He'll oblige you a midnight run to Black Friars. From there, you should be able to dodge your way through dark alleys to your lodgings."

Staring down at her, he smiled, could feel it growing, wicked and unpleasant. *My, my, Mrs. Neville, you're tryin' verra hard to get rid of me after such a pretty plea in the shed.*

"I'm no' crossing the river, nor do I care if anyone sees me in my kilt."

"Have you lost your mind, Will MacDonald? If

it is a matter of paying the ferryman, I will give you the coin."

His impatient huff was worthy of a dragon. "I'm no' taking your money. It's time you explain yourself. I've waited long enough."

Her laugh was sharp. "Have you now?"

She marched on, her heels decisive clicks on stone.

Catching Anne at her doorstep was easy. Getting the slippery woman to spill her secrets was the greater task. He was glad the hour was late and the lane vacant. A passerby would think a madman was accosting the widow of Bermondsey Wall. With his shirt in tatters and hair unkempt, he was a fright. He was haranguing a woman who'd made it clear she didn't want his services after all. That about-face was puzzling enough. Life held little value for him these days, but this was different. Anne's appearance at Marshalsea shook him. Badly.

Her key poised to unlock the door, he stretched out an arm and blocked her.

"Eight years I don't see you. *Eight.* You'll no' dismiss me like some errand boy."

Her hot regard speared him. "Don't you mean you dismissed me?"

A sane man might tuck tail and run. He considered it, until he caught a telltale sign: Anne's thumb rubbing circles on her forefinger. She followed his sight line and jammed her hand into her cloak.

"My refusal," he said. "I hurt you."

"Not at all."

Liar. She was nose-in-the-air proud, but truth

be told, he was in no rush to let down his guard either. The river's tranquil hush and laughter from a distant tavern cooled their collective ire. This should be a simple, honest conversation despite the fact good deeds rarely happened at this hour. Harlots and housebreakers roamed late-night streets. What did that mean for him and Anne?

A patient man, he waited, his father's voice in his head. *No good decision was ever made after midnight.*

"When I heard you were in Marshalsea . . ." Her speech broke and she averted her eyes. "I—I couldn't bear the thought of you imprisoned again."

He stared at nothing in particular, his shoulders sinking under the burden of damaged pride. No boy dreamt of going to prison, yet he'd been there. Twice.

After the war, the English had locked him away on a prison hulk with two hundred other common rebels. One year or so, it was, and each month, he'd endured the ritual of guards descending into the dank hold, a beaver hat filled with nineteen slips of white paper and one slip of black paper. Each month, twenty men took their turn, reaching into the hat. Being reckless, he'd stepped forward often. The prisoner who drew the black piece was tried and executed. Simple as that.

At first, he'd cravenly prayed for the white slip. Later, he'd cravenly prayed for the black slip.

One morning the guards called them all on deck, daylight scorching every prisoners' eyes.

Soldiers pointed the business end of their bay-
onets at him and the other rebels, telling them
to seek shelter elsewhere. *Shelter!* As if rotting
below deck was time spent on a pleasure barge.
The Act of Indemnity had freed them. Left them
as cast-off goods by the River Thames.

The same ancient waters tapped the wall outside Anne's house, and his nape prickled.

She'd said *imprisoned again.*

Did Anne know his whereabouts after Culloden?
At the shed, she'd rubbed his arm and spoke of his
working the docks.

He hadn't said a word about the docks.

"There's no harm in lettin' me in for a wee bit
of conversation and warmth." He attempted a
cordial smile. "My tackle is fair to freezin'."

"Oh, Will . . ." she groaned.

His charm was rough at best, but it worked. A
smile ghosted Anne's mouth.

"I'll let you in under two conditions. First—"
she checked the road from whence they came
"—you listen to what I have to say about a highland league—"

"A highland league? Are you mad? It's—"

"Dangerous."

"It's sedition!" he whispered vehemently.

His peace of mind faltered under the weight
of Anne's firm defiance. Scotland's loss had unhinged him. He knew that. He'd lived with de-
spair and was prepared to stay a forgotten man.
But the determination in Anne's eyes was born of
stark rebellion. He'd seen the same in his mirror
before the Uprising.

Anger balled his right hand. He would pummel

the man who'd snared Anne, Aunt Maude, and Aunt Flora into a losing proposition.

"If it takes the starch out of your spine, I'll listen. But it doesna change the fact that rebellion is sheer folly."

"So says the man willing to molder in prison over a kilt."

Mouth clamping, he eased his stance. As logic went, she had him there.

"My demise, my choice. But, bringin' down others . . . Your leader has porridge for brains, and I'll be the mon to tell him."

Her lips curved beguilingly. "You shall have your chance. The league meets tomorrow."

"Good." He cupped his hands and blew into them. "What's your second requirement?"

"You take a bath." Anne coughed delicately and set a gloved finger under her nose. "You smell awful."

He chuckled, rubbing his hands for warmth. "I could use a good scrubbin'."

"Finally, we share common cause."

Anne unlocked her door, and he entered a humble home etched with signs of wealth and poverty. While she locked the door behind him, he dragged a dirty boot across an iron scraper. A faded mural of sloops covered one entry wall with London Bridge and river barges painted on the other.

"Follow me." Anne wasted no time, leading him through a small dining room to the kitchen.

Embers heated four modest cauldrons at the hearth, and a dented copper tub gleamed in one corner. Anne dropped her cloak and gloves on the oak table while he waited. She stirred life into the kitchen's dying fire, a gold medallion on a black ribbon teetering from her neck.

"The tub," she said, tucking the medallion into her bodice. "Bring it here."

Glad to be of use, he dragged it across the kitchen and set it down with a *thud* between the table and the hearth. "That'll wake up the house."

"No one will bother us. Aunt Maude is exhausted from preparing a chamber for you and—" smiling like a conspirator, she hoisted a pot off its hook "—Aunt Flora nips brandy before bed."

She emptied one cauldron after another into the tub. He should help, but his feet were lead. Warmth, imprecise and imperfect, seeped into his bones. It came from faint light dancing on stone floors. From water's cheery splash and the plum skirts hugging Anne's bottom. He stood by the hearth, kneading his aching shoulder, weakened by a canny woman. Her weapons of choice were clean linens, a hot bath, and a cake of soap she set out for him. The comforts of home.

"You knew I'd follow. That I'd have to see where you lived."

Was his voice hoarse?

Anne was an enchantress, her fingertips swirling bathwater. "You're a free man. That is what matters."

Shadows and light played on her bodice, and like a starving wretch, he took his fill. Steam anointing her skin. A tiny freckle blooming on her breast. Her cleavage, an enticing trail and the plump mounds pressing it. A man could spend all night drawing his finger through that mysterious line and count himself content. Even her collarbone's silken ridge begged to be traced.

Anne glowed. A widow's independence became her.

She stretched upright, firelight slanting across her face. "Your bath is ready."

He ceased his shoulder rubbing, the artless moment sinking in. He was about to take off his clothes, which wouldn't be bad except that he'd been inside Anne. He'd tasted her. Their past whispered a sensual language he longed to forget. The same couldn't be said of Anne. She was remote, as if tending a half-naked man in her kitchen was commonplace.

Could be it was.

Let her host all of Southwark. He was miserable, stretching angrily to free himself of his shirt. It was halfway off when he flinched, a groan curdling in his throat. Every cut and welt branded him.

Warm hands urged his elbows down. "Let me help."

Arms heavy, he did.

Mellow light licked the column of Anne's neck and crafted her lashes as ebon fans. Her attentive hands checked a frayed seam. Slowly. Agonizingly. He burned to be irked with her for reappearing after all these years, but she was kindness itself with glossy midnight tresses.

Black-haired lasses . . . his weakness.

Her touches were innocent; his thoughts were not.

Heat from the kitchen's fire raked his legs. Sweat popped from his skin. He fancied himself stuck between Limbo and Lust, the First and Second Circles of Hell.

"It's a lost cause," she murmured and ripped his shirt in two.

He lurched, a silent howl bursting in his chest. Linen slipped off his shoulders. So quick, there and gone. A woman tearing off his clothes was savage. Primal. Made his blood pump, erratic and loud in his ears.

Anne's dark-fringed eyes met his. "It was the best solution."

Tell that to my reeling senses, lass.

The ruined shirt sailed into the fire. Molars gritting, he felt his nipples pinch to needy points, and he knew who he wanted to touch them. Or kiss them. He wasn't particular. Instead, his efficient dark-haired temptress dusted threads off his shoulder and accidentally skimmed his ribs with fingertips wispy as dandelion tufts.

In short, a woman utterly unmoved at touching him.

He eyed the ceiling, sweet agony rippling to his toes. How much more could he take?

"Now the kilt," she said.

It was the splash of cold water he needed.

"Oh no." He grabbed his belt with both hands. "You're no' gettin' my kilt."

"You plan to bathe in it?"

"I'm no' lettin' you toss it to the fire. That's blasphemy."

"You cannot be serious. It is beyond repair."

He glowered his best for a man sleep deprived and lust addled. "I agreed to your demands. Now honor mine."

Anne's slender nose nudged higher, and her eyes sparkled. She *liked* that he wanted to keep it.

"Let me see what I can do to save it." And bold as she did eight years ago, Anne hooked two fingers into the waist of his tartan and pulled him close, *trust me* flashing in her eyes.

He grunted, a wee bit soused on her lavender scent and those tugging fingers. Trusting the woman was the rub. With his senses scrambled, he couldn't think straight. If Anne removing his shirt was intoxicating pleasure-pain, her undoing his kilt was ruthless torture.

Chin to chest, he *had* to watch.

Pale, ringless fingers brushed grit off his belt. Dirt clods rained on his boots. Her hair grazed his forearm, black ropes tethering him. He could do with a night of tethering. A feminine body tucked into his. The friction, the softness. Filling his hands with silken hair. Breathy moans against his—

"The league would be willing to purchase your passage to the colonies and give you a handsome bag of gold to boot. If you help us."

His lust landed with a *thud* on the kitchen floor. Nothing killed a mood like talk of sedition.

"You know as well as I do, there's no' enough gold in England for us to be in the same room for long."

Her green gaze pinned him. "It has been eight years, Will. I require certain talents you possess, not social parley."

"I said I'd meet your league," he grumbled.

There was a jingle. Leather slackened at his waist, and the belt fell to the floor. His kilt drooped but otherwise stayed in place thanks to dried mud and ample sweat's gluing effect.

Anne nudged his belt aside with her foot. "Have you heard of Bonnie Prince Charlie's treasure?"

Muscles below his navel clenched when her hands invaded deeper territory between kilt and flesh. He concentrated on the far wall, heaviness in his ballocks reminding him his lust hadn't vanished entirely.

"The lost Jacobite gold? A myth. About as true as dragons and fey folk."

"What if I told you about seven casks filled with gold? Over a million French livres."

Anne's eyes sought his, but the wall was safer while she unwrapped his kilt. "I'd say that's a story meant to keep rebel hope alive."

"It is alive."

He dared to look into her eyes. What glittered there was bright, expectant, and hard as any gemstone.

"Anne," he said with all the patience he could muster. "The only gold to reach Scotland was thirteen thousand gold livres. Gold lost to the English."

Gold they'd desperately needed with two hundred soldiers in tow to help the fight. Gold that could've turned the tide of their scrabbly rebellion.

"A spoil of war lost in March before the Uprising ended. But I am talking about a greater treasure." She paused unwinding his kilt. "A treasure brought to the west coast in May . . . *after* the war ended."

He knew of the French ships, *La Bellona* and *Le Mars*, coming with promised aid. Every rebel did. The Uprising had been gasping its last breath when those ships ran a gauntlet of English warships, trying to deliver supplies. The promised guns, ammunition, and brandy he could believe—Frogs were always good for a tipple. But the French king giving up that much gold after the first shipment was taken by the English? For ragged highlanders who couldn't unite? It defied reason. His own clan chief had stood with the Government while the chief's son and heir had fought for the Bonnie Prince.

They'd been doomed from the start.

"I know of the ships." His voice was gruff and tired. "But the gold? A fevered tale, best forgotten."

"It's not a fevered tale."

The last yard of wool fell from his body. He was naked save his boots and a draft nipping his arse. This would be laughable, except he smelled worse than a gutter. Anne turned and folded his ruined tartan in silence, her back an unflagging line. He knew that posture. The subject of Jacobite gold was far from over. Toeing off his boots, he released a gusty sigh. The leather, like him, was well-worn, the shaft on both boots slumping badly. He nudged them aside and climbed into hot water.

"Tell me," he hissed between clamped teeth. "If the French delivered that much gold, why hasna the Government taken it?"

Anne set his kilt on the table. "That Butcher, Cumberland, and his men were looking for it. The gold had to be moved."

"Never to see the light of day . . . the same as all treasure that doesna exist."

He slid under the water's surface and sprang up fast. Heat prickled his limbs, sinking in muscle deep. Cleansing wetness sprang from his pores. He grabbed the soap and began scrubbing off the odor of prison and bad decisions.

"It did see daylight," she said. "The MacPherson of Cluny started spending it."

He dunked for a rinse, counted to five, and came up sputtering, "A highland chief spending money? That doesna prove a thing."

"It was enough for the Bonnie Prince. He sent Dr. Cameron to the highlands to retrieve the gold."

"And the poor mon was executed for his loyalty." Eyelids heavy, he settled back in the tub. "Yet, no one has found this fabled treasure."

Sadly, Dr. Archibald Cameron's death was not a fable. As a rebel of high status returned to Scottish soil, he'd become a hunted man. The *London Daily Advisor* had reported English soldiers chased the good doctor in the vicinity of Loch Arkaig. The same newspaper later trumpeted his grisly end in June. Disemboweled *and* hung because the Government couldn't resist making a point—all the more reason to knock sense into Anne's league.

"As to Dr. Cameron," Anne said quietly. "There was nothing we could do."

He sank deeper in hot water. "Don't fash yourself. I heard the Government had him locked up tighter than a vicar's virgin daughter. No visitors."

Suds trickled down his cheek. His beard would smell of Anne tomorrow, a twice-widowed woman with treason on her lips who owned a warehouse and had enough funds to pay a costly bribe, yet her house was a step or two above ramshackle. A woman he should leave to his past.

"Oh, Dr. Cameron had a visitor," she said over her shoulder. "A woman who claimed she was kin of the MacDonald chief of Clanranald."

He opened one eyelid. "Was it you?"

"No."

His vision narrowed on uncombed curls spilling down Anne's back. "How can you be sure of what this woman said?"

"Because my source of information has never disappointed." She turned around, a confident hand on her hip. "Of course, any sapscull would know what Dr. Cameron's visitor was after."

"Jacobite gold?" Reluctant words were thick on his tongue. His mind refused complete surrender, not until he saw the gold and touched it.

"The league found some of it." Anne crouched beside him, zeal bright in her eyes. "Will . . . it's here. In London."

Shock muted him. He sat up, needing to digest this, but Anne brimmed with excitement.

"And we want you to help us steal it!"

He dragged both hands over his scalp. After all these years, Anne sought him for theft. Not his heart nor his body. How lowering, to sit naked in his former love's kitchen, battling lustful longings, while she asked him to commit a crime. He'd done things he wasn't proud of. Thievery was never one of them. He'd been the clan chief's enforcer, for goodness sake, the one to keep law and order. But the Jacobite treasure had been found, and highlanders were going to take it.

Steal their own gold?

Justice was a devious wench.

The Government would see the matter differently, which shined a light on something he couldn't ignore. Dr. Cameron's mysterious visitor was no English spy sent to trick the prisoner. If the Government had gotten their hands on a single rebel livre, they would've gloated about it in every newspaper from Plymouth to Aberdeen. Their silence could mean only one thing.

Anne had another rival for the gold—someone worse than King George.

Water dripped coldly down his neck. Whoever bribed their way into that prison cell was wealthy, powerful, and unafraid of the crown. And a highland league crossing them? Easily crushed.

Chapter Three

*S*malls landed on his bed—clean, patched, and thankfully his. Morning's first greeting was followed by more garments flying through the air. Breeches, *plop*. Waistcoat, shirt, burgundy coat. *Plop, plop, plop*. His unstarched neck cloth was a well-aimed streamer falling silently on the jumbled pile. A sylph in green petticoats roamed his bedchamber, her hem tapping slender ankles while she went about her business. Dishes clinked. Water splashed. Drapes were snapped properly open.

He winced at teeth-jarring daylight shocking his body.

"I am glad you have seen fit to greet the day." Anne tied back the drapes, a blur of feminine efficiency to his sleep-hazed eyes.

He scooted upright and scratched his chest, a nearly sated man. One should never underestimate the power of a good night's sleep to set a body right. It was almost as satisfying as sex.

Almost.

"Good morn to you," he rumbled, entertained by his morning visitor.

"You mean good afternoon. It is a quarter past one."

"Is it?" He wrestled a sheet from the bed, tied it around his waist, and padded to the window to see for himself.

Gray skies beckoned the brave to crawl atop St. Paul's Cathedral and touch heaven. A peaceful place above the sprawl. The rest of the world was not so disposed. Wherries, light boats delivering passengers, beetled the river's surface. A pleasure barge sliced a path near the bridge, the oarsmen working as one. In the distance, docks were a hive. Barrels rolled and stacked. Fat merchants and customs men scuttling around dockers, warehousemen, and clerks. All paid homage to London's other cathedral, the Custom House.

Worship of the almighty coin. The City's lifeblood.

Money's fever plagued the best of men. Would he be counted among them?

His breath fogged cold glass. He could almost feel Anne's breathing. The quiet, the steadiness. A soldier in silk, she betrayed nothing of what beat within. Did her heart flutter over Jacobite gold in London? He'd fallen asleep to that refrain. Last night's tempting offer of passage paid and a fat purse would set him up nicely in the colonies. Or he could leave Anne's house an honest man and shed the last vestiges of the rebellion.

It meant going hat in hand to his employer, Mr. Thomas West. Being four days gone without so much as a by-your-leave didn't put him in good stead. Five years of honorable service and solid friendship might. He'd earned his keep and then some, laboring for Mr. West's modest whaling concern. Now, all that good will was probably lost.

His world was out of sorts . . . because of a woman.

"With your hair uncombed and that sheet around your hips," she said, "you look like a foreign prince in those tales Aunt Flora reads in the *Gentleman's Monthly Intelligencer.*"

"Yet, my comforts are far from princely." His voice scraped low.

Anne's stare skimmed his navel, and the tingle on his skin reminded him *You are naked under this sheet.* Her eyes were fascinated by the place where skin and bedsheet met. The mystery wasn't in what was behind the linen, but how that landscape of skin might've changed—if at all. He'd wondered the same about flesh hidden under swishing green skirts.

Their past was a third person in the room, a reckless visitor stoking a fire that had no business burning. Anne had to sense it.

"I hope you will feel at home here for the duration of your stay." She looked at the world outside. "However long that might be."

He drank in the sight of her. Midnight was for shadows and secrets, daytime for honest folk. Different intimacy. Especially those with shared history. Daylight christened Anne a fine lady in a lace-trimmed gown and fat garnets swaying from peach-soft earlobes. Her attention was on the road, the corner of her mouth curling up.

"You're staring at me, which means you must be deep in thought and have forgotten where you're looking because we both know you're not a besotted man."

Male pride beat a new drum in his chest. If this was a game, Anne just made a play, possibly the second one since she opened the drapes. His sleep-grogged mind had some catching up to do.

Shoulder braced on the window frame, he hooked a thumb in his makeshift garment. "I'm considering my options."

"About meeting the league? Or something else?"

A small hitch broke her confident voice. Anne didn't ruffle easily. Could be him, or the pressure to make sure he met with the seditious league gathering in her house today. For some reason, she wanted him there, ardently so, despite their pained history.

He'd never been one for coy games. It's why he decided to deal honestly with her.

"It's the gold," he said at last.

"What about the gold?"

"I've no' acquired your comfort with theft."

The road outside forgotten, she looked at him, her eyes brimming with hauteur. "But murderous rebellion is quite acceptable?"

There's the woman with fire in her veins. He couldn't stop his smile. "Battle is face-to-face. Straightforward effort. Theft? Work done in the dark."

"All of it done without violence or bloodshed."

You have a bruise on your head, lass. But he'd keep quiet about that, for now.

"I've earned my keep with honest hands. Life is better that way. A mon can go to bed content he's done his best."

"You followed me last night because you wanted the truth. I gave it to you. Do you wish me to take it back?" Anne's chin tipped higher. Hauteur delivered with smooth, defensive tones.

That was just like her, combative even when currying favor. The woman never gave up.

"I wouldna dream of asking you to hold back."

"You will at least keep your word," she pressed. "And meet the league."

Her hand was almost hidden in her petticoats, but there it was. Her thumb worrying her finger. An arrow of need shot through his heart, gluing his feet to Anne's floor. He couldn't leave now if he tried.

"Have I given you reason to doubt me?" Want thickened his voice.

"No, you haven't," she said softly but something flickered in her eyes.

He was at once aroused and irritated by his ferocious appetite for this woman and her inborn calm. Couldn't she look just a little affected? Skin flushed, eyes darkening with desire, the hint of a quickened pulse?

Something? Anything?

Hair swept high off her forehead and curls perfectly pinned, Anne was poised. She'd maneuvered things to suit her needs. Could be she was maneuvering him. He had to be careful, but with his boots cleaned, the leather oiled, and the square toes pointing at him beside his satchel, Anne had him neatly in place. A well-traveled edition of *Dante's Inferno* and his collection of pamphlets were stacked on the mantel. Near the washstand, a familiar stropping leather hung, ready for the day.

His things, here. It was the splash of cold water he needed.

"I see you've gathered my personal effects."

"A sunrise ferry ride to Wapping Wall. Easy enough."

He considered asking how she'd gained entry to his lodgings, but at five shillings, two pence a month, his meanly furnished room above an exotic animal dealer's shop was no palace. His randy landlord would let her in for the price of a flashed ankle.

"You took liberties, madame."

"And you are naked in my home. After I rescued you from prison, thank you very much."

She was tart tongued and tetchy, but there was more at stake than a satchel of measly belongings. Pride, maybe. Yearning, perhaps. Or something else deep, deep within, something refusing to retract its claws so firmly embedded in him that there wasn't enough ale to drown it.

He knew that fact with ale to be true because he'd tried.

And now he and Anne were in an awkward standoff, last night's progress on shaky ground.

How was it they managed to be honest in the dark and skittish by day?

He was at a disadvantage to answer his own

question—hungry, undressed, and facing the one woman who'd ripped his youthful heart to shreds. When his stomach rumbled, she stepped aside to reveal a steaming bowl of porridge on a mahogany table with a single chair facing the window.

"Your breakfast." Anne announced the meal as if announcing a truce.

He walked to the table, his arm a hair's breadth from hers. She stiffened. Heat leaped off her body but her mouth pressed a firm line that brooked no compromise. *Definitely tetchy.* He'd said he'd listen to her league, but he was his own man. Best she understood that.

Grinning, he picked up the bowl and gripped the spoon like an oaf for no other reason than to goad. Anne was a reservoir of control that needed stirring.

"My boots cleaned, my clothes delivered. Are you making my bed next?"

"Make your own bed."

"You're sparing with your tender mercies, Mrs. Neville."

She crossed the chamber, tossing words over her shoulder. "You want tender mercies? Go find Red Bess."

"But the companionship wouldna be nearly as stimulating."

Miss Stiff Skirts, indeed. He laughed low and shoveled food into his mouth. Hot porridge dusted with nutmeg and sugar melted on his tongue. Just the way he liked it.

She remembered.

He traced her movements through narrowed eyes, taking one bite after another. Anne was fidgety, adjusting the mantel's clock just so and wiping her flawless sleeve, twice. Her thoughtfulness gave him something else to chew on. Why the small kindness with his morning meal? She got what she wanted—he was here and he was going to meet her seditious league. Could be the room was making him twitchy. He was certain he'd spent the night in her late husband's bedchamber. Portraits of sloops and frigates lined the walls, and there was the adjoining door. The brass handle showed the patina of use.

His spoon clinked overloud on porcelain. *How often did Mr. Neville pass through that door?*

Molars clamping, he didn't want to know.

Anne fished inside her petticoat pocket and pulled out a black ribbon. She was winding it when her gaze caught his in the mirror above the washstand.

"It's for you. To club your hair." Her chin's tilt set blood-red earbobs swinging.

He took another bite, but the porridge lost its flavor. Years ago, she had wound another black ribbon for his hair—the day she'd promised him, *Wherever you go, I am with you.* Anne's vow to run away with him had soothed his brash heart. Enough to make him believe they'd be together forever.

How wrong he was.

She placed the coiled silk on the washstand. Did she remember that day? Feel the pang of loss? It was hard to say. The woman before him was supple and confident. A vision of fortitude. Untouchable. Not war nor widowhood or youthful indiscretion had crushed her.

"When you are ready," she said. "Come find us in the salon."

Anne quit the room, a whisper of silk and sedition. Belowstairs, muffled voices carried in her house of secrets. Muffled voices with dangerous plans and Anne hosted them.

His porridge forgotten, he stared at the Custom House a good long while. He was no greenhorn to grand hopes and crushing disappointments. What he couldn't overcome, he made peace with in his way, the blessing of imprisonment. A sharpened mind and stilled spirit were unexpected gifts he found while living with two hundred men in a prison hulk. Watching London's somber sky, he drank from that well again.

A stubborn creature had indeed hooked its claws in him, a hungry creature climbing to the surface, hunting a single need—the part of his past left undone. He wouldn't fight it. Since stumbling out of Tilbury Fort, life had been a haze of regrettable decisions and hard labor, all to numb wounds slow to heal. But heal they did, and for the first time in years, he knew what he wanted.

And damn his eyes, he'd sell his soul to get it.

Chapter Four

"Are you good at spotting lies? We can't presume Will MacDonald's motives are—shall we say—pure." Cecelia. With lips painted an intractable shade of carmine red and her character limber, she served the league well.

"I haven't acquired your particular talents with men. If that's what you mean," Anne said.

She was standing by the salon window, red serge drapes grazing her cheek and curious stares grazing her back. Above her head was a casement with the city's arms in stained glass. Square panes the size of her hand offered small views of a larger world outside. Another dray passed her home, this one loaded with Mermaid Brewery casks. The third one today.

Gathered in her salon were her cousins Mary and Margaret Fletcher, Aunt Maude and Aunt Flora, mother hens to their band of thieves, and of course, Cecelia MacDonald. The tight-knit group was on tenterhooks at footfalls overhead—Will, the interloper they badly needed.

It was a tad ironic, Cecelia, his nearest flesh and blood, was the one to cast doubts about him.

"Cecelia makes a fair point." Mary sipped tea, her gray eyes pools of self-possession. "You said this morning, the man you found at Marshalsea struck you as mildly unhinged. He could very well hie off to the colonies with our gold."

"'Mildly unhinged'?" Cecelia smirked. "Either one is or is not."

Anne's breath steamed a circle on the window. Tension camped between her shoulder blades and nothing could unwind it. She badly wanted to reach around and rub the spot.

"A fortnight ago, the lot of you argued for Will to join us—against my wishes. Now you're singing a different tune."

She had been the lone voice against seeking Will, though Aunt Maude abstained from that debate before grudgingly admitting they did need Will. Then there was Will's surprise imprisonment. Like her, they would not tolerate him in chains for donning a kilt. There'd been a scramble to gather resources and find the right warder with the right offer at the right place and time. Bribery was a delicate skill and should never be rushed. Hence, Will's three days in Marshalsea's shed instead of one.

Stepping away from her vigil, she addressed Mary. "Speaking of gold, the purse you gave me was full of 1703 VIGO-stamped half guineas." She arched her brows in reprimand. "Really? Must you?"

"I must." Mary set down her cup with a firm

clink. "It's nothing more than giving the English a dose of their own medicine."

"A dose, I think, that's quite lost on them."

Mary reached for the teapot, an *I don't care* moue on her mouth.

Anne sighed. VIGO minted coins celebrated England's seizure of Spanish gold boldly taken in Spanish waters. It wasn't an exact analogy, but she understood the message. The English had crowed about plundered gold with minted coins; Mary, in her way, crowed about French livres in their possession. There was no need to argue the point. Instead, she'd try a measured approach.

"Would you consider stamping a more recent date?"

"I will not. If the Government arrests me, it will be for coins struck before the union, never after."

Mary. Elegant, meticulous, well educated. A dear friend and cousin who excelled at nearly everything she touched. She was the staunchest Jacobite in their fold. But, oh, once her mind was set, heaven help the body who got in her way. It took certain skill to shepherd the woman.

"Then at least make the coins look as if they were minted in 1703. Ledwell, daft man that he is, commented on their polished state." She ventured across the room, side-stepping a battered sea chest. "We have got to do better. All of us. No detail is too small."

A frown etched Mary's forehead. The admonition struck a chord.

"I could tumble the finished coins with rocks, but the noise . . ."

"Dears, Mary and I are in a precarious state," Margaret chimed in. "The coal boy asked if we were eating our lumps of coal. It is August, after all."

Mary and Margaret were sister proprietors of Fletcher's House of Corsets and Stays. By day, stays and corsets were their shop's custom. But Mary, the daughter of one of Edinburgh's finest silversmiths, was skilled with more than needle and thread. By night, she converted French livres into guineas and half guineas. A tedious, but necessary, process done in the back of her shop. Passing French coins, they'd feared, would attract attention.

After Dr. Cameron's arrest, the MacPherson of Cluny had contributed to their cause. Anne's knife at his ballocks convinced him. He'd smiled through clenched teeth and given up one hundred thirty-five gold livres, the last of the money he'd filched while supposedly guarding it for the Bonnie Prince. Dr. Cameron had already taken the rest.

Where he hid the money was the question.

At Callich burn, in a fresh grave he'd found in Murlaggan private burial grounds?

In the woods near Loch Arkaig?

Or right under Clanranald noses in Arisaig's beaches, fields, and woods?

None of them had answers until shortly after Dr. Cameron's death. That's when an explosive rumor reached the league: Jacobite gold had traveled south to London.

Anne had returned to the City with the MacPherson of Cluny's one hundred thirty-five gold livres to fund their hunt for the rest of the treasure. Their chief, Ranald, 17th of Clanranald, was supposed to search in Scotland while she and the league searched for stolen gold in London. But, she suspected the burden of old age and managing the clan wore on their chief. Thus, hunting for the treasure fell squarely on the women presently seated in her salon.

And hunt, they did. Like lionesses.

One by one, Mary Fletcher melted their cache of coins, poured them into a small bronze cast, and stamped them with a new identity.

Recasting gold. Not quite counterfeiting.

Anne reached into a cracked vase on the mantel and retrieved foolscap folded at the bottom. The crown would hold a different opinion, but the dye was cast. No sense in worrying over the past, youthful love included. She had a duty to fulfill. She was on a mission and God spare the man or woman who got in her way.

"Ladies, these doubts are nothing more than our collective nerves talking." The foolscap in hand, her gaze traveled to each woman perched in her salon. "We are ready."

"But can ye say the same of Will?" Aunt Maude. Iron haired and iron willed. She'd been the first to question Will's residence in London. Many of his kin had left for the colony of Virginia.

Why did he stay?

The room groaned a peculiar silence. Will was the unknown. By the apprehensive eyes peering at her, one might think the ceiling would fall. Once or twice, she'd checked the plaster medallion overhead for fear it would fall on her head.

She'd checked doors and windows too—for English soldiers.

She dusted off the seditious piece in hand. "He doesn't know everything."

"Then this would be a good time to tell me." Will's voice shot across the salon.

Shock bolted through her.

"If you want my help," he added.

Will lingered in the unlit hall, a beast transformed into a Greek god. A sculptor had chiseled his square, clean-shaven jaw to perfection. Ditto, his lips. With his hair clubbed and imposing height, Will would turn heads. Burgundy velvet stretched across wide shoulders. Threadbare and well traveled, the wrinkled coat might be an effort to blend in with mere mortals. The same could be said of his shirt opened carelessly at his neck.

Both ploys would never work. The women stirred like harried hens.

"Mrs. Neville." His nod was spare.

"Mr. MacDonald."

She was equally cool, though the pulse in her ears beat louder. Hands clasped behind him, Will was baptized in shadows. *A dark blond Hades, deity of the Underworld, come to pay a call.* Tan and virile. Thoroughly in command.

The exposed flesh at his neck irritated her.

Truly, Will? No neckcloth? For a meeting this important?

His lack of neckwear was pure defiance. Neither a woman nor proper decorum could contain him. He stared into the room, a man with all the time in the world, while in hers a clock was ticking. Cecelia coughed delicately. One glance and she was smacked by Cecelia's smug smile. Introductions were expected.

"You remember Aunt Maude and Aunt Flora." She waved vaguely at the pair seated at a mahogany table with Cecelia. "I believe you are already acquainted with your cousin, Miss Cecelia MacDonald of Kinlochmoidart."

Clanranald MacDonald land sprawled from the west coast of Scotland to the Hebrides. Some kin never met.

She pivoted to a yellow brocade settee. "And these are my cousins, Miss Mary Fletcher and her sister, Miss Margaret Fletcher, both formerly of Edinburgh."

Will sketched a bow. "Ladies."

"That's not how you referred to me years ago at a summer fair." Cecelia was coy. "I believe *saucy article* was your preferred sobriquet."

He winced. "Words of a misguided lad. Please forgive my bad manners."

"There is nothing to forgive." She saluted him with her dish of tea. "You were quite right about me."

The salon was a hothouse of ruffled femininity, the balance of nature having subtly shifted with Hades stalwart as a ship's captain navigating stormy seas.

"Won't you join us, Mr. MacDonald?" Mary motioned to an empty chair. "There is plenty of room."

"I'm no' joining anything. No' yet."

Anne slid the foolscap behind her back. Hades had come to bargain. There was nothing to do but corral him, one step at a time.

"It's true. Last night Will agreed to meet with us and hear what we have to say," she said to the room. "He hasn't agreed to join us."

Will showed no sign of appeasement. His broad shoulders remained just outside the salon doors.

Mary hummed sympathetically. "You have hesitations about our league. That's understandable. But, should you help us, know that you will be well paid."

"Keep your money. I don't want it."

Cecelia searched the other women, her light laughter sprinkling the air. "Well, that answers my fear of him stealing from us." She turned keen eyes on Will and spoke in crisp, untrusting syllables. "Though I can't imagine you're here out of the kindness of your heart. In my experience, men always want something in return for services rendered."

His smile was predatory. "Never said I wouldna take payment."

"Then . . . you will join us?" Mary asked.

"If Anne gives me what I want."

Furniture creaked, and six pairs of eyes veered her way: five of them curious and the sixth, exultant. A conqueror come for his due. The hearth's fire blazed at her backside and her hands holding the paper she pinched so harshly it'd scream. A fine reminder that foolscap. They were so, so close—and Will was literally the key.

A drop of sweat trickled down her spine.

"Pray tell, what do you want?"

Will's eyes burned molten gold and his voice singed, uniquely soft. "My demands are best made in private, madame."

Her skin tightened. *Madame?* Will reserved
the title for when angry or battling for control
and curse the man, he had it. This was primi-
tive. Barbaric. Before witnesses, no less. She
should be properly offended. Instead, a vibra-
tion swirled inside her, hot and prodding to
meet Will's challenge and toss back one of her
own. At the moment, she couldn't think of one,
but this awkward standoff was . . . stimulating.

"And I am supposed to yield, whatever it is
you want?"

"Easy as that." Will's brogue danced around
each word.

One could say Hades was amused, and she his
current toy.

She flushed, felt it rising up her chest and landing on her cheeks. What game did he play? She
refused to be cornered by a deal with the devil,
but Will consumed the air. He commanded it. A
ploy for power? Knowledge of the league?

Access to her body?

Pinpricks vexed her skin. Testy, seductive little
sparks under layers of clothing. This was battle,
and she stood in the fray. She'd planned every
step of stealing back their gold. It was her mission, planned and delegated accordingly. Will
was the unknown, the factor she'd resisted, and
his jaw jutted the longer she held silent.

She knew that look; he wasn't giving an inch.
He didn't have to.

"I do not like nebulous demands," she said.

"And I do no' like being ambushed."

Her belly knotted behind her stays. *Then you
will hate me for what I require of you.*

Guilt was a sword at her back, irony a whip. Head down, she contemplated the floor's wood planks. Cecelia was in her side vision. Her pitiless, round-eyed visage shouting *Tell the man you'll give him what he wants!* Her gaze swept to Mary's neatly linked fingers. Small burns scarred what was once pretty skin on hands which toiled late at night with searing metal. No woman of substance and courage left this world unmarked. Life battered the brave.

Her run-down properties, her body, her soul, she'd give him all.

Whatever Hades wanted.

Raising her head, she met his gold-chipped stare. "As God is my witness, this unnamed demand of yours, I shall pay it."

Chapter Five

"*We*'re settled, then." The deal struck, Will strolled into the salon, a beast among the delicate.

A voice of reason warned him. *She didna honor her last promise. What makes you think she'll honor this one?*

It was a gamble he'd take. A fair arrangement in a new venture, however short or long it'd be. He claimed no unique skills. He repaired ships most days, unloaded cargo on others. He could only conclude Anne and her league needed a strong back, which was the one thing he could provide with ease. Rough around the edges, he didn't belong in this temple of refinement with mirrored sconces and lime-white walls.

Aunt Flora with her merry blue eyes was his lifeline. She was cheery in black wool. Like her sister, she wore the same severe gowns they'd favored when he was a boy. Aunt Maude was surly as usual, her mouth pursing disapproval. He was certain she came out of the womb with a sour expression, but that sameness comforted him, the good parts of his past visiting the present.

He touched Aunt Flora's shoulder and dropped a gentle kiss on her round cheek. "It's good to see you, ma'am."

Her work-scarred hand touched his. "Wee Will, what a sight ye are. An' so braw an' handsome."

His heart pinched. More gray hair than ginger was pinned around her mob cap. She was Clanranald's favorite spinster aunt, the one who tended unruly, motherless lads at large gatherings, lads such as he. Quick to wipe skinned knees and soothe troubled brows, Aunt Flora had an answer for all the world's ills. When words wouldn't do, a warm hug did. If she used the endearment given when he was a sprite of a boy, so be it. She'd earned the right.

"I canna believe you're in London." He tossed back his coattails and took a seat in a great chair between the table and the settee.

"Been here a few years now, but I want tae go back tae MacDonald lands." She was quiet, reverent. "I miss the green. It's no' the same green in England, is it?"

"No, ma'am. Nothing like it."

Longing blossomed in his chest. He missed her Ayrshire accent. Aunt Flora and Aunt Maude had spent their youth in Ayrshire with their merchant father, and the accent stuck. Hearing it was like going home. It was good to be among his people, to get a whiff of Aunt Flora's verbena perfume and smell bread baking in the kitchen.

He was as ravenous for kinship as he was food.

Aunt Flora leaned closer to him. "The gold we're stealin' . . . some of it will buy sheep for our herds. They were wiped out you know."

"Yes, ma'am. I heard." Hands in his lap, he could be a youth again, listening, nodding, paying respect.

"Some of the gold we'll steal will buy passage for our kin who want tae go tae the colonies." Her eyes were dim and watery. "After the war, many were desperate tae leave but they couldna pay the passage. Indenture was the only answer. Boys sent tae one colony, mothers and fathers tae another." She dabbed her eyes with a handkerchief. "It breaks my heart."

"A fair number of our indentured kin are in the colony called New York," Aunt Maude said in a sad hush. "Do you know of it?"

"Only what I've read in newspapers, ma'am."

Guilt stabbed him. Words of theft coming from the tenderhearted old spinster, it wasn't right. Nor was it right, his clansmen selling themselves. He knew only of his father and others living free and well in the colony of Virginia.

"After the war, English sailors came ashore and put Moidart to flames. I canna go back. I have no home and my father is dead." Cecelia rubbed her thumb across the rim of her cup, her polished English curiously gone, replaced by clipped western Scots. "I want to spite the Government. That is why I am here."

"The English hunted forty Clanranald men on the Isle of Eigg," Anne said across the room. "Our men, lured by false promises, trusted the English and surrendered in good faith only to be put in irons and sent to one of the king's plantations."

Aunt Flora dabbed wet eyes again. "They're gone, Will. Lost tae us forever."

He reached out to comfort her weathered hand, but Aunt Flora gave him a reassuring squeeze. This was a lot to take in: gold for sheep and gold for his kin's safe passage out of Scotland. The state of MacDonald lands was worse than he thought.

His first months on the prison hulk, he'd been desperate for news of home. Near the end, he'd been desperate to forget. Hadn't they forgotten him? Vague reports of trouble had been whispers in the wind. Skirmishes of a few hardheaded highlanders. He'd become lost to his people, an abandoned foot soldier. Severing the past was akin to cutting off a rotting limb. He'd done it to survive. Now his people were calling him back. His kin. Their cry was soft, the weight of it heavy. He shifted in the fine upholstered chair, this new burden a very real yoke on his shoulders.

Aunt Maude poured a cup of tea and nudged it toward him. "I hear yer going tae the colonies once yer done helping us."

"Yes, ma'am. I'll make a home there." He cupped the steaming dish with both hands and sipped.

"I canna blame ye. Arisaig is no' what it once was. Farms burned. Houses empty. An' the isles . . ." Aunt Maude wiped glistening eyes. "It's no wonder ye canna go back," she said in a watery voice. "Only the strongest heart could."

"There, there." Aunt Flora patted her sister's hand. "Wee Will's heart is strong and good. He'll find a wife in the colonies, an' get a passel of bairns in the bargain." Aunt Flora beamed at him. "Ye can start by practicin' with Anne."

He nearly spewed his tea, while his cousin giggled behind her hand.

"I—" he set down the cup, coughing hard "—I'm no' sure what you mean."

"She means you will play my betrothed," Anne said blandly. "It's part of the plan."

He faced her, his throat and lungs giving him fits. Surely, he was red faced. He could feel the hard coughs watering his eyes.

"No need to look so pained," she drawled.

Lacking a handkerchief, he swiped a sleeve across stinging eyes. "What you see is shock, madame."

"Blame me, cousin. It was my idea." Cecelia could be innocence in white muslin. "You are to play the part of an up-and-coming merchant courting Anne."

He pinched the front of his coat. "Wearing cast-offs from a rag-n-bone mon? No one will believe it." He relaxed in the chair. "I thought you needed a strong back. To haul things and such."

"We need that too, but it must be a well-dressed back." Cecelia stretched her arm toward an old sea chest, a silent squatter in the room. "Your new wardrobe awaits. You'll be pink of the fashion. After some alterations, of course."

The chest's lid slanted open from clothes crammed to overflowing. Silks and gold embellishments winked in the light, top of the mode by the look.

He'd never worn silk a day in his life.

"The rightful owner left my home in a hurry. The law was on his heels. It turns out he was a bigamist and will not return to London anytime soon." Cecelia's eyes were bright with mischief. "You will be comforted to know, he's still alive."

His gaze traveled to Anne. So she told the room about his refusal to wear a dead man's clothes. He was twitchy about those things.

"I'll wear whatever you want." He answered Cecelia, but his eyes were on Anne, the color high in her cheeks.

Anne's betrothed. The tables had turned in his favor. He sat back, knees wide, fingers loosely linked. The league practically served him Anne on a platter. Could be why she kept her distance, tense and straight.

Her blood-red earrings twinkled darkly. "I'm pleased that you will join us. Now, can we get on with the plans? We've dithered too long already."

The battle cry given, the women took action. Quick voices bounced instructions around him. Tea implements were cleared. The Fletcher sisters collected wooden chairs off the wall. Anne strode to the table, unfolding foolscap. This mirrored meetings in West and Sons Shipping. Mr. West unfolding paper, the men gathering round the diagram to get their orders.

A life of crime never looked so efficient. Or so feminine.

The elder Miss Fletcher touched her sister's arm. "Please fetch the wax from the kitchen."

While Miss Margaret Fletcher nipped out, his cousin regarded him with wily eyes. "Are you drowning in this sea of women?"

"It hasna escaped my notice that there's no men."

"Our league has none. That is until you. It's

better this way. Women are barely noticed," Cecelia said. "Maids, wives, shopkeepers. We are the cogs of Society."

"We keep our mouths shut and our ears open," Mary said wryly. "We excel at it."

"Our clan chief knows about this?"

"Knows about it?" his cousin said archly. "Once we promised to secure the *sgian-dubh*—"

"*You* promised to steal the dagger." Anne was beside him, holding the paper close.

His cousin steeled herself. "Yes, once *I* made that promise, our chief practically pushed us out the door."

He whistled low as Margaret Fletcher scurried back to her seat and set a lump of wax on the table. "The ceremonial Roman dagger, you say?"

"The very same." Cecelia MacDonald sat taller, quite pleased with herself. "But first we get the gold. Taking back the *sgian-dubh* comes later."

The *sgian-dubh*, stolen during the Uprising, or so he'd heard. The tale of its loss was hazy, its beginning, however, was clear. Every lad was told the tale of the ancient iron dagger, pride of Clanranald MacDonald. Lore said a Roman general gifted the knife long ago to a MacDonald warrior chief. Their agreement being, *You barbarians stay on your side of the bulwark. We Romans will stay on ours.* Clansmen accepted it, cocksure in the knowledge the great invaders feared them.

Like him, the dagger had lost its way.

"I'm surprised our chief gave his blessing," he said. "He didna support the Uprising."

"What happened at Moidart and the Isle of Eigg convinced him." Anne was solemn. *A town burned, our herds destroyed, and forty men unjustly taken.* The unsaid words were a firebrand in her eyes.

His hand curled to a fist. Her fervor was putting a fire in his belly. It wasn't enough that Scotland surrendered. The Government had to rub salt in the wounds. "This is why you do it," he said for his own edification. "To make Clanranald lands home again."

"Yes. First the gold, then the dagger." Anne was quiet, the only one standing at the table as if she couldn't bear to sit down on the job.

The women gathered round the table were a force, their manner confident, their ages unimportant. Brave and beautiful, war had branded them, but loss would not define them. Their courage put a great yearning inside him—to be the hero they needed him to be.

In scanning their faces, there was no mistaking Mary Fletcher and Cecelia MacDonald capable of leading this league. With full curves, chestnut hair, and a cleft chin, Mary Fletcher was a beauty . . . as his purely male opinion went. By her plain fashion and prim hair, she wouldn't tolerate her appearance as her stock in trade. His cousin, however, thrived on it. She was a brazen piece. Proudly so. Honey-gold curls in flirtatious places, a heart-shaped patch on her cheek. Cecelia MacDonald would play her features to the hilt and give as good as she got.

Wise men would look deeper and find their true worth.

"And your leader is . . . ?"

Anne set the foolscap on the table. "Me."

A half-cocked smile formed. He should've known. Anne was unafraid of firm decisions. She was his past, and for the next few days, his near future. She smoothed the paper, a pretty wisp of hair gracing her cheek. Someday a better man than him would earn the right to brush it aside.

"Lead on," he said, but the salon was oddly quiet.

Not a rustle of petticoats or creak of a chair.

The women glued their attention to the foolscap. Forearms bracing on the table, he did the same. It was a detailed floorplan of a grand home. The league's rival for the gold, no doubt. Someone with a lot of quid and an appetite for more. Eyeing it, a vague remembrance teased him.

"We do this in two parts," Anne said. "Tomorrow, we make a copy of the key holding the gold." To him, she said, "The gold is in a cabinet built into a wall, secured by a Wilkes Lock."

"I know how they work." He craned his neck for a better view of the floorplan. "A tricky lock with a numbered dial etched in the metal. Keeps count each time it's opened."

"Which is why we will have one chance to open it."

He honed in on the room marked with an X where the gold was stored.

"When you find the key, press it into this." Mary passed over a block of wax.

The whitish lump was cool in his hand. He would make an impression of the key?

"Have a care when you pull it out," Mary said, finishing her instructions. "Or I won't be able to make an exact reproduction."

He rolled the wax across his palm. "We're no' stealing the gold the same day?"

"We cannot. There are nearly seventeen hundred livres. The cover of night is best." Anne slid the map closer to him. "Tomorrow is the servants' half day. Only the housekeeper will be in residence. That is our day to imprint the key."

"When do we steal the gold?" he asked.

"There will be an evening entertainment, two hundred people or so, attending an art salon about a week from today."

"You want to take the gold with that many people around?"

"It is the perfect time. The more in attendance, the better." His cousin regarded him with cynical eyes. "It is the law of social events. The bigger the crowd, the more they preen and posture. *Especially* in London."

Could her drawl have been any more dramatic?

"Everyone will be so concerned with how they look and what they think everyone is thinking about them that they won't notice what's right under their noses," the elder Miss Fletcher said.

"Aunt Flora will be in the kitchens, and Aunt Maude will be an attending maid in the ground floor retiring room. A signal will be given, and that's when you and I shall go to the study, unlock the cabinet, and pass the gold to Mary and Margaret through the window here—" Anne tapped the paper "—where they will be waiting with a cart."

"That particular window is at the side of the house but near the mews," Miss Fletcher added. "We should escape notice."

He scrubbed a hand across his mouth. "It doesna matter how fine the clothes I wear, I'm no' a mon for such events."

"You are exactly the man we want."

Something in Anne's gentle voice and demure lashes gave him pause. Anne had never been demure. Why the sudden show now?

"You will be fine," his cousin assured him. "Wine and champagne will flow. And not all in attendance will be the genteel sort. The guest list includes artists and the women they paint in the nude. Those paintings, among others, will be on display."

Miss Fletcher's lip pressed with mild disapproval. "It will not be an evening for overfine manners."

He was slow to tear his attention from Anne's staunch profile. The tiny hairs on his nape were twitching. Blasted woman. She was hiding something.

"Where is this house anyway?"

He snatched the foolscap and studied it. Heat began to coat his skin, the pained rush of embarrassment combined with a strong desire for the ground to swallow him whole. *Upper Brook Street* buttressed a grand house facing a familiar garden square. The address written at the bottom scalded him: Grosvenor Square.

Silence pounded his ears. His past was in the bile creeping up his throat. Outside, a driver yelled at a team of horses clip-clopping along

Bermondsey Lane, but inside the salon no one made a sound. He rose from the chair, his limbs sturdy despite the quake within.

He loomed over Anne and held up the paper, his fingertips bloodless and his voice dangerously mild. "Who has the gold?"

"The Countess of Denton."

The beast inside him raked vicious claws the length of his soul and laughed.

Chapter Six

$\mathcal{W}$ill's gaze distilled the air to its simplest form. Breathing hurt. She touched fingertips to the table for balance. The need for Jacobite treasure shimmered blindingly, but she'd just asked Will to pay a hefty price by returning to his shame.

To the woman who'd kept him like a favorite possession.

It had been an honest contract with Lady Denton. That much she knew, and while certain men reveled in the role, Will had not. At present, he burned with shame and ire, twin flames threatening to scorch her. Everyone in the league had sacrificed in one way or another, but his past was the currency they needed most.

Will set the paper on the table with heartaching carefulness and stalked across the room. Male pride evened his shoulders, a majestic form at the window. Thank God the glass stopped him. At his nape, his queue's black silk ribbon taunted her.

Promises made, promises broken. Their legacy.

She clutched her stomacher. Behind tasteful embroidery, pain twisted and pressed as if someone had drawn back their booted foot and kicked her.

Her eyes stung. She'd hurt Will again.

"Ladies, please give us a moment."

In her side vision, fluent glances spread around the table. Chairs scraped and the women exited in respectful silence, their footsteps a hushed clutter until the salon doors squeaked shut.

Will's dignity was on the altar.

The Countess of Denton collected braw men the way others collected soft-paste porcelain figurines, though her tastes ran afoul of her class. Former soldiers, thief takers, the odd dockside brute. Gruff men hungry for coin and a warm bed, men good in a fight. If an attractive woman from Society's higher places came with the offer, it was fine by them. *Her private footman.* That's what the countess called the man who attended her, though no livery was worn. And her ladyship never kept a man beyond six months.

She'd kept Will for a year.

Their arrangement was no mystery; how it began and ended was.

What happened?

Anne rubbed her nape, the knot in her back palpable, the tension growing. If she wasn't careful, she'd be a hunchback, worn out and old before her time, and at the moment, time was not her friend. Daylight waned in the glass framing Will. The gloaming hour would soon come.

A well-executed crime required precision and confidence in one's partners.

Was he in? Or out?

"Will," she called as gently as she could.

Not a twitch.

"Will." She was louder this time, and he, a statue.

Head high, his stance brittle, she feared he'd break. A ridiculous notion for a man like Will. He'd always been mighty. Nothing could crack him, not a lost war, nor imprisonment. Still, she sped across the room only to stop short, skirts swinging, her heart in her throat when Will spun around with a glare to cut stone.

"You played me falsely, madame."

"No," she cried. The pounding in her chest cleaved fact from fiction. There might be *some* truth to his words.

"Aunt Flora's presence was a masterful move."

Did he not understand? Her feet itched to move, but she dared not go any closer. "Aunt Flora is not a chess piece."

Will scoffed. The brooding beast gone, Hades had taken his place, an angry deity framed by red serge drapes and late day London skies. Gray, gray, and more dismal gray while he flared brilliantly. The god of the underworld looked ready to smite her, but she'd not retreat, regroup, or reassess. The moment was upon her to carve a path forward. She'd seize it.

"Everything you've heard, the herds in need of replenishment, the Clanranald men unjustly taken, our kin desperate for safe passage to the colonies . . . it's all true."

"With certain details conveniently left out."

He advanced on her, slow and menacing, but she stood her ground, a chill camping on the knot in her back. Wonderful. More discomfort.

She deserved his ire, but she would not cower. Necessity was a harsh taskmaster. One learned quickly or was trampled by London's barbarians, and London bred the best of them. Silk-clad, bejeweled barbarians were particularly cruel. The skirted ones, the worst. They played fast with the law and hid behind privilege and petticoats after dealing vicious blows. Will never functioned that way. He was honest, loyal to a fault, and he fought face-to-face just as he'd told her abovestairs. Skulking in shadows and trickery were cowardly to a man of his high standards. It's why he fought the rebellion openly.

When he stopped a half pace from her, she wished he wasn't so forthright.

It hurt to be this close to his proud, beautiful face. The angles sharp, his skin smooth. The severe line of his mouth told her how great the divide between them. She'd do well to start bridging it.

"I tried to tell you in the shed—"

"You didna try hard enough." Arms crossed, Hades was in no mood to listen.

"—and then you followed me home."

Muscles tensed under wrinkled velvet pulled tight over shoulders and arms. Will needed that reminder. His flinty eyes burned a tad less bright for it. The two of them trod a careful line of thrust and parry, of argument and persuasion. All the same, she'd touched a nerve and wanted to soothe it. The irritating desire to smooth every inch of ruined velvet lingered too. She buried both hands in her skirts to resist the urge.

"You may recall, I spent considerable effort

last night convincing you the Jacobite gold is real. And when I saw how exhausted you were, I thought sleep the better thing."

Will's eyes were topaz chips. "Do not maneuver me, madame."

"I wouldn't dream of it. We are equals." An economy of words usually worked with Will. Direct, plain. When they didn't suffice, she reminded him in patient tones, "And I already agreed to your . . . payment."

His visage was stony.

"There is that."

Silence was a gift, a blessed moment to reassemble.

"Then, you understand," she said quietly. "You are not the only one uncomfortable here."

Will stalked to the fireplace, and she exhaled air she didn't know she was holding. A gate had been opened. Wasn't that how progress worked? A little give, a little take. She was sure more giving on her part would be required. Much more giving.

"I know why you came to me after all these years," he said.

She stilled. "You do?"

"Because I know where Ancilla keeps the Wilkes Lock key."

She squeezed her eyes shut a split second. Hearing the countess's Christian name set her teeth on edge. "It's in her study," she said. "I had planned to search for it if you wouldn't help us."

"She keeps the key in a hollowed-out book. You'd be old and gray afore you ever found it."

"A book." There were hundreds of them in the woman's study, thousands more in her library.

"But you don't know which one Ancilla uses." Will swung around, his smile pure satisfaction. "Which means you need me. Quite a lot, in fact."

"We need each other." Walking toward him, she enunciated each word, adding a surly, "And would you please address the woman properly? Despite her being a heinous gargoyle."

"A gargoyle?" he chuckled, and she swatted the air.

"Ignore that."

Of course, he wouldn't. Will rested an elbow on the mantel, a cocky smile wreathing his face. Her vision narrowed on him. *Hades is gloating.* It had a maddening effect because she *did* need him, and Will, full of swagger, was dangerous fun, a glimmer of the man she once knew.

"There's the matter of getting into her home," he said. "The countess is no' going to welcome me with open arms."

She cocked her head. What an interesting morsel of information. Her ladyship and Will at odds? She'd save that for consumption later.

"The countess is presently in the countryside, hunting grouse and not expected to return to London until the day before hosting her art salon."

"I recall . . ." he said vaguely rubbing his chin. "She likes the hunt."

For treasure and men. Especially if that treasure doesn't belong to her. Hands folded neatly, she tamped down her ire. Will was not a commodity to fight over, especially with that woman from his past. Facing him, Anne acknowledged another disconcerting truth: she belonged to his past too.

Three sharp knocks and the salon door flew open. Cecelia bustled in, a gray cloak in hand.

"Anne, we must go." Pensive eyes sought the darkening window. "We're late."

Will stepped away from the mantel. "You havena told me how I'm getting inside the house."

"I will tomorrow morning."

Cecelia handed over the cloak. "He could meet us tonight."

Oh, Cecelia. She almost groaned aloud.

Cecelia flashed a mischievous grin. "It makes perfect sense."

Will and her at a public house? Horrifying. They'd have to converse. Socially.

"Tonight is business," she said.

"Every night is business with you, Anne. I worry about you. You need some fun." To Will, "We shall be at the White Lamb on Crown Alley. Do you know it?"

"Do I know it? It's a den of thieves and cut-throats!"

"Indeed, it is." Cecelia winked at him and fairly danced her way out of the room, a flurry of white petticoats.

Anne tossed the cloak over her shoulders. People depended on her. Of course, duty to the clan came first. She'd not apologize for it.

"The idea has some merit. You could meet Mr. Horatio Styles."

Will's brow puzzled.

"Our means of entry to Lady Denton's home

tomorrow," she said, looping the frogs under her chin. "Meeting him might make you feel better about working with me."

"Me going with you now. That would make me feel better."

Will's moody glower softened her. She itched to brush clean the tension framing his mouth. A man worrying over her was adorable, though Will would chafe at being told as much. She could tell him their clan chief hadn't fretted over her since the '45. Neither had her father, or her brothers, bless their clodhopper souls. She'd grown used to her strength and independence for seven years and counting; change was impossible.

"At the moment, Aunt Flora is laboring in the kitchen to make sure you're well fed. I'm sure you'll have no trouble obliging her, and the Fletcher sisters need you here." Her gaze led his to the sea chest. "Some alterations will be necessary."

"I don't like it." His voice was a deep, protective rumble.

"I shall be fine. Your cousin will be with me."

"That's supposed to make me feel better?" he scoffed. "My cousin thinks the White Lamb is an adventure."

Something akin to delight flickered inside her, a treacherous little flame that needed watching. Will wasn't trying to stop her. She was more than capable of taking care of herself. Will grasped that. Even better—and this was the alarming part—was how he handled her authority. He was fierce but respectful. Will didn't swoop into the league, the proverbial male taking over and showing the females (the lesser sex, of course!) how things should be done. She had a keen mind, and Will didn't try to stop her from using it.

A dangerous flame, indeed.

"We'll be safe, I assure you." She tempted fate by rubbing a threadbare spot on his sleeve. "We need you looking the part of a merchant on the rise."

Will's big hand folded over hers, his warmth seeping into her skin. She shivered nicely when he leaned in and his lips grazed her ear.

"No, lass. You need me looking like your betrothed."

Chapter Seven

Moorfields was the common man's pleasure garden, where good and evil met. Open-air markets and traveling shows, criminals and Methodists all mingled as one. Ha'pennies flooded the torchlit green, passing from one grubby hand to the next. So many, Will crossed trampled grass, tasting copper's dirty tang.

The dance of vice and virtue. The night was rife with it.

A bored fortune-teller shuffled cards inside her open tent. Yawning players in patched clothes traipsed a makeshift stage. The drunk and aimless gathered and they weren't particular about their entertainment. Anything would do; in its absence trouble brewed. West End nobs knew this. The idle poor rioted.

Keep them numb, Ancilla would say from the comfort of her gilt-trimmed carriage.

He'd watched and learned in those days. The Countess of Denton was older, smarter, and accomplished, a beauty to seize a man's breath. Or his ballocks. Sometimes the countess took both.

She'd taken in a young forgotten foot soldier, a wild highlander and molded him. A quiet hulking man who read more and pondered things took his place.

One lesson in particular stuck: survival was primal, and it often came well dressed.

Him wading through Middle Moorfields was about another confounding woman, and he'd traveled a long distance these years to find her. She had something he wanted. Tonight, he'd get it. But the crossing was gritty, a dogged journey that began on a doorstep in Edinburgh and landed him here, in Crown Alley.

Tall, dark, and bricked, the alley was busy. Men hanging candle lamps to ward off night, boys roping barrels. A pipe-smoking, thrum-capped sailor slouched beside the alley's lone door. Music and laughter swelled behind it.

"Ye here for the weddin' feast?" the old man asked. "Or the bare-knuckle brawlers?"

Will stepped back and checked the tavern's sign. Faded letters spelled White Lamb, but an impudent soul had recently painted a lush, red-lipped smirk on the wee animal.

"Neither. I'm meeting a woman."

The seaman let loose a salty laugh. "It's all the same, lad."

He eyed the door. The latch was rattling as if straining to hold a raucous tide of merriment.

"It starts like whot's in there—" the sailor pointed at the tavern "—and ends like that." He jabbed a thumb at the roped-off ring. "If yer lucky, she'll give ye a kiss and a tup—" he opened the door with a flourish "—no leg shackle required."

Will tipped at waves of noise, color, and the scent of women washing him. Deep within a fiddle sawed a rustic tune. Feet were stomping. Hands were clapping. Breasts were heaving, plump and ripe for the picking. Pale and dark skinned, the public house welcomed all comers. Sirens, all of them. Their eyes sparkled with invitation: *Sex is here.*

He stepped inside, a carnal current vibrating from the floor up his legs.

A leg shackle never looked so desirable.

He didn't bother to bite back a grin of male appreciation. Women were everywhere. On the stairs and above them, crowding the railing, flirting with crane-necked men below. Silk petticoats mashed between balusters, skirts too fine for this establishment. Somewhere a tallyman had made a year's worth of coin renting gowns to the women here tonight. Those skirts were meant to be seen—and lifted. Tamer crowds milled the room's perimeter, pints in hand without a table in sight. The center was for dancing—if that's what one called the melee of bodies. Men tossed up women and twirled them close. Partners passed in messy lines. Torsos rubbed and necks arched to receive a carnal kiss.

Even the primmest preacher would throb with lust should he cross the White Lamb's threshold.

"There you are!" His cousin sidled up to him, breathless with excitement. "Quite a lively reel, isn't it?"

Thumb hooked in his waistcoat pocket, he soaked in the revelry. "Been to my share of country assemblies, but I've never seen a reel like that."

Which made his cousin laugh. She linked arms with him, and he smelled spiced rum. It had been a long, long time since he'd last set foot in the White Lamb. It was quieter then: thieves and cutthroats, harlots and humble travelers, all taking respite from the thirsty business of life. If what he was witnessing tonight was how a newborn marriage came about, he needed to get out more. Perhaps he'd kept too much to himself laboring for West and Sons Shipping. Most days, once the work was done, he'd find a chophouse, get his fill of food, and find his bed—alone.

A deep itch grabbed hold, and he searched the dancers for a seditious raven-haired woman. All and sundry in this establishment would test the limits of their bed ropes.

Why shouldn't he do the same?

"Mr. Gladwell's daughter, Hannah, wed one Mr. James Hadley." His cousin stood on tiptoe and pointed. "There they are."

A ginger-haired man tossed a laughing, comely maid high in the air. Flowers crowned her head, and pink ribbons twined blond locks.

"He looks happily leg shackled."

His cousin leaned against him, her visage wistful and soft. "He most certainly is. Mr. Hadley was part of a company of rogues. The best Spruce Prigs in London, and he gave it all up. For her." She sighed. "Now he's going to help Mr. Gladwell, owner and proprietor of this establishment."

"True love, I'm sure."

She eyed him. "Too quaint an emotion for you?"

"Too costly."

His cousin's mouth curved, worldly and wise.

"Well, you're sure to find whatever your heart desires . . . to the extent your purse can pay for it."

Was that a warning? Did she see him as a sheep among wolves? Could be he still exuded rustic highlander, the kind who spent more time hunting wild game than chasing pretty women. Or his cousin swam regularly in a pool of iniquity and was quite jaded.

A pair of smiling blondes ambled by. Lips rouged, cheeks flushed, and one with a red flower in her hair. She gave him a come-hither look before blending into a cluster of friends. Her blue-eyed stare cut across the room past bobbing heads and found him once more.

His cousin's voice floated artfully beside him. "And there are plenty of women willing to oblige your company without benefit of payment. I could make introductions."

He briefly held that blue-eyed connection, then severed it to watch a smiling groom dance with his joyous bride. Blue-eyed women were everywhere and not so desirable.

"I'm here to watch over you and Anne."

"Of course. The night's business," his cousin said, smiling coyly. "You'll need a drink for that." She tugged his sleeve and led the way, speaking over her shoulder. "While you're watching over us, have a care with your coin purse."

He patted his pocket, the coin purse still there.

Spruce Prigs were a cunning lot. Pickpocketing wasn't their usual mode, but one could never be too careful. Well dressed and well mannered, the rogues sneaked into the City's best social events and robbed the master of the house blind. A particularly bold band of Spruce Prigs had opened a store off Threadneedle and sold the goods back to the owners for twice their value.

Smart and pretty or scarred and vile, the White Lamb hosted rogues of every order.

His cousin cut a path through the hive-ish mob when her arm slipped free. A clutch of thrum-capped sailors claimed her. She smiled grandly and pointed at a corner, "Over there!" before melting into the crowd.

He hesitated, but her full-throated laughter was the sign he needed. Cecelia MacDonald was just fine, which was a good thing. Another woman called him, one with firm command of her life and a vexing way of stirring his.

Something happened when they were alone in the salon today, and he hungered to finish it.

Slogging through the crowd, he was hot and impatient. The music loud, the voices louder. Ale was spilled on the toes of his boots. Elbows jabbed his back. He plowed on, scanning faces as if he'd waited eight years for this night. His journey had taken him through rebellion, imprisonment, and a string of unwise days frittered in London. Now it landed him here, his final steps in this boisterous public house.

Until he saw what he wanted. Anne tucked in a corner, hair tumbled, skin sheened.

Dumbstruck, he breathed in her magic.

Could a man see a woman for the first time, twice in his life?

Anne must've danced a reel or three or four. Ruby-red lips parted, and she drank from a pewter cup. He would feast on this picture except his vision expanded. Two men flanked her, the taller one whispering in her ear. A first mate, he guessed, by the cut of the man's coat and his stance.

A peal of laughter was her answer.

Both hands curled into fists. The men would leave, or he'd hammer them.

Patrons jostled, and he moved, the planked floor sticky against the soles of his boots. Hands clapped in time to the music. The beat matched his pulse. Winding around giggling harlots, he waited for Anne to feel his presence. He felt hers, the fey night creature exposed, her darkness brightly fascinating.

She made everything vivid. Songs were spirited, colors clear, and touch . . .

His mouth quirked.

Lasses with the right touch . . . his weakness.

But touching her was only a memory. A wise man would leave the past where it belonged, yet standing in the White Lamb he was far from wisdom's gates.

And only Anne had what he wanted.

Watching her, he knew when awareness struck. The hitch of her body, her rum-glistened mouth still until her reckless gaze found his.

Like flint to steel. He burned.

She drank again from her cup, her fearless emerald eyes locked with his in a blatant carnal stare. Sensuality fused to his skin. His joints taut, he pushed past throngs of couples until the last, a young man trying hard with a serving wench.

"Not now, Thomas. I'm working." The harried

woman wiped her brow and tucked a rag in her apron pocket.

The poor lass blocked Will, but he'd wait impatiently.

Anne called out a neutral, "I'd given up on you coming."

"Why wouldn't I? We are *betrothed*," he said with relish.

His reward was her eyes rounding and one man's face draining color. Had she forgotten their ruse? Apparently. His chest swelled with satisfaction at reminding her, while pewter clanked and the serving wench between them sped off, mugs in her clutches and an ardent swain in tow.

Finally, Anne. Except . . .

Anger and lust bolted him. "What the devil . . ."

She was perched on a barrel, slender legs crossed with skirts foaming around white-stockinged knees. A black silk shoe dangling off her toes, Anne was sin and innocence.

She wasn't waiting for trouble. She was looking for it.

Chapter Eight

$\mathcal{W}$ill's bone-cleaving stare traveled from one man to the other.

"Leave."

She was shocked to her toes. At his harsh command and her dancing pulse. At Mr. Gunderson's hasty exit (no loss there, the man was a trifle dull). At Mr. Harrison briefly sizing up Will before bidding her adieu with a neat bow. She expected more from him. Mr. Harrison had sailed around the world twice and fought pirates, if his tales were true. How could he give up so easily?

It might be the tiny detail of her sudden betrothal, but she couldn't fully countenance that. A woman at the White Lamb was fair game until she was wedded and bedded, and even that was negotiable to some. Men were wolves on the hunt, seeking where they might scatter their seed.

Or was it the hulking beast who scared them off?

Will. Upon spying her legs, his calm humor coiled to a snarl. His size would daunt the heartiest, and his hair was on the mussed side, the queue loose with hanks of hair framing a handsome, if unfriendly face. Definitely not Hades. That version of him was rough refinement. This man was nostrils flaring, eyes burning, tension on two legs. He prowled. A great grace surrounded him and she fell into the depths of his amber eyes.

The beast she'd unchained from Marshalsea was back. He'd cleared the field, and by the look, he'd walked all the way from Southwark to do it.

New heat washed her limbs, sounding an alarm. No rules, save one, existed in their new arrangement. She was to give him something in return for his service to the league. Beyond that, theirs was an open field, tenuous and un-negotiated.

She needed to . . . reassemble.

She sipped rum and twirled her foot. "You might as well post a no trespassing sign."

"Your garter is showing, madame."

"So is your ill temper." She couldn't stop from peering at her knee.

A red silk bow peered back.

"Do you always conduct business with your petticoats at your knees?"

"When I want to, yes."

Will leveled a hard look at her.

She feigned innocence and tucked her hem an inch higher. "Should my hem be here?"

Will's gaze locked on the bit of skin exposed at her knee.

"Or . . . here?"

She baited the beast, nudging her hem another fraction of an inch. So her skirts had climbed that high. Blame the potent drink coursing her veins.

She was deliciously light and free. It had been, well . . . forever since she'd last danced. Dancing was a frivolous pursuit when there was much work to do. A household to run, a warehouse to manage, Jacobite gold to hunt and steal. A woman's work was never done.

And if she was perfectly honest, it had been forever since she'd satisfied that *other* frivolous pursuit.

"No man will ask me to dance. Not with you hulking about." She toyed with lace trim on her underskirt. "It's getting rather lonely . . . me and my hand."

"What did you say?" he asked incredulously.

She dragged a finger over rum dripping down her cup and sucked her soft wet fingertip.

"A woman pleasuring herself." Defiant words rolled off her tongue, fueled by rum and frustration. "The widow's consolation prize."

A slow grin fought his scowl. "What have you been pouring down your throat, lass?"

"A toddy."

Will checked the bowl. Nutmeg dusted a mixture of rum, water, and sugar.

"Don't you think you'll need a clear head for tomorrow?" His voice roughed with concern.

"I'll be fine." She raised her mug in salute. Duty was her middle name.

Her spine hit the wall, and she was grumpy again, slouching as best a woman could in stiff stays. Neither of her two dead husbands ever worried over her. The newness of it was rather like tasting a foreign dish for the first time—did she like it? Or not?

"You could dance with me."

She jerked at his gruff invitation. The beast would devour her, and by the currents snapping under her skin, she'd welcome it.

His mouth on her. Anywhere.

Everywhere.

Yes. That is the problem. Will was delectable and masculine with a tender underbelly, though few saw it. The outside was just as tempting. Light touched each teeth-achingly beautiful angle of his face, and tomorrow, they were supposed to work together. If sex muddled clear thinking, dancing with Will would baffle her senses. Hands touching, bodies brushing, faces close.

She gulped rum. "No."

"Suit yourself." He grabbed a Mortlake jug of ale and poured it into an empty tankard, muttering, "If you did, at least your legs'll be decently covered."

Her Catholic highlander was such a Puritan. His offer to take a turn at the reel was born of propriety. In the White Lamb? Where harlots flashed knees and thighs?

"Take a look around you. No one is going faint at the sight of my shins."

His grunt was primordial. Will angled himself just so, shielding her from the rest of the tavern, and drank his ale. The beast on watch. No poaching here! His back stretched impossibly wide, narrowing by degrees to his waist. He was comfortable in his cast-off velvet coat, and she liked that about him. She always had. No airs, just Will being Will. A common laborer and one-time warrior, an unashamed man of the land. By day he worked with his hands, and by night he read, as evidenced by his collection of pamphlets and lone book, *Dante's Inferno*. An interesting choice.

Will had depths worth exploring; their summer together she'd barely scratched the surface. But he was better suited for tame country assemblies with harmless punch and proper reels, though she couldn't be completely sure. She'd never danced with him.

A crack split her heart. She never would.

Will would go his way, and she'd go hers. Again.

The room hazed. Duty was a lonely banner to carry. Leaning over, she dragged her mug through the toddy bowl atop a barrel beside her, her table for the night.

"This evening was supposed to be fun."

Will braced a hand on the wall, his coat falling open. "I thought it was supposed to be work."

A black waistcoat hugged him. The vee of his waist distracted her. Flat, narrow, flouting symmetry of an otherwise large male frame. Eyelids drooping, she stared.

"It was." She cleared her throat and conjured her best woman-of-business voice. "I bought a drayage and two horses. They'll be delivered to Cecelia's house in three days."

"A legitimate purchase?"

"I'm afraid so."

"That's no' very exciting, buying a big side-less cart and two horses."

She took in the width of his shoulders. "A necessity."

Will took a swig of ale. "Why, Mrs. Neville, you make a life of crime sound almost boring."

His brogue trilled warm and resonant. The little things about him got her. His slouching old boots and gilded-gold hair. And Will was so close. So touchable. She ran her fingers along his shirt's open neck, the seam worn, the linen a textured grain.

"Most of my purchases are legitimate, Mr. MacDonald." She stared at his mouth, the width and fullness of his lower lip. "There's been only one illegitimate purchase."

The tankard stopped halfway to his mouth. "Only one?"

"Yes. Though I prefer to think of him as a troublesome hire."

Will's eyes were glossy and black, ringed with amber. She could swim in their depths.

"Him, you say? And how do you keep this troublesome mon in line?"

She gripped his shirt with one hand and filled the other with velvet. "By giving him what he wants."

"A perilous plan, lass."

"Not any more perilous than committing a crime."

Time slowed. She searched his face, his eyes fierce and clear. Theirs was a dance of stillness, him on the brink of crossing a boundary and her ready to smash them all. The tension was agony.

"What do you want from me?" she asked.

His chest expanded and contracted with a mighty gust as if she'd laid a boon at his feet, yet he'd stay a gentleman. She didn't want a gentleman; she wanted the beast. Or Hades. Both were versions of Will, and she wanted to taste them.

She scored old velvet with her fingernails, an image flashing: grabbing Will's hand and racing out the door for the nearest dark alley. She'd lift her skirts and he'd take her against a wall. An act of steamy, grinding sex.

"Now is no' the time or place for that," he chided, thick voiced.

She begged to differ. Matters of the flesh had never been their problem.

Will set aside his ale and touched his thumb to the corner of her mouth. "You have a small mess here." A gentle swipe and, "No thief should sport nutmeg on her mouth. It's distracting. About as distracting as you talking about touching yourself."

Lust danced like the devil between them. She was acutely aware of touching his clothes. If she touched him, she'd incinerate. Somewhere in their conversation, music had stopped and her legs had uncrossed. Her limbs, in fact, had a mind of their own. Her skirt was properly down but underneath her jellied knees were wide open. Will was between them.

His lips parted, a magnetic pull.

Her mouth was drawn to his, as necessary as breathing.

She tipped her head and—

"This is my cousin, Mr. Will MacDonald."

Her shoe clattered to the floor. *Cecelia!* What piss-poor timing.

She grasped more velvet, stretching the cloth

to its limit. Will checked her, a tense frown her answer. His private smile did nothing to erase her jagged edge. They untangled themselves, him smoothing his coat, and her hot skinned, tossing back unruly curls while wantonness streamed her veins.

"We were discussing today's purchase," she said as dignified as one could, sitting on a barrel with one shoe on and one shoe off.

"Of course, you were." Cecelia's cat-that-ate-the-cream smile stretched wide and introductions were made.

Cecelia was arms linked with Mr. Horatio Styles, cozy and friendly as was her way. Anne worked hard to be agreeable, but lust clung like a vapor, clouding her head. She liked Mr. Styles. He took his profession seriously. With gentle manners and a tutor's mien, his past was unknown. Scholar? Actor? He could've been both or neither. Gray haired and smooth skinned, his age was uncertain, but his talent legendary. When he didn't work, the man dressed well. Pink of the fashion.

"Mr. Styles is a counterfeit crank," Cecelia explained to Will. "The best."

"Thank you, Miss MacDonald." Mr. Styles beamed. "I am happy to use my skills to help a friend."

"A counterfeit crank?" Will's brow furrowed. "How is your pretending to have the falling-down sickness getting me inside a house on Grosvenor Square?"

"Because I shall play the part of a rag-n-bone man afflicted with the falling-down sickness."

"While you and Anne play a newly betrothed couple out for a stroll," Cecelia said to Will.

Will nodded, appearing to digest this. "There's go' to be more."

"There is," Cecelia said. "Do go on, Mr. Styles. My cousin hasn't heard all the details."

Anne tucked a wayward lock behind her ear. Will pivoted well. She couldn't. Her jangled nerves and lust-drenched limbs needed to recover. At least there was nothing to worry about here. Chatter swelled inside, the perfect place to converse about a crime. No one would hear them. No one would care. The White Lamb was crawling with harlots and rogues of every stripe.

"Of course." Mr. Styles was bright eyed, speaking to Will. "Tomorrow, at half past one, you will see me steer my handcart to the doorstep of Denton House at Grosvenor Square. I shall climb the stairs while chewing a piece of soap. A froth will form quickly. At which time, I shall fall down at the front door, appearing to foam at the mouth. That will be your cue to come to the rescue and pound on the front door." Mr. Styles beamed at his audience of three. "Easy enough?"

Will shook his head. "It won't work. West of St. Martin's Lane, all rag-n-bone men go to the kitchen or the mews. Never the front door."

"For this outing, he will be at the front of the house," Cecelia insisted. "Your pounding on the door will bring the housekeeper—"

"Who will slam it shut when she sees trouble on her mistress's doorstep." Will was mulishly certain. "And let's no' forget that Mrs. Goodspeed knows me."

Anne watched him. Interesting, his knowledge of the habits of rag-n-bone men.

"Mrs. Goodspeed is no longer housekeeper of Denton House. Mrs. Brown is." Cecelia's voice firmed. "With you and Anne dressed in the height of fashion, Mrs. Brown *will* oblige you."

Anne touched Will's sleeve. "Once the door is open, you will pull Mr. Styles into the entryway—"

"The housekeeper will have a hard time removing you then," Cecelia put in.

"—and that's when you will offer to fetch a cup of water from the kitchen."

"But I won't go to the kitchen. I'll go to the study and make an imprint of the key," Will finished the plan neatly, intuitively, his eyes on Anne.

"While Mr. Styles and I will do our best to detain the housekeeper."

She let her spine rest against the wall. Rum and the late hour were beginning to sap her. In a matter of minutes, Will grasped what had taken weeks to orchestrate. Every twist and turn had been argued and counter-argued with the league. Nothing could go wrong. The alternative, if Will had refused to join them, was her hunting for the key in the study.

"When you return, I shall make a miraculous recovery and be on my way." Mr. Styles winked. "None will be the wiser."

"All the servants will be gone on their half day, save the housekeeper," Cecelia said. "You will be in and out in a matter of minutes."

The four of them made a tight circle. Will, eyes on the floor, rubbed his nape. Crime didn't sit well with him. A moral man, he was goodness from the crown of his head to the soles of his worn-out boots. She'd hardened her heart, but Will's return scraped off calloused parts. His presence was a reminder: she used to wake up to honest, carefree days.

She gripped her mug with both hands. Prison terrified her. The cold finality, so bleak and hostile.

How did Will manage to endure it? A man who aspired to do good had ended up in a dank prison hold, while she worked ferociously in the shadows to skirt the law for a good end. There was no fairness in what life had dealt them. Yet Will was fearless as ever, a solid presence beside her.

"It sounds easy enough," he said.

"It will be your quickest workday ever." A cheerful Cecelia dipped her cup in the toddy bowl. "Nothing can go wrong."

Chapter Nine

*T*heir wherry glided through inky waters.

One Mr. Henry Baines had met them at Tower Stairs close to midnight. There was none of the usual "Oars and sculls! Sculls and oars!" cries of ferryman. Only one man waited with a candle lamp. At their approach, Mr. Baines had doffed his tricorn and swept a bow worthy of a queen for Anne and Cecelia. The ferryman left his lamp at Tower Stairs, his vessel guided by moonlight alone, a surreptitious passing since The Company of Watermen and Lightermen required well-lit ferries.

Whether driven by coin or a smitten heart, this wasn't the first late-night ride he'd given these women. Probably wouldn't be the last.

A well-mannered counterfeit crank and an obliging ferryman. What else would Anne and her league produce?

Will wouldn't know. She'd gone conspicuously tight-lipped since their near kiss at the White Lamb. They'd entered a tacit agreement, the word *later* hanging in glances between them.

Raw and restless, he didn't regret a thing.

His cousin blathered amiably with Mr. Baines. The ferryman, barely twenty and broad of back, obliged her. They gossiped of ships and sea captains and pleasure barges (and who took them privately). Cecelia was intriguing to watch, harvesting tidbits of information from Baines. Her moue was an expressive language all by itself. She was laughter and light, or teasing and coy. He doubted she possessed a serious bone in her body. That his cousin was part of Anne's league was quite surprising.

The next seat over, Anne's spine was a ramrod, her face an artful sculpture within her hood. When the City's lights faded, her eyes met his, vivid, direct, with a touch of wondering. The woman had ensorcelled him with her talk of a widow's consolation. A kraken could swim upriver, swarm their slender vessel, and he'd be none the wiser of the fabled sea beast's approach.

All from a plaguing image.

Rumpled sheets. Anne, hair loose, her face turned into a pillow . . .

Head high, he forced air into his lungs.

. . . underneath the bed linens, halfway down her body, the smallest stirring.

Loins heavy, he let the rush consume him.

Red lips opened wider. A soft moan, a louder one. The bed creaking, the stir hastening, and the woman, her pleasure cries a sweet song.

Anne sat an arm's length from him, gentle winds carrying her not-so-innocent lavender and spiced-rum scent. He laughed, a low rusty grumble. He knew how *her* song ended. She had sung it for him many times in their lust-crazed youth.

Of all the White Lamb's sirens, she lured him. Her emerald eyes haunted him from the shadows of her hood. Same as she did in Marshalsea's shed while the warder babbled on about kilts. Anne was the only woman he could talk to yet never say a word.

Staring into her eyes was like that, one fluid conversation.

He'd known what it meant to be understood.

Gripping the wherry's rail, he stared at the river. Their summer together had also been a long, fluent conversation in sex. But, he'd loved Anne. Fiercely. He'd been the same age as Mr. Baines when making that proclamation. Love had flowed like milk and honey then, an easy exchange in the give and take of youth. Now he could barely comprehend its vastness.

What does a young man know of love that an older man doesn't?

No answer came from stygian waters.

His hold on weathered wood tightened. The beast within didn't care. It wanted only to be fed.

Mr. Baines halted his drive and turned his face skyward. "Wind's picking up. I hope it's not more rainstorms."

Spring and early summer had inundated the City with rain. Recent days had been a pleasant reprieve.

Anne searched the heavens, moonlight caressing her face. "It's not a storm. There's gentleness and warmth to it."

"Not too warm, I hope," Cecelia said over her shoulder. "The gutters will be a stew of awful smells."

Will looked up and speckled stars stared back. "Wind is nature's way of saying it has somewhere else to be." When three faces looked at him curiously, he shrugged. "Something my father used to say on blustery days."

"I like that." Mr. Baines dipped the oars in water, his grin pearly white.

His cousin twisted around on her bench. "I recall your father knew quite a lot about nature and whatnot."

"He did. He taught me about hunting, fishing, how to properly shear a sheep—"

He stopped abruptly. Shearing was women's work, but lacking a mother meant he and his father had to muckle through chores together. Cooking, washing dishes, a fair turn at the laundry, he could do it all. Growing up as such gave him a better understanding of a woman's load. Except for childbirth and nursing a babe, household chores didn't care who did them. Sharing tasks made work light. Could be why he'd tolerated Anne's take-charge spirit.

Danger to his manhood didn't worry him. Talk of home did.

His cousin had a peculiar look in her eyes as if she sensed the subject was perilous ground, but she'd test boundaries nonetheless.

"Do you miss it? The wide-open land, I mean. It must have been a trifle hard to live in the City after life in the highlands."

Try life in a prison hulk, lass.

"The City grows on a mon."

"I find that surprising. You liking the City."

"It's no' a matter of liking. Learn the lay of the land and a mon can survive."

"The way you learned to live off the land in the highlands before you were twelve," Anne said quietly. "But there is a difference between surviving and thriving."

A flutter stirred in his chest. "Indeed, there is."

He'd become skilled at putting away memories of Clanranald lands . . . of Berneray and Benbecula and all the islets a lad with a skiff and a nose for adventure could explore. He'd grown up not far from Arisaig, but the isles had called to him. During midseason's quiet, his father let him go for a day or two or three. The rugged, wide-open land had been in his bones, their whispers lingering to this day.

"I remember giggling madly about the name for sheep mating. Autumn is their season for it, is it not?" His cousin searched the air. "The name for it . . . it's something sailors and soldiers use, something about a ram mounting—"

"Tupping." Anne's voice shot like lead from a flintlock. "It's called tupping."

"Yes!" Cecelia cried gleefully.

He grinned. Anne and her terse tones. She'd tolerate no talk of mounting. Did she wish to find a private place and be done with certain unmet needs? The seditious widow's house loomed ahead, a lone candle lamp flickering beside the front door.

"When is the last time you saw your father?" Cecelia asked.

He fisted his hands on his thighs. Her question startled him, a rapier sharp cut to his heart.

"Summer of '45," he managed to say. "Afore I went to Edinburgh."

On an errand to fetch the lass who changed me forever.

Anne fumbled with her hood, a shadow crossing her face. Was it guilt? A woman remembering the summer she'd been promised to one man while falling in love with another? Such a tale was not uncommon. She'd been no more ready for what happened that summer than he. Love had come at them like a mallet. It nearly destroyed them like one too.

"No wonder you want to go to the colonies." His cousin was wistful, her gaze downriver.

Eight years since he'd last seen his father, and eight years since he'd last seen Anne. Visitants from his past, the two were inexplicably entwined. He looked downriver, a breeze cosseting his cheek. The water was a formless void save the narrow moonbeam striking its oily, onyx skin. That light pointed the way he would go once his promise to Anne's league was done.

Why did it feel impossible?

"No' sure he'll have me," he said roughly. "Last time we talked didna go well. We were . . ." His words faltered, and a hard swallow recovered them. "Our parting was . . . vicious."

All eyes were on him. He shrugged heavily, the weight of youthful mistakes returned.

"He couldna understand why I supported

the Uprisin' and I couldna understand why he did no'."

"He'll have you, Will. With open arms," Anne said. "I'm sure of it."

A knot twisted behind his breastbone. The same knot came from talk of home, his father, and Clanranald. Like other men, he'd lost a great deal more than the war.

Relief flooded him when Mr. Baines announced, "Bermondsey Wall."

The younger man leaped into the water, and Will joined him, glad to help. Bermondsey Wall lacked the usual boat-to-stairs landing, thus the wherry had to be hauled ashore through sludge. Water slapped his legs. Mud sucked his boots, but he needed to put his back into something. Exertion got his blood flowing. He was taut as a bowstring. Restless and cagey. Neither talk of home nor the bread of idleness sat well with him. A man was meant for labor, and a son to honor his father.

His heels dug in and sweat popped at his hairline. Could be the green-eyed woman watching him. Thoughts of Anne began to harass him again. Her hand moving under bed linens. Her sweet cries. His booted feet in cold water could not quench the fire.

An appointment with his hand might.

Molars grinding, he gave the wherry one last heave 'til it was half on dry land.

A panting Mr. Baines touched his hat. "My thanks, sir."

His cousin, petticoats plucked high, picked her way over narrow wooden benches. She chattered on, veering toward Mr. Baines while Anne stood in the back. On impulse, Will sloshed through knee-high water and offered his hand.

"Mrs. Neville."

"Mr. MacDonald." A breeze caught her hair. "This is very gallant of you."

He felt a smile creeping over his face. Standing in water, his arm out, he was in danger of turning into a fool. "You mean my sparing you from walking the length of this little boat?"

She smiled back. "It's not that little."

And you're no' a fragile woman, but I want to take care of you all the same. The thought swirled inside him with stunning force. What would Anne say if he said it aloud?

"If you don't mind, my feet are a wee bit soggy. An' I'll have a devil of a time cleaning my boots."

She set her gloveless hand in his. "Perhaps someone with tender mercies will clean them."

His chuckle was rusty as an old saw. He liked her dry humor. Subtle and rare as London's cloudless blue skies but worth the wait. Anne balanced a foot on the rail and stepped up, an act of trust, warming him down to his chilly toes. The wherry wobbled, and he swept her into his arms. For the second time tonight, she grabbed handfuls of his coat and held fast.

Her rum-sweet exhale fanned his cheek. "I wasn't expecting that."

"In the auld days, I'd've tossed you over my shoulder."

"The City has tamed you."

Maybe Anne wanted to be tossed over a man's shoulder? His shoulder. In this, he couldn't claim knowledge of her mind, but he knew exactly why he'd trotted into midnight waters. To feel her hand in his. To hold her.

"Might be because I'm aulder," he said.

"You are twenty-eight. Hardly long in the tooth."

Anne was a slender piece, engulfed in cloak and petticoats, yet his feet sank deeper in soft, hidden soil. Currents buffeted his legs, a reminder to get moving. He savored her body against his. The embrace wasn't the same as lust and sex. It was holding. An arm hooked under white-stockinged knees hidden by voluminous skirts, the other supporting her narrow back.

His nature ran to elemental things. The powerful need to protect and provide. To earn a woman's lifelong respect.

Anne rubbing his back was nice too. When she reached for his cheek, he stilled. Their faces were close, her hood fallen. Moonlight glossed ink-black hair and painted her a touch mysterious. Anne had never been mysterious in her youth, but how much did that young man know of her?

The older man craved deeper knowledge. He let himself forget his cousin and Mr. Baines watching them. He hadn't moved from knee-deep water. Anne was dociling him, the great hulking beast holding a maiden fair.

She tucked loose hair behind his ear. "I forgot that you know about sheep."

Quivers traipsed his back when her fingertip traced the shell of his ear. He'd never been so grateful for that narrow strip of skin.

"A lad doesna forget his education," he said

gruffly. "You go' yours by way of tutors. Mine came in a barn."

He waded ashore, squeezing her close. *Don't think about tupping. Do no' think about tupping.*

She studied him intently. "You get a certain tone when you speak of home, yet you've stayed among the English."

With Anne, a statement could be both declaration and question. He wasn't sure of the answer. Emotions wanted to drown him. Why he couldn't leave, yet why he'd believed now, years after the Uprisin', he should. Answers bubbled near the surface, popping and breaking before he could grasp them.

"You don't hate the English," she said. "I don't see it in you."

"Prison changed that. They're no' all good and they're no' all bad."

"Yet you hate that I had an English husband."

His gut clenched. He had no words for that. None at all.

"You're not bitter? About the English?" she asked.

"A wasteful emotion." Out of the water, he eased her onto firm ground and called out, "Mr. Baines, hop aboard. I'll give you a send-off."

Talk of English husbands unsettled him. He needed to shove something.

"Thank you kindly." The ferryman jumped into his wherry and found his seat. Oars in hand, he nodded. "Whenever you're ready, sir."

Will seized the opportunity to put his shoulder to the vessel. To burn his restlessness with a good, hard push. Feet digging into soft sand, he did push. And push. Limbs and muscles tensed and strove. Mud scraped the red hull and with a final thrust, he sent it swaying into the river.

Mr. Baines shouted a farewell, and Will waved from the water's edge. A drop of sweat ran down his back, stinging a cut from the beating he took at Marshalsea. Last night Anne saved him from that prison. Now she waited for him, cloaked and quiet, at stairs that rose from the beach to Bermondsey Lane.

Skin on his chest pebbled. Night brimmed with intimacy, a different flavor than the White Lamb's variety. Anne had to feel it.

Did she have more questions for him?

He had one for her.

Chapter Ten

$\mathcal{W}$ill ambled across loose soil, a breeze teasing his mussed queue. Talk of family brought ghosts of questions past. Of mistakes made and lessons learned. Though Will trod on English soil, he was every inch a proud highlander. Not years nor a lost war could change that.

"That was kind of you to help Mr. Baines," she said.

Will mounted the bottom step and stopped, eye level with her. "It was the decent thing to do."

She didn't move. He was heart-achingly decent.

One side of his mouth curved up, and her traitorous breath hitched loudly. Will's mouth twitched, victorious at his effect, no doubt.

A tender gauntlet had been thrown, and she was not one to shirk a challenge.

With a bold hand, she brushed back a lock of hair batting his cheek. The texture was thick gold and twice as smooth. She tucked it behind Will's ear and he stilled, a lion tamed.

"You really are a good man, Will MacDonald."

"You say that like it's a new discovery."

"I might have known it once before, but it bears repeating."

"A mon never tires of hearing it."

"Is that an invitation to stroke your pride?"

"Stroke whatever you like, lass," he said in a feather-soft voice.

She huffed at her own weakness. She'd walked right into the snare of innuendo and Will was not one to let opportunity slip from his fingers.

"You are the worst flirt, Will MacDonald." A reprimand delivered with a smile, while her hand rested on his shoulder.

"Flirting is good for the soul. Flirting with the right woman, even better."

Her heart sang. He managed to say playful things yet be endearing. Complex emotions flooded her lust-addled body. *The right woman?* Dangerous words, indeed. And like a woman reaching for her own calamity, she petted his velvet-clad chest.

"Ours is a . . . particular arrangement."

"Playing your betrothed," he said agreeably.

Midnight enfolded them, the river's hush their only companion. Will's big hand slipped inside her cloak and found her hips. Five fingers and his palm, the warmth an imprint she'd remember for the rest of her days. Will sought her chest-petting hand, brought it slowly to his lips.

He touched a knee-watering kiss to her wrist, the same as he did the first time he kissed her years ago. She was crushed and elated, her body pliant, her soul stiff.

How could he do that? Give so reckless a kiss? If she was lost, Will was equally taken. His eyes a torrid storm, his breathing that of a desperate man. Their mouths touching was inevitable, yet they stood in the unknown. Their past dust; their future without hope.

A connection lost forever.

Will's grip on her wrist tightened painfully and a tempest broke fast and furious.

Their mouths met, hot and agitated. Longing and need fused them. Will was velvety smooth, salty and sweet. He was life and she kissed him deeper for it. His strong hand cradled her hip, wooing her, drawing her close, as if to say *Your body belongs right . . . here.*

With me.

She gloried in being close to him. Will's arms holding her. The moon and the stars blessing them. It was a kiss to melt a woman's resolve and scatter her wits, a kiss that ended too quickly. Eyes closed, she held fast to the pleasure of her passionately kissed mouth. To simply *feel* again.

But life demanded her presence.

Sand crunched under restless boots. Will.

When she opened her eyes, her gaze found his haunted glare.

He was once again the man she'd found in Marshalsea Prison.

KISSING HER WRIST was a bad idea. A carnal kiss to her mouth alone . . . that's what he should've done. Lust easily sated. Now, he was stuck with the fragile glow on her face—the moment too hallowed for Anne to open her eyes. Women put such emphasis on first kisses and how they happened.

Maybe he did too.

He fidgeted, irked with his rash behavior. If there was a message in kissing her wrist, he refused to think about it.

"My feet are cold and wet," he said.

Anne checked his legs, her tender glow fading. "We should get you inside before you catch a chill."

A brief walk up the stairs and across the lane, and they found Anne's iron key in the door. Cecelia must've left it. He'd forgotten about her and the others inhabiting this house. For a span of time, no one else existed save Anne and him. Even the beast within had been docile and drugged by that kiss.

But the key . . .

It looked the same as another woman's key, the one he would press into a lump of wax tomorrow. Crossing Anne's threshold, he was two parts restless and one part practical. If a man was on the eve of a crime, he ought to get a good night's rest. For the time being, getting the gold was his job. With muck too thick for an iron scraper, he removed his boots and stockings in the entry hall. Anne locked and barred the door, her sand-encrusted hems in view. He was barefoot, rolling his stockings and ruing the moment Anne freed him from Marshalsea.

"Give them to me," she said. "I'll see them cleaned."

"No need. I'll hang them over a chair."

"You won't require me to do that for you. In your bedchamber?" Her question came with grave hesitation.

"I was teasing you about the tender mercies, Mrs. Neville. You're no' required to do anything for me." He balled the stockings, irritation building.

"Isn't that what you want?" Eyes wide, she looked genuinely startled.

He squeezed the knot his stockings made. *I want a lot of things, lass.*

A pair of sconces caught the shine in her rich black hair. Somehow a mere hand's breadth separated them. Anne's mouth was a ripe red curve, her eyes a fascinating green.

"It's what you bargained for. Today, in my salon." Her pretty mouth moved, saying astonishing things. "I'm prepared to give you what you want, but I ask a boon. That we wait until the gold is in our keeping. Otherwise, sex might become a . . . distraction."

His bare toes pressed hard on the cold floor to keep him from toppling over. His mind was reeling over one fact after another. Only one of them needed absolute clarity.

"You think I'm helping you because I want sex?"

She blinked. "Isn't it?"

He flinched, the blow like a punch below the belt. Holy Mother of . . .

She thought *that* of him?

A carnal creature roared inside him. He could take her. He still ached behind the placket of his breeches, but another beast reared its head, long of claw and cruel in nature. Anne was the one to satisfy both . . . just not the way she was thinking.

She raised her hands to touch him? To comfort him?

He manacled her wrists, his voice whip sharp. "Don't."

Anger came off him in waves, evaporating all tenderness. Anne gawked. She was the heart of his fury. Her petticoats tangling his shins, black hair wrapping his hands. They were confoundedly, inexplicably tied together. He couldn't let her go. In eight years, he never had. Truth slammed him like a musket ball.

He *still* loved her.

Eyes wide, he absorbed this astonishing fact.

He'd not left England these eight years because of Anne. Since his release from the prison hulk, he'd made a habit of donning his kilt and closeting himself with the best ale and whisky his money could buy, then drowning his woes on a certain August day. Until this year, he'd committed his kilt-wearing crime in private. But this year he'd been desperate.

And the reason was standing before him.

The woman in his clutches, stunned, beautiful, and utterly maddening.

He let go of her and stalked two, three paces by the salon door where their bargain began. He was exploding inside, his body restless, his heart worse. Emotions ricocheted like black powder set afire by a dozen fuses. This should be a glorious moment. Rare was the day a man realized he loved a woman. For him, it happened twice . . . to the same confounding woman.

His back to her, he rubbed his chest. Everything ached. He wanted to break something and not think, not feel. This morning, in her late husband's bedchamber, he knew what he'd wanted. Sex was never part of the arrangement made in Anne's salon. After their blistering kiss, he understood why she'd think as much. But, bartering her body? To get his help to steal the gold?

Pacing again, he couldn't be sure which was worse: love unreturned or her body traded in a bargain. With him.

"I canna believe it." He swung around chewing words. "You've gone all day thinking I bargained to use you for . . . *reitheachas*." He practically spat the word.

Reitheachas. Rutting. Ramming. Base use of a body.

Anne's eyes were sharp slits.

"I see you understand me," he said, breathing hard.

"Thanks to your cousin, my Gaelic education continues."

Her tone was formal, lady-of-the-house, while he could barely contain his rage. His armor was off, splintered in a thousand pieces.

"Don't hide behind your coolness, madame. Tell me the truth," he said in a harsh voice just above a whisper. "You were going to trot me up to your bedchamber and play harlot for the sake of stolen treasure?"

"I wasn't going to trot you up to my bedchamber," she hissed back. "Cecelia's there."

He felt his jaw drop. "You were going to lie down with me . . . in your late husband's bed?"

Shock got in line behind frustration. Which was

the greater crime? Anne coldly selling herself for gold? Or taking him to her dead husband's bed? Lips curling against his teeth, he couldn't say.

"Forgive me. I misunderstood your intentions." Her mouth pursed. "Most men wouldn't find my offer difficult to swallow."

"I'm no' most men." *I wanted to marry you.*

Anne flinched as if he'd spoken his fierce thoughts aloud. The curse of intimacy came in understanding someone yet remaining far apart in accord. Why couldn't they breach this wedge between them?

He raised frustrated fists to fight it, asking a furious, exasperated, "What happened to you?"

Silence crashed the entry hall. Anne's eyes were hollow. Black holes in midnight forest trees held more light. She was far from reach, and he didn't know how to get her back.

Door hinges whined on the floor above their heads. Footsteps pattered, bringing Aunt Flora's voice with them. "Is something amiss?"

Anne smoothed her palms down her skirts. "It's me and Will."

"Oh?" Floors creaked. More footsteps.

"Go back to bed, Aunt Flora. All is well." Anne recovered enough to sound commanding.

The barest pause and, "As ye say, dear."

They waited until a door clicked shut. It was enough time for tempers to cool and for him to see Anne in a new light. The line of her mouth was stalwart, but her eyes were shaded with emptiness. Twin candle stubs were guttering their last. Soon they'd be in the dark, and Anne would have an excuse to slip away, the same as she'd slipped away eight summers ago. Years of hardship had battered him into the man he was today. Prison's solace had chiseled his mind. Shipyard labor had molded his body. He'd gained a new trade and put war and rebellion behind him. Anne had not.

She had one thing right. His help came with a price—her answer to the question which had racked him all these years. A question which stirred the beast of pain and rejection inside, a question that waited eight years for an answer.

"Why didna you come to me at Castle Tioram?"

Chapter Eleven

*H*er knees buckled. Insults, threats, and arguments with those most dear had never stopped her. Neither did greedy men and ham-fisted rogues. Nothing could sway her from a goal once the seed was planted. But, Will's question . . .

She slumped against the entry table and clutched her stomacher from cruel, phantom pain behind the cloth she gripped.

"Of all the things to ask me." She hardly recognized her paper-thin voice.

Will took a half step forward. "Are you going to be ill?"

She was, but not the kind he could heal.

Why did that day matter anymore? A lifetime had passed.

Hadn't it?

Wounds of the soul were treacherous things. They scarred. They toughened. They generally made a body wiser. Until one day, a letter, a memory, or in this case, a pointed question ripped them wide open. What she was satisfied to bury, Will sought to unbury. Their natures couldn't be more different. But the wretched war had taken more than her young love. It had stolen from Will too. He deserved to know what had happened; telling it was her challenge despite the spinning hurt climbing higher inside her.

A secret wanted out.

Her tongue was heavy with it. "This is what you bargained for. To know why I didn't run away with you."

"Yes."

She looked beyond Will, dragging in a ragged breath that cut her insides. It hurt, how good and different he was from other men. Will's ambitions swam in deeper waters: he preferred truth over gold. His patience in seeking an answer was equally astounding when all this time she'd thought he didn't care.

At the moment, impatience clouded his brow and banked rage lit his eyes. Will was done waiting.

"Do you remember the day I was supposed to meet you?" she asked.

"It's branded on me."

His ferocity startled her. A sconce candle died, its smoke trailing thinly beside Will. In the gloom, he was no more than a beastly scowl with hair askew and the white of his shirt showing. She braced a hand on the table. Fresh beeswax glossed the surface, buttery smooth, supportive and friendly, if furniture could be that.

"It was the nineteenth of August. The day the war started."

"I know," he ground out. "I was there. Waiting for you."

She saw Will as he was then. The windblown highlander, kilt swinging, long hair buffeting his back, a flintlock tucked in his belt. He belonged to Scotland and Scotland belonged to him.

Her finger found a tiny bump of excess beeswax. She rolled it between thumb and forefinger, the past coming forth in brilliant color. The grass a rich green skirt around Castle Tioram, the skin of Loch Moidart a restful blue. The tides were out and the sun full. Will had boldly gone to gather the cache of weapons and ammunition in daylight, weapons he'd stored in the castle's ruins. The Uprising was upon them, and her desperate need to be with Will outweighed distant voices. Her family in Edinburgh, the man she was to marry yet had never met . . . all vanished when she found the highlands. Her first nineteen years had been as nothing. A wisp of memories, not full-bodied life.

She'd been adrift and Will became her anchor.

But passing into life with Will wasn't all a pleasant dream.

"I was packing my things when Morag stopped me," she said, strength growing in her voice.

Morag was the innkeeper who'd hosted them while they waited in the village near Castle Tioram for instructions to journey to Skye, as originally planned, or to journey instead to Arisaig. Her betrothed, Angus MacDonald, had gone missing. Apparently, he was no more interested in marriage to her than she to him.

Tarrying near the castle ruins was no hardship. More time with Will, more summer-blessed freedom. From the moment they'd left Edinburgh, she rode a horse alongside him every day. By Linlithgow, they'd kissed. By Stirling, they'd fallen in love. By Drummond Castle, she'd given herself body and soul to the landless golden-eyed highlander.

Will had shared enticing plans—if she'd go with him.

She was not noble blooded. Her father was a merchant, increasing his circumstances. Her marriage had been about gaining purchase in Western Isles trade. Her rebellious choice to run off and marry Will was brazen enough, never mind that it would happen during a war.

The Uprising had been an argument of principle which faded quickly under the fair skies of young love. Will was a cocksure rebel. He'd been equally sure of persuading the MacDonald of Clanranald to make him a tacksman, to secure rent for the clan chief. The chief, he'd boasted, had already offered him land on the Isle of South Uist. Land he had no reason to take until her. Will had spoken of them being together forever, and she drank it in as a maid of nineteen would.

There was no going back.

Until Morag stopped her.

The pebble-sized wax forgotten, she hugged herself, comfort for what was about to come. Will watched her intently, curious, frustrated, his nostrils flaring as if he'd rattle the truth out of her. Her heart beat strong and true. She was no delicate lady to be rescued. She was hardy enough to follow the drum, but that August day, her eyes had been opened. Others did need rescuing—the weak and the innocent, those who couldn't speak for themselves.

"Morag told me it is the duty of the strong to look after the weak and fragile."

Will was a thunderstorm. He couldn't know a stony lump was rising inside her, so dark and hard yet formless.

"Morag had brought water for me to wash with. She'd seen blue veins on my breasts," she explained with astonishing quiet.

"Blue veins?" His face twisted in confusion. "What the devil does that mean?"

She swallowed hard. Her secret was fighting for a path to her tongue.

"I was . . . with child," she whispered.

There. It was out. She was lighter for it and freer than she'd been in a long time. A burden shared. Will, however, sagged, his brawny form reduced by hearing of his unborn child.

"But . . . it was—we were barely two months . . ." Will's tongue stumbled and he went starry-eyed and mute.

Nothing silenced a man like the shock and wonder of fatherhood. At least that's what Morag had said to her. It took eight long years to finally see for herself.

She laughed softly. "We were worse than rabbits, though I suspect your seed was planted our first time together."

Will's gape was comical. Eyes wide, jaw loose. Speaking of their assignations unburdened her.

"We weren't as secretive as we thought," she said.

Was it possible to hide young love? Its beacon shined stronger than a lighthouse on a clear night. Only the daftest person would miss it.

Aunt Flora had been her chaperone across Scotland along with Will and another outrider. A patient clansman drove Aunt Flora and all Anne's worldly possessions. With Anne on her horse, the cart trailed far behind. She'd never been so unrestricted. Freedom was an elixir served to her by a handsome, attentive highlander. Aunt Flora was a dear. Talented with young children and healing tinctures, she excelled in many things. Escorting willful maidens was not one of them. The old spinster napped daily and slept soundly. Aunt Flora lacked the stern fiber God gave her sister in spades.

The wee life that once grew in Anne's belly had proved it.

She rubbed a circle over her womb. "Morag warned me not to follow the drum." Her eyes sought his. "A war camp is no place to bring a babe into the world."

Will dragged in a long deep breath and righted himself. His eyes offered tacit agreement.

"It was no longer just you and me. I had a child to think of." Her throat clogged. She couldn't cry. Her well of tears had gone bone-dry long ago.

Yet, she still hurt. Breathing, standing, talking. Old secrets carried crushing agony. She'd been drowning under the weight too long.

"Where is the child now?" Will's voice was a spare rumble.

Hands trembling, she clutched her stomacher. "She died in my womb. Not long after you left."

"She?"

A jerky shake of her head and, "I just . . . knew."

The final piece of her secret was out—the loss of her unborn daughter. A tear threatened to come. How she missed that little girl. She still dreamed of her. In quiet times, her heart conjured images of what could've been. The girlish giggles. Running with her in the sun. The sweet childish kisses on her cheek.

Will's head hung low. "I'm sorry, lass."

She wanted to stroke his hair, to comfort him, but theirs was a connection weathered by time. A lustful touch would satisfy the flesh, but a cosseting touch, with her soul laid bare and his defenses weak?

Frightening.

She could lead him into her unlit salon, lie down on her narrow settee, and bare herself to him. To what end? Touching Will would lead only to hurt. Once she had the gold, he would leave to find his kin and she would go north, as planned. Will was destined to find his father; she was destined to save their clan. Their futures couldn't be more opposite.

Will was still staring at the floor, his hand covering his mouth. What more could he say? Eight years put much distance between them. What were mere words spoken to him equated to a new life that had once grown inside her. There was no joining, no erasing, no healing. Relief in the telling washed her clean. Her secret would quietly ebb as sad secrets did.

With careful hands, she opened a drawer in the table and touched a taper to the sconce. The humble flame showed Will had come a step closer. One pinch and the stubby sconce candle was out.

"Why did you marry Angus MacDonald?" he asked, his voice peculiar and calm.

She stilled. *Don't do this, Will.*

"The babe was gone before I married Angus."

Not a direct answer to his direct question, but it got the job done. Wild dawning flared across Will's face, probably from the notion that she could have married Angus with Will's babe in her. She wouldn't have. Therein, was another tetchy point—having been the one left to face the consequences of their choices. It rankled then and it rankled now.

But Will was hunting a meatier point. He held her gaze, his jaw tense.

"Couldn't you have waited?" Each word was razor sharp.

Couldn't you have waited for me? was the message in gold eyes burning bright.

She trembled anew, with anger this time. The emotion welled up and burst. "I could ask the same of you! Why didn't you wait for me?"

Her hair fell across her eyes. They were toe to toe, their harsh voices low in deference to the household. Morag had delayed her running to tell Will because the older woman feared she'd throw caution to the wind and follow Will after all. She'd brought Aunt Flora as reinforcement. Had it been an hour? Half an hour that she'd spent stunned at the news of a child, then assuring Morag and Aunt Flora that she wouldn't follow the drum?

Such costly minutes those were.

"I ran to tell you about the babe but . . . *you* . . . *weren't* . . . *there!*" Her words sliced with accusation.

Will's eyes were stern slits. He was flint to her steel.

If he wanted to go down this path, then by all that was holy, she'd take him.

"I searched everywhere!" she hissed. "A passing shepherd boy had to tell me you'd already left with two outriders." She gripped a handful of his velvet coat and yanked with all her might, but Will was a fortress. He hardly moved. "War and rebellion . . . that's what you really wanted." She breathed against him in cold fury. "You couldn't even wait for me!"

Brows heavy and teeth bared, Will was feral. "I did wait."

"Not long enough!"

"You knew I was supposed to bring weapons. Men were counting on me."

She tried shaking him. "*I* was counting on *you.*"

"I left because I thought you had second thoughts." Will huffed a noise worthy of a lion. "Why didna you write to me? An' tell me you were with child?"

"I did. Three letters and none were answered."

Will's mouth was a grim line. "I didna get any of them. If I had, you know I would've answered you."

She *had* tried. The need to reach Will had fueled her legs when she ran to Castle Tioram's ruins, and it had fueled her letters: the first full of longing, the second full of need, and the third full of desperation. By the time she wrote the last letter, her unborn child was gone, taking her heart with it.

"I needed you," she said, letting go of his coat.

Will flinched. She'd thrust a dagger into the heart of the matter—Scotland or their young love. All the fiery speeches and impassioned arguments came down to that one simple thing. Her best laid plans had gone awry years ago. Trouble happened. A seasoned woman accepted this and learned. A strong woman fought back and forged her own path. Only fools and untried innocents believed life was an even field to tread.

Anger was a form of baptism. In it was the power to hone the mind. She had a duty to think of the stolen highland treasure. A duty to their kin who were hungry for what those gold livres would bring.

But she'd send this final bitter salvo. "The rebellion was first for you. Always."

"The war was for Scotland. Our home."

Will's brogue was rich, the cadence of tranquil days tracking red deer and golden eagles, of tasting Western Isles sea spray, and walking through wide open glens. Clanranald MacDonald lands. Home to many. Heaven to her. She'd do whatever it took to save it. The irony—Will letting go of Scotland, and her, holding fast—was not lost on her.

"I've often wondered, what bothered you more?" she said, righting his coat. "The loss of Scotland? Or the loss of me?"

Will was frightening, his face pale and eyes burning, a touch of the half-crazed soul she'd found in chains at Marshalsea.

"The war divided us from the start." His voice was a deep rumble.

"Perhaps it did, and we were too blind to see the truth." She was sad, tired, and in need of a good night's sleep. Cupping the taper, she walked around him and stopped at the foot of the stairs. "You can come with me or find your way in the dark."

Stubborn pride tensed his shoulders. Hers was not a carnal invitation. Will's eyes pierced her all the same, reading her, wondering. Though near in body, Will may as well be miles and miles away. Out of reach. Forever.

How lonely.

She turned to hide what must've been her own blanched features and went stiffly up the stairs with Will behind her. No hint of the evening's sensual flirtation remained. Whatever had been between them could never be resurrected. It was as dead as the dream of Scotland's independence.

Will now knew why she was late to meet him at Castle Tioram that fateful August day when a war started, and an unborn babe was revealed. During that same war, she'd fallen in love with Clanranald MacDonald. Their tenderhearted chief, the hardy crofters, and gorgeous isles. Aunt Flora had healed her broken heart and her ailing body after she'd lost the babe. There'd been so much blood.

She eventually honored her father and married the man he had chosen, then she buried Angus three months later when he died of a war camp fever. She'd learned, and she'd loved.

Duty burned brightest in her now. Loyalty to the end. Pure and direct, no messy emotions with those ideals. Love was a luxury she could ill afford. She'd had her chance and lost it.

Tarrying in the hall, she gave light for Will to find his way. His footfalls sounded an even tread. He would sleep alone, her part of their trade done. Tomorrow, Will would deliver the key, the first part of his promise to help the league.

The world was falling neatly back into place. As it should.

Will pushed open the door to his bedchamber and waited. Skin around his eyes softened. With his stockings and boots gone and hair half-loose, he could be a world-weary, barefoot philosopher.

"I know what you're trying to do," he said. "You've lost much and you're itching for a fight."

"Am I?"

Her words delivered more challenge than inquiry. Will appeared to consider them, the orange glow of a welcoming fire lighting his room and limning his silhouette. He filled the doorway as if he would impart wisdom yet hadn't found a way.

The best he could offer was, "Let it go, Anne. You canna save Scotland."

"Watch me try."

Chapter Twelve

$\mathscr{A}$ ridiculously ostentatious carriage carried them down South Audley Street. The interior exploded robin's egg blue. Polished brass buttons shimmered. Gold tassels swayed. Will stroked the butter-soft squab where he sat, its tufted leather a cushion running from behind his calves to the ceiling.

"Have a care where you touch," his cousin warned. "This carriage belongs to a courtesan. It's her favorite vehicle for assignations." She batted a tassel in the corner. "Equipped to meet diverse appetites."

Anne and his cousin were crammed in the seat facing him, their panniers bunching.

"It doesna look big enough for sport of any kind."

Cecelia giggled. "She manages."

His cousin poked her nose out the open window, basking in sunlight. It was a perfect late summer day, if overwarm. With most nobs still in the country, West End streets were clear. To all and sundry, they were a harmless trio out for a lazy drive.

"What glorious sunshine. I hope it stays." Cecelia flopped against the squab. "There's a cricket match this week at the Artillery Ground. It's London's club versus the Marylebone men. Could be fun."

"Cricket . . . fun?" he intoned. "Turtles move faster."

She cast a worldly, knowing look at him. "One doesn't go purely for the sport."

"Sport? Try tossing a caber. That's sport."

"Men throwing a log. How original." The carriage rolled to a stop and his cousin dashed on lace gloves. "Everyone knows the best part about cricket is drinking beer and watching *all* the interesting people."

A footman opened the door, allowing her to pass. Outside, she set a straw bonnet on her head and tied a flirtatious red bow at her left cheek.

"Think about it, will you?" Her gaze flittered from Will to Anne. "A little gambling and whatever else we can stir up."

"It's the stirrin' up part that gives me pause," he said.

His cousin *was* fun. Barely two days in her company, and her appetite for life was infectious. The woman didn't possess a solemn bone in her body, yet she'd disembarked at a somber pile of gray stones known as St. George's Chapel. He checked the road. Not a soul in sight. Their carriage, in fact, was the only conveyance on the street.

The footman shut the door, moved from view,

and a thump signaled the driver onward. Cecelia yanked her bodice lower and called out, "Wish me luck."

Lace trim on her bodice fluttered, revealing a tartan rosette pinned underneath. Clanranald MacDonald tartan. The knowledge pleased Will, a fine secret shared. A hefty one already followed him since midnight. Extra baggage, and he ill equipped to carry it. He'd slept poorly for the weight.

Him . . . almost a father.

Alone with Anne, he stared out the window and watched Cecelia swan into the chapel's courtyard.

"It's Thursday," he said. "What the devil is she up to?"

"Prayer and supplication." Anne's voice was a smoky purr, the aftereffects of too much rum.

"Humor, Mrs. Neville. I wasna expecting that." *Not after last night.*

Her brows arched. *I don't scare easily* was her message. If ever a driven woman existed, Anne Fletcher MacDonald Neville was first of the mold.

"Do you find it hard to believe in your cousin's piety? Or my sense of humor?"

He rested gingerly against the squab. This might be a test.

"Why do I feel like answering that is a trap?"

Hands folded demurely on her lap, Anne was the very picture of a woman who belonged in carriages with supple leather and velvet curtains. Peach petticoats covered the seat and pretty silk shoes poked out from her hem, but he knew better. She had a knife up her taffeta sleeve. Anne was as nimble with weapons as she was with words, which left him staring at the clean cut-stone faces of passing homes.

"Cecelia is meeting a contact in the burying grounds behind the chapel."

He turned from his survey of houses. Was Anne offering an olive branch?

"A man of the cloth?"

"No, she's meeting—" brows pinching, she snapped open a lacy fan "—I dare not say. The less you know, the better."

"You didna hold back last night, madame. No need to hold back now."

"Last night was personal."

"No, it was an act of trust. The same as today." He looked pointedly at her. "I'm part of this."

I'm part of you was the deeper message.

They'd spent the morning navigating an unspoken truce. Her scratching notes in a ledger while he stood, arms out, in her salon with Aunt Maude and Aunt Flora fussing over him. The final product wasn't bad. His coat was brown velvet trimmed in gold at the sleeves. The matching velvet breeches felt good on his thighs (velvet—one thing nobs got right). The bigamist's shoes pinched his toes, but for a few hours work, they'd do.

Appreciation gleamed in Anne's eyes, but he'd rather see faith in him.

She fluttered her fan with an indolent wrist. "Cecelia is meeting someone who works at General Seward's School. They talk over the stone wall that separates the school from the burying ground."

"Clever."

"She is indeed." Anne's carmine smile was pretty. "Cecelia cultivates contacts throughout the City and places beyond."

They trundled into Grosvenor Square, daylight blessing Anne. She reminded him of a proud mama, warming to her topic with words of genuine respect and friendship. She was the league's leader, but each woman was a talent in her own right.

"Cecelia negotiates for information with the French coins reminted by Mary, or—" she gave an eloquent shrug "—she uses whatever means to accomplish her goal."

"Who would've thought, my cousin, procurer of information and queen of the barter."

"Don't crown Cecelia yet. You've not seen Aunt Flora at work. The woman contrives her way into places Cecelia cannot."

"Aunt Flora? I thought she was just keepin' your house."

"Have a care or she'll box your ears. Aunt Flora may be an older woman but she's no less capable." The carriage rolled to a stop. "Both Aunt Maude and Aunt Flora are the perfect foil. No one would ever suspect them."

"What about you?"

She looped her fan around her wrist. "I am exactly what you see. Leader, organizer, general shepherdess."

The door opened. Anne exited the carriage, her garnet earbobs swinging like great drops of blood against her neck. He followed, mild unease in his belly. They were at the mouth of Duke Street. At the next corner was Denton House. Its slightly superior three-story height was a sniff above the neighbors, and its five bay windows, dismissive despite pots of cheery red flowers and a bright blue door.

Never thought I'd cross that threshold again.

"Meet us by St. George's Chapel in an hour," Anne said to the coachman.

The coachman touched his hat. "Aye, ma'am." And the garish vehicle rolled on.

The Garden Oval at the center of Grosvenor Square was just as he remembered. Low hedges, trimmed lawns, and elm trees. A little girl and her nursemaid admired the statue of King George I on horseback in the garden center. It was by that statue he'd bade farewell to Ancilla. Her tears had flowed, tiny droplets rare as diamonds. She'd sniffled and whined (another rare occurrence), but when he gently disentangled himself, she'd cast him out with the fury of a flaming cherubim sealing the Garden of Eden.

Black railing encircled the exclusive oval, a reminder that neither he nor Anne belonged. Only keyholders who lived here and paid for the privilege gained entry.

He donned his hat, the wax lump solid in his pocket. Another key was more important.

Anne was tying a peach silk bow under her chin, scanning the environs. A sharp-eyed treasure huntress.

She was most important of all.

Letting Anne know this—how and when, in particular—was the hard part. It required skill and thoughtfulness after what she'd gone through, and he'd be the first to admit, finessing matters of the heart was not his strength. Her secret rocked him. How was he going to overcome her sense of desertion?

His desertion . . . committed in ignorance under the belief she'd deserted him.

"Mr. Styles is not in the square," Anne said.

He consulted a pocket watch which he'd found at the bottom of the bigamist's sea chest. "He has five minutes."

"I don't like it."

His gaze shot from one corner to the next. "I don't either, though I canna be sure if it's Mr. Styles or something else."

More pigeons than people inhabited the square. It was quiet. Too quiet.

"This could be nerves," Anne said. "Since we're about to commit a misdeed."

"Misdeed?" he snorted. "A genteel way to put it."

Anne linked her arm with his. "Walk with me. We're supposed to be a newly betrothed pair out for a leisured stroll, remember?"

Scouting for battle was easier than this. A man could at least use trees and bushes to his advantage. Anne was a natural, slim fingers in the crook of his elbow, her stroll sedate. The brim of her hat covered all but soft red lips and pale skin, badges of a gentlewoman. He wasn't fooled. Anne would brandish her knife and charge Denton House this very moment if she thought it best.

A bored footman walking a scrap of a dog crossed the road. The little girl in the Garden Oval shrieked gleefully at a squirrel. A lady of quality exited her home and ensconced herself in a waiting sedan chair painted with roses. Two men dressed in claret-colored coats bent their knees, lifted their burden, and off they went, the lady they served fanning herself languidly.

Anne's petticoats brushed his legs, and his cares melted with each gentle swish. She walked with grace, her face tipping companionably to his. The bruise at her temple was the only thing out of place.

"Tell me about the night you were attacked," he said.

"Why?"

"Because I will track them down and see justice done."

Her grip firmed on his arm. "You can't go to the magistrate."

"I wasna thinking of that kind of justice."

"Oh, I see."

It struck him right then: he was good at protecting, and this skill, the strength of his back and his ham-sized fists, might be the door to winning Anne once again. His rough charm only went so far.

"You opened this door, Mrs. Neville. I intend to be fully at your service."

"Helping with the key and the gold is more than enough," she said quietly. "Your brute strength is best served there."

He chuckled. "No false flattery from you."

A squirrel scampered from a hedge behind the garden's black railing. The wee beast flitted its tail and darted across an ostentatiously wide street.

"Your about-face is . . . curious."

Ancilla's house loomed. "Consider it atonement."

Her breath caught. A good sign? Or bad?

He slid two fingers in between his neck and cravat and tugged. "Maybe it's my better nature wanting to protect a clanswoman."

Because I'll do whatever I must to win you back.

He'd wooed her as a headstrong maiden of nineteen. Wooing the older, wiser woman at his side would be another kettle of fish. Ardent words and passionate kisses worked once; both ploys wouldn't work again. The test was how to win a twice-widowed woman? She already knew the dance of courtship. Freedom and independence appealed more than anything a man could give. Nor was Anne drawn to money. She was on the cusp of stealing a treasure to give it away.

"And how do you propose to do this?" she asked. "'See justice done' as you say."

"I don't know."

"I'd forget about it, if I were you. The attack was happenstance. Life on the wharfs."

"You're the shepherdess of a seditious league. Anything bad happening to you is no' happenstance."

"I really don't need protecting," she muttered.

A poorly dressed man entered the square off North Audley Street, wheeling a squeaky handcart.

"Mr. Styles," Anne said under her breath, her relief palpable. "Let's go."

He stopped and clamped a hand on hers. "Tell me."

She tried to pull him along. He didn't budge. Carmine lips pressed into a rigid line.

"You're incorrigible."

"You're no' the first to say that."

"What if I don't want you to investigate my attack?"

The stubborn lass had held too many cards for too long. He could argue a million things, but with Anne, it wouldn't work. Actions always spoke loudest. The squeaking cart neared Denton House. Birds chirped and Will pulled out the pocket watch, sunlight blindingly bright on the silver.

"One minute and counting, Mrs. Neville."

Her bosom heaved. She was indignant, her eyes green chips shaded by her straw hat. A stooped rag-n-bone man stopped his cart at the stairs of Denton House. Will had a direct view, but Anne, angled toward Will, couldn't see, though she could certainly hear the goings-on behind her. The ruse was afoot. Mr. Styles had indeed transformed himself. Soiled shirt, patched breeches, hair untidy. He scratched his head and rifled through a pile of clothes.

"There's nothing I can say to convince you?" she asked.

"Nothing."

Sweat trickled under Anne's gossamer kerchief tucked into her bodice. Could be he was pushing his luck, but time wasn't on his side—for finding the men who hurt Anne or winning her heart. He tucked the watch into his pocket where the lump of wax waited. A footman marching toward them eyed Will, his gait slowing. The servant changed course and crossed the street, giving them a wide berth.

"Mr. Styles just popped something white into his mouth," Will said in a voice for Anne's ears alone. "At least we're getting this part right. Betrothed couples have the odd spat, don't they?"

Her slender nostrils flared. "And you're making my heart race, but not the good kind."

"It's a start, lass."

To which she glanced peculiarly at him before glancing at Denton House over her shoulder. The counterfeit crank was making a show of rummaging through his cart of clothes, his jaws working.

Anne linked a stiff arm with his. "You want information? Start walking."

He did, which loosened Anne's tongue.

"I was alone in my warehouse at Gun Wharf. It was late and there was only one lamp burning. Three men with dark scarves covering their faces entered my warehouse. Two of them ransacked stored goods, though nothing was stolen. The third man came at me. We fought. He knocked me into a post which is how I got hurt. That blow left me dazed and disoriented. I recovered . . . couldn't have been more than a minute, but when I turned around, all three were gone."

Foam squished out the corner of Mr. Styles's mouth.

"Did you notice anything different about the men?"

"Will!" she hissed, her arm taut against his.

"Anything at all?"

Mr. Styles mounted the steps to Denton House. Anne shook with nerves and anger, her head swiveling from Denton House to Will.

"Calm yourself, lass." His voice was even but copper's flavor coated his tongue, the familiar taste of prebattle madness. They were seconds away from committing malfeasance—if only to take back what was rightfully theirs. While Anne's steel nerves were fraying, his were going cold.

"Take a deep breath," he coaxed.

She obeyed. Her arm's rise and fall against his evidenced it. His satisfaction at her listening to him was a victory best gloated over later. A crime was in play. When Mr. Styles banged the door's brass knocker, their stroll landed them near Denton House. He touched Anne's fingers tucked in his elbow. She bumped intimately against him, Anne's hard swallow her telltale sign of fear.

They stepped as one onto the wide street, sunlight blasting their heads. Mr. Styles banged the knocker again and slumped convincingly against Lady Denton's bright blue door.

Anne's straw bonnet tipped a thoughtful angle. "You know, there is a particular detail that I forgot. The man who fought me had the letter *T* branded on his thumb."

Will picked up their pace. "Let's get our key."

The letter *T*, brand of the common thief. The irony wasn't lost on him.

$\mathcal{T}$he ruse began with frightening ease. A simple choice, him trotting ahead of Anne and racing up stone steps. He left behind regrets at forcing her hand. They were good at butting heads. Any worthwhile partnership would experience a see-saw of wills. It was part of the climb to higher ground. At present, that meant mounting Lady Denton's stone steps where Mr. Styles thrashed.

His falling-down disease act was worthy of Drury Lane. Foam frothed at his mouth. Limbs went stiff. The man arched his back while his eyelids fluttered madly. Will dropped to his knee, convinced.

He banged on the door, bellowing, "Help! Come help, at once!"

Anne knelt on the front step, fanning the rag-n-bone man. Seconds passed, expanding to a minute. A small crowd was gathering off Brook Street. A butler at a neighboring Grosvenor Square home poked his head outside his door, while Denton House's door stayed shut.

"Where the devil . . ." Will cursed under his

breath and banged an open hand on solid wood with all his might.

"Open up! Help—"

The door swung open. "What in the name of all that's holy is going on?"

Beady blue eyes glared at him from under the frill of a large mob cap—the housekeeper—if he read her starched gray skirts and pristine apron right.

He pointed down and spoke in his best man-of-business voice. "This mon has fallen ill on your doorstep. He needs water."

Wispy brows pinched in disapproval. "Why, he's—"

"He is ill, and it is your Christian duty to help, ma'am."

Mr. Styles's shaky hand grasped the housekeeper's hem. "Waaa-terr."

Mr. Styles had a fine grip. The housekeeper, a stern-visaged woman, tried to yank free her petticoat. Pulling Mr. Styles in wouldn't work. The housekeeper's stout body was planted in the doorway.

"Waaa-terrr." More bubbles and spittle dribbled from the corner of Mr. Styles's mouth.

"Please! Help the poor man," Anne cried, fanning him with all her might.

The woman gawked. "What am I supposed to do?"

"Hold his hand, stroke his brow," Anne said. "I will cool him."

The woman eyed the filthy rag-n-bone man, miserable to her bones. "But, he's . . . ghastly."

"Is he not fit for the kindness of your bosom?" Will asked with righteous indignation.

Emerald eyes glinted with startled humor. Anne's head dipped fast. She was a straw hat and a furious fan. The housekeeper blinked at him, at the gathering crowd, and at the man holding her hem.

"I will fetch a glass of water while you guard your mistress's front door," he said.

"Cover his hand with yours and rub," Anne said. "It will surely loosen his fingers."

The housekeeper was keen to free her hem. Knees cracking on her descent, she lumbered downward and the front door swung wide.

"He smells awful," the housekeeper whispered. To Will, she nodded at a passage flanked by ferns. "Go down that hall. You'll find a narrow plain white door on the right. The kitchen is through it, belowstairs."

She sniffed at the half-dozen onlookers, people of quality by their dress, people she could scarcely order away.

Will was off, his footsteps echoing on the black-and-white marble floor. Cold and cavernous, Denton House was the height of fashion. Everything was big. Wainscoting panels, the height of the wall. Pedestals with flowing plants. Darting to the left, carpet dulled the sound of his rapid footsteps.

The study was the last door on the left at the end of the hall. He trotted to it, his heart kicking faster.

Sweat dampened his cravat. He turned the familiar brass knob and the ghost of his past came to call. Ancilla's perfume. The heavy scent, akin to dark red wine, clung everywhere, exquisite and expensive like the complex woman who wore it. It had taken him months of scrubbing whaling ships to blot out the smell. Ancilla, his great sensual mistake. She'd been a means of survival and the plummeting of his pride. They'd sealed their bargain in this room.

Daylight flooded the carpet's twisting yellow vines. It was second only to the quality sprawled across her bedchamber floor. Walking across it felt like walking on clouds, which he did in a bigamist's shoes. How out of place he was—then and now.

He sidled between the bookshelf and a satinwood desk, sunshine streaking its polished surface. He faced the cabinets and crouched lower, a desk corner scoring his back. Copper's tang hit his tongue. He was face-to-face with the gleaming Wilkes Lock. Polished brass, a guardsman etched in metal, his pointer directed at a numbered dial for the owner to count how often it was unlocked.

Jacobite gold sat behind it.

He itched to take it now. A wailing moan trailed down the hall. Mr. Styles giving a warning?

Sweat trickled down the back of his neck. He was wasting precious time.

He searched for Dr. Colombo's book. The countess usually hid it in plain sight on one of these three shelves. Plain black leather, the embossed gold worn with time.

He scanned book titles, and . . . there it was.

Osservazioni anatomiche con enfasi sull'Amor Veneris, within arm's reach of the desk.

"You're getting lazy, Ancilla."

He snatched it off the shelf and flipped open the book. Inside hollowed-out pages sat the key. A silver filigree bowhead, its teeth a square with defined cutouts and indents, which set it apart from other keys.

From the open door more moaning carried. Louder this time.

He pulled the wax from his pocket and mashed the key inside it. Was the housekeeper getting suspicious?

His mouth was dry and his skin hot. Velvet on a hot day. He should've listened to Aunt Flora. She'd cautioned him, silk was better in summer.

He was careful, removing the key by the bow head as Miss Fletcher had advised. He rubbed all vestiges of wax from the filigree too. A wipe to his temple and he returned the key to its nest in the book.

Back it went to the shelf and he trotted out of the study, careful to shut the door.

The hall was still empty and light. His race to the kitchen was quick, the wax lump safe in his pocket. He retrieved a cup of water and climbed back up the short stack of stairs to the ground floor, his heart thumping.

They were nearly done.

He coaxed calmness, his feet flying over the hall's carpet. Not a drop spilled. Flush with victory he rounded the corner, and a sherry gaze collided with his.

A chill grabbed him by the throat. A slender, elegant woman stood in the doorway, raven haired and ruthless.

"Will?" His former lover's voice was a shocked wisp.

"Ancilla."

Chapter Fourteen

Anne's stomach could be rotating torturously on a medieval spit. The Countess of Denton had taken no notice of anyone else, her visage morphing with stunning speed. And Will . . . saying her Christian name for all to hear. The tableau was awkward and endless. Afternoon sun beating the road. Crowds gossiping. Impeccable servants waiting. A second later the countess speared Anne, her eyes glittering pools of speculation. Her gaze drew a line. Anne to Will, Will to Anne.

The countess did the math and she did not like the answer.

Lady Denton tossed aside years of breeding, stepped over Mr. Styles, and swept through her marbled entry, a moth to the flame that was Will MacDonald. Never mind her ladyship's current private footman standing on the steps, the flustered housekeeper kneeling in the doorway, or Anne.

It'd be comical, but Anne wasn't laughing. She was hot and jealous.

A big paw crossed her vision. "Let's get you up, ma'am."

She took it and clambered upright, her silk-covered whalebone corset sticky against her ribs. *Wrong day to wear a new corset.*

"Thank you, sir."

The paw held on. "Name's Rory MacLeod."

A Western Isles brogue—and he was a Mac-Leod.

Her panniers jammed unprettily against the door frame. Perceptive crystalline blue eyes searched hers. Scarred at his eyebrow and chin, Mr. MacLeod was the rough sort. He chewed a long blade of grass at the corner of his mouth, and dust coated his boots. Thickly built, nicked knuckles, a bull of a man who probably made his coin as a bare-knuckle brawler—and he was a MacLeod.

Her mind reeled. *What is he doing here? And still in possession of my fingers?*

"My hand, if you don't mind."

He released it. "This is where you tell me your name, miss—" his gaze slid to Will and the countess talking in the entry "—or is it missus?"

"Mrs. Neville." She smoothed her skirts, calling out. "Will, water for this poor man if you please."

They were atrocious actors in this ruse, thrown off step by the Countess of Denton's sudden appearance. Mr. Styles, however, played his part with aplomb. Mr. MacLeod helped the coughing rag-n-bone man to his feet, then went two steps lower and retrieved the older man's battered tricorn.

"For you, sir." Will handed over the cup of water.

A shaky hand accepted the boon. "You are too kind," Mr. Styles rasped. He wiped a dirty sleeve across his foam-caked mouth and gulped water.

This was the housekeeper's cue to bustle down the steps and clear the riffraff. A grand carriage with the Denton crest on the door loitered in the road. One of the attendants held the reins of a large bay horse.

"Take the carriage to the mews, and I shall supervise the unloading there." She pushed the wooden cart with its hodge-podge of garments to Brook Street's corner and dusted off her hands as if the matter was done.

"What a surprise, Mrs. Neville."

Anne whipped around. Centuries of quality flowed in Lady Denton's blood. She was perfect in butter-hued silk, her rapier glare put away. Hair impeccably coifed boasted one silver-white lock in otherwise midnight dark hair. Anne felt dampness growing under her chin, no doubt darkening her bonnet's wilting peach ribbon. This was a baptism of fire.

"You two know each other?" Will couldn't curb his astonishment.

There were layers upon layers Anne wanted to explain, but the countess home early was a rug swept out from under her. She was battered and off center. She should've prepared him. She would have . . . before the art salon.

"Why, yes." The countess's pink fingertips grazed Will's sleeve. "Earlier this summer, Mrs. Neville and I were in discussions regarding my purchase of the Neville Warehouse on Gun Wharf." She looked benignly at Anne. "Why ever did we stop our negotiations?"

"You had business at your country home."

"Yes, summer." The countess wrinkled her nose. "The City is abominable in July. The smells and such." She looked gently to Mr. Styles. "You are well enough to . . . travel?"

"I am much better, milady." He touched his forelock and Mr. MacLeod held out a battered tricorn.

"I believe this is yours."

"Thank you, my good man." Mr. Styles exchanged the cup for his hat.

What a motley band they were. Anne forced her spine upright. Perhaps the corset was just the thing to keep her standing and prevent her from becoming a crumpled heap. Mr. Styles smiled to all, touched his hat, and trod with care down the steps. He performed well under pressure, having stalled the Countess of Denton from entering her home. Anne owed him dearly.

The housekeeper bounded up the front steps with age-defying agility and reached for the cup. "Let me take that, Mr. MacLeod." To the countess, "Shall I arrange for tea and refreshments, milady?"

"Excellent idea, Mrs. Brown." To Will and Anne, "Where are my manners? Dawdling on the front door like a rustic." The countess claimed Will's arm. "You will join me for tea especially—" her feline smile touched Anne first and Mr. Styles second, watching him grab his cart "—after what must have been a trying interlude."

"We wouldn't dream of bothering you, Lady Denton," Anne said.

"No bother at all. We have reason to celebrate. Mr. MacDonald informed me a moment ago that the two of you are betrothed. Does that make this . . . marriage number three, Mrs. Neville?"

"It is. Perhaps third time's a charm."

Will was again Mr. MacDonald and the ungentle barbs were out. Anne wanted to parry her ladyship's verbal thrust, but she had nothing. Nothing at all. Speaking her mind was a talent she possessed, but cruel wit was a level to which she'd never stoop. Words mattered, even in the face of overwhelming odds. But all was not lost. She breathed in Will's presence, his sunshine and steadiness. He had an imprint of the key and he had her secret. Both were in his safekeeping.

Hope lifted her chin. "Tea might be just the thing, my lady."

The countess's brows rose a fraction. Anne smiled back. She'd studied her adversary. Agile in the art of set downs and intrigue, her ladyship knew when to regroup and retreat. The countess watched Mr. Styles drive his handcart down North Audley Street.

"How odd. A rag-n-bone man coming to the front door." A regal hand settled in the crook of Will's elbow. "Shall we?"

The countess had staked her claim. From the doorstep, Anne watched their amble. Only a sliver of light squeaked between her ladyship's head and Will's upper arm. Wretched emotions and late summer's warmth coated Anne's skin.

She needed a bath and a brandy and to unpeel that woman from Will.

"I prefer beer." MacLeod's eyes sparkled with amusement. "But tea it is."

A flirt, a ruffian, and he was her ladyship's *very* new private footman.

"Indeed." She set a hand on his sleeve, and they stepped inside the cool marble entry.

Why wasn't Will putting distance between himself and the countess?

An inner voice taunted, *Why do you care? You've got the key, now get the gold. Just make sure the countess doesn't ask too many questions.* Anything to divert her ladyship was good. Wasn't it?

Low laughter rumbled beside her. "Careful, Mrs. Neville. Your glare could melt ice."

She willed her legs and her attitude to match MacLeod's relaxed nature. This was only tea. She could do this. When they passed through a gilt-trimmed doorway, her face was forward but her gaze dropped to MacLeod's dusty boots. He must've ridden the bay. Could he not tolerate long stints alone with the countess in her carriage? Or was her new private footman simply an outrider? Mr. MacLeod's role with the countess didn't matter. One singular fact did. A new actor—a highlander—had entered the stage, and he was probably after the gold.

Chapter Fifteen

$\mathcal{W}$ill folded himself into the small carriage, gusting a long exhale.

"I was afraid I'd have to send a search party to find you." His cousin scooted over for Anne, who was presently squashing herself onto the shared seat. Cecelia's bright smile faded at Anne's grim visage. "Something went wrong."

"Verra wrong. Lady Denton returned home earlier than expected." He tossed aside his tricorn and planted himself beside it. "Something about poor grouse hunting."

His cousin banged the ceiling, and the vehicle lurched forward.

"The countess," Anne said, ripping off her straw hat. "Couldn't find creatures to hunt in the countryside. So, she came to the City with a mind to hunt for something—or someone—else."

Her gaze pinned him. She was in a mood with tendrils sticking to her cheeks, and stray hairs haloing her head. One side of her gown was off . . . wilted, he'd say. Her skirt drooped off one hip while puffing properly on the other. Anne was in a tiff and the walk back to St. George's Chapel didn't burn her ire. Their walk fueled it.

Conversation had been a balancing act, him soothing her ruffled feathers while otherwise holding his tongue. Grosvenor Square, and by extension South Audley Street, swarmed with servants returning from their half day. They had to be careful. Anne, however, had been a hissing cat once they left Denton House. In her anger, she'd thrown caution to the wind, while the countess, in the safety of her home, had thrown veiled insults over tea. Sharp darts. Subtle digs. The Countess of Denton had hunted for Anne's weak spot during their brief respite—all delicately done as was her ladyship's way. Anne's clothes, her station, her lack of wealth, and classic beauty. Anne had gamely absorbed them all, smiling blandly, engaging in a verbal swerve and deflect. He knew why. She focused on the prize: taking back Jacobite gold.

Ancilla was another story—a woman crossing paths with the man who'd scorned her.

Her poor behavior was pride, simple as that.

Both women would recover. More importantly, with the wax mold in his pocket, their task was done. A good day's work.

"We should celebrate." He shrugged off his coat. The carriage was stifling.

Cecelia clapped. "Yes, let's do!"

"No, let's not." Anne's mouth pursed.

"Do we have an imprint of the key, or not?"

"We do, but there's a new wrinkle. Lady Denton has a new private footman," Anne said. "One Mr. Rory MacLeod."

Cecelia fell back against the squab. "Oh dear."

Will scratched a pattern in his velvet breeches. Perhaps a celebration was premature. MacLeods and MacDonalds, be they Clanranald or another branch, shared a long strident history. Centuries' worth.

When God made the earth, He'd formed isles aplenty in *An Cuan Barrach*, the Sea of Hebrides. More than enough for two clans, yet the two could never share. Dominance had been their watchword. A recent eruption came in '39 when he was a lad of fourteen. Norman MacLeod, 23rd chief of the MacLeods of Dunvegan had kidnapped nearly a hundred seaside crofters with a plan to sell them as slaves, three pounds a person. MacLeod had done it with the help of that slithering bastard Sir Alexander MacDonald of Sleat. Most of the stolen spoke only Gaelic and most were MacDonald. A storm had wrecked the MacLeod's iniquitous vessel on Ireland's north coast, ending the ugly venture.

Lore claimed somewhere between Scotland and Ireland's coast, the MacLeod was having second thoughts. It didn't matter. Damage was done.

Will untied his cravat, hoping Mr. Rory MacLeod wasn't a young man seeking his fortune with the MacLeod chief in '39.

"I will ask about him," Cecelia said.

"His presence won't change our plans." Anne ripped off her gossamer neckerchief and used it to dab her nape. Her medallion rested high on her stomacher. Sunlight glinted harshly on inscribed gold.

"We work each problem," he said. "One at a time."

Anne's dabbing slowed. "Yes. One problem at a time."

The blessing of joint-loosening heat was its ability to sap fiery emotions. Anger was simply too much work. He unmoored the top three buttons of his waistcoat, all the better for his skin to breathe.

"Do you think the MacDonald has been working with the MacLeod of Lewis?"

"I don't know. Our chief hasn't written a letter since June," Anne said.

Cecelia pinched the fingertips of her lacy glove. "Maybe Mr. MacLeod is here to help bring sheep back to the highlands?"

Will chuckled. "The mon we met is no' sheep herder. He'd cuff the wee beasts afore leading them through green pastures. No' like a good shepherd . . . or shepherdess would."

Anne gifted him with a grateful smile. Sun rays cutting through the carriage bathed her skin and bleached her blue-green bruise. "MacLeod bears watching, but we keep to what's next. Creating a new key."

A knee bumped his. Anne's. So innocent that contact, like a promise of more to come. They trundled across Westminster Bridge, late afternoon sun casting gold on the water. It felt good to feel good. A daft observation, but he grinned all the same. Anne and his cousin were deep in conversation while peach-colored petticoats brushed his legs. He tempted fate and slid his shoe under her hem. Intimate heat washed the top of his foot, the center of a private world. A man found different balmy heat under mounds of silk skirts. A woman's heat. Anne's. Sensual, sweet, a scent and warmth unique to her.

The carriage's gentle sway rocked him nicely, putting him in a fine mood. Best of all, he'd given Anne what she wanted—the key—something only he could give. A victory roar was in order, but he'd settle for a victory kiss.

Chapter Sixteen

A rattle jolted him. He opened his eyes to his cousin staring out the window and Anne tucking her medallion between her breasts.

"You napped all the way across Lambeth Road and Blackman Street," she said.

"Did I?" He scrubbed his face and looked outside.

They were in the bowels of Southwark. While they'd managed a good day's work, others labored at theirs. More traffic. More people who couldn't flee the City for grouse hunts and house parties: costermongers, their vegetables half gone, and carters and drays rolling by. A golden tassel danced beside his head when they approached the Iron Bell. He caught it and held on. Harlots roamed the walkways like colorful birds in drab cages. Their custom was coming: clerks, sailors, warehouse men whose workday ended soon. For these women, work was just beginning . . . if it ever honored set hours.

Red Bess lounged hip cocked, her calculating gaze climbing all over their passing vehicle until her stare met his. Sharpness faded from her visage and she blew a kiss. Flirty thing. A woman like that would be a fount of information. She'd know who came and went off the docks and who might have been inclined to raid Anne's warehouse.

He'd talk to her. Tonight.

When they rolled up to Anne's brick-and-flint stone house, a cut on his back throbbed. He reached around and gingerly touched a sticky spot under his waistcoat. Blood and bodily humors coated his fingertips from a wound re-opened when he banged against the desk's edge. The countess had left her mark again.

"During the Uprising, did you fight alongside any MacLeods?" his cousin asked.

"None that I recall." He gathered his things and followed her out of the carriage.

The MacLeod of Harris had stood with the Government, the same as their clan chief, but like Clanranald MacDonald, the MacLeods had their dissenters who fought for Bonnie Prince Charlie.

Anne's heels were firm clicks on flagstone. "You have friends in the City who might know, don't you?"

"No' many. I kept to myself."

She opened her front door, a magician of sorts. More sunshine flooded the house but not what the eye could see. It was in the pristine feel and the aromas of beef stew and baked bread, in the friendly feminine voices, a peculiar music with the power to knit bones and heal souls. He'd carried on in his room above an exotic animal dealer with wafts of unseemly smells. A word with his landlord fixed that, but no amount of scrubbing could match this.

His hand curled against the velvet coat draped over his arm. This was . . . longing.

All the king's riches could buy a house, but never a home.

A home was made with gentle hearts and acts of kindness. Anne and her seditious league had made one. Women, young and old, caring for one another. It took a moment before he crossed the threshold and shut the door. This was hallowed ground.

The ladies tossed hats and sundry on the entry table, their chatter dancing between league business to his cousin's staunch belief a day of cricket would be good for all. He was subdued, withdrawing the wax from his coat.

Anne pivoted to him. "Surely you have a few."

"A few what?" He added coat and hat to the pile.

"Friends in the City," she said patiently.

He smiled. When men built a conversation, it was a ladder, one rung to the next. Women built theirs as a rambling garden, planting seeds here and there. The listener was expected to jump nimbly from one patch to the next.

"I'd count Mr. Pidcock, my former landlord. A few men at West and Sons Shipping."

"Funny little man, your landlord," Cecelia said. "I'd ask him about MacLeod."

After today, he wasn't surprised she knew Mr. Pidcock.

"Five years, I minded my business, and Mr. Pidcock minded his."

"Yes, well, time to change that." She was bright

and encouraging. "Just talk to him. A man like that knows a lot of people, but you'll have to be friendly."

"I am friendly."

"And don't be so . . . broody." His cousin wrinkled her nose. "That and your size puts people off."

"I don't brood." But he knew no truer words had ever been said. "And why am I all of a sudden asking about MacLeod?"

"Because while you napped, I decided two heads are better than one." Anne smiled, but he didn't miss firm notes in her voice.

"You decided, madame?"

He could argue he wasn't part of her league, more employee than partner. He had things to do—a former employer to see and men with *T*-branded thumbs to hunt. He wanted to begin his hunt tonight at the Iron Bell. Red Bess knew him, if he counted her flashed stays. He was sure the lass would be happy to share a pint and conversation if he paid for her time.

His cousin pinched her skirts and tossed back an airy, "I shall leave you both to sort the details, all this lurking about has made me positively famished."

Anne waited until Cecelia's footsteps crossed the dining room into the kitchen. A lack of privacy was both a blessing and a curse in cozy homes. Anne's mouth was soft but set, a combination only she could achieve.

"Lady Denton's party is on the twenty-eighth. Less than five days. We cannot afford to be caught off guard again."

"Despite the countess's early return, we made it work. Today was a success."

A slight nod. "It was a victory."

"You don't have the look of a victorious woman."

Heat flowered on her cheeks. Wrinkled skirts and messy wisps from ripping off her hat betrayed her normal mien. This victory came at a cost: a verbal flogging done by the countess. Anne had to have been gritting her teeth while the weight of the world was on her shoulders.

When her gaze met his, a pang bottomed inside him. She was vulnerable. Another chink in the armor of Anne Fletcher MacDonald Neville.

"I won't feel victorious. Not until I have the gold and am on a ship bound for the Western Isles."

The league. The clan. Couldn't she be a little needy for him? Just once?

He was wooing a complex woman. He had to remember that. Brash emotion defined their past. Anne's heart, the heart of an older and wiser woman, would have to be won a little at a time.

"Then, you'll need this." He took her hand in his and set the wax mold in her palm. "Don't be so hard on yourself. Celebrate your victories, lass."

Her head bowed, she was almost angelic, looking at the block of wax, its center an empty shape of a key. It was like Anne, a woman fully formed in wisdom and character, yet void in certain parts. He wanted very much to be the one to fill those parts.

Patience, mon, patience.

"Did you know, I am in the midst of negotiating the purchase of our clan's sheep from a Frenchman?" Her voice was small and quiet.

"That makes you a true shepherdess."

"It does, doesn't it?"

She lifted her head, her smile blessing him better than the noonday sun. A shared secret, something of a positive nature, broke through her ever-present armor of duty to the clan. Her face tipped to his, her lips free of carmine's emphatic color. More black wisps fell forward, and this time he gave in to the temptation to brush them back. Her hair was silken onyx threads. Lock by lock, he tucked them behind the peach-soft shell of her ear. The tiniest hairs inhabited her earlobe. He gloried in touching them. Soft and sweet. Tender as summer fruit. Why didn't men spend more time on a woman's ears?

Anne's breasts strained against her bodice.

Because men were slathering hounds there.

"I—we, the lot of us—have met with success because we've worked every detail," she said. "But the countess coming home early and Mr. MacLeod's sudden appearance cannot be good. Especially when we are so close to getting the gold."

"Don't look at it so darkly," he chided.

"I prefer to call it cautious."

His ear-exploring fingers dipped to her neck. Her eyes were liquid, pliant, open. Slowly, he followed the trail of her ever-present black ribbon necklace. Tracing the ridge of her collarbone.

Tracing the hollow well at the base of her throat. Tracing the high curve of her breast, sanctified territory usually guarded by her neckerchief.

Pale skin pebbled everywhere he touched.

"That's better," he murmured.

"Will you ask about Rory MacLeod tomorrow?"

He dragged his finger along the black ribbon into velvet warm cleavage. "We need to negotiate new terms, Mrs. Neville."

Her breath sawed quietly while merry voices rang from the kitchen. Dishes clanked, and cutlery jingled.

"New terms?"

Heat bloomed in his breeches. Her skin was soft, soft, soft. The freckle high on her breast, a tiny bump. Stolen moments were as exhilarating as a tumble in the sheets, anticipation in its purest form, a hint of what was to come. If he wasn't careful, he'd miss the beginning of dinner to spend himself in his bedchamber.

"You go' the imprint of the key. Next comes the gold. Anything else is subject to discussion."

He was possibly the worst man. Last night he'd been outraged at her believing he'd barter for sex. Today was another story. Today her cleavage was his plunder. Until he touched hard metal. The medallion. He pulled it from her bodice, the thumbprint-sized gold warm from her skin.

Seduction evaporated with a flick of his wrist. A curlicued nine in the center of a diamond had been etched in gold. The Curse of Scotland, the nine of diamonds, its lore long and lethal for highlanders. Feared and hated, even sober-minded lowlanders avoided it. The symbol carried a weighty history.

The Earl of Stair, villain of the massacre at Glencoe in 1692. Nine diamond lozenges was the man's crest.

Every ninth King of Scotland had been a tyrant and a curse.

A thief in Queen Mary's court stole Crown Jewels—nine diamonds—causing heavy taxes on all of Scotland to recover the cost.

Mary of Guise, Scotland's French regent, swindled many a Scottish noble of land and money with her game Comette of which the nine of diamonds was the winning card.

Cumberland had scribbled "No quarter" on a nine of diamonds playing card after Culloden. Some claimed this was false, but he believed it was true.

And these were but a few of the tales of the number nine's scourge.

"We all wear a nine etched in Jacobite gold," Anne said. "As a reminder."

Anne's unflinching sense of duty gained new meaning. They'd not stood on the same side when the rebellion began, but they stood on the same side now. He acknowledged this with a solemn nod, the slim black ribbon a gentle tether from her neck to his hand.

He couldn't let go. He was undeniably tied to Anne and her league.

Her eyes shined with gratitude. "I shall have a care when I negotiate with you. Last time I labored under false assumptions."

A rumbling chuckle vibrated in his chest. "You talking like a proper woman-of-business does things to me. Makes me want to unwrap every layer covering you and find out what's underneath."

Her breasts grazed his knuckles from a slight inhale. He noticed them and he noticed her eyes glossy and sensual. It was the curse of a man in love, wanting to spend equal time on a woman's breasts and her eyes. Both augured good fortune and happiness and all the lustful things that made him tick.

"You already know what's underneath," she said.

He could feel a wicked grin spreading. "That was young Anne. The wiser woman you are today offers a new and better reward."

Her mouth's sweet wobble gratified him. He said something right.

"Yet, for all my wisdom, I can't seem to get one stubborn highlander to do what I want."

"You mean chase down information about MacLeod."

"Yes."

"We're of one accord, lass. I'll ask about MacLeod, no new terms required."

He was becoming putty in her hands. He'd worked with the stuff, sealing windowpanes on ships. It was pliable and formless one moment, useful and strong the next. It stood against the fiercest gales and angry squalls, all that the seven seas could throw at it.

"There is another reason I want the matter of MacLeod settled," she said.

"Mmm . . . what is it?"

"Once we have the gold, I will deliver it to Clanranald lands. Two days after we take it."

Her lips parted, a hesitation, as if words refused to form.

"I won't come back to London." Anne squeezed his medallion-holding hand and looked into his eyes. "I will stay on Clanranald lands for good."

Queasiness sailed into his stomach. The floor was less straight, possibly slanted. Anne let go of his hand as surely as she'd let go of him at Castle Tioram years ago when she thought he'd deserted her. To her, he'd turned his back on her for the good of Scotland. How ironic, this ugly twist. Anne would depart for Clanranald lands, while he would set sail for Virginia. She was the one people counted on. She'd been at the heart of her father's home, taking care of him and her brothers. She was the hub of this league, and like a good shepherdess, Anne didn't want the women preyed on by MacLeod—if the man was a wolf.

Now she dared to make plans for her future.

Chairs scraped in Anne's absurdly small dining room. Shy Margaret Fletcher poked her head around the corner. Cheeks blushing, she eyed their intimate stance.

"Dinner is ready." And the young woman slipped from view.

He was sure he'd arrive at the table and find her face a shade of scarlet.

"Your requests will be honored," he said, tucking the medallion into her pretty cleavage. "I want them done more than I want all the Jacobite gold in England."

Chapter Seventeen

His shoes were off and he was shirtless again in Anne's kitchen, nursing a Mortlake jug stamped with windmills on its glazed brown belly. He needed the jug to quench his thirst. Aunt Flora was at his back, her touch like wasps stinging his flesh.

"Oh, wee Will, yer back is a mess." Her kindly face popped into view. "Brace yerself."

She daubed her greasy unguent on a new spot low on his back. He winced. Searing pain peaked and then, *ahhhhh*. The viscous slime oozed into his skin, leaving a tolerable simmer and an awful stench in its wake.

"Healing is it?" he teased. "Then why do you torture me with a foul potion?"

She chuckled. "It does smell something awful, but ye'll thank me in the morning." One final dab and she circled him, checking her work. "All done, laddie. No bandage tonight. Best tae let the wounds breathe while ye sleep. I'll wrap the worst of them tomorrow."

He tipped the jug and drank. He wanted some-

thing stout, something he might find at the Iron
Bell along with answers to his questions about
the night Anne was attacked. Surely someone
heard something? Saw something? Those plans
were thwarted the moment Aunt Flora slathered her stinky unguent on his back. At present,
her gnarled hands held up the once-fine shirt.
A dozen candles lit the kitchen, illuminating
smears of blood and bodily humors.

"Is the shirt still good?" He cuffed ale at the
corner of his mouth.

Aunt Maude looked up from her work. "It's
cotton."

"An' verra expensive," Aunt Flora said. "Let me
see what I can do tae save it."

"Donnae waste yer time, Flora. Toss it tae the
rag heap and be done." Aunt Maude shucked
peas with a steady cadence. She scored each pod
with her thumbnail. Then a pinch, it split open,
and her finger sloughed green peas into a bowl,
the empty pod discarded.

Both women were his companions for the night.
The whole evening was agreeable. Everyone had
lingered over dinner, the company pleasant, the
food satisfying, but to say that wouldn't suffice.
Lots of dinner tables had amiable people and
good food.

He'd looked around the table when chatter
swelled, a question coming to mind.

Do these women know what they have?

Did he know? Was it family? Contentment? An
accord that ran deep?

Their voices had ebbed and flowed, his heart
caught in their rhythm.

Anne and he had regaled them with their tale of the day's adventure. The beauty of Grosvenor Square's private garden. The countess's early return to London had met with clucks of concern, and Mr. Rory MacLeod with mixed reactions.

Was he friend or foe? Every woman had an opinion.

The wax lump had been passed to Mary Fletcher who in turn regaled the table with her excitement at making a silver key. She had a half ingot of silver, and she expected to begin work on the key that night. His cousin yawned first. Chairs scraped regretfully back. Dishes were cleared, and Mr. MacLeod's appearance was relegated to a minor detail. No great cause for concern, Aunt Maude had said. They should bear up and move on. The gold would be theirs in a matter of days. With that, the Fletcher sisters and his cousin disappeared into the night.

He'd gone to the kitchen, commenting on his back's discomfort, and Aunt Flora whipped out her unguents, insisting she have a look.

Before he knew it, his shirt was off and Anne had vanished.

When he asked about her, Aunt Maude had clucked, "Never mind her, lad. Anne is a grown woman, twice widowed. She can come and go as she pleases. But you? Yer back is festering, and we cannae have you catch a fever. Sit there—" she'd pointed at the kitchen table bench with the authority of a general "—and let Aunt Flora tend ye."

He did, taking a Mortlake jug with him.

Aunt Maude had settled down with her bowl of peas, muttering, "It's a wonder. Why didna Anne take care of yer back yer first night here."

He could've told her Anne was too busy taking off his kilt, and he was too busy trying to survive it. The back of him hadn't been his concern. The front of him . . . well, that was another story. Being well mannered, he drowned his words with another swig of watered-down ale.

Aunt Flora settled on the bench near him, wiping her hands with her apron. "It's best ye sit here awhile and let the unguent soak in."

"I'm no' going anywhere, no' smelling like this."

"I shoulda warned ye of the smell," Aunt Flora said, but something in her smile told him she had him right where the dear old woman wanted him.

He craned his neck to see over his shoulder. Light glistened on his skin. "Thank you, ma'am, for taking care of me. For always taking care of me."

Her aged eyes softened. Aunt Flora had been as close to a mother as he'd ever had. She'd taught him to read and tended youthful cuts and bruises. Companionship with her was easy. If life was a weave, she was the ever-present thread in his boyhood, steady and kind, never a harsh word. And understanding . . . always understanding.

Her keen eyes took in his discarded shoes. She bent over and hooked them with her fingers. The bigamist's shoes hung like awkward specimens.

"An excellent pair," she mused.

"They are."

His was polite agreement only. The heel was too high and the cut too tight. They would never be his. He preferred his loose boots, the leather worn and brown, the soles repaired twice by a cobbler. Staring at those black shoes, their sparkly paste buckles mimicking diamonds, he faced a new fact. Anne's many changes these eight years might include the wish for a man who liked diamond buckle shoes, even the paste variety.

"They don't quite fit, do they?" Aunt Flora said sagely.

"They never will, ma'am."

Understanding ran deep, and that was a currency worth more than diamonds. Aunt Flora knew he'd live and die in his old boots.

"Let me see what I can do tae make them comfortable while you have tae wear them." She turned on her seat. "Maude, would you be a dear and fetch Mr. Neville's shoe forms? The largest pair, of course."

The rhythmic shelling stopped. "But all his things are stored in the cellar."

"I know that. You grumbled about it when you put them there. But wee Will needs his shoes stretched." She held up the bigamist's shoes as evidence. "They're tight on his feet."

Aunt Maude rose with a laborious huff and set her bowl on the table. She lit a taper and crossed the kitchen. "At least it's no' raining."

She opened the cellar door and dank smells invaded the kitchen. Aunt Maude's sturdy footsteps sounded her charge into the underbelly of the house.

Aunt Flora's eyes twinkled under her mob cap. "It floods when'er there's heavy rain." She chuckled. "It floods in light rain too."

The cellar's dank air brought the ghost of another man into the kitchen. Will hooked the Mortlake jug on his finger and rested his elbows on his knees.

"Mr. Neville, he was a shoemaker?"

"His father was a cobbler. Mr. Neville apprenticed with a ship's captain when he was fifteen. He saved his father's things, for sentimental reasons, I suppose."

"And what was Mr. Neville like?"

He was prying, which made him worse than a gossip, but he had to know about the man who gave his name, a house, and a warehouse to Anne. The bench jiggled. Aunt Flora was studying her jar of foul-smelling unguent, probably considering how to answer him.

"Well . . . he was older than me. A kindly, lonely man. He'd never married until Anne. They were introduced by her grandmother who, I think, wanted the union for Anne's security." Her mob cap's frill fluttered from an emphatic nod in his side vision. "Yes, I am certain that was the reason."

He took a casual swig. "Anne loved her grandmother, I collect."

"Indeed. She doted on Anne. The issue of inheritance was, I think, a sore spot."

"Oh?" He toed a crack in the floor.

Aunt Flora corked her unguent with care. "Her grandmother believed a woman's fortune should be found with her husband. Her worldly goods passed on tae her sons, though she did bequeath garnet earrings and a manageable old man as husband for Anne."

"A pair of earrings and a docile husband. Every woman's dream."

A wise chuckle shook the bench. "Out with it, laddie. What exactly do you want tae know?"

He turned his head slowly and met mischievous blue eyes.

"Why do ye think I sent my sister tae the cellar when I coulda gone myself?"

"I didna want to be rude."

The noise of clanking bottles rose from the bowels of Neville House.

"The clock is ticking. Ye best get on with yer askin'."

He breathed deep, ribs swelling as if bursting with questions. Clamor from the cellar threatened to shove each question back into place. The odd pressure was astounding. Confusing. He wanted what he couldn't have. What he could never have. All of Anne's happiness, love, and passion. Oh, God help him, he wanted her passion. Her body against his. Her tart kisses and the sweet ones. He wanted her past, her present, and every bit of her future. And he wanted, *needed*, to atone for his grievous, youthful error—for unknowingly abandoning her.

Staring at the flagstone floor, he could almost see that August day unfold. The weapons and ammunition loaded. The two outriders, pressuring him to get going. Men were counting on him. Anne was too. He could picture her, wind-tossed hair, her determined legs cresting the ridge near Castle Tioram, the land empty.

And him, gone.

How could a man make right that wrong? It was a question for the ages while another nettled him.

"Did they love each other?"

"They were kind tae each other. Mr. Neville had affection for her. He was glad tae have the three of us here. Anne managed the warehouse. Took care of him. She made his last years pleasant." Her voice touched a respectful note. "With no family, Mr. Neville didna want tae die alone."

"And Anne?"

Aunt Flora sighed. "She married him for our clan. With few funds tae our name, it made things go faster. Our league needed tae be in London. Tae track down the *sgian-dubh* and the gold. What livres we have only came tae us this summer."

And the league had spent a hefty share of them to free his foolish kilt-wearing arse.

He stared into the hearth's dying embers. Marriage to Mr. Neville meant the clan gained a foothold in London. Without it, their progress would have been stunted.

Anne. Ever sacrificing quietly for others.

Aunt Flora rose from the bench. "I've seen her eyes shine only once with love. Her summer with you. After that? No more."

He drowned his gullet with watery ale, but nothing drowned his pain.

HE CLIMBED THE steps two at a time in stockinged feet, a waistcoat in one hand, a candle stub in the other. He'd finished the Mortlake jug, plying

Aunt Maude and Aunt Flora with questions of Anne's whereabouts. She shouldn't be out alone in the City, even with that blade up her sleeve.

Did they not trust him?

They chuckled, while tending light evening chores, and reminded him, "Anne is—"

"I know," he grumbled before quoting their refrain. "'A grown woman twice widowed. She can come and go as she pleases.'"

He considered searching for her, his odorous back be damned, but on the top floor landing, he got his answer to Anne's whereabouts. Light glowed under her bedchamber door. A shadow moved, plank floors creaked. He studied the sliver of light like a hawk.

Had she sneaked in? Or had she been here all night?

"Anne," he said from the hallway.

Fool! Go knock on her door.

Then what? Ask where she'd gone? What had she done this evening that was so secretive even sweet Aunt Flora all but told him to mind his own business while she slathered the devil's brew on his back?

Which begged a better question: Did he have the right to ask?

If he did, he was far from presentable. He smelled and his back was sticky and there was an oozing wound. Not a woman's dream of romance and courtship. Nor did Anne answer his first call. Unless her ears were stuffed with wool, she heard him. The house was quiet and their bedchambers the only rooms on this floor.

She was avoiding him.

He padded to his bedchamber and shut the door. Anne couldn't miss that noise either. He cocked an ear, and . . . nothing save those infernal muffled thumps. Light under their adjoining door shined brilliantly. Anne had to be burning a month's worth of candles. He tossed his waistcoat onto the bed and jammed his candle stub onto an empty iron candle holder at his bedside table. Plank floors groaned anew from Anne's bedchamber because the Neville household possessed no cloud-thick wool carpets to hush one's feet.

Another thump came, louder this time.

"That's it." He walked to the adjoining door and knocked. "Anne."

He rolled his eyes. *Fine, romantic greeting.*

"It's Will." He rested forehead and hands on the door. "Of course, it's me because you put me in this bedchamber and you're in that one . . . doing whatever it is that you're doing."

He cringed. Love turned men into utter blathering fools who talked nonsensically to closed doors.

"Do you need something?" she asked.

He lifted his head off the door and grabbed the latch. "I'd like to talk with you."

It was bolted.

Against him? He tried it again.

"Please . . . can it wait 'til tomorrow morning?" she asked.

The latch was a staunch soldier guarding Anne. There'd be no passing here. He let go and stepped back, her bolted door a slap in the face. He'd wager all his measly coins that she'd locked the hall door too.

"Will?" Her voice was tentative.

This wasn't a coy game. She had no reason to fear him. They were in a partnership of sorts, yet he was left out in the cold.

"Yes. Tomorrow morning."

He'd asked if she and Mr. Neville were in love and got his answer. He didn't ask the indelicate *Did Mr. Neville exercise his husbandly rights?* The possibility scorched him with a fresh wave of jealousy. If what Aunt Flora said was true, Mr. Neville passed along his house and his business, giving Anne security.

The man had married her, while he had deserted her.

After their parting, Anne at least had sent three letters—letters he never got. Blame the mess of war and his constant movement for that, but he never wrote to her. At first, a young man's indignation kept him from picking up a quill; news of her marriage to Angus MacDonald stopped him for good.

He turned his back on the adjoining door and stared at nothing in particular.

He'd thought . . . what? Helping her league would erase the past? Make all things new? He owed a debt of heavenly magnitude with no earthly way to pay it. The bolted door was but another piece of evidence stacked against him. He crossed the bedchamber ruthlessly unbuttoning his placket. Once loose, his breeches dropped to the floor. He applied the same ferocity to removing the bigamist's silk stockings. Stockings in hand, he gathered the breeches and was about to throw them at the lone mahogany chair.

His hand froze midair. Black wool stockings hung there. The same Will MacDonald, dockyard laborer stockings he'd left in a soggy heap downstairs last night.

He checked the floor beside the washstand. Moonlight from open drapes showed his boots had been cleaned, the leather oiled, the square toes pointing at him beside his satchel tucked against the wall—the same as his first morning here.

Anne?

Had to be.

He dropped the clothes on the table and sniffed his old stockings.

What a miserable sop he was, sniffing his stockings. But they smelled good, freshly laundered with a hint of lavender.

Hope stirred in his chest.

"Well, well, Mrs. Neville. You're no' so sparin' with your tender mercies after all."

This was another olive branch.

He closed the drapes and made his way to the bed. Clean stockings and a bolted door, an unexpected combination but a man had to work with what he had.

He sank facedown on the mattress, the bed's creak lonely. He drew the sheets over his arse but no higher. No need to ruin them. From the other side of the wall, mild bumps sounded. He answered by thumping his pillow with a frustrated fist.

No one was above the draw, the beauty, the sheer strength of love. It molded men. It shaped women. Rebellions erupted from it with heart-carved passion for the land of one's birth, but love for a woman was a different matter.

Rare was the man who walked an easy road to win his true love. And winning the same woman twice in his lifetime? A feat. Especially elusive, dark-haired lasses who moved mysteriously in the night.

Lasses with secrets . . . his weakness.

Chapter Eighteen

Anne's quill didn't impart ink; it stabbed it. Ungraceful zeros and smeared ones lined two columns of her ledger as if a battle took place on the page. Perhaps this morning it did. Neglected ledgers, Aunt Flora's shopping list, and correspondence cluttered her humble escritoire. The Countess of Denton had sent not one but two missives, hand-delivered by a footman (the liveried variety). Both letters stared with pompous authority, a styled *D* stamped in red wax, the drips reminiscent of blood.

Was she being dramatic? Twirling her quill, she couldn't decide.

The Denton name carried a long history of power, seized in great legal swipes. When the correct channels wouldn't suffice, shadow work did. Centuries of rank distilled their blood, arrogance inbred.

She fiddled with the black ribbon at her neck. A vise was closing in on her. On one side, the countess's grasping hand reached into her home via the unopened correspondence. On the other, Will, the prize her ladyship wanted.

He was a patient statue in her salon with Aunt Flora bustling around him. A tuck here, a pin inserted there. His waistcoat for the night of the art salon had to be just right.

"You must be majestic." Aunt Flora dipped to check a seam.

Burnished amber silk rippled like watery flames fitted to his body, and this was the waistcoat turned inside out. If clothes made a man, Will would be a king resplendent in morning sun spilling through her windows, strong and tall, hair clubbed, a shadow of whiskers adding a rough, storied touch until one spied his old boots. Firmly on, they were. Clean, proud, the loose leather folded under knees and thighs prone to caber tossing.

Definitely not a cricket player's legs.

"This needs to be the final fitting, ma'am. At least for today." His voice was a respectful rumble.

"What? You have things tae do?" Aunt Flora asked. "You cannae dash off now. Aunt Maude is organizing a tray of tea and biscuits."

"I have errands."

Anne checked the direction of the kitchen. Breakfast was not but an hour ago. What were the sisters up to, orchestrating a cozy morning tea?

Aunt Flora hummed and pinched the waistcoat. "Ready tae be off, are you? Seems my unguent did the trick."

"Your potions have always worked."

"Will ye need more tonight?"

"No, ma'am."

"Didna think you would," she chuckled. "It's near magic, though the unguent carries a wee essence of the bogs." She nudged his elbow up. "Arms out." She circled him, starched skirts rustling. "All the same, yer back will need checking. Every night."

"No need to fuss over me, ma'am."

She snorted loudly. "Ye need a bit of fussing, Will MacDonald."

Anne pivoted in her seat, her mouth curving with commiseration. She'd been on the receiving end of Aunt Flora's mother-hen nature. Will's head tilted a message of acceptance over Aunt Flora's head: *She is who she is.* Daylight spiked around him and one could almost believe summer would last forever until his gaze traveled to the letters.

Will's brows arched. *Aren't you going to open them?*

She bristled. Duty called, and for once, she chafed at its yoke. When it came to the league, everything was fair game, even quiet mornings in her salon.

Aunt Maude swept in, a tray rattling with unmatched Lambethware dishes. "Ye'll have him looking like a prince, Flora."

"I was thinking Hades," Anne said dryly.

Three gazes speared her. Startled and confused from Aunt Maude and Aunt Flora while Will managed an amused smirk. *All that lordly attire is sinking into his veins.* She waved gracefully, a gesture to make her grandmother proud.

"It's all the black and gold. I'm not sure of it."

Aunt Maude set her burden on the table and

turned to inspect Will. "He looks fine tae me, but goodness knows I don't cavort in higher circles."

"None of us do, except Cecelia," Anne said. London's lofty addresses had been her grandmother's ambition for her, not hers.

"Well, Cecelia's no' here tae educate us." Aunt Maude began setting the table as if the matter was done.

"I like the black and gold," he said.

Anne eyed Will who eyed her boldly back. A silent skirmish was afoot.

"With his size, shouldn't we consider something paler? A creamy yellow or a sky blue?" she suggested.

Creamy yellow? Will mouthed.

"And have him looking like a cake?" Aunt Maude huffed. The woman had stern opinions about London's mincing fops. Tartans were dark, serious shades, which met with her approval. "What do ye think, Flora?"

"Oh, I don't know."

Will was the center of a feminine universe, arms out at his sides, his smirk growing as if he could do this all day. Rather sure of himself. Or was he glad to needle Anne? Revenge at finding her door locked last night? She'd heard his thumping.

"Pale colors are the height of fashion," Anne said defensively. "I'm sure we can find something else in that sea chest. Something better suited to make him look more . . . or perhaps less of—" her hand flapped inelegantly "—of this . . ."

"Of what?" Aunt Maude pursed her lips.

Aunt Flora waited, and Will was the devil's own, his smirk increasing.

She was in a verbal pit, and shoveling herself in deeper. "Lighter colors would be safer." She hesitated. "Black and gold simply is . . ."

"Is what?" Will goaded.

She was on a knife's edge, her thumbnail digging an indent into her quill. Irritation flared. Other indescribable emotions surged.

"You look dangerous."

There. She'd said it.

Will's predatory smile spread. "Black and gold it is."

She dropped the quill and sorted papers. The admission cost her dearly, though she couldn't name why. It was clothes they spoke of after all. Aunt Maude shrugged off her explanation and finished setting the table while Aunt Flora freed Will of the incendiary waistcoat.

Another certainty struck her this morning: Will was once again the man she'd found in Marshalsea. Rough voiced and a little off. She shut her ledger with a firm snap. Will visiting Mr. Pidcock, or doing whatever errand he had in mind, was a good idea. It was possible he'd planned to devote his day to chasing the man with a branded thumb. In London, that would be hundreds of men.

The sooner he left, the better—if he could unshackle himself from Aunt Maude and Aunt Flora's attentions. Aunt Flora was no surprise; Aunt Maude was. The older woman went out of her way to attend him. It might be the appalling stripes on his back. She'd grumbled vociferously about them over breakfast.

Anne rose from her chair and tidied her desk to neat stacks of paper and ledgers, while Will retrieved his waistcoat. He bent over and a pristine bandage showed under his shirt, a hidden badge of honor for wearing his kilt. She should've taken care of him, but his first night here she'd been too busy convincing him the Jacobite treasure was real. She watched him slide braw arms through armholes (his waistcoat, not one of the bigamist's). A charcoal-hued patch swayed until the waistcoat was tamely buttoned. The patch's color was a near match, yet missing the mark.

Like the two of them.

Will deserved a woman to coddle him. A docile woman who waited by the hearth, darning his stockings and mending his clothes. A woman who would've tended his back right away. A woman unlike her.

She needed to escape, to clear her mind. Aunt Flora's shopping list. She held it up, her ticket to freedom.

"Aunt Flora, I'm off to purchase these for you."

"Now? No need tae rush off, dear."

"Have some tea afore you go." Aunt Maude scraped back a chair and took a seat. "And bring those letters with you. Goodness knows you've dawdled over them long enough."

She stifled a groan. There'd be no private consumption of her correspondence and no quick escape from Will. He settled in, looking just as curious about those letters. The Countess of

Denton was the league's nemesis. Whatever the woman had to say should be known to all.

With a reluctant hand, she scooped the letters off her escritoire and found her seat. Will sat across from her, no less glorious in faded green broadcloth, his patched waistcoat mostly hidden. She propped the letters against her plate, the waxen *D* facing him, and sipped her tea. How appropriate. Hades was also the god of gold dug up from the ground, and Nemesis the goddess of revenge. Remorse was not in that deity's vocabulary, the same as Lady Denton.

Comforting conversation flowed, mostly Aunt Maude and Aunt Flora, talking of the day's chores, while Will was silent. The reprieve was bolstering. Her throat properly warmed, she set down her dish and broke the first red seal. Quiet descended on the table while she scanned the first correspondence.

"It's an invitation to her art salon." She tossed it aside and snapped up the next note. "Her ladyship must be loose in the head. She already invited me before she left for the country."

"Odd," Will said. "She's usually no' forgetful."

She pinned her gaze on him. "She usually doesn't chase a man either."

An easy grin creased his face. "You overestimate my charm. Lady Denton doesna want me."

No sooner were the words said than he knew them to be untrue. She could hear it in the playful timbre of his voice.

"Oh?" She lowered the unopened note. "And what would you call her actions yesterday? Friendly?"

"Acquaintances getting . . . reacquainted."

To which she snorted. "Reacquainted?"

Aunt Maude and Aunt Flora faded in the way seconds at a duel would. The conversation's subtle turn had the weightiness of a flintlock slowly loaded. Ball and ramrod at the ready, the cock half-cocked, and black powder poured into the muzzle.

Anne felt the second letter bending in her grip. "How interesting."

"Why do you say that?"

"Do you wish to rekindle your past? Because the man I saw yesterday didn't disentangle himself from a certain woman's clutches."

That ramrodded ball and powder.

Will's eyes narrowed. "Easy, Mrs. Neville. You seem to've forgotten that I was at Denton House yesterday for no other reason than to help your league."

Ready . . . "Yet, you barely supported our false betrothal."

"I told her about it."

Aim . . . "Once."

Will's fingers pinched white on the Lambethware. He eyed her keenly as if sifting through his thoughts while trying to make sense of hers.

"Next time, her ladyship will have no doubts about who holds my affections, madame."

Fire . . .

Will landed his shot. Searing, precise.

A peculiar sensation cascaded, something which threatened to swallow her whole, at once thrilling and dreadful. Of all the things Will could have said.

Who holds my affections?

She was drowning in those four words until sound reason saved the day.

Of course, their false betrothal.

Will was mocking her gently. An odd combination, but he managed it. She'd lit a fuse, and there was no tamping it nor could the sparks be undone. This should've been addressed yesterday. She'd meant to. Will's finger in her cleavage might've thwarted her best intentions.

A regrouping was not out of the question.

"It's a matter of details," she said defensively. "Nothing is too small."

He raised his cup. "For you, I shall have a care with every one of them."

More nerve-calming tea was consumed. The table's edge pressed Anne's stomacher. A downward glance confirmed she was leaning forward, her hair on the table, the black curl taunting her. Since her second marriage, she was in the habit of pinning it. Yet, the night she freed Will and again today, she wore her hair down.

Because that's how she wore it when she was nineteen.

Why did women do that? Why did *she* do it? The answer was quite simple. She'd done it to please a man. Eight years ago, Will had stroked and praised her unbound hair. She'd gloried in his touch then as she did yesterday when he tucked a lock of hair behind her ear. His tenderness had been achingly dear. A terrible weakness, that.

She sipped her tea, deciding to use every pin in her arsenal of pins.

Aunt Maude cleared her throat. "There is more correspondence that needs reading."

The second letter had fallen into Anne's lap. She steadied herself, picked it up, and broke the wax seal. Two imperious sentences delivered a message in elegant script.

"The countess writes, 'Meet me at your warehouse tomorrow at one o'clock. I want to renew our negotiations.'" She held up the note. "It's signed 'The Right Honorable, The Countess of Denton.'" Her smile was close lipped. "How kind of her to order me to meet her."

"Strange that she's taking an interest again," Aunt Maude said.

Anne eyed Will cradling his tea with both hands. "Not so strange, I think."

"I'm surprised the countess gave your warehouse any consideration," he said. "I remember her rebuffing small business concerns as no' worth her time."

"You have it backward. I didn't seek the countess. She sought me with an offer to buy it."

"When?"

"Last June. I told you about that yesterday at Grosvenor Square."

Will scowled. "I thought you went to her man of business with an offer to sell." His scowl deepened. "You say she approached you in June?"

She refolded the note, dogged by foreboding. How confident she'd been that her league was too small to draw notice. But a woman powerful enough to bribe an audience with Dr. Cameron might be canny enough to find out women, commoners no less, had been asking about her.

"Yes, she approached me in June."

"Afore or after Dr. Cameron's execution?"

"After."

Will scrubbed a hand across his mouth. "There's a chance she knows."

Anne tapped the letter on the table, absorbing this blow. Three slender, plain gold rings glinted on her fingers. Graceful and fierce, she would fight. A shift in her chair and she met Will's gaze.

"It doesn't matter if she knows about the league. It won't stop us."

"How can you be so sure?" Aunt Maude asked Will. "Lady Denton's family is steeped in shipping and merchant trade."

"They are. But ask yourself, why would a woman whose father was among the first directors of the United Company of Merchants of England trading to the East Indies be interested in Anne's little warehouse on Gun Wharf?"

Aunt Maude set down her biscuit. Aunt Flora's aged fingers worried her dish. They had no answer.

"Her brother, the Marquess of Swynford, has a seat at the director's table now. Through him and the family shares, the countess has more money than we can imagine to have in our lifetime." He paused. "Do you really believe a woman with that kind of wealth would want an insignificant dock? In this part of Southwark?"

The older sisters exchanged worried glances. Will tried to reassure them.

"She may no' have taken notice of you two."

Aunt Maude smiled at her sister. "Because, dear, you and I are old."

"All the more reason for Cecelia, Margaret, Mary, and me to look after you." Anne's smile was the *cheer up* variety.

Aunt Flora patted Anne's hand. "I've lived too long tae be afraid of that woman."

"That's the spirit." Anne rose from the table with renewed purpose.

Nothing was going to stop them from taking back Jacobite gold—not king or countess or one cautious highlander. Thus, she walked to her kitchen and fed the morning's missives to the flames.

Chapter Nineteen

They crossed Horn Yard onto Stoney Lane. Sunshine sneaked through gritty clouds, shining grandly on the road's questionable muck and more questionable puddles. He was a man on a mission, following a woman on a mission to shop as quickly as possible. If Will didn't know any better, he'd say Anne wanted to lose him in the late morning crowd.

"Why the hurry, Mrs. Neville?"

"I had planned to shop alone." Anne stopped their progress to let three carters pass. "It's easier that way."

"And deny me the privilege of carrying your basket?"

She gave him the side-eye. "If I didn't know any better, I'd think you're holding it to make sure I don't give you the slip."

"You could be on to something." His ham-fisted grip on her basket garnered a queer glance or two, but a sharp glare back reminded Southwark's good citizens to mind their own business.

Anne pinched her skirts higher and they crossed the road. "Why are you so set on shopping with me?"

"Why are you so set on getting rid of me?"

"I needed to clear my head."

Drays rumbled by. Two hawkers, scrabbly lads with holes in their coats, took turns crying, "Cockfight, King's Head Yard!" and "Bareknuckle brawlers, Morgan's Lane!" A red-faced matron yelled at a costermonger selling his wares too close to her front door.

"You do your thinking in this?" Which earned him a giggle.

"I make do, as one must."

Anne was beautiful, mussed hair trailing her back. No straw hat and no carmine lips today. Her humble gray gown reminded him of grisettes, French worker women, shop assistants, servants (and erstwhile lovers) to university students. He'd seen grisettes in Edinburgh. A few inhabited Spitalfields where French Huguenots staked a claim in London, women of lowly circumstances but no less canny in their gray gowns of small cost.

"And why are you with me? I thought you had errands of your own to attend," she said.

Because I want to win your heart, lass. Risky words to say aloud. Instead, he chose the safer, "Because I want to talk to you and enjoy the pleasure of your company, Mrs. Neville."

"Oh?" Her stride was easy, companionable.

Pattens made Anne four inches taller, putting her head very near his shoulder, like their kiss on the stairs. They approached St. Olave's Street where vicars and harlots and red-coated soldiers patrolled the road. A pair of mail coaches trundled by. Pretty young flower girls, their baskets brimming, sold their wares on busy corners. Anne pointed to a wooden sign across the street with a white mortar and pestle painted on a field of black.

"That's my last stop. The apothecary." She spoke above the road's noise, her shoulder bumping his. "There's a quiet spot on the other side of Black Ravens Court. I'll take you there and you can explain this business of wanting the pleasure of my company."

A thrill bloomed in his chest. This was promising.

They set off across the street, Anne at one side and her basket of candles and coffee beans on the other. Last time he wooed her he was on horseback in wide open country, but if he was honest, there wasn't much wooing. By day, conversation had flowed without purpose, words seeding their love from boundless curiosity. By night, their conversation was passion sheened with hot need. A simple tale of young love.

Years and hardship changed their stories. Would the battering they'd taken make them less open? Or more so?

Anne dodged a rotting cabbage in the road and reached for the door with the unlettered black-and-white sign above it. Inside, the street's noise was blessedly muffled.

"The quiet," she sighed. "How nice."

"The improved smell's even better."

Dried plants secured by twine hung from rafters. Jars clinked behind the wooden counter, matching the soft grunts of someone maneuvering goods out of sight. Glass jars lined shelves, the labels on some of them as fascinating as the contents.

"Mermaid tears. Shark fins." He squinted at a clay jar in the corner and snorted. "Bat's eyes. What the devil are you looking to purchase, Mrs. Neville?"

A tall, slim man, his ginger queue neat and his smile bland, stood up. He wiped his hands with a cloth, his sharp gaze bouncing between Anne and Will.

"Good day, Mrs. Neville."

"Good day to you, Mr. Erskine." She gestured to Will. "Allow me to introduce my betrothed, Mr. MacDonald."

"I heard the news."

"You have? When?"

He waved a vague hand. "A few days ago . . . one of the elder women in your household told me."

"That would be Aunt Maude."

"Yes, yes. I believe she came to purchase a restorative for her bowels." The apothecary's voice pitched thoughtfully. "But I'd wager that malady is not why you're here."

Anne rummaged for her list. "No, sir."

Mr. Erskine's eyes narrowed on Will. "Your betrothed looks healthy enough, but appearances can be deceiving."

Will made an assessment of his own. Mr. Erskine was an educated Scots, east coast, Stirling or Edinburgh by his smoothly trilled *R*s.

"Like your jars of bat's eyes and mermaid tears?"

Mr. Erskine's smile was brisk. "'A wee thing amuses the bairns.'"

Hearing the old Scots proverb was a taste of home. "Simple people are amused by simple things."

"Indeed, the people of London seem quite taken with the display behind me. Ignore it. As long as I cure their ills, I could claim to have dragon's blood and people would still pay good coin for it." He reached under the counter and produced a scarred wooden box. "I keep my better remedies in here."

Anne pulled folded paper from her petticoat pocket. "We have a small list."

"Is the problem of a marital variety?" Mr. Erskine steepled his fingers above the box. "An inability to—shall we say—rise to the occasion?"

Will choked on a shocked laugh. "My tackle rises just fine, sir."

The apothecary looked to Anne. "Then, his is a problem of completion."

Anne giggled like a schoolgirl, her eyes bright and her cheeks pink. "Mr. MacDonald's needs are numerous, but I can vouch he is very capable in both rising to the occasion and completing it." She unfolded her list, adding an impish, "At least that was the case long ago."

Mr. Erskine hummed, deep in thought. He no doubt conversed daily on this delicate topic with the fine people of Southwark.

"A healthy specimen, you say? And there are no concerns with longevity? Or the like?"

Will was hands-on-hips indignant. "There are none."

Mr. Erskine set his box under the counter with a righteous, "Any woman about to be leg-shackled has the right to know."

"I couldn't agree more." Anne was all smiles, sliding her wrinkled list across the counter. "If you would be so kind, and fill this order for Aunt Flora's headache powder."

The apothecary donned his spectacles and read the list. "This is all you need?"

"It is."

The older man disappeared to a room behind his impressive wall of mystical remedies. Glassware clanked and there was a gentle *pop*, a jar uncorked by the sound. Will set both hands on the counter, his voice low for Anne's ears alone.

"You wound me, lass." Though his mouth could barely contain his grin.

She giggled again and he shushed her.

"It was funny, Mr. MacDonald."

"Because it was at my expense."

Anne poked his belly, her voice matching his. "Exactly. And you're man enough to laugh about it. That's what I like about you."

"*Like* you say? This is promising."

She sobered a little. "Despite our ill-advised kiss, there is nothing beyond our mutual liking, which bodes well for the next few days. Wouldn't you agree?"

"As you say, lass."

She playfully stroked the spot she'd poked. "Admit it. You were about to laugh. I saw the corners of your eyes creasing while Mr. Erskine carried on."

"He is serious about his business."

And Anne became serious about avoiding any further conversation that hinted at emotions. She withdrew her waistcoat-stroking hand and put distance between them as if struck by the intimacy of her hand on his body. A pall clouded her visage while she wandered the store, touching herbs and glass jars crammed with unknown contents.

He'd let things simmer. Anne needed to laugh after this morning. He'd not press his pursuit. Not yet. Another raven-haired woman was a persistent presence, a beautiful spider spinning a web of deceit.

How much did the countess know about Anne and her league?

Chapter Twenty

*T*he apothecary visit ended their market day. Anne was distracted, claiming her ledgers needed some tidying in preparation for the countess's surprise visit the next day. He never got to dance with her at the White Lamb and he didn't get to see the hidden place behind Black Ravens Court. If he was a cricket player, his strike rate would be zero.

While on St. Olave's Street, they begged a ride from an empty dray with Mermaid Brewery branded on the wood. They rode, legs dangling off the back like rustics newly arrived from the country. He didn't press conversation on their bumpy ride. The youthful Will MacDonald would've plowed forcefully onward, but the older and wiser man knew better. Sometimes a woman needed to be alone with her thoughts.

The dray eventually found Bermondsey Lane where the driver delivered them to Anne's broken gate.

Will passed coins to the driver and walked

backward, touching the brim of his tricorn. "My thanks for the ride, sir."

A smile creased the driver's weathered face. He dropped the coins in his pocket and snapped the reins. "Good day to you too, sir."

Anne waited at her gate, the basket tucked in her elbow. She'd taken back the basket and her conversation when they left the apothecary's shop. At present, her brows knit as if a remembrance teased her.

"Near St. Olave's Street, you said something about wanting to talk to me. Was that idle chatter?"

"No' idle chatter."

Winds were picking up. Anne's hem stirred and black tresses blew across her face. He dared not brush them off her cheek. A greater wisdom warned him to tread with care. Today's laughter had been as intimate as kissing her wrist. Playfulness was an innocent bond yet its threads could run as deep as any shared secret. For that reason, he reached around Anne and pushed open the gate, careful not to touch her.

She lifted her face to his. "You're a good man, Will MacDonald. I sometimes wish things could've worked."

His smile felt rusted and out of place. This was the scourge of a man who wanted love. Anne *wished* things could've worked—past tense. Those were the words of a woman who'd weighed their circumstances and found them lacking. Or him.

Hope shriveled in his chest.

"There is no higher compliment."

To be a good man in her eyes, to win that certain glow she bestowed on him would suffice for now. He was a fighter after all. He'd charged into war, facing incredible odds. His time with Anne and her league wasn't done. Nor was he.

"One question has been plaguing me about your league and the countess."

"But my display in the salon this morning squelched that." She stared at the river, chastened. "It is only natural that you would want to know more. And it's not as if I've been entirely forthcoming. Not on purpose mind you, but the effect is the same." Arms crossed, she wedged the basket between them. "Ask your question, and I will answer to the best of my ability."

Between Anne's high pattens and him down a step, they were eye level. Her directness was refreshing, a trait he appreciated.

He kept his hand on the gate. "How did you come to know the countess was behind the Jacobite gold in London?"

"That's what you want to know?"

"It's a good place to start."

She toed a pebble on flagstone, squeezing her basket close. "It is."

Her feet shifted and small jars rolled and clinked within her basket. He gently took the burden from her, wanting nothing between them. No objects and no secrets. Arms limp at her side, Anne seemed to understand. He wasn't an accomplice to her league. He was part of it. Part of her—his unsavory past included.

"The countess gave herself away when she managed to get into Dr. Cameron's cell." Anne brushed hair off her face and looked to the river. "The guards refused all bribes. A mark of how serious the crown was about the good doctor."

"But you told me someone bribed their way into his cell."

"They did, but not with money. With fear." She turned her gaze on him. It was vivid and sharp as a blade slicing to the bone.

A nasty shiver chilled his spine. Seven years ago, he'd witnessed Ancilla meeting unsavory men, wretches with empty eyes and no mercy in their souls. Men who would do anything for a price.

"The countess threatened a guard's family. Her bribe, if you will, was their safety and well-being." Anne hesitated, her eyes squeezing shut. "I won't tell you what she threatened to do."

A sigh gusted out of him. He knew how cruel men and women could be.

Anne grabbed the gate near his hand and held on tight. "Cecelia obtained the names of Dr. Cameron's guards and we watched them. Their habits, possible weaknesses."

"I believe you, lass, and I believe the countess was one step ahead of you."

"She was. By happenstance, I approached the guard, Mr. Wickham, while he was in his cups at a tavern. He told me a cloaked noblewoman armed with ruffians threatened him and his family. He said he had no choice but to let her in to Dr. Cameron's cell in the middle of the night while he was on watch."

"And he listened to the conversation and told you."

"He did. When I asked for the name of this noblewoman, all he could say was he glimpsed a white streak in her black hair." Anne eyed the bustling river. "That was enough."

"Does she work alone?"

"We don't know. Nor do we know how she got Jacobite gold to London and how much of it is out there," she said, her chin tipping at the City where rooftops bit the sky with uneven teeth.

London was good at chewing up its people. None save the rich and nimble could survive. Anne and her league were to be counted among the latter. Quick and agile, they had forged onward with their clan's reward in sight, and they were so, so close. The league's mission added vibrancy to his step—to do good for others. For his clan.

Anne's voice rose quietly beside him. "I want to go home."

He flinched, her words punching him. Anne leaned against her crooked gate with longing in her eyes. The same yearning pulsed in him. He'd fought it, denied it, and found rest in various places, claiming them to be his home. But he knew better. Home was more than where a man laid his head. It was in his heart, his soul, in the air he breathed and the kin he shared a life with.

But he couldn't go back to Scotland. An untenable stance, yet true.

Heavy in spirit, he touched her shoulder. "Let's get you inside."

They entered her house more tangled and unclear than when they left it hours ago. He'd sought to deepen his bond with Anne, to woo her. Their shop day journey through Southwark did nothing of the sort. They walked into Anne's salon pensive and quiet where Aunt Maude and Aunt Flora were altering the bigamist's clothes.

"Yer back and hale and hearty for the outing," Aunt Flora said.

"It was our visit with the apothecary. Quite stimulating." Anne winked at him and offered a wobbly smile.

Aunt Maude set a shirt aside and rose from the settee. "Let me take that." She took the basket from Will and peeked under white cloth. "Got everything, I see. And it was fun?"

"It was informative, ma'am."

Anne's small laugh was the fresh air he needed.

"Good, good." Aunt Maude bustled off to the kitchen with promises to bring cider for Anne and watered ale for him.

Anne collected her ledgers, her ink, and quill and took a seat at the table. He'd seen her on a horse. He'd seen her navigate Southwark and navigate the countryside, but he'd not witnessed her working. He took a seat at the table for the joy of watching her nibbling her thumbnail, dipping her quill twice in ink, and blotting it once before committing to the page. She was pretty, apple cheeked and wind mussed. He nursed the watered ale Aunt Maude delivered, enjoying this respite. The Iron Bell wasn't going anywhere. He would go later to ask his questions about men with *T*-branded thumbs. They were all chattering about the day, the mood easy and relaxed when the front door banged open.

Miss Mary Fletcher flew into the salon, hair

disheveled, her eyes wide. Her mouth rounded with all the drama she could muster, which had to be considerable since the woman didn't strike him as having an ounce of drama in her body.

She charged the table, nearly falling on it. "We are in terrible, terrible trouble."

He grabbed a chair off the wall and positioned it with an indecorous, "Sit."

She flopped on the chair and set her elbows on the table.

"I shall get the brandy." Aunt Flora sped off with speed belying her age.

Miss Fletcher was in a daze. Charcoal smudged her cheeks and acrid smoke clung to her clothes. Red-striped petticoats fanned out, burn holes pocking the fabric. She rested her head in both hands, announcing, "I set fire to my shop."

Chapter Twenty-One

*C*ollective gasps were followed by a spray of questions.

"Is Margaret hurt?" From Aunt Maude.

"Did everything burn to the ground?" From Anne.

"Was anyone hurt?" Aunt Maude again.

Aunt Flora scurried in, a cup and a bottle of brandy in hand. Will was useless. Inner wisdom told him to take a half step back and let the ministrations take their course. The succoring flurry, the flutters, and cooing reassurances. Aunt Flora poured brandy, and Miss Fletcher upended her cup, gulping it with the skill of a thirsty sailor. He couldn't stop his gape when she slammed sturdy porcelain on the table and swiped the back of her hand across her mouth.

"More."

To which Aunt Flora obliged her with a second restorative dose. Miss Fletcher took this portion calmly with steady swallows while everyone watched. They surrounded her, a worried, cosseting circle ready to jump at Miss Fletcher's slightest twitch. Emotions were bowstring tight. With this second cup half-gone, she was fortified. Almost. Char-stained hands hugged Lambeth-ware like a long-lost friend.

Aunt Maude gave a verbal nudge. "When you're ready, dear."

The fraught quality of Miss Fletcher's face lessened. A tiny nod, and her brow smoothed. Another gulp (air this time) and she began her tale.

"Margaret is well. She is . . . unharmed." Miss Fletcher's voice snagged as her face crumpled in pain. "I left her alone in the shop to come here."

The notion of what could've been silenced them. Agonized glances shot between Aunt Flora, Aunt Maude, and Anne. A shared history bolted this league together. Will was a bystander, present but not accounted for, and like any outsider, he took another polite half step back. The women filled the gap.

Aunt Flora rubbed Miss Fletcher's back. "There, there, dear. These are tears of gratefulness. Let them fall, and when you're done, we'll all say a prayer of thanksgiving that you and your sister are unharmed."

Fat tears rolled down charcoaled cheeks, which Miss Fletcher promptly smeared with her hand.

"I am relieved. And thankful," she said with a firm nod this time. "Neither my sister nor our neighbors were harmed. The fire was thankfully contained to the back of my shop." Another sniffle and Anne passed a handkerchief. "The bricks are charred, of course, and the room in ruins."

"What happened?" Will asked from his place outside their intimate circle.

Miss Fletcher dabbed her eyes, her chin tipping his way. Had she forgotten his presence in Anne's house? Daylight showed delicate purple skin under her eyes and her mouth, a tight line. An unpleasant admission was coming.

"The hour was late. I was preparing the coal. My forge is no bigger than—" she raised her hands with six inches between them "—this. My work room is about as cramped," she said dryly. "I must sit on a dairymaid's stool to work the forge."

Anne tossed a curt explanation over Miss Fletcher's head. "Her forge is a tiny pile of bricks low to the ground. Nearly impossible conditions."

"The forge must be small," she said defensively. "All the better to build the necessary heat. As to my work room, I can hardly expand it." Her indignation vented, she slumped in the chair. "Really, it was all a misunderstanding."

"With a neighbor?" Will asked.

"No. With the metal." Miss Fletcher folded the handkerchief into the smallest square. "In particular, its melting point."

"The melting point, I see," he said, not seeing anything at all except Anne shooting a frown over Miss Fletcher's head.

Miss Fletcher was more charitable. "I was working by rote, unfortunately. I overheated the forge. Gold requires a greater degree of heat to melt than silver." She sniffed and dabbed her nose with the newly folded square. "Too much heat and silver melts into unsalvageable drips lost in the fire."

He hummed his understanding.

"I was already working the silver when I realized my error," she said flatly. "I grabbed the tongs too quickly and knocked over my worktable. That's when my hem caught on fire."

Shifting in her chair, she reached for the back of her petticoat. Part of her hem was missing, as if a fire-fanged beast had taken a bite.

"Oh, Mary. How awful," Anne gushed.

"Embers landed on my worktable and the thing went up in flames. I yelled for Margaret and started dumping positively everything on the fire. Water, my flux powder, stomping on embers . . ."

Miss Fletcher's spine wilted again. Aunt Flora cooed encouragement and sloshed more brandy in her cup.

"You are a dear," Miss Fletcher said. "But I should not have any more. I need my wits about me."

"You could do without them for a day," the older woman muttered.

Will smiled against his balled fist while Miss Fletcher's eyes rounded.

"Surprised, are you?" Aunt Flora was in high spirits, jamming the cork in the bottle. "You canna keep working your fingers tae the bone. Neither of you," she said in a huff to Anne and Miss Fletcher. "Every woman needs a little fun. It's good for the soul."

"Cecelia understands this." Aunt Maude was a stern rustle of starched skirts. "You could learn from her."

Glowing respect for Cecelia's hoyden ways? From Aunt Maude? Now he'd heard it all.

Aunt Flora pointed the brandy bottle at Anne and Miss Fletcher with the skill of a seasoned tutor. "Beware, ladies. If you're no' careful, you'll wake up one day with a head of gray hair and no memories tae speak of."

"I appreciate your wisdom," Anne said, wiping biscuit crumbs into a neat pile. "But with the gold in our sights, fun is the least of my concerns. Returning the gold is our promise, our duty to the clan."

"Duty," Aunt Flora grumbled under her breath.

"It is the reason for our league," Anne said.

She was the good shepherdess, herding her flock back to the goal at hand. Murmured agreements and grudging nods came from the aunts' mob-capped heads. Will, standing in the background, reveled in the small rebellion. Their seasoned words struck an unexpected chord.

Fun! Imagine that!

Anne sat properly tall in her chair, her hands linking a tight knot on the table. Order had been restored. "Is there anything else you need to tell us?"

"There is one detail." A line creased above Miss Fletcher's nose. "With all the smoke, I opened the small window at the back of our shop."

"Did the neighbors notice?" Anne asked.

"No. But the Night Watch did."

Will groaned.

"I know," Miss Fletcher said, her gaze acknowledging him. "He yelled from the back alley. I called out through the window that all was well, but he insisted on coming into the shop. Margaret managed to keep him in the front and assure him the fire was out."

"That's good," Will said.

"I'm not so sure." Reluctant words rolled off Miss Fletcher's tongue. "He was suspicious of my claim that I was trying a new method of bending whalebone. It's done, of course, but you can't tell a man that. I fear he will come back, with the alderman perhaps, who can insist on inspecting the back of the shop."

"It's understandable. Fires in London, dear . . . they put everyone on edge." Aunt Maude held out her Lambethware dish to her sister. "Some brandy. I fear I need it."

Aunt Flora uncorked the bottle and poured a few drops.

"Last night it was the Night Watch, this morning the ward beadle." Miss Fletcher's face was baleful. "I've already hidden my tools, but for the near future, I won't be able to work metal."

"What about the wax mold?" Anne asked. "Did it melt?"

"It's right here. I was able to save it." Mary fished the wax out of her petticoat pocket and set it on the table.

Smoke and ashes had turned its milky hue a tepid gray. One end—the bow head end thankfully—wilted in the way wax did under transformative heat but mostly kept its form.

"You saved it," he said.

"A lot of good that will do us. I have no means to make the key."

Aunt Flora's fingers wrapped tightly around the brandy bottle's neck. "Surely, dear, you know a blacksmith? Someone who might let you use his forge? You do still have the silver?"

"The ingot is malformed but I have it." She

combed both hands through unruly hair. "Where am I going to find a blacksmith? One who will let *me* work his forge and not ask questions while I smith a Wilkes Lock key?"

Her challenge weighed on their small group. Will crossed his arms, an idea forming, though he couldn't be sure which obstacle was more daunting: A smith lending his forge, no questions asked, or a smith lending his forge to a woman.

"Have you no one in the City you trust?" Anne asked. "Think, Mary. There must be someone."

"None."

Aunt Flora's cheeks puckered. "You could try dressing up like a mon. If you put your hair under a cap, bind your bosom, and keep your face smudged . . . it could work."

"The imprint of a Wilkes Lock key in wax is too unique. People would ask questions. It would give me—us—away."

Will stepped up to the table. He was back in the fold. "I know a forge you can use, and keep your skirt on. It will help."

Chapter Twenty-Two

A week gone and he'd already forgotten about the smells, tar on the boil and sea-damp wood. They'd slipped from memory under the heady fragrance of lavender on Anne's skin, an intoxicating scent. Whale blubber was another story. When it sat in barrels the month of August, it was a whispered scent, harmless as beeswax, as was nature's way. Getting it was another story.

Grubb Street presses did their best to seduce readers with tales of bold whalers and floating ice vaster than the king's palace. The men of Howland Great Wet Dock knew the truth. It was written on the gaunt, feral faces of returning sailors. The arctic was a cold, cruel woman. Everyone knew she preferred the Dutch to the English. The English she spit out, killed, or simply denied them her bounty.

London's criminals weren't fooled by Grubb Street either. Upon release from prison, whaling couldn't entice them, though some had worked the Howland Great Wet Dock, a few with *T*-branded thumbs. None stayed long. The criminals who worked the yard eventually skulked away from West and Sons Shipping, singing a common refrain: "There has to be an easier way to earn my coin."

If a man wasn't ready to put his back into a day's work, West and Sons Shipping was not the place to be. There were barnacles to scrape, tar to spread, damaged hulls to piece back together. If unloading rotting whale parts in barrels didn't flatten a man, the brute strength needed to careen ships did. Backbreaking labor, it was, because the sea reminded all who crossed it: they were guests, and no more.

If capricious seas didn't devour the whalers, the Royal Navy might. Press gangs hovered, an everpresent threat, to sailors and dock workers alike. The King's Yard was downriver where work thrived apace. Storied ships needed hearty sailors. Will's first summer at West and Sons Shipping showed him that. Pressmen had slinked past Mr. West's office, sharks on the hunt.

He and Mr. Thomas West had beat the shite out of those turds—the genesis of true friendship.

Five years ago, Mr. West had waited while a prison hulk dumped Jacobite rebels back onto dry land. None accepted his employment offer. A year later, after suffocating in Ancilla's perfumed prison, Will gathered what remained of his pride and left. With a highlander's brogue and no letters of reference, he had one chance at honest work. His dignity in scraps, he'd sought the stoic Englishman who had to be either desperate or mad.

To his credit, Mr. West was neither.

West now stood on the selfsame dock. Coatless, hatless, sleeves rolled to his elbows, a large paper held wide in both hands. A ship's diagram, no doubt.

Will smiled, the familiar jump of friendship running in his veins. Men like Thomas West were rare, their blood two-parts honor and one-part grit, and West was the only Englishman he deeply, deeply respected. He wished his father could know him.

When Mr. Baines scraped his wherry along the dock stairs, the friendship would be tested.

Desertion had its price.

Mr. West squinted over his plans. He hailed no greeting, save slowly rolling up those plans. Mary Fletcher and Anne took the stairs with grace. Will followed. Anne slipped coins into Mr. Baines's outstretched palm, and the friendly wherryman scurried off to find more custom.

A grim Mr. West tucked rolled-up papers under his arm and waited. The sun on his face couldn't hide the skeptical glare in his eyes.

Guilt and dread took turns with each footstep. He should've sent word the first day in Anne's house that he was alive and well. While his absence might be overlooked, his request might not. It was a big one.

Will you let us forge a Wilkes Lock key?

He hadn't figured out how to broach the subject.

Thomas West was a good man. His reputation was golden in a city fat with greed and slim on honesty. Memory of the South Sea Company, a failed merchant partnership and whaling concern, still hung in people's minds. Stock criers selling shares in the streets followed by families stripped of home and hearth when the bubble burst. A man with ships who courted investors must be scrupulously honest.

The South Sea Company had been rife with money-lust and lies, its lines drawn directly to the crown. Mr. West's father had labored hard to keep his reputation spotless. His son carried the same banner. Will had been proud to be a part of that for five years.

Now he walked the sun-bleached docks, swallowing his resistance. Introductions were made. Anne and Miss Fletcher curtseyed, while pinching wind-buffeted straw hats to keep them in place. Mr. West, well-bred despite tanned forearms and a crooked scar on his cheek, tipped a fine bow.

"A pleasure to meet you, ladies. It's a rare day the fair sex steps foot on my docks." His eyes lifted to Will, sharp as a file. "A rare day indeed."

A healthy breeze fluttered lace on Miss Fletcher's gown. Near her heart, she, too, wore a tiny rosette of Clanranald MacDonald tartan pinned to her gown.

Emboldened, Will said, "We're here because I've a favor to ask. A grave one."

West's sharp eyes narrowed a fraction. "Then let us seek the privacy of my office."

"That is very kind of you, Mr. West." Miss Fletcher smoothed river-mussed hair as they made their way toward a two-story building.

Faded white letters, WEST AND SONS SHIPPING, emblazoned the riverside wall. The ground floor housed barrels of hooks and harpoons and the slanted desk of Mr. Anstruther, company clerk. Sun-warped stairs angled outside the building, the entrance to Mr. West's office.

At the bottom step, Will paused to greet the company clerk through an open window. "Mr. Anstruther. Good day to you, sir."

A snow-white head lifted from its sums. "Mr. MacDonald. You're back!"

The old clerk gawked behind his spectacles. Might've been Will's reappearance. Or it might've been the petticoats passing by.

"Good to see you, mon." Will waved and took the stairs two at a time.

In West's office, the yard's perfume diminished. Wood and whisky replaced it. Everything was the same. A paper-strewn desk, two plain wood chairs on one side, a heavy four-square leather chair on the other. A small door led to a storage room made into a humble sleeping chamber for the dedicated man of business.

A symbol of West's ancient profession hung on the wall behind the desk. A legendary harpoon.

The women were certainly fascinated.

Windows on three walls afforded a view of the River Thames and the King's Yard in the distance. They shot to the windows overlooking Howland Great Wet Docks. Below, men beetled over two careened ships, scratching the vessels' bellies with iron tools. Four ships were in dry dock, propped up in locks void of water. Over a hundred ships nestled in Howland's man-made inlet. Low-roofed workhouses lined one side, barrels of whale oil and whale parts hugged within.

The yard was a majestic sight, and West and Sons Shipping was but a small part.

Mr. West dropped the rolled-up plans on his desk and spoke with quiet venom. "Jemmy Brown ran three days all over Wapping, trying to find you. I did the same." West's jaw flexed in anger. "Apparently, you fared well despite our worst fears."

Will stiffened, bracing for a deserved blow. "I owe you a grave apology."

Neither man took a seat. Mr. West's gaze landed on Anne's and Mary Fletcher's backs. The ladies were pointing in awe, discussing the orchestrated chaos below. The sheer number of tethered ships was dazzling.

"Does your sudden disappearance have anything to do with your annual habit of donning your kilt?" West asked.

"It does. The same as every nineteenth of August when I get drunk as David's sow, alone in my lodgings."

"Except this year, apparently, you paraded about in your kilt. I was able to get that much from your landlord." West's mouth firmed. "Do you have a death wish? The rebellion is still fresh on the minds of those who lost husbands, sons, and brothers."

"The same is true for highlanders," Will said tightly.

West's mouth pinched a fierce line. The Uprising of '45 was their sore spot. The only place they couldn't find common ground. Simply, there was none. West, a man of reason, pushed past this.

"Am I to collect that your sudden reappearance has something to do with these ladies?"

"It does."

West eyed his desktop. "And this favor of yours . . . it pertains to them as well?"

"It does."

Will felt a smile grow. Their conversation was a hush over the desk. Across the office, Anne and her cousin's voices rose and fell, a musical lilt. By their carefully offered backs, they understood the need for this exchange. A hopeful prelude. Will's sudden return was troublesome enough, the risk of his request, greater.

West crossed his arms, a sturdy gesture. He wasn't entirely won over.

"Our current game of questions and answers will not suffice. You want my help? Tell me the *full* story today. Privately."

"Consider me at your service."

West snorted but his mouth curved, close-lipped and congenial. Calculations ticked behind West's blue-green eyes. Sounds of a thriving dockyard drifted through shut windows. Hammers and saws, men calling out to one another . . . a certain music. Mr. West kept the hum running smoothly. A blessed man, he walked to the windows, aware of his place in this world.

Curiosity angled West's head; confidence squared his shoulders. West was a hunter politely assessing his prey. *What kind of women has Will MacDonald brought to my yard?* had to be running through the man's head. By manners and speech, Anne and her cousin were educated. By their gowns and unpinned hair, they were unusual. Intriguing yet accessible. A story was here, and Thomas West hungered to know it. He murmured the offer of a tour, and feminine faces lit brightly.

"Indeed, Mr. West, we would enjoy that very much," Anne said.

"Especially your blacksmith's forge," her cousin chimed.

To which Mr. West's brows arched. He studied Miss Fletcher, storing her request and resetting his focus.

"Your accent, Miss Fletcher . . . Do you hail from Edinburgh?"

"I do, sir. My sister and I have called London our home for a few years now. I am the proprietor of Fletcher's House of Corsets and Stays on White Cross Street."

Her Edinburgh accent was refined, a genteel back-of-the-mouth treatment of her words. When her passions rose, as evidenced in Anne's salon today, Mary Fletcher trilled her *R*s dramatically as if she could barely control the rush.

"A woman of business," West said. "Have you a trade card?"

"I do." Miss Fletcher's mouth twitched. "However, you don't appear to be a man in need of a corset—if you will allow my boldness."

West laughed, a pleasant sandy sound. "Very kind of you to say, Miss Fletcher. I am not asking for my sake, but for my sisters."

Her face shined approval. "Ah, I would be pleased to have their custom." She fished inside her petticoat pocket and passed over her trade card. Mr. West read it, a glimmer softening his stoic eyes.

"It says you are also a member of the Worshipful Company of Glovers."

"I am. I purchased my placement in the livery not long after setting up shop on White Cross Street." She inhaled a morsel of air to impart reluctant news. "But we only make women's gloves."

"How unfortunate for me."

He tucked the trade card in his pocket while keeping eye contact with Miss Fletcher. Sunlight shined on his waistcoat's brass buttons, the only nod to his status. West's chin dipped a split second. A moment passed, the hum of life outside, matching the honeyed hum of . . . flirting? Will had never seen hardworking Thomas West dally in conversation with a woman. Ever. But this appeared to be the age-old male/female sport of flirting.

Cheeks blooming prettily, Miss Fletcher cocked her head. "Have I had the pleasure of making your acquaintance, sir? Before today, I mean?"

A boyish smile creased West's features. Arms crossed, Will eased his stance. Five years knowing the man, and he had never seen the like. His former employer pushed open the window, which forced him a quarter step nearer Miss Fletcher.

"I've not had the pleasure of formally making your acquaintance, but we have crossed paths." He reached outside and rang a brass bell, its clatter loud. "Jemmy," he bellowed to the yard, "when you're done there, come quick."

Anne inched away, her shoes softly scraping her retreat. She set fingertips on the window facing downriver. Was Anne recalling a time when she'd flirted sweetly with him? Will wanted her to turn around and tell him *I remember when we did this.* It'd be new intimacy if she did. But Anne's shoulders hunched, her only message, which could be any message. As for reading it, he wouldn't try.

He planted a hip on West's desk, vaguely adrift. Emptiness was palpable in his chest.

In the corner, Miss Fletcher studied Mr. West. "You know . . . it's coming to me, sir, where I last saw you."

West abandoned the half-closed casement, keen on the conversational hook he'd baited.

"It was last fall at Mr. Dorrien-Smith's King Edward Street warehouse. I was purchasing last season's bones and baleen." Mary Fletcher smiled her satisfaction. "To make corsets and stays, of course."

"Of course," he intoned.

That was a jiggling fisherman's hook, inviting her to fill a void. Would Miss Fletcher bite? West's stance, confident yet affable, hugging both arms to his chest, told Will the man knew exactly when and where he'd seen Miss Fletcher—the first time and possibly others.

Miss Fletcher looked outside, awareness a glow on her cheeks.

"Did I . . . purchase some of your goods, Mr. West?"

"Alas, you did not. My bones and baleen did not meet your exacting standards," he said in the driest voice.

"I see." Miss Fletcher touched her lace-trimmed bodice.

No, she stroked it.

West's gaze couldn't help but collapse on bountiful curves pressed high, presented prettily sans the annoying neckerchief. A smart man, West built a quick ladder back to her face. Miss Fletcher granted him a smile for his effort.

The art of flirting: notice, appreciate, but not too much.

"Well, the new season is nearly upon us," she said. "I have no doubt I shall be most enthusiastic . . . to peruse your goods, sir."

That sandy laugh again. "I am not sure how we can arrange that. Mr. Dorrien-Smith's warehouse will in future be dedicated solely to lumber."

"Fine goods, but not as solid or long lasting." Miss Fletcher's smile was feline. "Bone is far more satisfactory. It is considerably *harder.*"

"Indeed." Mr. West grinned, his arms falling loose at his sides.

"Have you found a suitable replacement?" Will asked.

Mr. West eyed him, the flirtatious spell fading. Life was intervening.

"Not yet."

"I have a warehouse, Mr. West. At Gun Wharf." Anne was solemn, turning from the window. "You are welcome to it." She looked at Will, an unspoken invitation for him to use her warehouse as a bargaining chip. "Will can tell you all about it."

"Have you a trade card, Mrs. Neville?" West asked.

"Unfortunately, not with me. You can find me at Neville Warehouse on Gun Wharf in Southwark most days, or seek my cousin." She finished by linking arms with Mary Fletcher. "She can help you find it."

"Cousins, you say?"

Footsteps thumped the stairs and the door flew open. "Mr. MacDonald! Welcome back, sir."

Jemmy Brown, the long-armed and knobby-kneed apprentice, launched himself at Will, his heels sliding to a stop just short of a hug. The lad whipped off his black wool Dutch cap and stretched out his arm, fingers splayed. Will clasped young Mr. Brown's hand and pumped it in friendship. The lad had won the tenderest spot in his heart with his hard work and eager spirit. Nothing could sink the buoyant young man.

Jemmy's eyes shined. "Thank God you are alive, sir. We thought you dead."

Will tousled the boy's wind-lashed hair. "I'm no' in the ground yet, Mr. Brown."

Chapter Twenty-Three

$\mathcal{W}$ill and Mr. West stood side by side at the office window, following the trio's progress. Jemmy burst with pride, pointing at the winch and pulley used to career a ship. The cap he wore barely corralled straw-blond hair. Tar etched his fingernails and hands which splayed with excitement. The women were an astute audience, standing at the dry dock's edge, looking up and down the *Mathilde* with timber angled into her sides. Mary Fletcher cast a careful eye at the blacksmith's shop.

Were they anxious? Or did Anne and Miss Fletcher want the yard cleared to have a go at the forge? They had to wait until the work was done. A woman in the forge would draw curious eyes. A woman smithing a silver key would draw curious questions.

The office's wall clock claimed the hour was well past three o'clock. More than an hour to go. West stared out the window, blissfully unaffected by time, whereas Will was a slave to it.

Atonement was messy business, especially

with an ardent woman constantly sacrificing on behalf of others. Anne, who had married into the clan, had done more for Clanranald MacDonald than most women born to it. Surely, she would see reason? See that she'd amply made up for losses from the rebellion.

A life with him in the colonies would be a fresh start. No war, no loss . . . just them and a new path. And West was but one more step on this path.

He cringed inside at his mercenary heart.

"Do these women have anything to do with your drunken August ritual?" West asked.

Will weighed his answer. He'd chewed on what to say and how to say it on the ride that went all too fast from Bermondsey Wall to Howland Great Wet Dock. He'd asked Mr. Baines to let him have a hand at the oars. Together, they rowed a blistering ride downstream. Will needed to put his back into something. Laboring with his hands freed him to think.

"Out with it, man," West coaxed, "But fair warning. If you tell me the intriguing Miss Fletcher has caught your eye, I shall drown you in the River Thames."

He chuckled. "She has not, but have a care. Miss Fletcher is a woman of sterling reputation."

West snorted. "No matchmaker said finer words."

They were quiet, drinking in rows of ships tamely moored. Mr. West was the canny sort who knew how to let silence breathe. West would give the necessary room for him to assemble his tale. His former employer understood the nineteenth of August was a difficult day. An IOU of the soul.

One side of his debt was the Uprising, due each year.

A green-eyed lass was on the other.

He stood before the open window and gripped where wood and glass usually met. He wouldn't tell another soul he loved Anne. Those hallowed words belonged to her and no one else. But his knuckles, white on the frame, might betray him. He wanted to tell her, to shout it from the window of West and Sons Shipping (as inglorious as that sounded).

Words weren't enough. There were things he needed to lay at her feet.

The key. The gold. A new life.

Would she want me? Her politely bolted bedchamber door was evidence that she did not. He was half-skilled in matters of men and women. Poorly prepared when it came to love. Other than protect and provide, he didn't have a clue how to win Anne.

One problem at a time. At present, he owed Mr. West an explanation. He stared at clouded blue skies and decided to be as forthright as a man about to commit a crime could be.

"Mrs. Neville used considerable resources to set me free after the Night Watch hauled me off to Marshalsea."

"So that's where you landed."

"It is."

"We didn't think to search this side of the river for you," West said, glossing over questions about Mrs. Neville's resources and putting a neat ending on Will's summary, until . . .

"I've never known you to let your August ritual

land you in prison." There was the rub, and West was poking it.

"Marshalsea was a respite," he said in breezy tones. "Time to stretch my legs, rest my back."

"Like taking the waters in Bath."

"Exactly." He grinned half-heartedly and turned the conversation. "What's this interest of yours in Miss Fletcher?"

West scratched his nape, affecting a casual demeanor. "I could do with a dalliance."

"Bored, are you?"

"She'd be a diversion. I'm plagued these days by warehouse troubles and missing laborers," West said with droll humor.

His grip on the frame tightened. A splinter might've slipped under his skin. "Forgive me for no' coming sooner. You've been good to me, hiring me, teaching me a new trade. I owe you."

West snorted. "That's a load of shite and you know it. You've outworked every man here and then some. I should've doubled your wages long ago." West slanted a look at him. "Nor have I forgotten that you saved my life. We both know I owe you the greatest of debts."

The past was in West's ominous tone. Another debt . . .

Seagulls screeched outside, landing on the *Mathilde's* mizzen mast. A memory floated in their shrieking cries, the keening wind of a cold dark night his first winter working the docks.

Iron tools had gone missing. Chisels, hammers, caulking irons one day. Boxes of nails and a gimlet the next. After a week of losses, Mr. West had decided to stay late, alone, since the men in his employ had already earned their wages and more. That's what men did at West and Sons Shipping. They went above and beyond, but that particular day had been brutal. A chill camping in limbs, men with the ague, miserable but still working. Like the others, Will had been bone tired and hungry that night. No one had wanted to stay late.

He had one foot in the wherry when air soughed through leafless trees rimming the Howland Great Wet Docks. The boat rocked men shivering under a primordial sky.

"Mr. MacDonald. We don't have all night," a man in the boat said. "I've got a pretty whore off King Henry's Yard waiting to see me."

"She's waiting to see yer coin, ye fool," was another's answer.

The men snickered, and a gust danced with white-caps on the river. The day had been loathsome, but the night would be worse, hallowed and dark, and there was something about those trees . . .

He stepped back onto the dock, his coat blowing sideways. "Go on without me."

Will walked to the blacksmith's forge, following a clanking noise.

He'd never forgotten that night.

Three rufflers, big and nasty with stony fists and foul breath, had come off Rogue's Lane at the back of the wet dock. They had the jump on Mr. West. One eye swollen, blood and spittle dripping from his mouth, West gave as good as he got. But against three men, one armed with an adze, the fight was getting ugly—until Will arrived.

Bones had crunched. A tooth had gone flying. Blood had puddled the forge floor. The thieves fought like men who'd neither give nor ask for quarter. A knife-sharp glance from Mr. West's good eye was a fast conversation. They were in it to the death.

Later when skies were pitch black, Mr. West and Will weighted three dead men with rocks, rowed them out far past the King's Yard, and dumped them in the river near the Isle of Dogs. They rowed the choppy river back to West and Sons Shipping. Utterly spent, they sank to the floor of West's office. Whisky was shared and a friendship born.

Down below in that same yard, Jemmy Brown introduced the ladies to everyone. Men balancing lumber on their shoulders stopped and touched forelocks. Friendly conversations rose, twined with the ping of a blacksmith's hammer. Mr. West's skirted guests were a pleasant distraction, twin confections.

The cheerful trio ambled near the smithy's forge, the afternoon sun showing a charred triangle of missing cloth on Miss Fletcher's back hem. Mr. West's neck craned for a better view.

"Is Miss Fletcher's skirt burnt?"

"It is. You could say that's why we're here." He faced his former employer, deciding bluntness was best. "She needs to forge a key."

"All this secretiveness over a key?"

He hesitated. "It's no' just any key. It's a Wilkes Lock key."

"I see." West watched Jemmy and the ladies disappear into the forge. "You won't need iron then."

"Miss Fletcher has an ingot of silver in her pocket."

"Of course, she does. Doesn't every woman?"

Will stood taller, the incredible need to defend Miss Fletcher jabbing him.

"Her father is a silversmith in Edinburgh. A well-established mon, I collect. She learned her smithing skills from him. She's quite talented."

He shut his mouth when tempted to share how talented.

Mr. West frowned his disapproval. "He would undoubtedly be displeased to discover his daughter is replicating a Wilkes Lock key."

A father figure to his sisters, West would say that. Learning about her role with the key might have tarnished Miss Fletcher's shine. Will could've told West these women weren't like his sisters. Anne didn't want to be ensconced in a pretty house like a doll on a shelf. She craved open land. She'd never tolerate a loss of freedom. Miss Fletcher had to be struck from the same mold.

West strode to his desk and dove into his comfortable world of business. "Go ahead," he said distractedly. "Ring the bell, and announce the workday done. The forge is Miss Fletcher's to use as she sees fit."

"Thank you."

West's gaze lifted from a stack of papers. His eyes were knife sharp on Will. This was a tremendous risk, but a debt was paid, the transaction done. There'd be no more questions about the Wilkes Lock key.

Will pushed the casement wider, breathing iron, grit, and sweat . . . his history on the Howland Great Wet Dock. He'd recovered here. Be-

come the man he was today for the new trade
he'd learned and a true friendship earned. A
pang uncoiling in his chest, he reached for the
bell cord and rang the end of the workday. Smiling men hailed greetings when they saw him
half out the window. He would go down and see
them. After today, he'd not come back here again.
He couldn't.

It was on him to leave the lightest trail. After the gold was stolen, Ancilla would trace his
whereabouts. He'd have a word with Anne when
they were alone in the forge. The league should
scatter after the art salon.

At the moment, he had goodbyes to attend.

The peculiar throb inside him rippled wider.
"I'll go down and say my farewells."

"Yes, do."

His hand was on the latch, the door ajar when
West spoke, his head down as he shuffled papers.

"You said Miss Fletcher is a capable smith,
but . . . I don't suppose Miss Fletcher needs a man
to help her with the forge, does she?"

"Neither Miss Fletcher nor Mrs. Neville need a
man for anything."

And that stirred the widest rift of all in Will's
chest.

Chapter Twenty-Four

*W*ill hadn't come home last night, though *home* wasn't precisely correct. Will MacDonald didn't live at Neville House. He sojourned here, a man passing through her life the same as he did eight summers ago. But that wasn't precisely correct either.

She rubbed her temple, the bruised one. Splitting hairs over Will MacDonald's place in her home was not a priority, yet it was all she could think about.

He was all she could think about.

It was maddening.

She'd never been one to dither about men. She liked them. They had their uses, certainly. Nor had she ever been the heartless variety of woman out to conquer every man who crossed her path. A rude return to her father's Edinburgh house at fifteen had taught her a thing or two about men. Her grandmother's staid, gentle home was one version of love. Another version existed with her brothers; theirs was a rough-and-tumble camaraderie thrown awry when she reappeared after years gone. To them, she was a foreign species. A sister.

She developed a backbone, as one does in a household of men. Steeled by order, primed with love.

It was all for the day she opened the door on Lothian Street and found a handsome, kilted highlander. Brash, broody, with a charm all his own, Will MacDonald was a gift. The harbinger of wide-open land and freedom.

He made her heart sing, and at the moment, he made numbers swim before her eyes.

Tiredness could be the issue. She'd stayed up late, a candle in the window, waiting. She'd kept her hands busy with mending. It was good for the soul, as Aunt Flora would say. It gave a woman hours to think.

At the moment, her thoughts ran to giving Will a sound drubbing.

She worried over him, big lug that he was with a brawny back and caber-tossing thighs. He was at heart a gentle soul, which made the numbers swim again. A foreign drop of wetness plopped indignantly on the page. She swallowed, or tried to. It was confusing, this dampness in her eyes and dryness in her throat. Her body demanded she acknowledge a simple fact: Will still owned her heart.

A pained howl wanted out. Venting wouldn't matter.

The man destined to seek his father in Virginia was destined to leave her behind. He had grand plans (not that he'd shared them). She wasn't in them. For the moment, her greatest task was to thwart the Countess of Denton. Throw the woman off from any hint of what Will and the league were going to do.

She wiped her eyes, free to concentrate on important tasks that didn't include wondering where Will MacDonald slept last night. Wondering if he had hit his head and fallen in the street. Or wondering if he'd availed himself to Red Bess's tender mercies.

She was free to ask important questions such as what color should a woman wear when meeting her nemesis? The question tumbled around Anne's mind all morning. She'd already changed twice. It was exhausting, taking as much focus preparing to meet an artful enemy as an assignation with a cherished man. Funny about that. Will had never cared what she wore as long as *she* was in the gown. When he was randy, her out of her gown was even better.

"Stop," she said under her breath.

"What's that, dear?" Aunt Flora hemmed an apron in the great chair by the window. The sunlight helped her stitching.

"It's nothing."

She was careful not to turn fully around. Aunt Flora might be across the salon and her eyesight dimming, but she had a talent for sniffing out emotions and demanding a body confess.

"I'm finishing the Neville Warehouse ledger . . . for my meeting with the countess."

"Excellent, dear." The needle wound in and out of pristine muslin. "I feared you might fash yourself over Will no' coming home last night."

"I'm not," she said tersely. "He's a grown man who can do what he wants."

Aunt Flora shifted in her seat, daylight shining on black petticoats. Her smile was beatific. "I seem tae recall saying the same tae Will—" the needle's hypnotic rhythm stopped "—about you."

She rolled her pencil. "This isn't his home. He is a guest. We should remember that."

"Of course, dear."

Anne scribbled on foolscap beside the ledger. It was her place to check her sums and draw aimless but satisfying pictures and shapes. Nothing of consequence. A rose, a swirl, a shape that morphed into a mess. She should concentrate. Will had stolen most of her night. He would not steal her day. There were things to do, such as deciding if wearing her garnets to the warehouse would be too much. To do what? Impress the Countess of Denton?

The garnets were out of the question. She'd worn them when the countess came home early, and she would wear them again the night of the art salon. They were her only display of wealth, save her three gold rings. She made a fist and rubbed them. Pretty, scrawny things that once belonged to her mother. They reminded her of a Roman *caestus*, fighters' gloves. Except these rings were too flat to be harmful and too thin for a show of wealth.

Confidence was all she had. She'd array herself in it. Armed with her ledger, proof she was a competent woman of business. She'd wear the plum fustian petticoats she wore when setting Will free from Marshalsea.

And seeing to his bath.

That made her smile.

Yes. The plum fustian with the stomacher and plain outer robe, all in the same unembellished fabric . . . save lacey elbows, all the better to hide her knife.

Another reason to smile. She could take care of herself.

She glanced at Mr. Neville's plain weight-driven wall clock. Half past eleven. Enough time to change from another version of yesterday's gray gown. This one had small red flowers painted on the fabric. She was scratching one little flower when a soft, metallic whine sounded. Her front door was opened.

Her pulse leaped. She sprang up from her chair and ran to the salon door.

"Will?"

Sunlight haloed a feminine form.

"No, it's me. Cecelia." She shut the door. "Where did he go?"

Tension spooled between her shoulder blades. "I don't know. He's been out all night."

Cecelia untied her straw hat, one arm clutching papers to her ribs. "He didn't come home?"

"This isn't his home," she said irritably. "He is a guest."

How vexing. The ladies of her league already thought of Will as a permanent fixture.

"A guest you want to keep around, I think." Cecelia tossed her hat on the entry table with a breezy, *"Chan eil an earball aige fo do choi."*

"I don't want to keep his tail under my foot," she said defensively. *Just know his whereabouts.*

Cecelia's eyes narrowed. "Did you cry over him?"

"I—" She touched the corner of her eyes.

Cecelia brushed her hand away. "Don't. Wetness spikes your lashes prettily, long gorgeous things that they are." Cecelia linked arms with her and they ambled into the salon. "Does he know that you've shed tears over him?"

"I don't . . . I didn't shed tears over him."

Cecelia snorted, an artful feminine sound that matched her kohled eyes and rouged cheeks. "Your lashes tell me you shed a few tears, prettily, no blotched cheeks, but you are terribly pale."

She touched her cheeks. Cecelia wasn't being unkind. She was being direct and helpful . . . and too insightful.

"It's written all over your face, Anne. You didn't sleep a wink, did you?" Cecelia led them to the settee where they both sank onto its lumpy yellow seat. "Good morning, Aunt Flora."

"Good morning, dear." The rhythmic needle didn't stop.

"Today, I am the bearer of bad news."

"What bad news, dear?"

Cecelia unfurled the papers she'd carried and slapped them on the upholstery with a dramatic flair. "It's all this sunshine, I tell you. It emboldens criminals."

Anne chuckled and picked up one of the papers. "Are we the pot decrying the kettle?"

Cecelia waved off her quip. "We need torrential downpours, same as we had earlier this summer. Heavy rain cleans more than gutters."

Anne scanned the paper, its blaring captions

and columns of print all the usual dire news and gossip. "What troubles you so?"

"Don't you see?" Cecelia rattled another paper. She punched an elegant finger at a caption.

Anne read a few lines underneath it. "A house-breaking?"

"Yes. A rather grisly one. The rise of violence and housebreakers has everyone talking." Cecelia started to fold the paper. "I tried asking about our man at Covent Garden and—"

"You asked about Will?"

Feminine brows arched and the folding stopped. "No, Mr. Rory MacLeod." Cecelia could've followed with *you idiot* but she kindly shook her head and continued folding. "You are lovesick," she muttered.

Anne bit her bottom lip. She checked the clock. It was almost noon. He still wasn't back, and she'd have to leave shortly. Seeing Will made her day better. His presence was amiable. *Amiable?* She cringed behind the paper she was supposed to peruse. Amiable was better suited for recommending a chimney sweep or describing a favorite costermonger.

She sucked in a deep breath and tried to read the paper. Cecelia was rummaging through the other papers, a line etched in otherwise smooth skin above her nose. Something had gotten her dander up.

"You've heard nothing about Mr. MacLeod?" Anne asked conversationally.

"Nothing. The man could be a ghost. Which is strange, don't you think? The person you and Will described would surely have stopped in a pub or tavern somewhere in the City, yet not a soul claims to have heard of him."

"Strange."

"Would you like some luncheon, dears?" Aunt Flora rose from her chair, her knees cracking.

"A little something would be nice," Cecelia said.

Aunt Flora headed to the kitchen and Anne refocused on the *Fore Street Journal*. Unlike the *Gentleman's Monthly Intelligencer*, which Aunt Flora hoarded in a basket in the corner of the salon, it did not print pictures. She skimmed a hyperbolic column dedicated to housebreaking incidents.

"It says, last night, there was a horrible housebreaking on Little Wood Street, another at Dean Street and another near Lincoln Inn Fields." Anne felt her eyes pop bigger. "Housebreakers moving to the West End? Rather bold of them."

"Read further."

She skimmed, which worked the same. Her mind could barely concentrate on a column of sums, much less a breathless recounting of terribly vicious crimes.

"What am I looking for?"

"The part that says the Duke of Newcastle summoned Bow Street's magistrate, Mr. Henry Fielding." Carmine lips twisted a pout worthy of Drury Lane. "Friends tell me the crown insists on criminal reform, and Mr. Fielding has been charged to see it done."

Cecelia's friends were a nebulous lot. She rarely expounded on who they were, and Anne never pressed. But that pout began to falter, and unease climbed into hazel eyes.

"You look worried. Don't be—snails move faster than the crown."

Cecelia shook her head emphatically. "No. This is different. Change is coming. Common folk are in an uproar. Look at what happened to you."

Anne touched the nearly forgotten bruise. London's aggressive tumble was part of daily life.

"I've been to Bow Street, Anne. I've watched Mr. Fielding in action. I've caught him watching me."

"Because you're pretty."

"Or because he's seen this." Cecelia peeled back a finger's width of lace, baring her tartan rosette.

A well-known fact: Mr. Henry Fielding wrote vociferously against the Jacobite cause. It was just like Cecelia to flounce into the gallery of the magistrate's court, her devil-take-you rosette showing. Anne sighed. From what she'd heard, it was just like Mr. Fielding to take note.

"He keeps meticulous records of criminals and their associates—even if they've never been charged with a crime." Cecelia worried a line in her petticoat. "This doesn't bode well for us."

Cecelia was lightness and cheer. She spoke the language of fashion and beauty. Fun and flirtation were her currency. That she pored over newspapers was troubling. An obsessive habit? A restless mind? She read positively everything. Perhaps their drive for the Jacobite gold had been too much? It could be she was cracking under pressure.

"Cecelia," she chided. "I hardly think—"

"He has a record of me!" Cecelia whisper-hissed.

Chapter Twenty-Five

The front door opened. Pleasant conversations rose, Aunt Flora greeting Aunt Maude returned from purchasing more candles, Margaret and Mary Fletcher joking about Neville House needing to lock its door, and not a manly brogue among them. Aunt Flora's refrain rang in her head: *He's a grown man who can come and go as he pleases.*

At the moment, Will should be the least of her worries. The league needed her. Cecelia needed her. The woman was white as a sheet behind rouged cheeks.

Anne squeezed her hand and said a quick, "Please. You and I will speak of this later. Not a word to them about Mr. Fielding and his meticulous records."

Cecelia gave a jerky nod. "None." Though worry was plainly writ on her face.

Anne rubbed trim on her skirt between her thumb and forefingers. It was difficult to think with the clamor in her mind. If Cecelia is in Mr. Fielding's book, she might be too. And the other ladies.

Had Bow Street's magistrate heard whispers of their league?

"I cleaned the key." Mary swept into the salon, smiling proudly and her hand open.

The silver Wilkes Locke key rested innocently in her palm. The key, still cast in wax, had gone home with Mary after their interesting sojourn at West and Sons Shipping. Will and Mr. West had taken Mr. West's small boat and seen Mary delivered to Billingsgate Stairs, and the sun had just set when they delivered her to Bermondsey Wall's beach.

Mary's hand inched closer. "Aren't you going to take it?"

She did. The metal was warm. Mary must have kept a firm grip on it all the way from White Cross Street. Silver twisted a pretty tangle on the bowhead, a nice recreation despite the fire having melted part of the wax.

Mary hovered near, hands clasped, her head cocked as if she sensed something was amiss.

Anne cleared her throat and closed her fingers around the seditious key. "Thank you."

"Are you well?" Mary asked.

"Will didna come home last night." Aunt Maude tossed out that information.

Mary mouthed a silent *O*.

Anne shifted irritably. "He *is* a guest." Which everyone ignored when a beaming Aunt Flora set a tray on the low table by the settee.

Will MacDonald was only a few days in their fold, but he'd won a permanent place in their hearts. Why shouldn't he? The man had knowledge of the key's whereabouts, had sneaked into a house where he dreaded to return, and imprinted the key in wax. If these feats weren't enough, he produced a forge—a forge!—for Mary to use when all seemed lost.

The man was a miracle worker. He should be an honorary league member.

She was happy calling him Hades. His absence was bedeviling.

Aunt Maude set aside her basket of market goods. Plain wood chairs were brought over to encircle the low table. The Fletcher sisters and Aunt Maude and Aunt Flora chattered on, balancing small Lambethware plates in one hand, while selecting from the luncheon offering of fruit slices and palm-sized slices of meat and potato pie. Cecelia quietly gathered the newspapers she'd brought, and Anne tucked the Wilkes Lock key into her petticoat pocket.

Life was a cheerful prospect for most of the league. Anne wanted to keep it that way.

"Anne, aren't you going tae eat?" Aunt Flora asked.

Cecelia put a flaky triangle on her plate and poked a fork at its gold-baked edge.

Anne checked the clock. Twenty minutes past noon. "I can't. I must leave in ten minutes."

"She's meeting Lady Denton at one o'clock," Aunt Maude said.

Cecelia stopped torturing her meat pie. "The witch of Grosvenor Square plagues you?"

"Such scorn, delivered with perfect manners." Mary smiled and elegantly wiped the corner of her mouth where a crumb sat. "It's why you are dear to me, Cecelia."

Hand over her heart, Cecelia bowed from her seat. "I do try."

Cecelia passed a fledgling smile to Anne. Jacobite gold wasn't their only binding tie.

"Lady Denton sent word yesterday. A letter calling for us to renew our negotiations for the warehouse," Anne explained. "Will thinks she knows something."

"She probably does." Cecelia set down her plate, her attempt at eating done.

"You think so?"

Cecelia curled one foot under her bottom and lounged as best a woman could in a whalebone corset. "You're good with ciphering, Anne. What is the outcome when you have a woman with tremendous resources and the morals of a snake?"

She didn't have to answer. Her league had done the math and come up with the answer.

"We've known the odds were against us since afore we left Scotland," Aunt Maude said.

There was a rustle of agreement. This small group of women was ready to change their part of the world, and not the crown nor a powerful, ennobled woman could stop them. Unfortunately, they'd labored unnoticed for so long that anonymity had become a warm blanket they'd taken for granted. But too many unfortunate intersections were colliding of late, intersections that could not be ignored. A change was needed.

"You aren't reconsidering our plans for the twenty-eighth, are you? We canna let fear of what the countess *could do* stop us. We are equal to the task." Margaret Fletcher, by far the quietest of their merry band, had spoken.

Anne smiled gently, adding stout-hearted to Margaret's qualities.

Forks scraped plates politely. Everyone waited for Anne. Knowledge glinted between her and Cecelia, shiny as quicksilver and twice as dangerous. The two of them were thick as thieves among genteel, skirted thieves.

"Quitting is not a choice," Anne said at last. "We go as planned."

"That's the spirit." Aunt Flora's fork plowed into a substantial bite.

Anne rose from her perch on the settee, fingering her medallion. She had less than five minutes to impart needful information.

"There is, however, one small twist."

The fork scraping stopped. Five expectant feminine stares sought hers.

"All of you must leave the night we take back the gold." Her gaze touched each woman. "It's best to assume our cloak of anonymity is gone."

"Do you think she knows about us?" Aunt Flora asked. "For all the times I've been tae her kitchen, she's never set foot in that room. Not once."

"It doesn't matter. Even if Lady Denton doesn't know exactly what we're up to at the moment, she certainly will once the gold is gone."

"But to leave . . . so fast?" Mary asked.

She was firm. "Yes. Do you have someone to watch over your shop?"

The best tactic was to herd the conversation away from *if* they left to when and how it would be done. A tidy maneuver, it worked wonders.

Mary rested her plate in her lap. "I did hire a shop girl last month."

"She's trustworthy," Margaret said. "I can vouch—her character is sterling."

Anne was pacing in earnest now. A glance at the clock: two minutes to leave.

"Why would the countess have any inkling of me or Margaret?" Mary asked. "Or Aunt Maude and Aunt Flora? We're invisible to the likes of her."

She set hands together. In supplication. To beg. To order, if she had to, though her shepherdess skills had grown legendary. Why be imperious when building accord was much more effective?

Trembling, urgent need rose inside her. She wanted to choose her words with care, but an ardent, "*Please*," was all that came out.

Young Margaret Fletcher's eyes rounded. Aunt Maude's mouth puckered fiercely. Aunt Flora and Mary's did too. The seated women checked each other quietly. A bridge of agreement was built one brick at a time. Anne was standing on a structure of trust which had been built long before this moment, and, God willing, would last long after.

Mary exhaled, her cheeks puffing. "Well, I've always wanted to visit Brighton. Perhaps this is our chance," she said to the room.

"Flora and I will go with you," Aunt Maude said, patting Mary's arm. "And you, Cecelia. Will you join us?"

Cecelia was coiling a curl around her finger. "I think I shall take the waters at Bath. It should be a fine visit this time of year."

"What about you and Will?" Aunt Flora's blue eyes clouded with worry. "And the gold?"

Anne strode to her escritoire where the ledger

waited, an innocent prop in this ruse. She knew the fate of the Jacobite treasure. If Will was here, she could ask him about his plans beyond the general *find his father in Virginia*. He'd certainly earned substantial payment to get him there, which was another matter to resolve. His payment. Answering his question about that August day eight years ago was not nearly enough.

"I don't know what he has planned." Saying that squeezed her heart. She opened the slender drawer that housed the Neville Warehouse key.

"He hasna said much tae me," Aunt Flora said. "But you'll be safe. Hauling the gold and all up north?"

The Neville Warehouse key nestled in a corner of the drawer. She dumped it in her pocket, shut the drawer, and collected the ledger. She hugged the account book to her chest and faced the women she'd labored with, colluded with, and generally grown to love over the past few years. She needed the book's gentle armor. Her heart was threatening to beat out of her chest and tears of a sudden wanted to spill.

"Mr. Harrison, an acquaintance from the White Lamb, helped arrange my passage on a recommissioned sloop named—" she held her breath because it was the oddest turn "—*The Grosvenor*."

"Oh, Anne." Cecelia's groan tripped into a delicious giggle.

She managed a wobbly smile. "It was Mr. Harrison's suggestion . . . who of course has no idea what I am taking to Arisaig."

Mary speared a slice of fruit. "Quite fortuitous, don't you think?"

"It is. I will leave at dawn the morning after we take back the gold."

She basked in the glow of friendship. Days like this were coming to an end. This unique, trying, and utterly satisfying time in her life would be no more. Taking home Jacobite gold was going to happen, which meant her life would change drastically.

She checked the clock and her pulse leaped unpleasantly. Twenty minutes to one!

"I must be off!"

She ran to the entry hall and jammed her straw hat on her head. While her nimble fingers tied a black silk ribbon under her chin, Mary was in the midst of recounting their visit to West and Sons Shipping. She was half out the door, nearly free to concentrate on the countess when she heard Aunt Maude.

"But what happened tae Will?"

Silence.

Anne clicked the door shut and soaked up blessed sunshine. *Will.* He was a heart-breaking puzzle. How could a woman long for a man, yet want to soundly thrash him?

She turned west, blending into Southwark's foot traffic: chimney sweeps, sweat streaking char-coaled cheeks, costermongers hawking vegetables already limp in summer sun. These were Southwark's foot soldiers, the common folk striving to keep impoverishment at bay. The Neville Warehouse ledger was her armor in that fight, clamped in her left arm, covering her heart. She was off to a battle of sorts, but her mind picked the bones of earlier wonderings. What happened to Will?

Was he in a ditch?

Did he spend his evening, thoroughly sotted with Mr. West?

Or was he hunting a man with a *T*-branded thumb in a misguided effort to exact justice for her?

Cut from a chivalrous mold, Will would strive hard to right a wrong—especially his wrongs. Guilt had colored his eyes the night she'd told him of the babe in her belly eight years past. He'd left her and their unborn babe to fight a war. A man would have to work very hard to atone for that. The matter was done for her. History.

A stubborn man, Will wouldn't see it the same.

Chapter Twenty-Six

*P*ink-arsed cherubs cavorting on clouds was too much by any standard, a treacle image for a woman who'd never been angelic a day in her life. Yet, the heavenly tableau adorned Lady Denton's gilt-trimmed door. On closer inspection, plump little angels decorated the entire vis-à-vis carriage, their innocent faces peeking from clouds on every panel. Excess run amok. Within the carriage, indolent fanning slowed.

"Mrs. Neville, how kind of you to join me."

Anne bent the brim of her straw hat for more shade. Pearl earbobs the size of thumbnails decorated the countess's ears.

Pearls. Doesn't every woman wear them to purchase a warehouse?

Swallowing her sarcasm, she strode to the carriage. Her legs were equipped with better manners than her brain. If she had her druthers, she'd walk to the warehouse door, and let the countess meet her there. Alas, her widow's independence ran only so deep. Good breeding was her bedrock, thanks to her grandmother. Thus, she found herself approaching the carriage for a better view of cloud-swimming cherubs on a field of blue.

"Lady Denton." A touch of mockery in her voice, she swept the deepest of deep curtsies and held it.

With strong and slender thighs, she could play the obsequious game all day should Countess Denton require it.

A snort sounded while she rose slowly, her gaze to the ground. The countess wasn't fooled by the display.

"You're late." The fan snapped shut.

Lady Denton was a face in her carriage, her black hair a fashionable *tête de mouton* mound of curls. Sheep's head curls were all the rage. Anne's hair was a horse tail down her back.

"I beg pardon for my lateness," she said. "But as you can see, Neville Warehouse hasn't gone anywhere."

"Humor. How refined." The countess rapped her fan against the window, and a footman in scarlet and royal blue livery scurried to open the carriage door.

"I find humor helps," Anne said, stepping back to give the countess room. "Makes the days pass amiably."

"Wine and sex do the same."

Her step hitched, the stumble slight. Well, *that* was unexpected.

"These cobbles, my lady. So uneven."

"Don't be a bore, Mrs. Neville. The cobbles are fine." The countess was silk unfurling, ice pink and butter yellow. "You were honest with me, it seemed fitting that I do the same."

So that was how it was going to be. There was a moment, the sun anointing their meeting while both women took measure of the other. A decision staked itself firmly in Anne's mind. Confidence would be met with confidence. A woman could fly no better flag.

"You already gave me a taste of your honesty at Denton House, my lady."

A fractured, artful laugh and, "I did, didn't I?"

The countess smoothed her skirts and rotated fully, taking in sun-bleached wood and seagulls squabbling over a dead fish. Gun Wharf was small by Southwark standards. Mostly timber and stone passed through here, raw materials for a master craftsman to create something bigger and better somewhere else. With only four warehouses, business was quiet. It always was. Even harlots at sunset sought their custom elsewhere.

Lady Denton eyed each warehouse, her bored gaze stopping at the fourth, its sign dirt smeared and faded. A *W* was visible.

"What is that one?"

"The sign says Wilcox, my lady. A deserted warehouse, I collect." She drummed impatient fingers on her ledger. "Shall we walk to my warehouse?"

Three male heads popped out behind a door at the other end of the wharf. The carriage was a head-scratching sight. The lady who'd decamped it, a floating confection, walking to Neville Warehouse.

"You might be surprised to learn that I have been looking forward to our meeting," the countess said.

"I wouldn't know that from your missive."

Her comment was a parry, left unmet. Lady Denton's admission was intimate, a door ajar, inviting entry. She was intrigued. That quip about wine and sex still floated feather-like through her brain, the words trying to find the proper place to land.

"You seek an honest audience with me," she said.

"It would be a fine beginning." Lady Denton tipped her head and read the faded blue-and-white sign above the door. "Neville Warehouse established 1733."

An iron padlock sealed the entry. Anne fished around her petticoat pocket, metal clinking. Her fingers brushed the Wilkes Lock key. She froze. Heat needled her scalp as she flicked away the dangerous, filigreed silver piece.

She'd forgotten that there were two keys in her pocket.

Lady Denton watched her, the sign no longer of interest. Brows like tapered half-moons pressed together with budding impatience.

A smile stuck to her lips while her hand closed over a plain bowhead key.

"Here it is." She held it up and rammed it in the lock.

Those tapered half-moons reset. Anne swung the door wide to let Lady Denton pass. She exhaled softly behind the lady's back.

Of all the blunders!

Eyes to azure skies, she steeled herself and went inside. Daylight landed on a shoulder-high stack of Bavarian pine and the countess, poking around the near-empty building. Eight crates were stacked on one wall. A dozen barrels nestled two abreast, MERMAID BREWERY branded on their bellies. Anne busied herself with unlocking the inside padlock of a larger, river-facing door. Heels digging in, she heaved the door, its rusty wheels *squeak, squeak, squeaking*. The Thames was on the other side, a modest wood crane and its iron hook overhanging it. The loft above housed the crane's treadwheel, which powered the crane.

A narrow strip of land, enough to stack two barrels side by side stood between her and timeless waters. She waited, more curious than alarmed. The key was in her pocket, and truth be told, she'd skirted more dire circumstances than a noblewoman mired in ennui.

Lady Denton approached, her face . . . charitable.

"May I see your accounts?" The countess stretched her smooth pale arm.

The innocuous ledger was passed, and the countess actually pored over it for several minutes, her manicured fingers skimming one page to the next. She'd guess the Countess of Denton cyphered accounts with diamond-like sharpness.

"You split your custom between factoring and rent," the countess said. "But in the last year, you've averaged less than five pounds a month."

Because chasing stolen treasure is time-consuming.

Instead she offered, "Your calculations are correct. As to my modes of custom, I prefer renting. It's easier . . . if one finds reliable people."

"That is the challenge." Corners of the lady's mouth curved as if Anne had passed a test.

Factoring was time-consuming, purchasing goods that might not be of the best quality (a trial by fire sort of education). A painful lesson learning the subtleties of English granite came to mind. If that risk wasn't enough, seeking buyers who might not deliver promised funds was another risk. Prime Bavarian lumber lounged in her warehouse, the casualty of a price dispute between two merchants. She wouldn't be paid until they resolved it.

The countess shut the ledger. "But no other custom than wood and stone? Rather dull, Mrs. Neville."

She smiled. There was the Countess of Denton's bite.

"Dull is fine, my lady. It keeps a roof over my head and debt collectors away."

She was glad she hadn't entered Mr. West in her column entitled Future Custom. Her ladyship had clearly scanned the book. For possible connections to the league? It wouldn't do to draw the man into a troubled web not of his making. She'd let her guard slip with the key. A bad mistake. Arms folding under her bosom, she'd not let another happen again.

Lady Denton, by contrast, leaned casually against the opposite door frame, her face to the river's breeze. "I've come to the conclusion that you and I are very much alike."

"Oh? How so?"

"We are seekers, you and I. We take what we want despite the silly rules that stand against us."

She weighed those words on a scale. There was

substance in them. A faint thread, drawing parallel lines. Her struggle, Lady Denton's struggle. Two women making their way in London.

Her chin tipped with doubt. They weren't alike. Not at all.

"You're skeptical," the countess said. "It's understandable."

"I'm assembling all your words. On the one hand, subtle insults. On the other, refreshing directness."

A feline smile spread. "You understand me. I knew you possessed a keen mind."

She pushed off the wall, struck by the idea of another test done and met with satisfaction. "Why don't I show you the treadwheel crane? It's in my counting house in the loft above."

"I've seen enough."

"Are you prepared to make an offer?"

"For this? Absolutely not."

Anne stepped impatiently to take back her ledger. "Then our business is concluded."

"Why the rush? Are you off to plan a wedding?"

She stopped and dug fingernails into her petticoats. "I don't know what you mean."

It was Lady Denton's turn to tip her chin with doubt.

"Don't play me for a fool. The two of you are hardly the smitten pair. You need help with this—" the countess arced her ledger-holding arm at the warehouse "—and Will has experience on the yards. It's a marriage of convenience."

Her jaw dropped. So, this was how her ladyship made sense of her connection with Will.

"My sources tell me you married Mr. Neville

and you gained a warehouse. I did the same but on a grander scale with the Earl of Denton, but that is where our similarity ends." The countess marched slowly forward, stamped earth submitting to her silk shoes. "My marriage settlement included one warehouse, a fee simple title. Freehold ownership, Mrs. Neville, and I nursed it like a child," she said proudly. "Now, I own all the warehouses between Arundel Stairs and Strand Bridge. My warehouses are filled with coachmakers, India paper manufactories and hangers, and soft-paste porcelain dishes. Pretty things, beautiful things. Things that sell for a great deal of money."

All on the other side of the river. The countess stopped an arm's length in front of her. Her brown eyes fevered, determined. A storm was building, the pressure about to blow. Anne braced herself.

"I intend to expand my circumstances, Mrs. Neville, and my purpose for seeking you is simple. I am inviting you to join me."

She shifted her feet, the ground less solid at the moment. The offer was disorienting to say the least. The countess must've sensed blood in the water, a weakening of resolve or simply the advantage of surprise. The lady's emboldened smirk slid sideways, though with the countess, boldness was the air she breathed daily.

"My offer astonishes you."

"It is stunning, to say the least."

"I have ample resources, but I need to employ someone I can trust. And you would be *well compensated*." Lady Denton delighted in delivering those last words. She relished them the way people relished clotted cream.

"Such an offer, but we hardly know each other, my lady."

"But we know *of* each other, don't we?" The smirk morphed, feline and sure.

Either the Countess of Denton knew more about her than she anticipated (and thus, outplayed her) and was keeping a close eye on an adversary. Or she had no idea about Anne and the league. This last possibility seeded her hope.

"I'm mired in disbelief, my lady, because you already have an army of servants to tend to your every need. You don't need me."

Lady Denton faced the water. In profile, her expressive mouth flattened. "Ask yourself how many women of commerce exist in the City. Then ask yourself, of those women, how many have a modicum of education and intelligence. Then ask yourself how many of those women understand and have experience in the business of warehouses, of factoring and rents."

"I see." This was one of the more flattering and honest conversations Anne had had in a long time, but she couldn't trust the woman.

"Between my brother and the minions who serve him, I battle men daily, Mrs. Neville. A woman with a keen business mind in my employ would change that."

"You mean someone else to do battles for you."

"The daily battles, yes." The countess shrugged an indolent shoulder. "It is the way of the world, except with me, you would be well paid. And you would live as independently as you saw fit."

Lady Denton smoothed a wind-teased ruffle. "I have considerable resources at the ready. Should you join me, I will make it worth your while."

There was the knife to her heart, driven to the hilt and twisted. The lady didn't have resources: she had stolen Jacobite gold.

"Your ledger, Mrs. Neville."

The ledger was again in her possession. She held it, the bottom angled on her plain gray stomacher. She'd been so concerned about what to wear, as if gowns made the woman. What a fraud she was. She'd allowed herself to be dazzled, flattered, and impressed. Temptation was the countess's version of independence, but it would come at a cost, namely the people counting on her.

Silk shoes crunched a soft retreat. The countess was several paces away when the footsteps stopped.

"There is one condition."

Her nape chilling, Anne met Lady Denton's resolved stare. Something awful was coming. She knew it with every fiber of her being.

"You can't marry Will."

Her stomach dropped. It was silly. The condition was just as farcical as her farce of a betrothal. But she had to ask, "Why? Do you want to marry him?"

"Marry him?" Lady Denton snorted. "And give up the astounding freedom a widow of my wealth and stature enjoys? To a commoner? Absolutely not."

"What about Mr. MacLeod?"

"A bare-knuckle fighter I found in Bristol."

The lady's tone suggested MacLeod was a shell found on a sandy beach, examined, considered, and soon to be tossed aside.

"But . . . why Will?"

"Because I want him."

There it was. A terse, mundane declaration. The countess could very well have placed an order with a draper: *I'll take ten yards of the red silk, twelve yards of green damask, and that highlander, Will Mac-Donald.* Will was a token bargained for like trade goods, which was foolish until another thought struck, this one landing with the heaviness of an anvil in her already-pained stomach.

"Do you love him?" she asked weakly.

"Love? No." Lady Denton was definitive until her gaze wandered and her mouth softened. "But there is a quality about him . . ."

"Yes."

"He's . . . well, he's . . ." The floundering countess searched the air.

Righteous ire squared Anne's shoulders and sharpened her tone with an inexplicable need to defend the man.

"You mean to say that he's a true gentleman, not the sickly version that permeates half of London. Will is a man of the land with a sense of honor that runs long and fierce. Brash at times, given to brooding when he can't put his back into hard labor, yet he possesses a discerning mind, one that wants to make sense of what's around him." Her hand curled to a fist. "And he is good, my lady, more good than you will ever know."

Her ladyship's eyes had gone wide.

"You do have a *tendre* for him." A tiny shrug

and, "Let your love for independence take its place." The countess back-stepped gracefully into a cloud of dust moats as she delivered her final blow. "You have until the night of the art salon to give me your answer, Mrs. Neville."

The silk enigma that was the Countess of Denton departed. Anne stayed in place a good long while. She couldn't move for the struggle to untangle an astonishing array of thoughts. The first, and safest, was her shock at what the grasping woman saw in her—that she was hungry for independence . . . over love?

The ageless river slapped the wharf, quiet and rhythmic, calling forth her past. A scramble of evidence spilled unkindly. Her first marriage had been an act of obedience. Her second, for a purposeful end. She'd pledged her troth to a lonely old man to gain a foothold in London for no other reason than to recover Jacobite gold and the *sgian-dubh*, Clanranald MacDonald's ancient ceremonial dagger.

She was as mercenary as a woman could be.

Nothing got in the way of her mission for the clan. Nothing.

Her hold on the ledger turned awkward, its armor of numbers and custom less appealing. She wanted love and a future the same as other women, save the Countess of Denton apparently.

And God help her, she wanted Will.

Chapter Twenty-Seven

*W*ill's boots were in her entry hall, square toes pointing out. Blessed relief that he was not dead in a ditch washed over her, however brief. Will needed a good push into said ditch for the worry he'd caused, and she'd be the woman to shove him.

A gust escaped her. This was exhausting.

Hat and ledger dumped on the entry table, she leaned over, pinched the boots together, and held them high with one hand for inspection. What sorry specimens. They could use a good cleaning. Bits of grass. Mud caked in cracked leather. Boots that had not tramped through Grosvenor Square to seize Jacobite gold driven by misguided heroism. Will had high regard for the league. She'd seen it in his eyes and heard it in his respectful tone.

She returned the boots to their rightful place on the floor. *Where had they been?*

"Aunt Maude? Aunt Flora?" Her voice reached into her home. No one answered.

She and Will were alone.

Her gaze wandered up the stairs. The quiet house meant Will was likely in his bedchamber. She sprinted up the stairs on agile feet, the soles of her low-heeled shoes slapping scuffed treads. Her skin tickled under her stays. A flush was spreading. She was going faster, breathing harder.

Anticipation was the crackle of a sparked fuse. She needed to hear his voice.

To see him and talk to him about . . . anything.

At the top floor, the hallway was quiet save her sawing breaths. Time and use had worn a bowed path in uncarpeted planks. Like a tree branch that path. It forked in the middle, leading to her door and the other, a finger's width open. She strode to it and knocked twice.

"Will."

A muffled, "Anne."

He sounded sleepy. She frowned at the door. A nap? Really?

She swanned in, petticoats swinging, confidence flying until her gaze landed on his arse. Moon white, curved stone, shallow indentations at the sides. She halted while her confidence made an about-face and fled. She wasn't sure if it was coming back. The day had been a trying one after all, and Will possessed the finest arse. Ever. Currently it nested in rumpled sheets which framed his caber-tossing thighs.

Another breathtaking part of him, those thighs. Long, solid. Crisp brown leg hairs, the sunlight striking them with gold. They defied the bigamist's breeches. Aunt Flora had told her so. Only two pair fit him. Which was why his legs belonged in a wind-stirring kilt and he belonged in Scotland. With her.

She touched her bodice. Under cloth and corset, her heart fluttered like a butterfly at that notion.

While heart and soul gloried over Will with her, the sheets fluxed, soft as clouds. With the drapes open, daylight blessed long manly legs and feet. Her gaze built a road along those legs, over his arse, and up his back to welts dispersing like watercolor. Inch by inch she went over his heavenly form until she came to molten eyes.

Ah, Hades. He showed a modest side and swathed his arse with bed linens—his mythical power no longer in view.

"Mrs. Neville." His brogue was graveled irony. "Why don't you come in?"

"Mr. MacDonald, I think I shall."

Stiff formality was her placeholder when lacking recourse. The idea of hearing Will's voice disappeared on the length of him stretched out lionlike. Even the soles of his feet were beautiful.

Will finger combed hair off his face. He'd been asleep, naked, as one does if his name is Will MacDonald.

"I came to talk to you. I thought you said my name in invitation." She gestured to the door as if it would give testimony. "It's why I came in."

Bed ropes squeaked, and Will sat up, his wonderfully meaty and sinewed torso revealed in all its glory. Hillocks and dales of smooth skin over knotted muscles. More sun-kissed gold hairs ringing male nipples. He grabbed a handful of the bed sheet as if to cover more of himself.

"What are you doing?" she cried.

He blinked sleepy eyes. "Trying to get dressed."

What blasphemy, covering himself.

"No. Stay just as you are. Please."

His brow furrowed. "It's no' proper, me like this and you in a bedchamber."

"Oh, but kissing me senseless and having sex with me in the countryside is quite acceptable?"

"We were young and foolish."

"And now we're older and wiser."

Will was doubtful, a lion's mane of hair falling around his shoulders. She advanced on him with cautious steps, so as not to spook her quarry.

"Rest as you were. You look a wee bit tired."

One side of his mouth quirked. "A wee bit is it?"

"Maybe more."

"I am tired, lass." He accepted her offer to throw propriety to the wind and stretched stomach down on the mattress. Will put his cheek on the bunched pillow, his face to her.

She took a seat at the side of the bed. Will rested comfortably, his body's gentle ebb and flow in time with his even breaths. She rested a hand in the field of white between them.

This was strange agony. To come this far yet know they had miles more to go. Where was the bold man who'd tucked her medallion between her breasts? The dance of man and woman was fraught with mystery and wonder. It left her with an inkling that Will had waited years for this moment, but she'd be happy to start with his whereabouts last night.

"Why didn't you come home last night?"

Will's eyes honed on her with the precision of a gimlet tool. "Home you say?"

"Do you deposit your dirty boots anywhere else?"

"You don't have to clean my boots," he said in a sleep-grumbled voice. "The men of West and Sons Shipping wanted to share a pint, which turned into three or four and a farewell dinner at a chophouse."

Their afternoon conversation took on the intimate feel of a minor marital spat, which was as discomfiting as Will naked in bed.

"They like you."

"Most people find me congenial." His mouth was a torment. Wide, sensual, framed by another day's whiskers.

"I find you congenial."

His answer was a pleased grunt, and appreciative eyes.

A fuse crackled in their stillness. Hot and weighty. She scratched her fingernails on the linen between them. Will took note, watching her over his shoulder's brawny summit. The move was hers. The conversation was hers. Yet, by the sheer force expanding inside her, she was incapable of talking. Her mouth was dry, her tongue heavy, and her hand slid closer to Will's body.

Will shifted his hips, the intimate whisper of sheets following. "I spent all night with the lads. No harlots, if that's what you're thinking."

Her relief was like the sun. His *No harlots* heralded a new and welcome turn. Will sensed it too, his big smile half-buried again in the pillow.

"We were out all night. Then I spent my morning asking about Rory MacLeod and men with

T-branded thumbs who might've been at Gun Wharf the night you were attacked."

"And? What did you find?" she asked, though Will stretching his arm across the sheet toward her was more compelling.

"Rory MacLeod is new to the City, a bare-knuckle fighter with a middling reputation."

She swallowed dryness building in her throat. "And the men with *T*-branded thumbs?"

"Too many to count," he sighed. "London's infested with rats and criminals. It's a race between the two, and I'm no' sure who's winning."

Her heart swelled. She couldn't stop herself from gushing, "You're winning, Will MacDonald, with your better nature and your sense of honor."

She brushed the side of his thigh. The unseen fuse hit a powder spot. Sparks danced hot and fast. Will was statue still.

Her hand ventured higher. "You have certain power over the gentler sex, you know."

"I flashed my thighs and bits at Marshalsea. You couldna help it, lass. You were overcome."

Her smile felt grand. "Your secret weapon, these caber-tossing thighs."

She rubbed crinkly hairs on his leg and touched his flesh. Will's ribcage expanded from a fast inhale.

He was *so* hard.

"What else can your thighs do?"

She exulted in the feel of him. Strong. Vibrant. Gooseflesh prickling where she touched. This was a different world, a cocoon, this bed with him and her in it. Clothed or unclothed didn't matter. This belonged to them.

The more she caressed, the more Will melted. Boneless, jointless, slayed by simple pleasure. Long, tanned fingers splayed in white sheets, the fingertips digging into the bed.

She bent over his hand and kissed each knuckle. Light, soft kisses. Seeds of affection. Sweet and worthy of a young girl kissing a young man for the first time in a summer glen.

Will slowly turned his hand, palm up. Her lips hovered above his wrist.

Their first kiss.

Amber eyes watched her. Will offered connection, to their past, to what they once had.

Could they try again?

Carnal tenderness was her answer. A gentle kiss on his wrist, to the fragile sinew and veins that made this not-so-fragile man.

His audible inhale was a gift. Her smile grew against his flesh. Her mouth wasn't ready to leave this warm, poignant skin.

Will grinned in return, though it was half-buried in his pillow.

This was fair. He deserved to be the center of pleasure.

She sat up, her limbs languid, her soul light. The sheets were cozy and they smelled of Will. Even touching his sheets gave her pleasure. She skimmed his thigh and her fingertips discovered the crease where thigh and bottom met. A barely there line. Skin soft, flesh firm. From the white of the pillow, Will's eyes pooled black.

Hades was pleased.

Her exploratory hand rucked the sheet over the finest hill any woman could conquer. But there was the rub. Will MacDonald was not a thing to be vanquished or a prize to be claimed. He was the gentlest of hearts . . . if one dusted off his rough charm and unwrapped layers of stubbornness and brood.

A man like that deserved more kisses. Everywhere.

She bent over and placed a sweet kiss on his arse, so tender, it bordered on quaint.

"What are you stirring up, lass?" His voice was a drowsy rumble.

Long hot kisses were her next answer.

His skin pebbled under her lips. Will's fingers dug into the bed, an eyes-closed clutch of pleasure.

Her hair fell around him, and her medallion landed on his skin. Her heart was galloping and the peculiar dryness in her throat was gone. With her mouth, she boldly sought the twin dimples at the small of his back. The curve of his arse. Will's hamstring and the side of his knee.

Her gown shushed against bedsheets.

Will's hips were grinding slowly on the bed. She leaned in and let his fine arse rub her breasts.

He was worthy of this . . . this worship. She dug her fingers in bed linens with furious need.

She wanted him. She scooted fully onto the bed, needful and desperate.

This was more than desire . . . it was—

A door slammed below. She dropped her forehead on Will's thigh, her breath ragged. She needed to collect her wits, scattered as they were.

Desire thickened her blood to the sweetest honey. Its nectar dripped through skin between her legs.

With a reluctant push, she sat up, the mattress moaning, Will moaning. She'd sprawled herself half over him.

Her feet hit the floor. She wobbled like a newborn foal and set a hand on the bedpost to steady herself. Will was in no hurry to change position. He lay as she found him, belly down, legs wider. The same ballocks which swung into view at Marshalsea were snug in the apex of his legs. Hairy and comfortable. How Will's bits ought to be.

Aunt Maude and Aunt Flora's voices rose and fell in sisterly rhythm. Cecelia was among them. The Fletcher sisters would follow. Dinner would be on the table soon. This would be their last meeting to go over the details for tomorrow night.

The time to steal Jacobite gold was almost upon them.

She tucked the medallion in her cleavage and cuffed hair off her cheek. Will's mirror showed flushed cheeks, starry eyes, and moist lips. Mussed hair was life on the wharf, but the former traits were all Will MacDonald's affect. Cold water splashed on her face would help. Lots of chilly water.

"Anne?"

Her name on Will's lips was a question laced with . . . hope? Did they have another chance? She grasped plain cloth between her breasts. It hurt too much to hope.

"Will." She turned around, and he noted her cloth-gripping hand.

The clench was necessary, it kept her together. She wouldn't tell him about the Countess of Denton's offer. It was beneath him, and she'd already scored Will's pride when he first met the league. She could never make up for her unintended ambush—could anyone? She'd hurt him, he'd hurt her. Theirs was the impossible spiral that wanted closing. True atonement was impossible, and forgiveness too deep and wide to comprehend.

Still, she'd try.

"Will, you don't have to wear the bigamist's clothes or his shoes. I know you don't like them, most of them, anyway. Go to that art salon as you are—dock worker, former highland rebel . . . take your pick."

His head lifted off the pillow. "I'll be whatever you need me to be."

"I want you to be you." Each word sunk an arrow into her heart.

For some reason, this need burned fervently inside, as if she would replay their history and see the brash, kilt-wearing foot soldier she fell in love with. But nothing could erase the years and change between them. Worn-out burgundy velvet shimmered modestly on a wall peg near the window. There was a history behind that coat. One day she would hear it. For now, she'd be content for Will to wear it. It made him happy, that coat and his boots.

That had to be true love—wanting someone just as they are.

Will rotated, a leisured turn in which he bunched linens strategically. Propped up on his elbow, dark blond hair at his shoulder, he was regal as a lion . . . or a pagan. Definitely a foreign prince, naked on his throne bed. They were both eyeing his favorite coat.

"Wear it every day," she said. "Wear it to the night of the art salon . . . I don't care. I want you to be comfortable and happy."

To which his head cocked and he watched her with a discerning gaze. If she wasn't careful, Will would see through her. Every flaw, every error and misstep.

"I'll see you at dinner." She fled his bedchamber and shut the door behind her. Its wood panels supported her back while she gathered her wits.

Be it through prison or the war, Will had gained the gift of understanding. Seeing more, doing more, living a good and decent life, despite bad decisions. It made him a better man. She, however, was crumbling inside, a castle built of sand assaulted by waves.

She was falling apart bit by bit.

But the fuse she'd lit with Will? Unfinished.

Chapter Twenty-Eight

Ancilla rolled her wrist, a lethargic effort to power her fan. The toil was hardly worth it. Her carriage baked in a shaft of sunlight, stalled as it were. Departing Southwark's narrow, labyrinthine streets required the patience of Job and the wisdom of Solomon. The roads were abominable, a fair number too narrow for a modern carriage to pass. Buildings leaned liked old drunks, lathe and plaster timbered relics in poor repair. Stuart kings were at fault. They lacked foresight. Many a man did.

And the odor . . . Appalling.

Clean streets? *Is that too much to ask?*

She winced when bad onions passed inches from her open window (she had a costermonger to thank for that). If the ramble-and-halt rhythm of her carriage didn't give her a *mal de tête*, the stench surely would. She mashed a perfume-drenched handkerchief over her nose. Reveling in victory might help. Her meeting with Mrs. Neville was a success by any measure.

The woman had been properly shocked.

Rich employment. The chance to make her name as a woman of business because she would be generous and encourage Mrs. Neville to seek her own custom . . . as long as it didn't interfere with *her* empire. When the time was right and trust ran deep, she would reveal just how intricate her trade ran.

All in good time—if she could get out of this forsaken part of the City. Her carriage lurched to a halt again, and a footman appeared outside her window.

"My lady, there appears to be several barrels in the road ahead. A few broken by the looks. Men are cleaning them up, but it may be several minutes afore we can move on."

Afore. His brogue sent a delectable shiver over sticky skin.

"Of course," she said, waving him off with her cotton handkerchief.

He bowed and took his place again at the back of her carriage. She did have a weakness for Scotsmen, highlanders in particular, and their supposed wild, uncouth manners. Some were dull as bricks with barnyard habits. Will MacDonald was the exception. He was the diamond in the rough, eyes like ancient amber and a body made for sin.

His curious mind and tender soul had burrowed deep inside her. He'd won a piece of her admittedly closed heart when he helped with her son. Normally she kept a wide berth between her private footmen and James. But Will sensed her frustration and offered to help. There was only so much a mother could do for her son. Boys needed a man to guide them.

James had been a gangly youth, his voice cracking, his confidence faltering. Her husband, the late Earl of Denton, never gave two figs about his son and heir. Will did. The two took to each other, thick as thieves, fishing, swimming, riding on her estates. Will taught her son to shoot, how to clean a fish, and shoot a bow and arrow.

For James, the sun rose and set on Will.

There had only ever been one man in her heart—her son, now at university.

Will had found a way in too.

His first days serving her, she found him in her library. He marveled at her wealth of books. He'd only ever read two. Their first months together, he'd read twenty.

She lavished gifts on him, which he refused, unlike other men who'd played the role of her private footman. Leeches, most of them, who quickly became tiresome. Not Will. His pride was horribly offended when she offered to purchase a house for him.

She'd thought it a step up. He'd thought it the worst hell.

A man kept by a woman.

Why? It worked well for thousands of women. But men could be particular.

She'd wanted a family. Will had never broached the subject of marriage. It was impossible. Her rank, his lack of it. Will had grown restless. She could see it in his faraway stares, and he didn't approve of some of the men she'd hired. But in quiet moments, she knew. There had to be another woman, someone in his past, but her investigators could find no such woman. Between the war and Will's clan scattered to the wind, reliable resources were hard to find. Few highlanders wanted to talk to her English agents anyway.

But there was a woman. She knew it in her bones. Will pined for her.

If she could find her, she would crush the woman. Find a way to make her disappear. She had resources. Will, however, didn't seek the woman.

She pressed perfumed cotton over her nose. He'd left with nothing more than a few farthings in his pocket and the clothes on his back. The same as what he had when she found him at Marylebone Pleasure Gardens. Like others of her station, she hired a guard to walk alongside her carriage while they traveled those dark, perilous streets on the garden's perimeter. Criminals destroyed streetlamps all the better to work in darkness. Brawny men like Will offered their services, to guide the carriages of London's best citizens.

Will had stayed by her window, his charm rough but endearing. When her carriage reached safer streets, she opened her door to him and he obliged her. Being with Will had been a near perfect year. She wanted him back. Simple as that.

Her eyes fluttered shut, all the better to remember.

"Lady Denton!" a woman called from the street.

She roused to scan the faces outside. Grizzled men walked by, hair graying, cheeks dirty, their clothes dirtier. Whores plied their trade, hands fanning shiny faces against the heat. One of them sauntered from the pack of torn hems and bored faces, her hair an alarming shade of red.

"I remember you from Cuper's Pleasure Garden, my lady, before it was shut down—" the whore waved a dirt-grimed hand at her own head "—it's me, Red Bess."

"Red Bess . . . I beg your pardon, but I cannot recall making your acquaintance." She was kind to whores most times. They had their uses and most were a wealth of information.

A giggle uncoiled. "You're a different one, milady. Fine manners and all." Red Bess crossed her arms casually under her bosom. "My hair is my trade card. A way to remember me. If not, you might remember my friend, Peg Boyle."

Ancilla could feel a wan smile spreading. Peg Boyle, a Cuper's Pleasure Garden whore, had been particularly helpful in the past, and she'd been rewarded for it. By the gleam in Red Bess's eyes, she wanted to be helpful too. A seller of information. But in this part of Southwark? The quality of it was doubtful. Ancilla dug into her velvet coin purse. A shilling would make the woman go away.

She passed the shilling out the window. "Here, a deposit."

The coin fell into Red Bess's open hand.

"You can do better than a shilling, milady."

"You're an insolent piece." She raised her fan to summon her footman.

"I have information you'll want, milady." Red Bess's tone cleaved the fat from their conversation. "But you'll have to pay more than this."

A frisson impelled Ancilla to sit up and take note. The whore was dead serious, tired (no doubt the hazard of her profession) but quite focused. Her thin-lipped mouth was void of false friendliness, and she had known Peg Boyle.

"Very well. I'll pay a half crown if your information is good."

"It's good, milady, and I'll take three half crowns for it."

Her blood spiked with irritation and interest. Red Bess was astonishingly confident in what she had to offer, confident enough to wave it like a juicy steak.

Ancilla was hungry enough to bite. She produced a half crown from her velvet purse and offered it.

"I said three half crowns, milady." Red Bess was mutinous.

"We'll build a bridge, you and I. If your first offering is worthwhile, you'll get more. If not, our transaction is done."

"Start diggin' in that velvet purse of yours because my information is about the widow of Bermondsey Wall, Mrs. Anne Neville—"

"I have paid better people than you to inquire about the woman." Disappointed, Ancilla's hand dropped to her lap.

"—and Will MacDonald." Red Bess smiled slyly.

She sat taller despite the road's atrocious smell.

So, the whore remembered seeing her with Will. She and Will had gone to Cuper's Pleasure Garden to watch fireworks when he'd been in her household. Will's sudden betrothal to the Southwark widow had been a surprise.

Her investigator had begun his work last spring and concluded it midsummer when she was still at her country estate. She wouldn't offer the esteemed position of managing her warehouses without a study of the woman first. The investigator's report painted a picture of a reliable woman of humble commerce with two older, unnamed female relatives in her household. He'd noted Mrs. Neville's visits, few though they were, to London's less savory taverns. The hidden message being, the woman might have a tolerance for working outside the law. Even better, there was no hint of interest in a third marriage, but Mrs. Neville was a handsome woman. A sudden, late summer betrothal wasn't out of the question.

"Go on."

"'Bout a week ago, I was standing outside the Iron Bell. It was midnight, the streets empty, no custom to speak of. Then who comes walkin' right here on Mill Lane, but Mrs. Neville herself with a gorgeous man in a tattered kilt 'bout ten paces behind her." Red Bess smirked. "A rare sight, it was."

"Thus far, I'm not impressed with the quality of your information."

The carriage's rear spring gave and the footman appeared. "Three more minutes, milady." His gaze slid to Red Bess. "Is all well here, milady?"

"Yes, yes," she said, waving him off. To Red Bess, "Go on."

"The next night, Mr. Ledwell, a warder from Marshalsea, was at the Iron Bell. He had some awful bruises round his eyes, but he was braggin' 'bout how *he* got the best of the other man, a highlander, dragged to Marshalsea, arrested for wearin' his kilt. I figured it had to be the man I saw the night before." She paused for dramatic effect. "But how did he get out of prison?"

"You need this—" Ancilla held up a half crown "—to continue your tale?"

"You and I have good accord, milady." Red Bess took the coin and stuffed it behind stained scarlet stays. "Another pint, an' the warder told me a woman paid thirty half guineas for the man's release and his arrest record."

"Thirty half guineas? A princely sum."

"A woman who pays that means business."

"Or she wanted this particular man." Ancilla's vision narrowed. Bribes greased the wheels of London's prison, a standard story, but thirty half guineas for a man Mrs. Neville had met this summer?

"That's what I thought, especially it being Mrs. Neville. She keeps her warehouse in good repair, but her house is not the house of a woman who can toss around thirty half guineas."

"Or the warder lied because he wanted to impress you," she said. In the matter of bribes and information, one had to consider all possibilities.

"No, milady. I have proof."

"Proof?"

"Show me your next coin and I'll show you my proof . . .'cause this is one you'll want to see."

Another half crown was passed. Red Bess took it and slid it into her stays. Then she did the oddest thing, pressing her body against the carriage, head swiveling to the left and the right, her hands fishing south on her person. A thump, and the whore stepped back, producing a shiny gold half guinea, clamped between her middle finger and forefinger.

"Mr. Ledwell paid for his tup with this. He took me from the back, which gave me time to look at the coin and think 'bout where I'd seen Will Mac-Donald's face. That's when I remembered you." Red Bess's voice dropped as if now the woman was reaching the meat of her tale. "Mr. Ledwell finished his business and I said how smooth and pretty was the coin he gave me. He said all of them were just as smooth."

"A smooth coin? Not exactly a scintillating fact, I'm afraid."

Red Bess's eyes were flinty shards. "How 'bout a fifty-year-old coin? Is that scint'lating enough?"

"Let me see." Ancilla snatched the coin and read 1703 on one side, VIGO on the other.

The coin was remarkably shiny and clean, its weight solid and true. A tin disc in the middle was a forger's trick to melt the coin and recast it with less gold. Yet, this coin was true. She'd held enough to know. Red Bess reached into the carriage and took back her coin. The impertinent grasp would normally get her knuckles smacked, but Ancilla's spine fell against the squab.

How did a five-pounds-a-month (before expenses) warehouse owner accumulate that much money?

"I can tell by yer face that yer beginnin' to see the value of my information, milady." Red Bess's jaw managed to be mulish and her eyes triumphant. "I'm thinkin' this last bit I have is worth two half crowns."

"You have more information?"

Red Bess nodded and Ancilla opened her velvet purse and paid the sum.

Red Bess's fist closed around two half crowns and she finished her late summer tale. "Yesterday, Black Horse Brewery's new man made a delivery. He's a Scot, hails from Linlithgow. Said while he was out making deliveries, he thought he saw a man he knew walking by Bermondsey Wall. A Will MacDonald, who fought in the Rebellion of '45. The Black Horse brewer is a talker. Says he fought in the rebellion too, but that's not the first time he saw Will MacDonald."

The open window framed Red Bess's face, a flushed and avid face about to impart two half crowns' worth of information.

Ancilla was at the edge of her seat. "Tell me."

"The brewer says first time he saw Will MacDonald was in Linlithgow summer before the rebellion . . . when he was kissing a black-haired woman. The very same black-haired woman the brewer saw with Will near Bermondsey Wall."

Ancilla squeezed her velvet purse hard enough that coin edges bit her palm. Anger, putrid and vile, threatened to overflow. Red Bess jumped back, her eyes flaring wide.

"Is there anything else?" she asked much too softly.

"No, milady."

"You did well," she assured. "I will not forget this."

The carriage lurched forward, all the better for her to stew over this stunning news. Red Bess watched her go, sunlight fracturing in her violent red hair. The woman missed a prime opportunity. She could've demanded all the contents of the velvet purse.

Ancilla would have given it to her and more.

Chapter Twenty-Nine

*W*ill scooped a generous spoonful of porridge into his bowl and reached for the chipped Lambethware pitcher.

"So . . . Mrs. Neville." He commenced swirling concentric circles of cream on his porridge. "It struck me, the day afore yesterday, you were putting distance between us. Being spare with your words and your doors bolted against a friendly visit, as it were."

"Both friendly visits?" she asked innocently.

"Both your doors." He was unabashed, setting the empty pitcher down. "I would add, your nefarious ploy to get me to wear butter yellow."

She fought a rueful smile and watched Will pick up the nutmeg grinder and crank it over his bowl. The man seated at her table was a vanquisher of breakfast and a common man's logician. A point would come. A big one.

"Perhaps I am distracted with my work, Mr. MacDonald," she said between nibbles of porridge.

There was safety in formality, a medieval wall of sorts, allowing one to hide behind it.

"No' too busy to barge into my bedchamber and kiss my arse. You've ruined the insult." The grinding done, Will armed himself with a spoon. "Next time someone yells *Kiss my arse!* I'll grin like a half-wit."

She snort-sipped her coffee and gave in to a hearty laugh. Only Will could do that to her. She dragged her apron hem across her mouth to wipe herself clean. It was good to have the house—and Will—to herself. With the sudden need to journey to Brighton, Aunt Flora and Aunt Maude claimed a dire trip to the laundress was necessary.

Will took a few bites, shovelsful it seemed, while keeping eyes on her. He wore his clothes this morning. Brown broadcloth mostly, though his neck cloth was a surprise. The knot was done just enough to say he cared. This could've been their future, sitting across from each other at the breakfast table, her with an apron, him with chin scruff. There was tenderness here. And fun. With Will, life would be. It was elevating and risky and beautiful. The indefinable pressure was growing, bringing prismatic wonder. Colors were brighter, the sky bluer, the sun shinier this morning.

Yesterday's kisses almost went unaccounted for—the blessing and curse of living with two aunts. Except now, they were five houses away, visiting the laundress, and Will's stare could char ice. Lust lurked behind his rough charm. It was palpable. A living thing she could reach out and touch . . . like his whiskers and smooth bottom lip. Had to be the nutmeg. She was eating more of it since Will arrived. The spice was considered an aphrodisiac.

Their first summer together, she'd asked why he devoured the spice. He'd answered that it tasted good. Like her.

"My first day here," he said. "I asked if you had any more surprises for me."

He invited her to pick up his conversational thread. If she did, she'd spill everything, good and bad: the reason for her locked doors, Cecelia's name in Fielding's books, the Countess of Denton's shocking proposition, and how much the woman wanted him.

Just your average breakfast conversation.

"Out with it, Will. What exactly are you after?"

Hers was a simple question. His was devastatingly direct.

"Why?" Will's amber eyes could singe wood.

Pressure inside sharpened. "You mean, why did I kiss you the way I did?"

"Yes."

She set down her spoon. "I had to . . . to touch you."

Will's mouth dented sideways.

"There is that, lass. There is that," he said quietly.

Stillness sat like a storm cloud. Will wanted a deeper admission, something not seeded in lust. He waited, his grin fading the longer her painful silence stretched.

Didn't he understand? It was *him* she needed. Will. To touch, hear, see, taste. To bask in his person the way flowers faced the sun and water quenched one's thirst. It struck her right then, sitting across the breakfast table from Will, something they'd once hoped to do for the rest of their lives, that they weren't very good at this. At the open-your-heart part of love.

And yet, she knew . . .

Will MacDonald owned her heart. He was her perfect match. No one else would ever, could ever have it.

Why were they so awful at letting that be?

She stared at her bowl, lost. She was drowning in needs: to soothe Will, herself, and the women of the league who needed reassurance with the sudden change of plans. And there was the single constant which brought them together—stealing Jacobite gold and taking it home.

Indulging her emotions in these final hours wouldn't do. The mission wasn't done.

Will rose from the table and took his dishes into the kitchen. She heard their gentle clatter as he set them down, and she heard his footfalls returning him to the dining room. He picked up his tricorn hat, which had been hooked on the back of his chair. She looked up and found him studying one of its corners.

"I have one more farewell to make afore I leave."

Will's *afore I leave* speared her. His eyes answered *for Virginia*.

"Will . . . the gold. I have a duty to finish it."

"I know, lass. I know." He set his hat on his head, a solemn man. "I'll be back in plenty of time for tonight. I'll no' let you down."

Again . . . the word hung in her dining room long after Will left.

In their youth, they'd been good at sex. Very, very good at sex. They were good at parsing debates on Scotland, England, the dilemmas of kings and realms. But a frank discussion of the whys and hows of their emotions didn't truly begin until . . .

Unlocking him from Marshalsea?

Telling him about their unborn child?

She sat a long while in her empty dining room in her empty house. Her idle fingers found a loose thread on her skirt and rolled it. Her grandmother had done a wonderful job preparing her for the wifely tasks such as tracking household expenses, arranging furniture to please the eyes, and advising her on the mark of a good draper. Needful things, but not the stuff of life.

Last night, Will had come to dinner and been fully present for the league's last reiteration of their plans. Then he'd retreated to his bedchamber. Without a word, she'd cleaned his boots. A week here and that wifely task was already second nature. It wasn't a chore; she wanted to do it.

Her tasks done, she'd climbed the stairs to her bedchamber, finding more than a wall and bolted door between them. Will had been quiet on the other side. Reading is what he'd said he was going to do. He probably had. Or had he thought about his journey? Everyone was astir about theirs. He'd been closemouthed about his arrangements. But everyone knew . . .

Will would leave for Virginia, and she for Scotland.

Once candles had been extinguished, and darkness descended, she was alone in her bed, and he in his.

That was the loneliest kind of dark.

HE COULDN'T SHAKE the sense that his breakfast conversation with Anne could've gone much, much better. He'd upended his life for her, and done everything he could to provide for her unique requests.

The key imprinted. Done.

A forge for Miss Fletcher to create a new key. Done.

A willing back to unload bags of gold through a window. Ready, willing, and able.

He'd carried her market day basket around Southwark for her and laughed after his male parts were called into question. What more did the woman want? There was the rub. Anne wanted the same thing he wanted—a heart cracked open and its contents poured out. All the things one person in love said to another. A simple thing yet vastly, vastly difficult. Nigh to impossible for some. In the best of circumstances, trust was built a little at a time.

The road to rebuild trust was trickier. No map existed for that.

He ambled along Wapping Wall caught in a vise grip. Anne's sudden midnight appearance at Marshalsea was at one end, her inevitable dawn disappearance on *The Grosvenor* at the other.

"*The Grosvenor*," he said.

Justice was, indeed, a devious wench.

The sloop was probably out there right now.

Sloops, schooners, wherries, lightermen boats, and brigantines jammed the river on one side of him. On the other was Wapping where Charles II's navy had lived. At present, the waterfront district was home to dockhands, laborers, sailors of all stripes, criminals, harlots, and one exotic animal dealer.

"Mr. Pidcock!"

A bandy-legged man was worrying over a wooden cage with a blue parrot inside. The man turned, squinting into the sun. "Mr. MacDonald is it?"

Will picked up his pace and extended his hand. "It is, sir."

A breeze batted crimped white hair that grew above his ears. Like twin banners, they were. The parrot squawked, its feathers ruffling. Pidcock pulled a bit of apple and fed it to the bothered bird.

"There, there, Mr. Wiggins," the old man cooed. "You'll be in a new grand home before you know it."

Mr. Wiggins had been a fixture of Pidcock's shop, but the old shopkeeper hoisted the cage and handed it to a waiting thrum-capped sailor. On the foreshore below, a lighterman's vessel was loaded with caged creatures. Another parrot, three monkeys, two ferrets, and a turtle. Mr. Pidcock sniffed and withdrew a wrinkled handkerchief from his waistcoat.

Pidcock dabbed his eyes. "Blasted wind's picking up. Must've got something in my eyes."

"Looks like you sold half your inventory, sir. Business must be good."

"Business is awful." Pidcock planted a fist on his hip and gave Will the gimlet eye. "My store's been broken into. No one bothered me when I had an oversized Scot living above my shop."

"I am sorry to hear that, sir."

"Ehhhh." Pidcock stuffed away his handkerchief. "It's not all bad. Made up my mind to move to Great Russell Street. Has a nice ring to it."

"Sounds better than Cock Alley and Maidenhead Alley."

Pidcock chuckled. "Indeed, Mr. MacDonald. Women will find Great Russell Street less offensive."

They both turned and faced the shop. The storefront boasted one mullioned window where a fat orange tabby pressed the glass from the inside.

"Is Fat George going with you?"

"Of course, I'd never leave him behind." Pidcock was one part feisty and two parts softhearted. The old man scratched white whiskers sprouting from his chin. "'Sides women like Fat George. He takes a good scratch anywhere, he does. Your lady certainly enjoyed petting him, and he liked your lady."

"My . . . lady?"

"The one who collected your things, dunderhead. A Mrs.—Mrs.—"

"Mrs. Neville."

"I'm bad with names, but that sounds about right." Pidcock sniffed and checked the skies. "I shall miss her."

Will went very still. "Miss her?"

For someone to be missed, there had to be visits to make the missing noteworthy.

"What did Mrs. Neville look like?"

A low whistle and, "Black hair, slender . . . a bit too slender, 'cause I like some meat on a woman's bones, I do."

"You sound quite familiar with her."

"Ehhhh. She's come to the shop now and again."

Anne? He couldn't believe it. His cousin might haunt Wapping Wall to cultivate sources with the criminal element here.

It begged the question. "Are you sure the woman wasn't blond, hazel eyed, well dressed but a bit of a tart?"

Pidcock jammed a fist on his hip, knocking back his coat. "Mr. MacDonald, ladies may not bang down my door to visit me, but I do know blond hair from black . . . especially if it's attached to a pretty woman's head."

He loomed over Mr. Pidcock. "What else can you tell me about this black-haired woman?"

"Easy there, Mr. MacDonald. You've never cared—"

"Details, man. What was this woman like?"

The woman could've been Ancilla, though he doubted it. She'd never set foot in Wapping Wall. But Anne? He was on tenterhooks. The possibilities of crossing paths with her exploded in his mind. He'd always thought she was living somewhere in Scotland, a woman done with him.

Anne, here in London . . . checking on his welfare? He couldn't breathe.

"Well . . ." Pidcock's caterpillar brows pinched a line. "She was a serious sort. Came in a time or two your first year here. I knew she wasn't looking to buy an exotic pet. She'd be all casual like, petting Fat George, asking about the Scot renting the room above my shop."

"And you never thought to tell me?" He was aghast.

"What am I? A messenger boy? If you remember, Mr. MacDonald, your first month here, barmaids, laundresses, and a married woman or two made the rounds to my shop." Pidcock batted his eyes and spoke in falsetto, "Oh, Mr. Pidcock, do ye know when Mr. MacDonald will return? Did Mr. MacDonald say he'll stop by the Three Sails today? Oh, Mr. Pidcock, please tell Mr. MacDonald that I'll launder his clothes at half price." A snort and, "You'd've got more than your laundry done if your head wasn't in your arse half the time." Another snort and Pidcock waggled a bony finger at him. "You, sir, told me to send those women away, and I did."

"Apparently, Mrs. Neville didn't get your message."

"Ehhhh. She's not St. James but she is quality by Wapping Wall standards. A pretty woman like that elevates my shop."

What would Pidcock have done if Countess Denton had come to call? Probably swooned. A bit woozy himself, he braced a hand on the window. Anne had been here, regularly by the sound of it, to check on his welfare. Wind scuttled a faded broadside past his feet. Ships listed gently in the Thames. He checked the skies and found lush clouds tumbling in. A storm was coming. He talked with Pidcock, of his plans and Pidcock's plans, the gusts picking up around them. Until the farewell came to its end, Pidcock hugged his coat shut. The thing was missing half its buttons.

"What was it your father's said? 'Wind is nature's way of saying it has somewhere else to be.'" Pidcock opened his shop door. "Looks like the wind is telling you and me, it's time to go, Mr. MacDonald."

They shook hands once more. Will walked along the river, his coattails blowing this way and that. Wind was indeed telling him it was time to move on.

But where to?

Chapter Thirty

$\mathcal{W}$hat does a man do with a woman full of secrets?

Kiss her?

Woo her?

Tease them out one at a time by building trust?

Answers were coming like wind-tumbled leaves, clusters of them spinning fast. It was his task to pluck them one at a time. Though they traveled in the night, he saw Anne clearly as if someone had swiped a cloth across misted glass and the woman on the other side was waiting to be seen. This might be the tale of all women, the desire to be seen, to be understood. He couldn't do that for all of the fair sex. He could do it for Anne.

Her heart had been established on a foundation of women and built in a world of men. The signs were there. A man didn't need to look hard to see them. Her grandmother's garnet earrings, swinging proudly from her ears. Her league's profound unity, evident in Cecelia's hand clasping Anne's at the moment. They were heading into sweet victory or foul disaster. The outcome was up to them, though many staggering factors were beyond their control.

It was the art of chaos. Control what one can control. It's what he'd learned since the rebellion. Prison's chiseling effect. A body learned quickly what to let go of and what to hold on to . . . and there was precious little worth holding fast to in this world. Anne, he was sure, had learned the power of secrets and trust. They were currency to her in the way silver and gold was to Ancilla and information was to his cousin.

His cousin, who at present, pushed back a velvet curtain of robin's egg blue to study the world outside.

"We're almost there." His cousin's red stomacher sank from her slow exhale. "Look at the line of carriages. Twelve deep. Bored of the country already, are you?"

Face to the glass, Cecelia chattered about crests on carriages, while he and Anne carried on a silent, needful conversation. They had not had a moment alone since his return from visiting Mr. Pidcock. He had things to say, questions to ask. She carried on a conversation of a different sort, twirling a lock of hair.

Her grazing stare was like hot coals raking his skin. Legs opened, shoulders back, his hands confident on the squab, he was a king on a throne. The barest upturn of Anne's carmine-shaded lips was a tome's worth of approval. The glint in her eye, a night's worth of seduction. That was the way it was with Anne. More said in quiet moments than a thousand spoken words, but love couldn't live by silence alone. Things needed to be said. Their first moment alone, he would.

"Oh look, Mr. Williamson is wearing scarlet stockings." Cecelia grimaced. "With shins like that, a travesty." She flopped back on her seat and looked at Will's shins. "Your choice of stockings, however, might set a new trend. That shade of gold matches your waistcoat, and with your calves, perfection."

"I bought them today. The haberdasher said it'd be a handsome pairing."

"Did he?" His cousin assessed the unseasonal black velvet he wore, its color broken with the burnished gold of his stockings and waistcoat and a plain white cravat. "When your coat opens, I think *ancient warrior with a plate of gold armor about the chest.*" She winked at him and spoke in a Western Isles brogue. "Verra handsome, cousin, verra handsome indeed."

He ran a hand over the waistcoat. The silk was liquid gold spun into cloth.

"How handsome, would you say?" Anne asked.

Cecelia's mouth puckered. "I was thinking Alexander the Great come back to life."

"Not someone more elevated? Such as a Greek god?"

"*Well* . . . if that's the direction you're going, then Apollo. Sun, light, and all that male beauty," his cousin said archly.

"I was thinking Hades."

Cecelia hummed thoughtfully. "The Underworld? Perhaps it's all that black and gold he's wearing."

"No. It's not the black and gold. It's the man

within." She smiled softly. "Hades was leader of the unseen, but tonight, he will be seen. Tonight, he leaves his mark."

His cousin's gaze sewed a line from him to Anne. A perceptive woman, she knew their history and understood the current running deeply. Where it landed was anyone's guess, though he had a certain destination in mind.

Their carriage rolled forward and Cecelia checked the window. "That was fast. We're already third in line." She fussed with her gloves. "Do we all remember what we're doing?"

"Looking at paintings and drinking champagne," he said.

"Not too much champagne," Cecelia cautioned. "And whatever you do, *do not* drink the red wine."

"We know. We've been through this a thousand times." Anne reached for Cecelia's glove-worrying hand. "We'll be fine. When the countess checks on the herd of guests gathering in the retiring rooms, that's our cue. Will and I will go to the study and get our gold."

In a matter of minutes, Cecelia would signal their arrival to Aunt Flora, who had been in the Countess of Denton's kitchen since noon. Aunt Flora would add drops of a stomach-upsetting tincture in red wine, which footmen would serve on shiny silver trays. Aunt Maude, who was working the retiring room, would tell a footman to alert the countess about the growing, indelicate situation. The threat of her event going awry would impel her to investigate. Once Lady Denton entered her ground-floor retiring room to check on her guests, the theft was in play.

Will patted his chest. "I've go' the Wilkes Lock key."

"Right over your heart," Anne said.

The carriage rolled to a stop and the door's click could be a pistol shot.

The race was on.

Cecelia took a bracing breath and exited first. She fairly glittered, a fireworks display of red and blond. She swept up the steps to Denton House, glomming on to a man's arm with a small laugh. No butler would announce the guests. The art salon was *that* kind of event—elegance with a hint of loose morals.

Anne decamped the carriage, a languid roll to her hips. Dark peacock green dressed her. If her gown had other embellishments, he couldn't say. He was following her silken hips to their place in line.

Anne craned her neck for a look ahead. "It appears Lady Denton is alone in the receiving line."

"She would be." Will offered his arm, and Anne set her gloveless fingers on his black velvet sleeve.

"But Mr. MacLeod—"

"Is either tucked away in a pub, or he's go' his feet up in his room, minding his own business."

"And you know this because . . . ?"

"It's what I did. Lady Denton's bold about keeping a private footman, but she doesna flaunt them. But you already know this, Mrs. Neville."

"How would I know that?"

"Because my cousin isn't the only person cultivating information, is she?"

Anne's head angled toward him, and door

lamps cast her face in a half light. She was shadows, softness, and secrets. But her eyes were emeralds, the fire and depth of which he'd yet to fathom.

"What do you mean?"

Ah, there it was. The velvet blade of her voice.

"I mean your visits to Mr. Pidcock to check on me these past five years. Were you checking on me when I lived here at Denton House?"

Her lips parted. The tiny opening between them was the most tempting spot on her body, and that was a feat because her breasts were pearled fruit spilling from her bodice, the ever-present medallion tucked between them.

"I was still in Scotland when you lived here. I could hardly check on you."

They were fourth in line from the countess. He'd get this out now because these words were years overdue and this was as close to being alone as he could get. Despite the league's well-laid plans, there was no telling how this night would end. He wasn't taking a chance, not with what needed saying.

"You managed to check on me while I lived above Mr. Pidcock's shop."

Anne's mouth firmed, and the small opening he coveted gone. He felt its absence all the way to his toes. It was a sorry victory he enjoyed, unfolding her secret. His feelings were mixed. Exultant and sad at five years . . . wasted.

"Why didna you come to me?" he asked.

There was fragile movement in her neck. A guilty swallow.

"I couldn't."

A polite cough yanked him from looking into her eyes. A gap swelled between them and the next pair greeting the countess. He led Anne over the threshold into the light. Fifty candles burned circles of light in a crystal chandelier above their heads. Light bounced off white marble floors, the effect breathtaking. It was a message from the Countess of Denton: *I'm a wealthy, powerful collector of beauty.*

Anne's profile was proud beside him.

"Why did you never come to me?" he asked again. "All this time, I thought you'd forgotten me."

"I have never forgotten about you because I have *never, never* stopped loving you." Shoulders square and chin proud, Anne was in high spirits, though her voice throbbed low. "I sought news of your whereabouts since the war. Any scraps I could find. Your time in the prison hulk, your time here at Denton House, and your time on the docks. All of it. But that's not what you want. You want to know why I didn't seek you out, and it's simple. I didn't think you wanted me."

Anne's eyes glossed wetly at the admission, and the beast that drove him to follow her out of Marshalsea sank greedy claws into his heart. The same beast which laughed at his rejection was cruelly laughing again.

"I pledged my troth to Mr. Neville. An old man who did no more than touch my hand. It was not a true marriage, Will MacDonald, but my vows were. And they always will be," she said fervently, quietly for his ears alone. "If I swear an oath before God and man to be faithful, it will be done . . . 'til death do we part."

Anne's pain pierced him. He was stunned and unaccountably angry. Life had been unusually cruel, stealing all that he had held dear. As a boy, his mother, gone. Then clan, country, and his father who he'd not seen since the war. And Anne, the most confounding woman to ever win his heart. She'd *known* where he was, yet she married another man to help their clan.

What a tangled web.

This woman he loved was layers upon layers of complexity.

Her loyalty was fierce and glorious. It rocked his soul, because wrapped within it was the real treasure he found in Denton House. Anne had never stopped loving him.

Chapter Thirty-One

*M*olten gold eyes burned with hunger. Anne ripped herself away from Will. She liked her arm entwined with his, but he pulsed with emotion. Anger, amazement, true, true amazement, and love. She'd take them all, though there were enough to make a woman forget where she was standing or if she was breathing. Naught else mattered. They would be together.

Not a war or a woman would come between them.

She touched Will's sleeve, a promise in it.

Later . . .

They had but one task tonight—take the gold. In that, they were united. Lightness rippled inside her. It felt like . . . victory.

She watched Will step forward in the marble entry. A fist curled against his midsection. He bowed from the waist.

"Countess, thank you for inviting us."

Anne's heart fluttered with pride. She needed to heal. They needed to heal. But true love was pliable and stalwart. She saw it in Will's handsome profile, more beautiful and perfect for his goodness. He smiled graciously at a woman who didn't deserve it. The countess basked in it. Anne took the moment to force herself back into the present. To hear voices cluttering, laughter spilling, the footmen scurrying with perfectly balanced trays. Music played somewhere too. Will was concluding the bland chatter one gave to a host. Hearts would quiver for Will MacDonald well into his advanced years, but she would be the one to walk beside him.

When he stepped aside, Lady Denton buried her hands in dramatic panniers, her wistful gaze following him. Perhaps love for the highlander lived in the woman's gilded heart. If it did, all hints of gentle emotions faded when Anne sashayed forward.

"Mrs. Neville. How kind of you to come." The Countess of Denton's voice dripped with ice.

Anne bowed her head and sank into a deep elegant curtsey. She held it longer than necessary, and her medallion swung forward, a golden pendulum.

"Mrs. Neville . . . must you?" Lady Denton's patience wore thin.

She rose slowly, her skirts a green silk froth. "I must, my lady. As a tribute to my grandmother, you see."

A politely bored, "Your grandmother?"

"Yes, the late Mrs. Elizabeth Wilcox. She taught me to show deference to my betters. Especially those of . . . experienced years."

A brittle smile stretched. Countess Denton was a vision of good breeding and perfect style.

Thanks to expensive creams and fastidious avoidance of the sun, she glowed with beauty and fine health. Her current gown of coppered silk and cream did wonders for the woman. Candlelight caressed the fabric and her sherry-colored eyes. Truly stunning. Her characteristic silver-white lock vanished in piles of curled black hair. The countess apparently had her unusual streak dyed to match the rest of her hair.

Imperious fingers flicked a summons. "Come closer."

Anne could hardly resist. She stepped into her ladyship's sphere of perfume and power. Countess Denton's head tipped forward and she dropped her voice for Anne's ears alone.

"You are swimming in dangerous waters, Mrs. Neville."

"Am I?"

"I know what you're about."

Dread seized Anne. With her ear cocked to the woman, guests traipsing the stairs and mingling in the entry would think the countess shared a secret with a friend. It was intimate, as only enemies in skirts would do battle.

"I can't imagine what you're talking about, my lady," Anne said lightly, but her palms dampened.

"You disappoint me, Mrs. Neville. I was prepared to open doors for you, to give you an opportunity. One that any other woman in the City would kill to have."

"I am not any other woman."

She parted from their tête-à-tête with a healthy dose of fear. She'd lived too long with its ability to separate the wheat from the chaff as it were. The countess, a creature of comfort, had not. The countess had lived too much with her confidence. It was making her careless with details. Thus, the upstart widow of Bermondsey Wall was one step ahead in their uneven race. It was an advantage Anne would enjoy while she could.

"I must decline your gracious offer, milady."

Spite flickered in the countess's eyes. They both knew why: all six foot, four inches of handsome highlander was why.

"Any doors opened will be of my doing and mine alone." Anne quieted her voice, lending the smallest smirk to it. "Another lesson from my grandmother, the late Mrs. Wilcox."

The Countess of Denton looked ready to smite her, yet the woman managed a polite, glacial, "Enjoy tonight, Mrs. Neville, for tomorrow, I shall crush you."

"Not if I crush you first, Lady Denton." Cold words delivered with knifelike precision.

Anne turned her back on the woman and swanned off with all the bravado a body could muster. She linked arms with Will. "Champagne. Now."

He kissed her bruised temple and whispered, "Whatever you said, lass, has go' her ladyship glaring daggers at your back."

"Good." She walked as close to him as her panniers allowed.

Will led them past gilt-trimmed doors flung wide. The drawing room–cum–art salon number one. The salacious art lived in the ballroom on another floor, where not surprisingly, most of the guests had migrated.

In this room, a quartet hid behind a wall of greenery, their stringed music serenading guests. Gorgeous paintings sat on easels placed around the room. For those who wanted to linger, damask upholstered chairs and settees had been arranged for comfortable viewing. Cecelia was planted on a beige settee. Her face tipped high while she conversed with an ardent, bespectacled admirer who owned neatly queued chestnut hair.

Anne dropped on the seat beside Cecelia. She was grateful the admirer answered a viscount's summons about a seascape, and even more grateful for the footman who stopped with a tray of champagne, not red wine. Anne took two glasses. The footman didn't bat an eye.

"Thank you." She emptied the first glass and tucked it under the settee.

Cecelia blinked at her. "Thirsty work greeting the countess?"

Anne gulped champagne from her second glass. She would've kept going, but Will slid onto the seat next to her.

"Calm down and tell us what happened." His voice was her lodestone. She could listen to it all night.

"Something happened?" Cecelia's brows pinched. She was fierce and exquisite with her piles of blond hair and artful cosmetics.

Her fingers were icy on the glass. "The countess knows."

"Knows what?" Will asked.

"When I greeted her, she said, 'I know what you're about,' which was followed with a threat to destroy me." A swallow of sparkling liquid courage helped. The first glass of champagne was already seeping into her limbs, uncoiling tight nerves. At least she imagined it to be so.

"Is that all?"

She looked into his face, each feature more prominent from his neat queue and smooth-shaved jaw. "She told me to enjoy the evening because tomorrow she would crush me."

Will's hand covered hers digging into expensive silk. His dockside callouses gently scraped her skin. His hand was a safe harbor in this new storm. They linked fingers, and he led their joined hands into his lap and cupped his other hand over hers for good measure. She would have to tell him about the countess's offer. Privately. Because that's what true love did.

"Crush you tomorrow, you say?" Cecelia's eyes narrowed. "Those are words of fear and jealousy said after you entered her house on Will's arm. I wouldn't be afraid of the woman, if I were you."

"I'm inclined to take her seriously. Call it an aversion to prison," she said and emptied the second glass.

Cecelia unwound Anne's fingers from that glass and she was struck by the notion of Will holding one hand and Cecelia holding the other. What a trio they made.

"I think that's enough champagne for you, dear." Cecelia tipped her closed fan at the doorway. "Look over there. Would you say that's the face of a woman who knows about our plan?"

More guests clustered in the ground-floor salon. The Countess of Denton, framed by gilt-trimmed doors flung wide, was in command of all she surveyed. She was laughing, a handsome artist at her side. A herd of pastel silks and velvets traveled upstairs. The countess and the young artist followed.

Footmen circulated, but not a single tray of red wine was in sight. Behind the latest gaggle of footmen, a fresh throng of guests appeared. Young, handsome upstarts. Well dressed, though at second glance, the coats were three seasons old and the shoes of one man scuffed. Anne studied these newcomers carefully, new dread landing in her stomach.

"Cecelia, what are Mr. James Hadley and friends doing here?"

"What do you think?" Defiance flashed in Cecelia's eyes.

"You invited them?"

Her peace of mind took another tumble. First, the countess's threat, which could or could not mean the woman knew their intentions. Now a gang of well-dressed thieves, Spruce Prigs as it were, had invaded Denton House, and Cecelia's mutinous frown told her who invited them.

Cecelia eyed Will. "Would you give us a moment?"

Will kissed Anne's temple and murmured against her skin, "Call me when you need me."

Tonight wasn't his battle to lead. It was hers,

and he was a foot soldier. How comforting that Will didn't try to take over, another sign of his respect for her. He rambled the room, his thickly muscled shoulders filling black velvet. A sturdy back, a sturdy man. Calmer now, she turned her attention to Cecelia.

"What are you about?"

"I am about our mission. The one we vowed to accomplish since we left Clanranald MacDonald lands. What are you about, getting scared and such?" Scorn twisted Cecelia's features. "Where's the woman I nursed after she was knifed in St. Giles?"

She touched her rib. A scar was the badge she carried from that night. Only Cecelia knew what had happened. She'd tracked down a source who might know who else in London hoarded Jacobite gold. After that night, she began to wear double stays. Not a perfect solution, but a helpful one. Her double stays had spared her another vicious cut when men attacked her in her warehouse. The very same attack before she freed Will from Marshalsea. Cecelia was her keeper of secrets . . . most of them. She was the one who'd take charge of the league in her absence.

She was certainly done with the City. When a woman wore double corsets for added protection, it was time to leave.

Cecelia's eyes softened. "Is your fear about Will?"

"What do you mean?"

"I see the way you look at him. You are in love and that, my dear, has compromised you." Cecelia patted her hand. "Before you were a fearless woman, the most fearless one I have had the privilege to know. You had nothing to lose before. Now you do."

A small inhale and, "You're right."

Fear would not get the best of her. But that wasn't all. Cecelia's grasp tightened on Anne's hand. Cecelia of frivolous shopping and the endless pursuit of pleasure and men had become very serious.

"There is something else."

Anne scrutinized hazel eyes. "You're not leaving for Bath tonight, are you?"

"I am not. I am staying in London."

Cecelia was staying to make sure Anne left safely with the gold.

She locked both hands with Cecelia. Faithful friend, ally, confidante. No finer woman walked the earth. If the Jacobite rebels had let Cecelia fight, they might have won on her tenacity alone. A fierce, loving streak a mile wide ran through her. She would be the first and last foot soldier on the field of battle. At present, her battle visage sterned, pretty and blond, her carmine lips curving with vicious determination.

"Tell me, Anne. Don't you want to grind the countess under your heel and ruin her?"

God help her, she did.

Chapter Thirty-Two

*H*e was perusing paintings of places he'd never seen and likely never would. Lush English landscapes, hedgerows, horses leaping over hedgerows, a manse vast enough to house a small village, and a quaint river with a folly beside it. He'd never actually seen a folly, but he knew of them. By virtue of their name, the men who built them and the men who paid others to build them, had to know it was foolish.

A playhouse for adults, follies were. The provenance of people with too much wealth and not enough brains to wisely use it. Hence, their foolish spending. No folly graced Clanranald MacDonald lands. Highlanders had the good sense to cry foul—or fool—as it were. If a castle was crumbling, it was because man or nature had a hand in it. No need to pay someone to build something and make it look like it was falling apart.

False things were a foil for the truth.

As a perfect example, there was him. An overlarge mirrored sconce reflected a man playing a velvet-clad guest. It was him playing a false game, not unlike his sojourn as *private footman* under Ancilla's roof when footmen slept below-stairs, while he'd lived abovestairs.

Thankfully, none of the servants trawling the room were here when he was in residence.

One of them slowed his stride. "Champagne, sir?"

The footman was liveried in a diminished spirit, eyes properly downcast.

"None, thank you." The footman turned, when Will asked, "Have you a good stout ale?"

The footman in scarlet and navy blue hesitated.

Will urged the lad's gaze to meet his. "You know, a hearty, dark ale. Something a man can sink his teeth into. Something you probably drink on your half day."

The almost blindingly white periwig edged up a few degrees. The lad looked to be eighteen, if he was a day. An obliging servant, he gave the expected response. "I can ask in the kitchens, sir."

Will already knew the answer. "Never mind. Can you tell me when red wine will be served?"

That set the lad's shoulders right. "No red wine tonight, sir. Her ladyship's orders. I can have a word with the butler. Lady Denton might change her mind if enough guests ask for it."

"No' if they're pouring her expensive cham-pagne down their gullets."

Which earned him a twitch on the lad's mouth. "I suppose not, sir."

"Thank you."

The footman moved on, and Will whistled low

under his breath. *No red wine.* The art of chaos. When it can, it will strike. Anne and Cecelia needed to know this news, but they were currently engaged in an animated discussion which centered on Mr. James Hadley. He remembered the newly wedded Spruce Prig, the sheer delight in his bride and his supposed promise to leave a life of crime.

So much for promises.

He continued his amble along the row of paintings. Boring landscape, boring landscape, another boring landscape until his well-heeled shoes stuck to the floor. This one took his breath away, a painting of a place dear to him. Sandy beaches, purple heather, and otherworldly standing stones.

The Isle of Benbecula.

Longing wrenched his heart. The artist captured sunlight on water, the beach's slope, and the scruff of land above it. The carpet underfoot became soft sand. He heard sand crunch under his boots and felt the sun shining on his head. He breathed deeply as if smelling the island's clean, briny air. He touched the painting like a desperate man. Fair distant winds whispered through it. Haunting him. Calling him. The whisper keened with bagpipes, a sharp, ancient cry.

Come home, it said.

He'd landed on that beach as a boy, many times, with his father.

The very same place he'd thought to show his son someday.

He tried to swallow the knot in his throat and tried to tear himself away. He couldn't.

Wild and wicked, that's what lowland Scots thought of their highland brethren. Picts and Norse-Gaels once carved out homes in the isles, history written in blood. The highlands ran in his veins, the brisk winds and peaty bogs. A place of pagan warriors. His ancestors. He could feel their roar at what had become of him. Of rebellion and loss. The City left its grit, a brand to be sure. Here were different warriors, the victorious ones and those who lost. Defeat was a scar that would stay forever, a reminder of what could have been. Yet, his forefathers had carried on in the land they'd loved.

Why couldn't he do the same?

These years had changed him with one constant in his heart, the woman he'd thought he'd lost.

"Anne . . ." Cecelia's voice rose in caution.

Anne was walking toward him. The woman was a warning and a prayer, snatching another glass of champagne from a passing tray. "I'm fine. If I can hold my own with sailors, I can certainly hold my own at—" her glass-holding hand arced at the room "—an art salon." Her last words were delivered with the faintest sneer. "What do you think?"

Anne took a drink, her eyes seeking him. Clear emeralds, cosmetics enhancing sooty lashes and sharp cheekbones. The near-emptied glass wore her carmine lip print on its rim. She'd leave her stamp. Always.

"I think you will do what you will, lass. You always have."

Her seductive laugh tumbled low. He watched

her delicate throat work while she finished the champagne, her green eyes sparkling through her lashes. Mr. Hadley's Spruce Prigs were spreading out. They blended in, making a show of studying the artwork. One Spruce Prig discussed the merits of a horse's portrait with an older gentleman. Others took the stairs, sharks on the hunt for silver and soft-paste porcelain figures, anything they could lift. Paintings were dull custom for the likes of them.

Cecelia watched them go, her eyes catching Will's.

"The two of you keep out of trouble, will you? I hear the countess changed her mind about serving red wine." She smiled deviously. "I am about to correct that."

His cousin sauntered off.

Anne reached out and came short of touching the painting. "Is that—"

"The Isle of Benbecula," he said reverently.

The gold medallion, its curlicued nine, rested over her bodice. Anne didn't bother to hide it. She was bold and wounded, as tortured and trapped in this gilt refinement as he. A black curl unmoored itself, this one resting high on her breast. The curl seemed to ride the swell, up and down with her breaths. When his gaze met her eyes, he found her wounds bared, her heart broken.

"Take me from this place, Will," was her hoarse cry.

"The gold," he murmured.

"Anywhere. Just away from this . . . Please." Her plaintive whisper was enough.

He took her hand and led her out of the drawing room and down the hall to an alcove near the dining room. Ferns and a marble bust on a pedestal provided cover, their oasis. He folded Anne into his arms or she folded herself into his. It was hard to tell with his heart beating out of his chest. She nestled her head under his chin and that was enough.

Contentment and satisfaction was a calm island in their storm. More truths had been shared this past week than one dare put in a lifetime, and they wore down the heartiest soul. Her hair under his chin, her hands on his back, the lavender she preferred. It all came back to him. The feel of Anne's body molded to his and the deep-seated satisfaction it brought.

She belonged in his arms.

His hands seemed to agree. They began to move with pride of ownership and remembrance. The slender line of her back and the stays hugging it. Beyond their slice of heaven, voices rose and fell, champagne-slurred, cheery, oblivious to the pair comforting each other ten or twelve paces away. Music drifted from the drawing room, but Anne's sigh was the sweetest music.

Her head tipped up, and he would nurse those sighs. Play them for the fine music they were. Down, down he went. His mouth to hers, soft and tender as spring. Falling into a peaceful place with the woman who held his heart. This was nothing like hot sexual need. Her arms around him, her mouth moving against his.

Softer than velvet. Warm and wet. A taste of Anne long overdue.

She quivered in his arms. The sensation rocked him. It went through silk petticoats to his thighs. He groaned in her mouth, feeling Anne and hungry for more.

Her hands circled his back and slid forward. They parted, a slight break.

"This is not enough." Anne's voice was a purr as she set both hands on his chest and pushed him against the wall.

With the wall at his back, his stance widened. He dragged Anne close—or she fell into him. Their reconnection sizzled. Her hands sliding over his chest, finding his nipple through silk and linen and stroking it to a fine point.

He bunched her skirts in one hand, desperate to hoist them and see her fine legs. To touch them, find the tender skin of her inner thighs, the slick skin high between them. Anne's husky laugh tickled his neck. She pushed up on her toes and nibbled his neck.

Her lips grazed his earlobe, and she sucked.

Soft, wet, suckling noises drove him mad. His cock began to swell.

Anne rubbed her body full against his. Silk against silk. She hummed, a languid music of pleasure until her mouth found his. He had to touch her hair, to see it falling gracefully. Black silk it was. He tunneled his fingers through it, slow and careful, feeling the wealth of his life right here. It was good to love a woman who reveled as much in understanding his heart as she did in pleasuring his body.

He'd revel in a lifetime of pleasuring her.

A loud cough on the other side of the pedestal

froze their kiss. Anne jerked back, a hand on her mouth.

"It's time tae begin." The whisper-hiss was Aunt Flora's.

Anne's eyes sparkled like emeralds in the shadowed alcove. Unmoored hair fell around her shoulders, as much of it up as down. She set a hand over his heart, where the Wilkes Lock key was tucked.

"I am with you. Always," she said in a kiss-drenched voice.

His heart was maddeningly light and pure—even if other parts of him weren't.

"And I with you, lass. I give you all that I have, all that I am."

Their words bound them, a tie no man or woman could destroy.

Chapter Thirty-Three

*H*ands clasped, they sped down the hall to Lady Denton's study. Anne—his Anne—laughed like a carefree maid when he pushed open the door. A body could think they were off to finish what they'd started in the alcove, not take Jacobite gold. No lights guided them, save the slivered moon's mean offering and a lamp in the mews. He reached into his pocket for the Wilkes Lock key. Silver glinted in his hand.

He breathed a prayer, *Let this key be true.*

By the mantel, the scrape of flint sounded, and a flame jumped to life. Anne lit a taper on a four-stick candelabra and was about to light the other three.

"No light."

"Not even one?"

"I've go' the moon to help me," he said, dropping to one knee.

"Sounds like you colluded with the heavens."

Footsteps padded over plush carpet. Anne crouched beside him, a sigh of silk and lavender.

She was the fey creature who'd rescued him from Marshalsea, her face awash in shadows. With her hair half-fallen, she resembled a woman who'd just tumbled from an assignation of clothed sex. Theirs very nearly was.

"Thank you," she said. "You are brave and strong, Will MacDonald. This couldn't have happened without you."

He swallowed hard. Her adoration was a gift. Words laid at his feet, better than Jacobite gold. To be the man she needed.

"You were doing a fine job without me, lass."

"We both know this would have been much more difficult without you."

An honest admission. He reached for her hand and kissed her fingertips, the back of it, a knuckle, then turning her hand over to kiss tender flesh where her pulse throbbed.

Her sharp inhale was gratifying.

Anne pressed against him, her forehead touching his. "Later," she whispered.

"Later."

The promise uncoiled them to finish their job. Otherwise they'd combust, gold or no gold.

Anne bunched petticoats about her knees and pushed off the ground. Her silhouette of slender calves in pretty shoes almost undid him. She opened the window casement.

"Get ready," she whispered hoarsely.

A horse snort was the answer outside the window.

"We've been waiting." Mary Fletcher's worried voice rose in the night.

He blocked their muffled conversation from his mind and concentrated on the cabinet. His eyes were fully adjusted to the dark. Brass gleamed the Wilkes Lock and its poetic, scripted warning.

If I had ye gift of tongue

I would declare and do no wrong

Who ye are ye com by stealth

To impare my Master's wealth

The warning was etched near the head of a man dressed in the garb of another century, his staff pointing to the number ninety-eight. The numbered dial, the lock's tracking system.

A tiny nob stood out under the figure's left foot. Will pushed it. The figure's left leg kicked forward, revealing a keyhole. Will inserted the filigreed key. He set a finger on the back of the figure's hat and gently tipped the hat while he turned the key.

The bolt released.

The numbered dial turned, and the cabinet clicked open.

It worked!

He released a long gust of air and opened the cabinet door, its oiled hinges quiet. Inside the dark cavern, he found a wooden box and a stack of leather folios. Ancilla's dark secrets were in there. Perhaps the secrets of other men and women. They were not his concern. The bulging leather bags, stained and well traveled, were. The bags were heaped in a careless pile, each one the size of Aunt Maude's pea-shucking bowl.

He grinned at the comparison. He really was a simple man. With a heave, he dragged one out of the cabinet. It clinked heavily on the floor.

"Open it."

"It's gold coins, Anne. You've seen one, you've seen them all."

She stood above him, hands on hips. "I've waited a long time to see these coins, Will Mac-Donald."

Outside light haloed Anne, a warrior in shimmering silk. Fiercely beautiful, she would not be denied. His pulse picked up, the cost of kneeling before plunder not yet theirs. The treasure was within their grasp, but they were still in Denton House.

He coaxed himself to outer calm. "As you wish, lass. But make it quick."

He untied one bag, and Anne knelt down to stare into it. He did too, finding reverence in the moment. The gold gathered light, its shine touching Anne's cheeks. So many French livres. Hard, flat, ready to be of service. These were old coins, their fluted edges worn smooth from use and their metallic tang, dirty. This gold, which was meant to win a war, would help those who'd lost it. Such was the matter of money. The hands that used it made the difference. Oddly, neither he nor Anne dug into the bag. The coins weren't theirs. Their mission was to return the treasure to their clan chief and then it would be given to those in need.

Never did he imagine the lass he'd loved at the beginning of the war would help him end it. But this was the end—of his losses and hers.

"Ready?" he asked with more hope than he'd felt in a long, long time.

"Yes."

He knotted the large leather purse, and cupping it with both hands, he carried it to the window where Mary Fletcher waited. Like her sister, she was dressed as a man, hair tucked under a Dutch cap, grime on her face. Margaret Fletcher waved to him from her place on the street where she petted the horses.

With the house's elevation, Mary Fletcher had to stand in a dray to receive the gold.

"It's heavy," he warned.

"I'm a strong woman. I can take it."

The burden passed, she almost dropped it. The bag slid down the front of her, but she caught it at her knees with a grunt of effort. Her eyes were saucers in her head when she looked at him.

"*Uh!* The countess could have shown better manners and parsed the gold into smaller bags." Her dry jest was punctuated with more grunts.

"Got it?"

"Yes. Consider me prepared."

"Good. There are seven more."

He ducked back to the cabinet to the sounds of her heavy boots clomping in the dray. Anne was on her knees, dragging bags from the cabinet and shuffling them along the carpeted floor.

She angled her body oddly, digging about her waist. "Bad night to wear new stays."

From Aunt Maude and Aunt Flora, folding

themselves into Denton House as occasional servants to Cecelia and her diversionary Spruce Prigs to the steady Fletcher sisters. All worked like cogs in a clock.

The *chink, chink, chink* of coins was the only noise they made. One bag after another was carried across the room and sent out the window.

"One left." Anne leaned on the cabinet door and levered herself upright.

Will closed the cabinet and pocketed the key. If the study appeared undisturbed, Ancilla's attention would be on the Spruce Prigs and not the Jacobite gold. He lifted the final bag with ease and went to the window. Mary Fletcher's hands were reaching for it when the bone-freezing cock of a pistol broke the quiet.

He turned to meet the pistol's owner, the bag still in hand. Anne did the same beside him.

"That's what you're up to," a male voice said from the doorway.

Rory MacLeod strode in, a well-traveled flintlock pointed at Will. His chest, to be precise. He made a big target and any lower the shooter risked hitting the bag of gold. Coins would explode in a mess. MacLeod stopped a foot from the other side of the desk, casting a curious glance at the cabinet.

"Mr. MacLeod, what a surprise." Anne took a half step to the left, shielding Will.

MacLeod gave a single nod, impressed by her bold move. His gaze wandered higher to Will's face. "Never had a woman do that for me. You are a lucky man."

Will stepped around Anne and strode to the

desk where he dropped the bag with a loud, decisive *clink*.

"I am."

Anne rushed forward. "You will let us go, Mr. MacLeod."

To which he snorted and waggled the flintlock. "I'm the one with the pistol, Mrs. Neville. I'll give the orders."

The room was dark, but Will caught movement in his side vision. Anne. She didn't have her knife. He knew this because his hands had been everywhere on her . . . unless she strapped it to her left thigh. He'd been too busy hitching petticoats on her right thigh to notice a weapon on her other leg, and panniers were the devil's own curse to a man with seduction on his mind.

"You don't need this gold," she said.

"And you do?"

Not a knife. Anne was gripping Ancilla's crystal ink pot. A heavy thing. It would do damage. MacLeod's flintlock would do worse.

"Let's calm down." Will raised his hands in a show of peace.

"I am calm. It's your lady friend who's about to throw that thing at my head."

Anne lifted the makeshift weapon. "It is at your peril, Mr. MacLeod. Never bring a flintlock to an inkwell fight."

MacLeod's smile cracked unevenly, its cheer matched by his low chuckle. "You're a rare piece, Mrs. Neville. Wherever did he find you?"

"Lothian Street in Edinburgh. My father's doorstep to be exact." She was clipped and efficient, his Anne. "I hope to go back there someday . . . after I deliver this gold to the people who need it most. Highlanders, if you must know."

"Regular Robin Hood are you?"

"I am afraid you've missed the mark again, Mr. MacLeod. Robin Hood was a man, while I am a woman."

"I've noticed."

Will did not care for the sensual note in MacLeod's voice.

"I caught a Spruce Prig lifting her ladyship's porcelain shepherdess. The two of you have anything to do with that?" MacLeod asked as if he needed to cross-reference the evening's criminal activity.

"Not . . . precisely." Anne was splitting hairs.

MacLeod *tsked* her. "A crime within a crime. Brilliant move, Mrs. Neville."

"I'm afraid I personally cannot take credit for the Spruce Prigs currently roaming Denton House."

"But you will take credit for lifting her ladyship's gold."

"Jacobite gold, yes," she said emphatically. "I most certainly do."

A stalemate stretched and by the set of Anne's profile, the lass wasn't giving an inch.

MacLeod didn't care about the gold. He was too busy staring at Anne, sizing her up, appreciating her. She had the look of a well-kissed woman with her hair in disarray. His flintlock-holding arm relaxed, and MacLeod pointed the muzzle at the floor.

"If you ever tire of Mr. MacDonald, come find me, Mrs. Neville. You and I would have a good time."

"That is very kind of you, Mr. MacLeod, but my affections are otherwise taken." She faced Will, her voice gentling. "For the rest of my life."

MacLeod's smile faded, small and sad. "Then you and Mr. MacDonald had better disappear through that window and find the rest of your life." When they didn't move quickly, he nodded a reassurance. "Go on, I'll watch the door."

Will lugged the last coin bag to the window and sucked in cool night air. A drop of sweat was trickling in his hairline. He'd fought with pistols and fists but never with the love of his life beside him. That interlude could've gone badly. He breathed a prayer of thanks it didn't.

At the window, Mary Fletcher was ghost white and her eyes round as dishes again. Horse hooves clattered in the distance and the confusion of men sounded in Grosvenor Square. Another lamp came to life in the mews.

"Please hurry," Miss Fletcher hissed.

He passed the bag into her hands. Anne was at his back.

"It's done, Mary. It's done," she said, a quiver in her voice.

Anne lifted her petticoats knee-high, and he helped her navigate out the window to the dray below. He was one leg over the casement frame when MacLeod called him.

"Mr. MacDonald."

MacLeod's head was cocked to the hall, an

ominous light shining on his flintlock's metal work.

Will balanced one foot on the floor, his other leg on the bottom of the window frame. A deuced place to be. Half in, half out, compromised as he was and with no weapon. Anne might've temporarily won MacLeod with her prickly wit, but that didn't mean the man wouldn't change his mind. They'd never learned much about him or his motives. The unlit room and falling into the dray were Will's best chance for a quick escape.

MacLeod took two steps into the dark study. "The Night Watch is on their way. Bow Street won't be far behind. Her ladyship has a few of them on a hook, I hear. You'll avoid them if you take Tiburn Lane."

"Thank you." Will leaped to the dray below. "The Night Watch is coming. Take Tiburn Lane and we'll avoid them."

Mary Fletcher snapped the reins and the vehicle lurched forward. He stretched out beside Anne in between barrels filled with gold and held her close. She gripped his waistcoat as if she'd never let go. He was coiled up inside, tighter than a child's wind-up toy. Much had gone wrong this night, but they were together. And they were free. For now.

House lights faded when the dray rumbled onto less refined Tiburn Lane. A turn to the right would take them to Tiburn Tree. He untied his cravat, the irony not lost on him.

Chapter Thirty-Four

They made it to Southwark. He knew this because star-strewn skies shed the best light where fewer streetlights were to be had. All the same, he was still on a bed of straw and out of sight. Mermaid Brewery barrels rattled, twin walls hiding him and Anne. The roads were less friendly but there was no other place he'd rather be. The woman he loved was tangled nicely with him, her head in the crook of his shoulder and her hand currently wandering to unsafe places.

He sent a prayer of thanks for the dark and the barrels between the Fletcher sisters and the goings-on in the back of the dray. It was torture because they still had a fair distance to go.

Anne's hand drifted lower. She rucked up the bottom of his waistcoat. A slow rumple of cloth and . . . her fingertips slid into the top of his placket. She played there. Little circles. Quiet. Soft. Just the feel of her body braided with his.

An image of her bending over and kissing his arse in broad daylight bloomed.

He hugged her closer and murmured in her ear,

"Careful, lass. I canna say what my tackle will do if your hand keeps doing that."

Her giggle was sweet. Her hand drifted with the same sluggishness out of his placket. "I cannot stop touching you, Will MacDonald."

"Because I'm the brawest mon you've ever met."

"By far."

"How handsome? Mr. Rory MacLeod handsome?"

Her head lifted and black wisps tickled his ear. She angled her head to see him better, the same as he was angling for a compliment.

She tipped her head this way and that. "It's a close contest to be sure, but we may need to go and find Mr. MacLeod . . . for comparison's sake only."

"You wound me, lass. Right here." He pointed to his heart.

Impish light sparked in her eyes. "For the best comparison, I may ask him to drop his breech—"

Will dragged her close and kissed her soundly. Hands in her hair, he nestled Anne between his legs . . . that stopped her tart tongue. It was a long kiss, sweet and dark, her tongue, her lips tasting of champagne. Anne was a mystery he'd barely plumbed. The young man had foolishly raised his fists in victory after their first kiss. His *Yes!* bellowed to the sky. A hard-earned first kiss, it was.

This was a mending of souls. Kindness, passion, love. An open-mouthed kiss melting into gentle nibbles, lips grazing, and tender noises lacing them together.

Heaven on earth. He'd find it wherever he was . . . as long as Anne was there.

Which begged a new, difficult conversation: she was leaving at dawn to go north.

Not a word had passed between them about him. Anne must've sensed his hesitation. She broke their kiss, folded her arm over his chest, and rested her chin there.

"Out with it, Will."

This was nice, the weight of her on top of him. Anne belonged there, her legs lolling against his while the dray rumbled on.

He hooked an arm under his head. "You're leaving at dawn."

"I am. To take the gold back to Clanranald lands. It's been my mission for years. You know that."

This was the next skirmish. The night seemed full of them, but if he had to do battle, he'd do it with Anne and for Anne. She was pretty, the stars a crown to her head. Her eyes big emeralds, her cosmetics smudged. His landlocked mermaid, her green skirts a tail flipping her impatience. Black curls fell in sensual disarray. He plucked straw from one and tossed it aside.

"We havena discussed you and me, lass."

He traced her collarbone to her shoulder.

"Because there's nothing to discuss."

He hooked a finger in her gown and tugged. Moonlight kissed her bared shoulder. The onyx curl slid lazily forward. It begged to be touched. He was fascinated with it, coiling and uncoiling her hair.

"We're together. Forever. You heard what I said to Mr. MacLeod." Anne's strong voice thinned. "I cannot . . . I will not—"

A catch in her throat stopped her. Anne's face crumpled.

"Will? You cannot mean to go to . . ."

The woman he loved more than life was about to cry and he would have none of that.

"Shhhhh . . ."

This wasn't easy for either of them.

Her cheek on his chest, Anne grabbed handfuls of his coat. "I saw the way you looked at that painting. The beach at Benbecula." Her head lifted heavily. "How can you not want to go home?"

"It's no' so easy, lass." He brushed his knuckles on her wet cheek. "My father . . ."

"We can figure something out." She cupped his head, her voice fierce. "I choose you, Will Mac-Donald. I choose us."

He dragged her hand to his mouth and shushed her.

He kissed her palm, the plump seat of her thumb, her wrist where her skin was fascinatingly soft. They'd given themselves body and soul to Scotland and their clan. Much had gone into finding the Jacobite gold which hardly jingled thanks to Mary Fletcher's clever burlap and wool packing. Anne had made her sacrifices, and so had he. If he couldn't be with Anne in the colonies, he'd be with her in Scotland.

Like an acorn seed must split to become a tree, his heart would have to break too. Only then would they have something better.

He touched a fat tear on her cheek. "As you wish, lass. We'll go home to Scotland."

Anne searched his face. The hope lighting her

eyes was enough to bring him to his knees. He didn't deserve her hope, her love but he'd give his all to earn it. The rest of his life, in fact.

"I mean it, Anne."

She melted onto his chest. Her muffled, sniffling, "We will be happy" tossing the sweetest tether around his heart.

This was the way of love. Compromise was a myth. Sometimes one gave his all and more to win true love. He'd been so set in his need to fight the war, he'd lost the only woman he'd ever loved. His second chance to have love would not be wasted on where he lived. He'd learned a new trade with West and Sons Shipping. He could do the same again.

With Anne's head near his heart, he closed his eyes and let needful rest come. He drifted off to an impossible vision of the Isle of Benbecula, a gentle wind blowing across a sloping beach, a scruff of land above it, and the sun shining down on his head.

Chapter Thirty-Five

$\mathcal{A}$ hand jiggled his shoulder. He grabbed it fast and sat up, blinking. Anne leaned over him, a candle lamp in one hand.

"My hand, if you please," she said in a husky voice. He did have a death grip on the hand that had shaken him awake, a habit of war and prison that stuck.

Air was stirring cold and unfriendly. He hugged his insufficient velvet coat tighter, closing the ends, turning up the collar. River water slapped, buildings loomed. He cuffed grains of sleep from his eyes, hoping to clear his head. They were at a wharf by the arrangement of buildings, the dock, and the river.

"Where are we?"

"Gun Wharf." She raised her lamp higher. "Neville Warehouse to be precise."

He scooted off the dray, taking a fair bit of straw with him. A blue-and-white sign confirmed they were at Neville Warehouse. Anne produced a key and inserted it in an iron padlock.

"You slept like the dead. We decided not to wake you."

"What about the gold?" he asked, squinting at his environs.

The padlock sprang open. "Mary, Margaret, and I removed it ourselves." She unhooked the padlock. "A force of habit, living without a man these years. We got used to doing everything ourselves. Besides, you've looked exhausted since Marshalsea."

Anne opened the sun-bleached door, and he was tempted to tell her he'd been exhausted since losing the war. Since seeing Anne again, he'd had the first true, bone-deep rest. Invigorating. Humbling. She was so competent.

He followed her into the near-empty warehouse, his voice echoing, "You do plan on needing me . . . someday, lass?"

The candle lamp swung merrily, its yellow glow crowning her mussed hair. "I need you every day, Will MacDonald. Close that door behind you and set the bar, if you please."

He shut the warehouse door and barred it. "We're sleeping here?"

"Until dawn. That's when Mr. Baines will take us to Mr. Harrison's sloop, *The Grosvenor*." She pushed up on her toes and kissed him. "Fate is a funny thing."

She was leaning so prettily against him, one hand petting his chest, that he couldn't think straight.

"You met him at the White Lamb." Anne tugged his coat to follow her through the dark. Three paces ahead, she glanced back coyly, "You will be cordial with him? He is, after all, taking us home."

Home. The word resonated as music to a man once lost but now found. Stamped earth was quiet under his footsteps. He followed Anne, a siren in green silk. Her shoulder was bare. She hadn't tugged her gown back up.

"We'll be safe here," she said.

Mermaid Brewery barrcls were stacked against a wall. One of them had to hold Jacobite gold. His Anne was quite a capable woman, rolling barrels with the Fletcher sisters, and him sleeping like the dead.

"What about the Fletcher sisters? Aunt Maude? And Aunt Flora?"

"I said my goodbyes to the Fletcher sisters. They unhitched the horses and rode them across the bridge where a hostelry has agreed to take them. They should already be at an inn at the edge of the City where they will meet Aunt Maude and Aunt Flora. From there, the four of them will travel to Brighton. They'll stay there until it's safe to return to the City."

"You mean when or if the countess cannot draw a line from you to them."

She set a hand on the rough bannister, her skirts snagging on rough wood. "It is the reality of our league. I put myself in first position as a possible target. Next will be Cecelia."

"Who is not leaving the City."

"Unfortunately, no."

"You're worried about her."

"I am but there's nothing I can do. The hazard of our choices, I'm afraid." Carmine had faded on her lips, but they were a definitive line. A determined woman, this lass from Edinburgh he loved.

Her smile curved seductively. "Follow me. I've something to show you."

She headed upstairs. He knew where they were going—her counting room. He crested the stairs and found a makeshift mattress covered in blankets, his satchel and boots (cleaned and oiled, the toes pointing out), another satchel (Anne's?), and a basket of victuals.

"What do you think?" Anne's smile was like the sun.

"It's good for the night."

There was a treadwheel, the smell of the river, of wood and labor and sweat. Home in many ways. Not a place for seduction but their love had been nurtured on less.

Anne groaned. "Take another look, Will Mac-Donald." She arced her arm over the simple bed.

His kilt.

It was folded in a big square in the middle of the bed. He went to the bed and dropped to his knees. He touched the tartan, raised it reverently, and held it up to scant light. The cloth had been repaired, some stitches neat and even, others jagged. Most places the thread matched the weave where the warders had done their worst. Other stitches were childlike . . . every one of them a stitch to put his heart and his life back together.

He stared at his kilt, marveling at it and marveling at the woman who cared enough to do this. For him.

Anne hooked the lamp to the wall. When she turned around, her eyes were vulnerable pools.

"It's why I bolted my door. I wanted to surprise you."

The thumping, the late-night candle burning, enough to break a Bermondsey Wall house budget. For him.

He fingered a long red stitch. "I will treasure it for the rest of my life."

CANDLELIGHT HALOED WILL. He was Hades on his knees before her. She caressed his golden head and pulled the black silk ribbon which bound his hair. His awe at her gift faded to one she'd seen on the faces of men in taverns and the streets when hungry for a woman. A scowl slashed his mouth. She knew how to tease and how to drive him mad. It would be a torture and a pleasure, a night journey to indulge for years to come.

Finally, finally they would be together. She would feed his needs and in the doing feed hers. Emboldened, she slid a hand over her stomacher, the silk whispering against her hand. Lower her hand went. To her petticoats. To the place between her legs.

Will followed her hand, his scowl twisting tighter.

She cupped her mons and rubbed. Rich, dark silk slithered, the only noise.

A triangle imprint formed in the silk. Will's molten eyes grew darker and blacker and hungrier the more she rubbed that triangle inches from his face.

Her heart pounded with thrashing wildness. The pressure that wanted out was back, the fuse lit. Fireworks indeed. Sparking, crackling, heat building.

She kept her hand working the delta between her legs, her fingers swirling over the tender mound.

"Lift your skirt, lass."

His rough command thrilled her.

"Fine words for a man on his knees before me."

His heart-melting grin slid sideways. "Seductive, teasing lasses . . . my weakness."

For that, she obliged him. Yards of peacock green silk swam upward, shimmering, dancing, a pretty cloud. Behind this cloud, her legs stretched. One of her finer features, her legs.

Will huffed, an enslaved man, running his hands up and down her thighs. "What a shame to hide such fair legs." He kissed her thigh, his fingers digging into her flesh. "It will be my privilege to worship them for the rest of our lives."

He buried his face against her thighs.

She gasped when his big, warm hands cupped her backside.

"Keep touching yourself." Will's voice was ragged against her skin.

She rubbed her mons. Crinkly black hairs springing against her palm. The pressure building in her nub of flesh high in the cleft. The throbbing. The need. Will's breath fanned her hand, her mons, her thighs.

A dark storm lit his eyes.

Its force stunning, invading. Domination of a different kind. His hands kneaded her bottom, the pressure so, so, so good. Her head tipped back. She could barely breathe. Air refused to stay in her lungs.

The pounding . . . in her heart, her body, her nipples tight nibs.

The ache was everywhere.

"Slide your finger through your cleft."

Will's order, steady this time. He was sharp and clear while she fell into murky depths. Night was velvet closing over her and her finger.

"Do it, lass."

Three of her fingers spread delicate flesh. The wetness kissed by Will's breath. She whimpered.

"Will . . . I . . ."

Delicious weakness flooded her limbs. She rubbed, her fingers circling while he watched. Slippery, wet snicks matched her touch.

"That's it. Move your fingers for me. Play with your clitoris."

"My wha . . . ?" Her head dropped, chin to chest. She couldn't hold it up because her three fingers controlled her body. Or the pink nub did.

"Your clitoris." Molten gold eyes stared up at her in the dark. "It's . . . here."

Will added his finger to her three.

She cried out and clutched his shoulder. Her knees didn't work. Will might be the one on his knees, but she was a slave to his talented finger circling her—whatever he called it—part of her body.

"Lie down, lass."

She did, an inelegant mess of snagged silk and crushed panniers. Her shoes on, Will's shoes on, they were clothed bodies mashing together with his clever finger stuck between them. Need was building. She knew what it was. Powerful, aching, desire. The fuse coming for its due.

"Hold on to me, lass."

She hooked an arm around his neck. She was desperate, her hips bumping his hand, her bared legs shaking. He kissed her. Wildly, passionately, the sadness and fury of years apart crashing in that one kiss.

Liquid silk dripped within her cleft. She was primal, animal, needy bumping hard against Will. His velvet-clad thighs rubbed hers with the sweetest friction.

"Keep going," Will ordered against her mouth.

"I ca—I can . . ." Her neck arched and the fuse which hounded her so fiendishly smashed and sparkled.

Pleasure peaked, shuddering her, ripping a hoarse cry. Sweat heated her skin. Her pink nub pulsed against Will's finger. He circled slowly, slowly as if to coil her into a neat circle of stillness. As if he could control her . . . *right there*.

But that storm brought another one with it. Hot pressure, deeper inside. More tender, commanding. Another need that refused to go away. Will sensed it.

He fumbled with her bodice. She fumbled with his placket. It would be an honest joining of two ragged hearts with hungry bodies.

Will grinned when her nipple popped out above green silk. He suckled it with the same teasing relish she suckled his earlobe.

"Oh . . . Yes. Like that," she murmured, hooking a leg over his hip.

They lay on their sides and no one, not all the king's men would stop their joining.

She thrust her breasts at Will. He got the message—he was rather good at unspoken messages—and he freed her second nipple too. The suckling was divine and teasing and ticklish. It was only fair that she free his cock—his tackle, as he called it—and put it inside her.

They *were* long overdue.

They pressed close, his cock nudging slippery flesh between her legs. She rolled onto her back, sinuous and ready. Will rolled with her, his mouth a wreath of satisfaction. Her legs were up, her skirts bunched, his placket open. With the tip of his cock, Will drew a line through her cleft.

The obedient skin parted for him.

His entry shocked them both. So needful, so carnal. So freeing.

"Oh . . . Will," she cried.

Will slid home, gasping for breath.

He looked into her eyes and rocked inside her again and again and again.

It was a naked connection, gazing into his eyes. Their flesh joined, their bodies as one.

This was love, life, a renewing. Until something hotter, a new tormenting fuse burned, needing to meet its end. They found their pleasure again with Will inside her this time. Years of denial obliterated in hot, melting sweetness. His seed met hers.

In their sticky, hot-skinned joining on Will's kilt, something new and better was born.

Chapter Thirty-Six

Anne woke in the dark, a hand over her mouth. Terror fluttered in her chest. Will's face loomed inches from hers. He set a finger to his mouth, an order of silence. She obeyed, catching the rustling and rummaging of men below. Their voices were not inclined to quiet and their manner not inclined to friendliness.

"There's nothing 'ere," the first voice whined. Higher pitched and petulant.

A barrel was kicked.

"We were told to search Neville Warehouse and that's what we'll do, mate." This voice was smoother, boasting of an education.

Lamps swung on squeaky hinges. Footfalls scampered, albeit slower for the middle of the night.

"We should go back to the woman's house. Give it another look-see." The whiney voice. Another kick to a barrel. A lid opened and clamped shut.

Will peeked through a crack in her counting house wall and held up three fingers, then four.

Four men in the warehouse? The countess

must've checked her Wilkes Lock cabinet. Dread cloaked Anne. The diversionary Spruce Prigs, while a fine idea, must have stoked Lady Denton's ire. The woman was out for blood if she sent men to ransack Anne's house. She yanked up her bodice, glad Aunt Maude and Aunt Flora were not as wayward as Cecelia. They had the good sense to leave the City.

The men rummaged through crates, their lights dancing in pitch black below. Will had extinguished their lamp before they settled into sleep. She lifted her satchel, her heel bumping the wall. She froze.

"What was that?" A new voice, deeper than the others. The third man.

"It's probably a mouse or a rat. This is a wharf after all." The second man with the smooth voice.

"It's London. Rats are everywhere."

"Only they have the good sense to sleep at this hour," a fourth voice said.

Another barrel was opened. Will mouthed *the gold*! Darkness couldn't hide his fury. She shook her head and mouthed *No!*

"You, Jones, take a look up there and see what you can find." The second man again, clearly the leader.

"I'd like to find me bed," Jones grumbled.

"You're not paid to sleep. You're paid to find things," the leader said. "Now go. Check whatever room that is and maybe by dawn we can be done."

More grumbling, louder. The men didn't try to be quiet about their search now. Barrels were upended, Bavarian pine kicked, and the piled logs tumbled with a crash. White fear seized her. The loud noise was her chance to grab her knife from her satchel. Will took a broom that had been leaning in the corner.

Will walked on stockinged feet to her counting room entry. There was no door. The narrow wooden stairs creaked and shook under the weight of the man climbing them. She had an inkling of what Will was about. His knees bent, he waited at the side of the counting room entry.

When a bald man's head poked up at the stairs, he raised his lamp, his eyes agog at Anne against the wall.

"Hello, sir," she greeted him.

Will greeted him by smacking the man's head with the broom handle. The bald man tumbled down the steps, landing in an unnatural bone-crushing heap. He moaned, his eyes rolling back into his head.

"Jones?" one of the men said in dismay.

With all the noise they made, they probably had not heard Anne.

"The clumsy oaf fell!"

Jogging footfalls sounded. All three men were coming. Will set a finger again to his mouth. She nodded, her eyes wide and her knife in her grip. Light spilled from below into a few feet of her counting room. Noises, had to be Mr. Jones's body being dragged and checked.

"I . . . I think he's dead." The whiney voice announced this.

"Somethin's not right," the deep voice growled. "Burn the warehouse. That'll chase out any rats."

"A fair idea, but we're supposed to be looking for the gold," the leader said.

"Gold melts in a fire and goes solid when it cools. The lady'll still get her gold. I say we burn this place to the ground."

"Mr. Little has a point," the whiney-voiced man said.

"We set fire here, and the Night Watch'll come. Is that what you want? A quick trip to Marshalsea?" the leader asked.

"Then let's set fire to that room up there," Mr. Little said.

Did the man intend to set fire to the stairs? Dry and old, the stairs would go up like tinder in a matter of seconds. She sucked in a quick breath. The men had gathered at the base of the stairs. Beside her, through the treadwheel, light from the new day cut through thin lines where door and warehouse met. The square door was just big enough for a body to crawl out on the crane and make the occasional repair.

She looked at Will and mouthed *Mr. Baines!*

Will was grim, his jaw set. He pointed to her and the crane door. He wanted her to leave. She shook her head adamantly. Will's mouth flattened in anger. He hefted the broom, pointed to himself and the stairs.

The criminals were arguing loudly below. Even the smooth-toned leader seemed to be swayed to set fire to the warehouse.

"Let's get it over with, but I'll be the one to tell her ladyship, which means it's my arse she'll take a piece of, not either one of yours."

From across the warehouse, another voice. "Mrs. Neville?"

Mr. Baines!

Will jumped to action. He charged halfway down the ladder and leaped. He landed on agile feet, the element of surprise on his side.

"Good morning, men." A whack sounded.

She raced across the narrow room and flew down the steps. Mr. Baines grabbed a barrel lid and used it against a tall man with black and gray hair neatly clubbed.

Will advanced on the whiney-voiced man who tripped over a lantern. The candle touched Bavarian pine that should've been too green and too damp from her riverside warehouse to catch fire. But unlike the previous, rainy months, August had been hot. Pitch glistened in the bark and flames sprang to life, which was close enough to her open door. The door, so old and sun bleached, didn't stand a chance.

Mr. Little, a mean-eyed ginger, drew a flintlock that had been tucked in the back of his breeches and pointed it at Will's back.

Chapter Thirty-Seven

*W*ill struck the whiney-voiced man. Theirs was a fight of fists which didn't last long. Will landed Mr. Whiney on the ground, and the man gave up, curling like a babe, both arms covering his head.

The warehouse door was ablaze. Outside, wharfmen made a line, passing buckets to put out the fire. He whirled around and yelled, "Anne."

He couldn't see her in the smoke but he heard the crack of a flintlock fired, its ball whizzing past his ear. Its trail left a sting. He ignored it, searching for Anne in the smoke and melee. He found her crouching beside a man with a knife in his back. Anne's knife. A foot away was a flintlock on the ground.

"He was going to shoot you," she said, a dull quality in her voice.

He'd wager Anne had had her share of fights, but taking a man's life was a first. Cold fear moved him. The fire was nearly out but the Night Watch would soon be upon them.

"We have to get you out of here." He dragged Anne upright.

"*We* have to get out of here." She looked lively now.

"Mr. Baines," he yelled.

The bloody-lipped wherryman picked himself up, his fight a draw with the black-and-gray-haired man. The criminal's eyes darted with rat-like assessment. Smoke was clearing, more wharfmen were coming. When his gaze landed on Will, the criminal cuffed blood off his mouth and ran out the door.

Mr. Baines picked up his hat, coughing. Smoke hung heavy and acrid.

"Take Mrs. Neville to Cecelia MacDonald's house," Will said. "Do not let her tell you to do any different. Otherwise you'll answer to me. Do you understand, Mr. Baines?"

"Yes, sir. I do, sir."

Will nudged Anne forward. "Go with him."

"No. Come with me," she pleaded.

He advanced on Anne, steered her roughly around a fallen log. She let him guide her, her steps faltering. She didn't want to go. He felt his face twist into a harsh scowl. There was no time to dither.

Mr. Baines approached, but she brushed his hand off her arm.

"Will—"

"Go," he bellowed and pointed at the door.

Anne paled under smoke tinged cheeks.

Mr. Baines murmured something to her, enough to put sense into the woman and let him drag her toward the door. She was an odd sight, green silk petticoats and her hair a mess. Anne looked every bit like one of the lost souls who inhabited St. Luke's. She was wildness itself, clutching the unburnt part of doorframe.

"This is not the end, Will."

Her cry ripped through him. He stood and watched until the doorway was empty of nothing but light and smoke. He got a whiff of lavender on his shirt. It would be enough. It had to be.

Full of resolve, he walked to the man with the knife in his back. Instinct made him kneel beside the man and check him. The criminal sported a *T* brand on his thumb but with so many men with branded thumbs, it was nigh on impossible to know if this man had visited Anne's warehouse before.

Still kneeling, he scanned the warehouse. The gold baffled him. It wasn't here? *Mermaid Brewery* branded barrels had been upended. The Jacobite gold wasn't in a single one. He was searching the man's pockets, his boots, when the Night Watch came. Questions would need to be answered. Anne could not be the one to answer them. Hands resting on his knees, he braced himself for what would come. Prison. Again. That was why he was here and not Anne. He couldn't bear the thought of her in a cold, dark prison cell.

Two of the Night Watch approached, one an older man, former army by his bearing. The other young and mean, with fists and jowls like hams. Despite his appearance, the young man was respectful.

"That your knife, sir?"

"It is. The man tried to shoot me." He was casual, telling one lie and telling one truth.

The younger Night Watchman glowered at him. "So you knifed him in the back?"

Will jerked his chin at the flintlock by the log. "I wasna about to give him a chance to reload and try again. Would you?"

The younger man clamped his mouth shut, and the older man stepped in.

"What about those men there? By my count, I see three dead bodies, a warehouse that was ablaze, but thanks to the good people of Southwark, the fire is out. What say you, sir? Sign on the front says, Neville Warehouse. Are you Mr. Neville?"

He wiped his ear and found sticky blood on the back of his hand. "No, but I wish I had been."

To which the Night Watch hauled him to Marshalsea and put him in chains.

Mr. Baines walked her to Cecelia's home on Swan Lane. He pounded thrice on the door of the pretty two-story stone house with a pot of flowers on the front step. Mr. Baines was about to knock again when the door opened. Cecelia's yawning maid-cum–household servant answered.

"Yes?" Her sleepy eyes rounded when she saw Anne. "Mrs. Neville? What happened?"

"I . . . I need to see Cecelia. Is she home?" One could never be certain with Cecelia MacDonald.

"Of course, ma'am. Come in, come in."

Anne crossed the threshold, more collected than when she'd left her warehouse. She had Mr. Baines to thank for that. He'd poured reason into her ear, urging her into his wherry and taking her across the river. True to his word, the young man delivered her directly to Cecelia's door.

"Thank you, Henry. I will never forget this."

His chin ducked and his smile was bashful. Addressing him by his Christian name seemed appropriate after he'd fought to save her warehouse and her life. He'd been a faithful part of her life for   was it four years now?

She dove into his arms and hugged him, which sent a blush as bright red as his wherry across his cheeks. He hugged her back.

"Thank you, ma'am," he mumbled. "I have to get back to my wherry, ma'am."

"Which is exactly why you are wonderful, Mr. Baines. You left your livelihood to help me."

He set his hat on his head, grinning from her praise. They parted and she watched him walk down the lane.

"What a surprising sight," Cecelia said behind her in a sleepy voice. "You hugging Mr. Baines like a long-lost relative, smelling of smoke, and dressed the same as you were last night."

She turned and shut the front door. Cecelia peered at her.

"You still have your earrings on too?"

Her hand shot up to confirm that yes, her garnet earbobs were still in place. Both of them. She breathed the confusion that was her life, glad for the sameness of her grandmother's earrings. Cecelia finished descending her stairs, a vision in white linen. She hadn't bothered with a robe of any kind, thus her merits were indirectly on display.

"I'm disappointed. I expected Will to remove every stitch of clothing from your person." Blonde brows arched prettily. "Are you telling me, you *didn't* . . ."

"Oh yes, we did." Eyes closing, her spine hit the door. "It was glorious."

"Then why are you in my house smelling of smoke?"

"Because the countess sent men to the warehouse. There was a fire, three men are dead, and the Night Watch hauled Will away. I saw that from the river."

"You've had quite a morning. Something tells me *The Grosvenor* will depart the City without you."

Anne groaned. "I can't leave without Will. I won't leave without him." She covered her mouth to smother a howl that wanted out. "I should've stayed with him."

Cecelia rushed forward and grabbed Anne's arms. "No, you should not have."

"But . . . Will . . ."

Cecelia's gaze locked with hers. "Will did the right thing. He got you out of there."

"But, the Night Watch . . . they're sure to take him back to Marshalsea."

"And you wanted to . . . what? Molder in chains with him? As if they'd put you two together." Cecelia huffed impatiently. "What is the first thing we learned when we came to the City?" She paused, then answered her own question. "That it's easier to bribe one person out of prison, than two. I, for one, am glad they took Will and not you."

"Oh . . . don't say that."

"This is hardly over, dear." Cecelia stepped back and called out, "Jenny?"

Jenny, the maid-cum-servant walked in, rag curls still in her hair. "Yes, miss?"

"Two morning chocolates. Extra silky smooth please."

"I've already started it, miss."

"Excellent." Cecelia took Anne's hand and pulled her into a salon cozier and far prettier than anything Anne could envision.

"Now, sit here and tell me everything."

Anne sank into a green damask chair and put her feet on the stool that matched it. Cecelia curled up on a floral print settee and wrapped a large shawl around her shoulders. They sat quietly for a time. Anne needed it. She covered her eyes, the strain seeping out of her.

"You anticipated this. The countess attacking so soon. You should've taken charge of our league."

"Me? In charge of the league. You have courage in spades. You run into a knife fight while I . . ." Cecelia waved a manicured hand. "I get wonky at the sight of blood. And yes, we both knew the countess would strike. So soon? I hoped it'd come after dawn when you and Will were on *The Grosvenor*, but that didn't happen. Shall we stop useless recriminations and figure out how to get you and Will and the gold safely out of London?"

"I don't care about the gold." Her hand dropped to her lap and a fresh wave of misery swamped her. She searched the wall, looking at but not seeing the birds and flowers printed on it. "I don't care about duty and responsibility or having a mission. I want Will."

Arms crossed, she was quite mulish. Cecelia pulled the shawl tighter and listened.

"He sacrificed himself for me . . . for the gold . . . when he never wanted anything to do with it in the first place."

Jenny entered with a tray of two dishes of chocolate. Anne took one dish, its heat nursing her.

"I should go to the magistrate and let him know Will is innocent."

"You cannot. For all my complaints of Mr. Fielding, he is fair. But Southwark is another story. You will *not* find justice in Southwark. The countess will dig her claws in Marshalsea, if she hears you're there. Will did the right thing in sparing you." Cecelia sipped her chocolate. "Did anyone see you?"

"Only Mr. Baines. A few wharfmen. The smoke was still thick in the warehouse and the fire was at the small north door."

"That's good." Cecelia sipped more chocolate. "Let's think this through."

Birds chirped their morning song outside Cecelia's window. One could almost feel hopeful from the sound. Until Cecelia set her cup on a satinwood table with a decisive *clunk*.

"I have a wonderful idea, but we must find a dead body first."

Chapter Thirty-Eight

*T*orchlight flickered over a beast of a man sitting on the ground dressed in black velvet. His braw arms were manacled to the wall of Marshalsea Prison's strong room, the shed as it was known to many a troublesome criminal. Midnight was the hardest hour. Light danced on the walls, dipping and swaying over scratches left by men driven to madness.

Anne stepped into the shed's close confines, scarcely believing how her life had changed since her last visit here. Will's eyes were molten gold but clearer this time, tender and lively. His whole person stirred to attention, the chains jingling as if his limbs leaped for joy at the sight of the woman cloaked in gray.

She lowered her hood, her gaze meeting his.

The beast smiled. "Well, well, Mrs. Neville, back again, I see."

"You know I couldn't stay away."

Will's chest expanded. "You shouldna be here. It's no' . . . safe."

Anne eyed the warder, lounging in the doorway, a big bald man named Mr. Bixby, who enjoyed picking his teeth and showing how little he cared about visitors to the shed. The warder had made a fine speech about truth, justice, and the Marshalsea way. But his eyes slanted when he spied Anne's earrings from the depths of her hood.

Word was, Southwark got the occasional high-value prisoner, and the highlander dressed in black velvet fit that description. She didn't blame Bixby. He was trying to play his cards right, and go home a wealthy man. He was cut from the same mold as Ledwell, which at the moment was not of interest to her. All she could do was look at Will, his legs sprawled and hair down. No visible bruises this time. A fair crop of new whiskers growing. The velvet coat fell open from his widespread arms. He still wore the burnished gold silk waistcoat, but no cravat, and his stockings were torn and filthy.

"Inspecting the goods, madame?" he asked.

"Last time I saw a good deal of the man I purchased. What do I get to see this time?"

His mouth dented sideways. "My charm?"

"It's rough at best."

"My steady devotion?"

"You're getting warmer, sir."

His lips parted, soft with emotion. "Would you take my undying love?"

"Sold." Her gaze on Will, she addressed the warder. "What will it take for you to part with this incorrigible prisoner, Mr. Bixby?"

"Well now, ma'am . . ." he began. "I'm thinking he ought to go before the magistrate."

"For what? He's done nothing wrong."

Bixby jerked his thumb in the general direction of the wharfs. "There's three dead men—that's enough."

"Vicious men, every one of them. Mr. Mac-Donald was trying to save me."

"Then you and he can tell yer story to the magistrate, ma'am."

And give the Countess of Denton time to retaliate? Hardly.

"What will it take for you to release this man to me?"

"Well, his *possible* crimes are a bit more serious than kilt wearin', ma'am." Bixby scratched his ear. "With the summer's spate of violent house-breakers and the crown looking to stop it, well . . ." His eloquent shrug signaled this trans-action would be harder to seal than her first visit to Marshalsea.

"I'm no' a housebreaker, Mr. Bixby," Will said.

"Tell it to the magistrate."

Anne sighed and addressed Mr. Bixby. "You heard about my last visit, did you?"

"Ledwell likes to talk."

"Then you know I will pay very well for this man."

His stare landed greedily on her earbobs. "I might be able to accommodate you but, ma'am, you have to accommodate me."

"Oh?"

"I can't sell his arrest record. Not for murder, but I could sell it to you for a lesser crime—"

"Such as kilt wearing."

"—such as kilt wearing. But if you could, say,

find a body to replace him . . ." Mr. Bixby's words trailed off on a lighter note.

"A dead body?"

"That would work, ma'am."

Now the warder was being reasonable and smart and smart men were rewarded.

"You are in luck, Mr. Bixby. What if I told you I could have one delivered by dawn?"

Bixby's grin was amiable. "Then you'd have a deal."

"About the issue of payment." She removed an earring and held it up for his inspection. "You know the value of rubies, don't you?"

"Anne!" Will's voice rumbled from the floor. "Don't do it. Those were your grandmother's."

She gave him a speaking look, one filled with longing and tenderness. The earrings were pretty stones, cherished stones, but they were no substitute for Will. She'd learned a hard lesson of late: no amount of gold, rubies, or treasure of any kind could replace love. But, it wasn't the treasure which gave her pause; it was her blind sense of duty. It had nearly destroyed her.

Love was bigger than duty. That was a truth to hold on to, like the stubborn highlander she'd come to save again.

Mr. Bixby scrubbed a hand across his mouth. "Rubies you say?"

"Yes." A lie, but she was desperate and willing to do anything to free Will.

Mr. Bixby reached for the jewelry, but her fingers curled around it. "Not yet, Mr. Bixby. Release him first. Then the earring is yours."

"Ah now, ma'am, I cannot release him until I have a body to replace him."

"And I cannot delay." She pulled the second earring from her ear. "Both are yours if you set him free this very moment. You have my word, a . . . replacement body will be here at dawn."

Bixby kicked the brick stairs, thinking about the offer. Voices from Marshalsea rose, a new prisoner delivered by the Night Watch. Anne slowly closed her fingers again.

"Perhaps you're right, Mr. Bixby. Mr. MacDonald and I should take our plight to the magistrate and throw ourselves on his mercy. And it wouldn't cost me a thing."

Bixby gaped hungrily at her fisted hand. "No. I'll do it."

The exchange done, the warder passed over the life-changing key to Anne—her third in less than a fortnight.

Chapter Thirty-Nine

The next day

There was only one thing Ancilla liked less than arrogant, obtuse men and that was a woman who thought herself supremely clever. The destruction of Neville House at Bermondsey Wall was unfortunate, but necessary. Unsurprisingly, Mrs. Neville wasn't there. The destruction of the Neville Warehouse was more vexing. The clues to finding her gold pointed to Neville Warehouse.

Anne and Will had been hiding there.

But the treasure was not inside.

Why else would they go there but to guard the gold?

Due to the unfortunate fire, she had to stay away from Gun Wharf another day. Some of the Night Watch here were cozy with the Night Watch on the other side of the river. Mr. Fielding unfortunately had the ear of the crown through the Duke of Newcastle. It wouldn't do to stir the pot too much.

With Will MacDonald in chains at Marshalsea, awaiting the Southwark magistrate (who was known to take much longer than three days before hearing a prisoner's charges), she didn't fear Mrs. Neville's disappearance. The slippery woman was somewhere in the City. It was merely a matter of finding her.

Find the woman and she'd find the Jacobite gold.

When her carriage pulled up to Neville Warehouse, a more capable band of men combed the building. Former army men, smarter than the last group. Mr. Wortley was their leader, efficient, hawkish eyes, a clear grasp of order. He was resourceful. She was in need of a new private footman with Mr. MacLeod's sudden departure. But something in Mr. Wortley's eyes turned her stomach. Something of a rabid dog lurked under a thin veneer of restraint with that man.

No, it wouldn't do to bring that under her roof. She had her limits.

The carriage door was opened, and she exited, plainly dressed in muslin as it was the unseemly hour of nine o'clock in the morning.

"Mr. Wortley, what have you found?"

His eyes were dark under the brim of his tricorn. "We searched this warehouse high and low, milady. Tore it apart in places. If there was gold here, we would've found it."

She marched inside and surveyed the damage. She wore men's riding boots this morning, all the better to tromp around Gun Wharf. Four men dug up sections of the stamped earth floor, Mermaid Brewery barrels had been disassembled, logs scattered. Mr. Wortley walked her through what he suspected happened with the first men.

He stretched a long-boned arm and pointed at rickety stairs. "The counting room is up there. We found a bed there." He gestured to another spot. "That's where the first man was felled. The next over there." He swung around and motioned to the door. "Then the fire was started here. An upturned lamp likely caused it."

"I don't want to know how the event unfolded," she said through gritted teeth. "I want to know the whereabouts of my gold."

Impatient, she strode out of the warehouse with Mr. Wortley in her wake. "I want answers, Mr. Wortley." She pointed to the Mermaid Brewery dray parked outside the abandoned warehouse. "My neighbor's valet claims he saw a dray parked on Upper Brook Street outside my house. There are carriages in Grosvenor Square, not drays, Mr. Wortley. Yet, I come to Southwark, and all I see are drays and almost no carriages."

Mr. Wortley listened patiently. She needed to clear her head. What he said next did not help.

"My guess is the man and woman with the gold are long gone."

She wasn't sure what to do with the possibly rabid Mr. Wortley. He said just enough to pique her interest and prove that he could be useful.

"That's impossible. Will MacDonald is in chains at Marshalsea."

His mouth curled up on one side as if he stored contradictory information. It could be he was toying with her. Mr. Wortley liked the generous pay she tendered, but the rules of working for her were, as yet, hazy.

"Very well, Mr. Wortley. You have some news you wish to share."

"You said Mrs. Neville attended your event. Did she say anything or do anything unusual?"

She snorted. "Do you find deep, sarcastic curtsies unusual?"

Wortley had the audacity to grin. "Don't know about curtsies, milady. But it seems to me, Mrs. Neville has been one step ahead of you. Could be worth it to consider every detail."

She was bemused, her gaze drifting from one warehouse to the next. "You want details, Mr. Wortley. I can give you details. Mrs. Neville mentioned her grandmother, a woman named—"

Ancilla froze. She felt blood drain from her face and had to grab Wortley's arm to steady herself.

Gun Wharf's abandoned warehouse loomed.

Wortley followed her sightline.

She pointed at the neglected building. "That sign over there. What does it say?"

"Wilcox, milady."

She stared at the old warehouse, words falling loosely. "Mrs. Neville's grandmother. She kept saying the woman's name. It was . . . Wilcox."

"Do you want to check that warehouse? I can round up the men, get you inside."

"Yes."

The call was given and Wortley's men pried open the warehouse door. Weather and time had ruined the wood, but the hinges were oiled. Ancilla walked past the threshold and found the abandoned warehouse clean and empty. Not a cobweb in sight. Dangling from a center post was a black silk ribbon necklace.

"Is that Mrs. Neville's?" she shrieked.

Ancilla ran to it and ripped it off the nail from which it hung. She turned the gold medallion over in her hand and roared a ferocious, angry cry.

Etched in the metal was a nine in a diamond.

Chapter Forty

Three days later in Loch nan Ceall

Dawn stretched wide, pinks and yellows and the palest blues—colors to paint a sky, not a man's clothes. Seagulls circled, their wings wide and proud. Will could say a seagull was a seagull, be it English or Scots. But his heart burst with joy at those birds, their song sweeter, their flight more majestic. Pride of home filled him. Arisaig was nestled on the horizon, a warm lady welcoming him back to the places he'd walked as a lad. He had not heard her beckon until Anne found him bound in chains of his own doing.

Anne. She would bedevil him 'til he was old and gray.

Her presence healed him. She'd asked him once what hurt more: the loss of Scotland? Or the loss of her?

It took years to find the answer. Anne was Scotland. Scotland was Anne. If a man cut a star in two, he'd find the same glorious shine on one side as the other. Anne was mysterious, strong, the song in his heart, the passion in his veins.

She was his life.

Anne nestled into her favorite place under his arm against his rib. It was the perfect spot for the widow to cuff him should he need it (and he was man enough to admit there were times he did). It was the perfect spot for his wife-to-be to tickle his secret places should he need that too. It was the perfect spot because Anne was there, her heart beating near his.

They stood thus, the water glassy in places, the blue pale with mystery and hope. A breeze lifted Anne's hair but she didn't catch it and tie it back. She was as awed as he was at the notion of going home. Three days they'd held each other on the narrow bed allotted them on the sloop. Their talk wandered aimlessly as dreams put to words do. There'd be days of wonder and dreams, words, and actions. Little by little, they'd build their life.

Once they were settled, he'd write a long letter to his father. It would be an honest letter from a son who fought a war and lost. He'd tell his father everything in hopes his father would come back to Scotland. It might be for naught, but a son had to try. His father was the final wound that needed healing. Anne sensed it in quiet moments when she held him late at night.

He was sure she sensed it now. She cozied up to him, warm and affectionate.

"Mr. Gunderson is a little troubled at your choice of clothes today," she said, a touch of humor in her voice.

"We're in the middle of a loch near our home,

and Mr. Gunderson has been paid to look the other way." Will's voice lost its smooth quality on *home*. He couldn't say or think the word without a dry lump rising in his throat.

"Mr. Gunderson's late wife was a Chisolm," she murmured. "He understands."

"For this one day, when I walk back home, I *will* wear my kilt."

"As you should, my love. As you should."

Raw emotion entwined them. It was on the breeze batting his mended kilt and the water tapping the ship. Last night's sleep had been deep but he couldn't eat much. Butterflies dancing in his stomach made food impossible, though he had no doubt his appetite would return, once they were ashore. Once he clasped hands with his clan chief, he would breathe.

Mr. Gunderson approached, his hands clasped at his back. He stopped to admire the horizon with them. He was captain of *The Marietta*, the sloop taking them home for a substantial sum.

"Fine morning," Mr. Gunderson said, bouncing on his toes. "We'll lower a boat soon and take you ashore. A few minutes, I think. Are you ready?"

"We are, Mr. Gunderson. We've been waiting for this for a very long time."

They'd marshalled their things to be ready for this moment. Her satchel (bulging a little), Will's satchel (bulging hardly at all), and an oddly heavy Mermaid Brewery barrel as high as Anne's waist. It clinked loudly when moved, which took two men to accomplish.

The captain took a bracing breath. "I'll see to it then."

Mr. Gunderson was a wee bit nervous around Will. Their first meet at the White Lamb was not so cordial.

Anne rubbed her cheek against his well-worn velvet coat. "We'll write to your father."

She did know.

Will's chest heaved a worthy sigh. "Yes, you and I, together. We'll write to him."

"And ask him to come back."

Will squeezed her tight. He was dammed-up emotions, threatening to spill. There were only a few things he wanted to bring with him: Anne, his kilt, and his velvet coat. Late at night, the first evening at sea, he finally shared why the coat was dear.

After his release from the prison hulk, he had little more than rags covering his body. A rag and bone man gave the coat to Will. That man's kindness had saved Will's soul. Desperate, alone, no kin to speak of in London, he'd walked its streets, a lost man. It was the kindness of one person who helped him recover, one day to next. A sort of talisman.

In time, he broke free of his chains. Kindness and love saved him, from others yes, from Anne, most of all.

Raven-haired Anne . . .

His weakness.

He couldn't say what made that true, but he'd have the rest of his life to find out why.

Acknowledgments

A huge thank you to my editor, Elle Keck. She took a chance on this series and dove in with full enthusiasm. Her edits are kind, pointed, and much appreciated. I'll laugh-snort at "zero to butt" for the rest of my life!

Thank you to the Avon team who made this book happen: Production Editor Brittani DiMare, Art Director Amy Halperin, Cover Designer Patricia Barrow, Illustrator Gene Mollica, and Copyeditor Joan M. (You had your work cut out with me.)

To my agent, Sarah Younger—Thank you for always having my back.

To my friend, author Alyssa Alexander—Thank you for your texts, calls, and emails. Sometimes you just gotta talk to another romance writer because no one else understands.

To my husband, Brian—You're a loving, generous man. You're sleeping with the lights on so I can finish this. Need I say more?

To my readers—Thank you for your patience. My career has zigged and zagged, but you've stayed with me.